Praise for *Onc*

"One Bad Intentions *is as au*
of South London urban life as I have read. It takes its place
among every black working class novel in the canon."

- Alex Wheatle

"This fabulous, unpretentious book has got me back into
reading after a long absence. The simple straightforward
honesty of this first person account belies the depth of feeling
and the many conflicting layers beneath the surface of the
narrative. The result is a genuine empathy with Stephanie
and the desire to try and understand her even though I
personally have nothing in common with her (apart from
living where the book is set)…It's just so refreshingly honest."

-Joe Thompson (Amazon review)

"This book had me captivated from the beginning to end.
Such a true and vivid depiction of South East London in the
1990's."

-TJ (Amazon review)

"This was a gripping read from start to finish, providing
an eye-opening glimpse into a part of society that is often
marginalised and reviled. The author's depiction of Stephanie
feels authentic, and even though her journey is sometimes
dark, the book is ultimately one about redemption and is
beautifully written."

-Joanna Brooks (Amazon review)

A LOVE STORY OF TRIUMPH AND REDEMPTION

ONCE BAD INTENTIONS

MONIQUE CAMPBELL

Published by Monique Campbell

First published in 2013
This second edition published in 2023

ISBN: 978-0-9927801-2-8

Cover design, illustration and interior formatting:
Mark Thomas / Coverness.com

This book is dedicated to girls defining their own destiny,
and to the guardian angels who show up in their lives to guide them.

And to my daughter, Monet,
whose existence I'm eternally grateful for.

PROLOGUE

Parts of London, like most inner-city areas, are a patchwork. Communities of diverse mix people and cultures weakened by dilapidated buildings, poorly kept shops, excessive gambling opportunities, homelessness, and crime.

I spent my early years living on a small estate in Lewisham. Some children as young as six played outside and ran free into the night, completely unsupervised. My sisters and I were no different. We were fearless. We often skilfully climbed trees and the roof of our estate building, sometimes falling but mostly not. My mum and dad had three daughters, Macy, Safire and me, Stephanie. We also had a fourth sister, Charlene, my father's daughter but not my mother's child. She was the second oldest and grew up in a separate household. She often visited us during the holiday periods when we stayed at Dad's and remained at home. Mum was good in that sense. Always kept our sibling family relation intact, irrespective if the circumstances in which our relation materialised was questionable.

In retrospect, my mother's decision to move to a semi-detached house on a quiet residential road amidst doctors and social workers in Lee Green, was a good move. The local council moved us from a two-bed flat to a three-bed house, so Mum could both flee from the danger my father presented to her and house three children from the age of eight to fourteen.

You see, I grew up in the 1980s, at a time where deprived areas in the inner-city became rampant with drugs and infested with crime. In the worst council housing, some young families, who were financially and educationally disadvantaged, saw the drug trade as a business opportunity. Yes, they had pride if this meant they could feed their family, buy them flashy designer clothes and jewellery, and not have to work a minimum wage job for The Man. In my household lack of money wasn't an issue. We didn't want for much. Neither my mother nor her boyfriend, Derek, had a visible job. As in, in the traditional nine to five sense. Yes, Derek would sometimes leave our home and later return with bundles of cash, but no-one provided any context as to how this money was obtained. He kitted out our home with expensive electrical goods, Chesterfield leather sofas and a hand decorated China table. We wore mink coats and hats as young as four years old. Wore diamond studs and necklaces. We mountain climbed and sunned down on family holidays in Europe, and at Christmas were given hundreds of pounds to splurge on presents.

Derek spoiled us as much as he could. He came into our lives when I was a wee toddler, a matter of months after Mum left Dad post an avalanche of domestic violence. His involvement in drugs was from both ends of the spectrum—the dealer who became the user. As children, we only saw the money and the material things the money provided. We had no concept of where the money came from or the negative effects of the drugs.

But then things changed.

My mother wanted to ensure things would be different for her children, that we would no longer be exposed to certain things, a certain way of living. She found Christ and wanted salvation. She gave away much of the material things Derek acquired. She became God-fearing. She wanted for her children to be saved and not punished for her sins, her bad decisions in life. Such as the type of men she chose, from abusers to drug-dealers, and the general criminal, but loving kind. The men who would reflect her own chaos, and between them and her, carve out an environment to raise children. Then set them free to society and hope for the best.

CHAPTER ONE

ESCAPISM

....

7th September 1993 – My First Day at School

Wha' gwaan, Di? I haven't caught up with you in a while. I was thinking the other day that it's been like five years since we started this thing with you carrying the mad weight I offload on you. You done know you're my bonafide bredren for life, just like Kid 'n' Play were.

Right about now I'm still tired. Mum woke me up this morning at 6.30 in her usual way: blaring some gospel shit. Trust me when I say Mum's not the same person you used to know! Her music choice and interests have changed nuff since she got 'saved' a couple of years ago. And it's getting worse. It's like she uses the music to get that Derek off her mind, but I thought if the church didn't do that, then at least time would. It's been over two years! Don't get me wrong, I know I didn't check for him too tuff when I was yout', but he was cool before he started smoking his shit. That's joke business, ah-lie? They say everyone's doing it now. Macy told me, and you know she knows allot. She's like 16 and three-quarters now. She was

1

the one who got me my first one of you…but I've already told you that, right? She thought it was a good idea for me to escape some of the crap we witnessed…but what did I know? Not what I know now for sure. That's why my dad goes on the way he does sometimes. You know he doesn't play. Sometimes I still have those flashbacks of musical periods at his house when we would stay there on the weekends and in the holiday periods. Like when I sang Billy Holiday's 'Lover Man' on the microphone whilst Dad played it on the saxophone and Safire harmonised in the background. I was seven or eight, which made Safire nine or ten. Or the time when Dad came to pick us up from our new primary school in his bright yellow 1960s BMW 2002 Collector's Edition (he regularly drummed that into our heads) before I got that thirst for fighting when things didn't go my way. Dad had that car since the early eighties, which is why I never got why it was called the 2002 Collector's Edition, though it still looked brand new. I remember that day because it was the first time Dad had picked us up since Mum moved houses and purposely didn't tell him. He drove us around Lewisham stewing for information, but when Musical Youth's 'Pass The Duchie' came on…it all suddenly stopped. So we 'bubbled to the riddim' loving Dad singing and being chilled for once. Mum used to have a good selection of 80s party tracks before giving her life to Christ and started religiously playing this gospel shit.

Mum's only gone an' pissed me off this morning. Making me do shit for my middle sister, Safire, like she's the baby. Always giving her special treatment. Always making her

special treatment be at a cost to me. Dis morning she's got
me going school vex! I dare someone to cross me. I dare
someone to test me today...

Let's start here. In the morning. With me. My diary. Coexisting as friends and dependents. I needed her to manage what you'll later learn as my rage. She needed me for her purpose. To be useful. She soothed me. Helped me to understand and release the chaos in my life. My diary was my best friend. I called her Di.

September 1993. That diary entry was the opening to my first day at Lee C of E School. We'd had a rough few years going through the transition of Mum separating from her boyfriend, Derek, becoming a Christian, changing our home and then our school, but ultimately changing our lifestyle. This change was rapid and intense, a boot camp of dictatorship. With no father figure in our home and the severed relationship Mum had with Dad, Mum felt obliged to lay down the rules. This fuelled a burning furnace that became a constant feeling inside me when I was ten. I was always ready to explode. At the slightest provocation, I was prepared to fight. My eldest sister, Macy, had this trait (as did all my sisters), but something softened within her when she had my nephew just over a year before.

On my first day of secondary school, though, things were no different for me. I was pummelling a boy in my new class at my new school who I considered an *eediot* (it was standard practice to over emphasize the 'e'). I didn't know this boy or even understand how it had come to that. My fist powered down on his left eye socket. Blood spattered from the battered eye the boy tried to cover. Every time he tried to shield himself from its force, my ready fist would connect with his face, split and swell the skin further. He lost his grip. His face became more disfigured. His blood coated my steady hand. I saw red. My eyes blazed with venomous stupor. This is what happened when my adrenalin rose to that level, when my anger became so uncontrollable, I thrived on the sentiment it provided: someone got hurt.

Suddenly one of my sister's voices started to egg me on. "Go on, Stephanie, deal with him! Don't let man chat to you like dat!" It was Charlene's. Sister number two. She was in year ten, four years above me, so she already had a reputation that was recognised in the Lewisham borough.

I unclenched my fist and felt for my bobbled hair, which I had sectioned into eight with the ends twisted. It was still as neat as when I'd done it the night before. Silk headscarves worked wonders for holding afro hair intact. I stepped back from the boy like a frightened child being phased back into reality. He was huddled in the foetal position against seemingly recently varnished parquet floors. I could feel my spectators' disapproval and their amazement accompanied by fear of my fighting ability. I shook off my unease, the acid that wept from my gut in rejection of my actions and the person I was just starting to become. I used their fear to springboard my efforts. I needed my actions, my newfound persona to make sense to me. I needed their respect. Even if it derived from fear.

I made for the corridor where Charlene was standing. She nudged me to express her approval as I passed her in the doorway. We headed for the ground floor.

"Steph! Dere you are. How come you took so long?" Shariece quizzed. She was a friend of my other sister, Safire. Sister number three. I knew her before I started secondary school because Safire would bring her and other friends home when Mum was at work. They would all talk about boys, events at school, and Safire would show off her piano skills, having had intermittent lessons since she was very young, when affordability wasn't in question. Shariece had widely spaced eyes, smooth, dark chocolate skin, and a curvy body.

Shariece stood with Maria and René, Safire's other friends. I liked them all and enjoyed hanging out with them as the 'bigger girls'. I explained to them all what I had just done, how I *had* to beat him up as I did. *I had to*. How else would I live up to the reputation I had inherited and gain his respect? Charlene added proudly to my story of events. She said that I "gave him no *blies* whatsoever!" And I didn't. Giving him a 'bly' would mean giving him a chance to challenge the reputation I had earned. That I could not do—my family would think poorly of me.

We walked through the main hall where the dinner ladies were cooking up a storm for lunch. It was actually more your chicken nuggets, chips, beans, mushy peas, lumpy mash potato, that kind of thing. The original school dinners before Jamie Oliver took his stand. We headed out into the playground where kids played.

"So, what 'appened for you to knock him over?" René asked.

"He called my mum a bonehead, innit, so I put my knuckle bone to his head."

We laughed as we crossed the playground. Trivial as the term 'bonehead' was, the disrespect I would have hung on to was of him cussing my mum altogether. Albeit a natural slip of the tongue, the aim was that he would think twice next time. We advanced the benches by the huts. This was the place where the school's talented stepped up to the 'mic' (well, actually the bench) and would lyrically defend their position with their rhyming skills. A crowd of us huddled round, bobbing our heads to the lyrics rhymed by one boy and beatboxed by another. Once they finished, we all cheered and hollered, let out hoots and other strange deep-toned noises influenced from the Caribbean that expressed our appreciation of Lee C of E School's talented MCs.

Sean went up next. He was part of a local gang named The Younger Ghetto Boys. They were admired, feared, and equally sought after by rival gangs. He rapped about his neighbourhood, ghetto tribulations, and his girl, which he described as his 'gyal'. That was when this bald, slim-built man who we described as *maaga* marched towards us with my name ringing from his tongue.

"You better duss-out. Mr. Ahmed's coming for you," Shariece warned.

"Who's dat?"

"The headmaster, and trust me, he don't *ramp*," René added.

I didn't know what to do. For a second or two, I was scared.

"*Stephanie!* Stephanie Johnson! Come with me NOW!" bellowed Mr. Ahmed.

I walked his way. No, scrap that. I bopped his way like the rude girl that I thought I was. Shariece and the rest of the group watched me shadow his lead. I waved to my audience. We stopped outside a small office, a nameplate on the door announcing it as his.

"Come in, take a seat and close the door behind you," he began as he leaned back on a swivel chair. He swung a pair of crossed legs from side to side.

I did as he requested and slumped into the chair in front of his desk. "Yeah, whassup?" I grunted.

He rested his arm on the desk and leaned forward. I thought he was invading my personal space, but I said nothing. "First and foremost, you do *not* speak until you are spoken to," he demanded. "Secondly, violence will *not* be tolerated in my school under any circumstances. Though I am disturbed by what I've been told. I am allowing you to explain your side of events."

"What're you talking 'bout? Dat boy Christopher?"

"Yes, I'm talking about 'that *boy* Christopher', who's lying in the medical room with blood being mopped up off his face! Now, would you care to enlighten me on your views of what happened before I take action?" he screeched. His eyes pulsated, and the veins on his forehead protruded.

"All right, dere's no need to shout, I ain't deaf, you know," was my reply. He expressed his fury. I sighed, taken in by his admirable attempt to reclaim authority, and continued. "He was pushing everyone as he came out of class like he's some bad-man," I explained, "den when I told him not to push past me, he started coming up in my face and told me to 'suck-out my mudder,' so I pushed him, den he pushed me back, den I punched him."

"Stephanie, three witnesses have said that you punched him three times in the face, and he did *not* hit you back." He opened a folder that lay on top of a pile on his desk. "One witness said, and I quote, 'He said something about her mum, and she punched him three times...he was wounded, holding his eye on the floor. She punched him again, and then she left with another girl.'" He raised his eyebrows.

"They're lying, innit; they're his bredrens."

"No, Stephanie, I think it is you who is telling lies. I know Charlene is your sister, and I know her temperament—I have had many dealings with her over the past three years. As do I know Safire's. And I also knew your older sister Macy very well. Before she became pregnant." His eyes lit up at that point, as though he knew all my family secrets. "I will be speaking with Charlene after you, so I hope that your stories match up. You will spend the rest of the day in the Isolation Room. And by all means, do not think this is over. Now get out of my office before I lose my rag!"

I didn't know where the Isolation Room was. This vexed Mr. Ahmed as it meant he wasn't rid of me yet and had to show me the way. I followed him once again as he led me through the corridor. Upon the sight of him, pupils stiffened, their energy zapped. We entered a small white room with several empty desks. A middle-aged woman with goggle eyes, varicose veins, and an unfortunate weight problem presided over this vacant class. I was seated. Mr. Ahmed whispered to the hefty lady and then left.

"My name's Mrs. Mitchell," she announced as though talking to an entire class. "The reason you are in here is because your actions have caused you to require isolation from other, better-behaved, pupils. You will now write a thousand lines on why you are here and what it is that you've done wrong."

"I ain't done nuffing wrong so I ain't writing a thousand lines nuffing," I roared.

"You will write a thousand lines, and it will be of a standard that your mother and I can understand. If you fail to do this properly, then I'm sure your mother and I can agree on further punishment." She voiced with total confidence of the fear children like me possessed for their parents.

I hated her for this. *How does this fat bitch know this is my Achilles heel?* I wondered how she knew misbehaviour at school or amongst Mum's family and friends triggered a darker side to my mum. I wondered how she concluded Mum was a woman of pride, and the embarrassment and frustration of her having to come my school because of my bad behaviour, would likely result in my demise. How she would know that the mention of her name in situations like this was likely to choke me with fear.

I scowled at Mrs. Mitchell as I took the A4 sheets of lined paper that she offered and started my essay on 'Where I Went Wrong'. Soon enough, Charlene joined me in that room to write her thousand-line essay. I thought back to the morning, trying to figure out how the day had come to an end in such a bad way on the first day in my new school. It all came back to how I escaped chaos within my life, which was in two ways: violence and my diary. Violence was a quick fix, a blissful release of frustration. My diary was a good friend to who I could reveal my darkest secrets and feelings without a comeback, a judgment, or an argument. Whether I wrote good or bad things, there was no reaction, just the pages of my soul.

*

That particular morning I'd been lying in bed, rapping with my diary, writing down my thoughts. Before I knew it, it was time to jump up. I cracked open my bedroom window. My mood was bright and the sky was a gorgeous pale blue. Fresh and crisp. I watched the clouds. The thought of God came to the forefront of my mind. This was almost a spiritual experience. Mum would have liked that.

I arrived at the school gate having loosened the knot of my school tie and the bop in my walk. I fixed my blazer, black and square-shouldered, so that I looked sharp. An uncanny sensation came over me as I peered up at the three-story building buzzing with hundreds of pupils on a mission. I'm now in the bottom year, I thought. This felt a little weird. I was keen to find my sister Charlene. She had already spent over three years in this school. Being in year ten gave her authority, coupled with her reputation, ensured immediate respect when introduced to others.

First, I bumped into Shariece. I noticed her dark, coffee-brown complexion and curves from afar. She brought me over to René and Maria. They were both in year eight. They were behind the history hut in the playground where smoking pupils resided. It was my first time meeting Maria. I was surprised that she was white. The few times we had spoken over the phone, the ruggedness of her tone, her patois inspired vernacular, implied she was black. Her parents, however, were Greek. She had long dark hair with big ocean-like waves, and extra-virgin olive skin that spoke of her Mediterranean roots, but she seemed as rough around the edges as any one of us.

Finally, I met up with Charlene. She galloped over to me in a boisterous mood. Her arms swung parallel from left to right. She threw me into a headlock, bowing me over, so her conker-beans hairstyle dangled above my face. And then she threw me back up.

"Get off of me!" I cried.

Charlene ruffled my hair to silence my plea. She was just very rough like that. Beyond her slender frame stood a tall, bourbon brown-skinned boy with crisp oval eyes. He sported a sloped high-top haircut. His lips were cracked, and exposed crooked white teeth that overlapped beneath his smile. But 'crisp' he was all the same. His name was Tyrone. During the vivid introductions, I learnt that the beautiful-looking young man was the brother of Macy's, sister number one, partner Jason. He was my nephew's uncle, and I had never set eyes upon him before, just heard of his name. Macy lived alone with Jason since Ricardo was six months, and our paths hadn't cross. My melting heart wished they had.

Charlene ushered me on to meet other members of The Ghetto Boys who attended our school. Their names were Sean and Donavan. They were nice enough, but I continued on to attend my first assembly and then my first class, Religion. I felt happy about this whole secondary school thing, despite leaving home aggravated. I was at a school that housed gang members mainly from a deprived area of council estates in New Cross nicknamed Ghetto. We were in secret admiration of its members, as we all respected the gangster culture in America. They, like us, watched and loved movies like *Boyz n the Hood*, *Menace II Society*, *New Jack City*, *The Godfather*, and *Scarface*. *Scarface* was the epitome of 'gangsterism' and that's what they wanted to be…it's what we all wanted to be… gangsters in our own movies. They recruited individuals from the area with the same fight, the same struggles, and the same needs. It was like an extended family, offering an acceptance and unity that probably didn't exist at home.

During the first break, the boy I considered an *eediot* bounced everyone out of the way as he emerged from the classroom. He thought he was the 'G' in gangster. I made him aware of what I'd do to him if he tried that again. I made him aware that I would physically punch off his face if he ever bounced me. He ignored the threat and powered his chest out to me. He was testing my nerve, trying to identify if I were genuinely senseless. I let it go. As difficult as this was, I made an effort to avoid confrontation on my first day. Then I saw Charlene descending the stairs onto the landing, and I told her what had happened. She was furious I wasn't defending the reputation. I wasn't driving the fear factor. She told me to go back inside the classroom and "run da punk," which I happily did. But the boy defended himself. Pupils hurried by. It was a break, and I was wasting my time on this fool. I shouted after him, "Shut ya mout' you bonehead!" to silence him, and waved my hand as I made for the door.

Charlene followed me. Her shoulders were raised, and she showed me the palms of her hands. "What, ain't you gonna…?"

"Your mum's a bonehead." The boy's words sailed over my classmates' heads, over their voices and colliding conversations, and then softly, ever so softly, tapped me on the back.

And then it was all over. I saw red and externalised it.

*

Like Mrs. Mitchell had promised, at 3:05 p.m. Mum came shuffling in. She wore shiny green leggings, an old T-shirt and flip-flops that exposed tough, dry-looking feet. I bowed my head in shame. While

Charlene waited her turn outside Mrs. Mitchell's office because her mother was at work and no one could be bothered to explain that Charlene was not Mum's daughter and we've only got the same dad, Mum, Mrs. Mitchell, and I sat in her tiny office. Mum read over my work with eyes that looked like they would burn holes into the paper.

"Like I was saying, Mrs. Johnson-" again, no one could be arsed to explain to her that Mum's surname was Henry. She was not and never had been married to Dad—"when Mr. Ahmed confronted Stephanie about the incident, she showed no remorse or—"

"Was you even dere, doh?!" I foolishly interrupted.

BLAOW!

Mum's fist smashed against my mouth, piercing the inside flesh. She gave me her evil eye, shook her head, and mouthed "you lickle devil", which she'd been calling me since I was six. I held my lips in silence. They were bleeding, swollen, and broken-skinned.

Mrs. Mitchell continued fearfully. She was taken aback and already somewhat regretful. She could tell this wasn't the end of it. She could tell I was going to get a level of beating outside of her comfort zone.

I gave her my best impression of Mum's evil eye and willed her to drop dead before us.

CHAPTER TWO

MR. WILLIAMS

1st October 1993 – Mr. Williams' Maths Class

Hey Di, whassup? Don't think I didn't get suspended for two days, because I did. And don't think Mum didn't bruck me up and then made me read nuff of the Book of Proverbs, because she did. And don't think I wasn't double pissed, because I was. She keeps bombarding my brain with lyrics from the Bible as a form of punishment. Plus I'm getting the beatings on top of it, as though reading that long, boring book isn't enough punishment! And you know we already do Bible Studies most days? OK, then. But I did it. I read as I was dictated to do. Proverbs, chapter one, verse eight. First, I didn't get what that book had to do with me until I read: "My son, hear the instruction of thy father, and forsake not the law of thy mother."

I thought she was trying to be smart. But then I read: "My son, if sinners entice thee, consent thou not. If they say, Come with us, let us lay wait for blood, let us lurk privily for the innocent without cause … let us all have one purse. My son, walk not thou in the way with them … For their

feet run to evil, and make haste to shed blood." Proverbs
1:10-19

Yeah, when I read that, I sat down and thought things
over for a bit. Yes I brucked up the yout' in my class, but
the boy was rude! The pressure was on me to rep my peop's,
and had the yout' not bigged up his chest to me he would
have got a bly!

I loved my diary for doing just that, venting my frustration. Bible-bashing seemed to be common practice at home. Mum used the Bible as both her answer and template for most things. I wasn't a follower; I thought of myself as someone who led the army on the battlefield.

Mum's wrath wasn't one to be reckoned with. It was this fear factor for my own mother that infuriated me. The fear I brought out in others, my mother brought out in me.

Weeks later and I was still incensed by anger. I fantasised about doing things any human being, let alone a child, really shouldn't. And even though I knew it was wrong, I couldn't help those images of me hurting Mum from manifesting. I couldn't help feeling a strong association with the word hate, then guilt for having that feeling. I didn't always feel that way, though.

I didn't always feel so angry, feel this daunting level of despair and frustration. Before this turbulent woe of misunderstanding and aggression, things were relatively good before that point in my life. Back when the Sabbath had no meaning. Before church on a Saturday became a regular routine, and the Bible became the core frame of reference for Mum's life purpose. A time when Safire, Macy, Mum, her boyfriend, Derek, and I would holiday in Corfu, have days out at the farm, weekends away by the countryside. A time when cinema visits, ice-skating, and swimming were our norm. When we still saw our dad regularly on the weekends and throughout the summer holidays, and we knew they loved us in both homes. When Macy told us extraordinary bedtime stories that we described as 'boom', expressed with that extra bit of stomach power that projected the 'oom' of the 'boom'. They were as dramatic and exciting as those stories told by actors on television like *The Lion, the Witch and the Wardrobe* or *Pinocchio*. Those were the days when life was carefree and supposedly without complications, despite our parents' lifestyles and whatever their involvement with criminality.

Sitting in my maths class a few weeks after the incident with Christopher, I reflected on all of this and once more lamented that lie I told when I was six. A lie that triggered the change between Mum and me.

Mr. Williams called out to me from where he stood in front of a whiteboard.

"What?" I replied, jarred that my thoughts were being interrupted.

"Do not answer 'what'; it's 'yes Sir.'"

"Yes... *Sir*," I retorted sarcastically.

"Right! Come to the front. And bring that book in your hand!" he yelled, putting what I thought to be unnecessary pressure on his afro. I knew that stress could result in hair loss.

I slouched my way to the front of the class. The rest of the class waited patiently. Mr. Williams was now sitting back at his desk. He leaned forward on his chair, cupped his lengthy brow in his hand, which suggested a lineage from Frankenstein's monster, and looked up at me disappointed.

"*What?*" I whined, like he was the one wasting everyone's time.

"Do you think it makes sense that from your introductory exams you showed yourself to be one of the brightest pupils in your year, you are subsequently placed in the top class, and yet are as disruptive, if not more so, than those in the academically lower class?" He sounded genuinely bewildered. "Now, let's see that book you have." He showed me the palm of his hand and for a moment I was tempted to clap it.

"No, it's private."

"I will not ask you again!"

"Den don't."

"Right! Class!" The class looked up eagerly. "Please turn to page 186. Geoffrey, would you take over for five minutes please?" A pupil stood to attention with enthusiasm. His eyes were framed with thick black rims. Mr. Williams turned to me, grabbed hold of my arm and attempted to drag me out of the room.

I pulled back. When he turned round to face me, I scowled at him with the same fiery look I gave Christopher before I put heat to his eye. "Don't drag me. I'll follow you, but don't drag me." He immediately let go of my arm and told me to follow, which I did.

He took me to the Isolation Room, a room that I had by now become quite familiar with. He left me there for a few minutes with Mrs. Mitchell whilst he fetched Mr. Ahmed who showered me with rage upon entering that room. I wiped the spit off of my face and kissed my teeth in disdain. He continued to shout at me, spraying me with his oral fluid. I relented. I had no choice but to give up my most treasured possession because I didn't want to get suspended again. I didn't want to endure the beating that Mum would give me. I handed Mr. Williams my diary. Mr. Ahmed and Mr. Williams left the room, but I saw them huddled in conversation through the glass of the door before their footsteps separated in direction.

The four walls started to close in on me. Moisture caught between the fibres of my shirt and dripped down the centre of my back. My teeth clenched shut. A vein that ran across the side of my temple pulsated, and my nostrils flared.

"I can see you're angry, Stephanie. Just take a few minutes to breathe. This is just about some time out in silence so you can think about why you are here." Mrs. Mitchell expressed in a warm tone.

An uncontrollable force took hold of my arms, which mechanically unleashed a round of blows to the wall. White flesh exposed itself beneath the gape of my brown skin and then spotted with blood.

"Stephanie! Now calm down!" Mrs. Mitchell shouted from the other side of the room.

Mr. Williams walked in, whispered to Mrs. Mitchell, and she left. I fell to my knees, clad in grey woolly tights, and banged my hands on the floor and cried with fury, heaving puffs of frustration through gritted teeth, escaping as froth sputtered from the corner of my mouth. I rolled my body into a ball. I knocked the spike of my vertebrae against the table leg. My body rocked back and forth. A deep, winded scream pressed for release from my voice box, but emerged as incessant humming. My mouth was dry and tasted of chalk. Engrossed by shame, I wondered how Mr. Williams would react to the material he had read in my diary. Would he show Mum or tell her of my violent thoughts? Minutes later, polished black laced shoes advanced me. I kept my head dipped low, attempting to masquerade any visible traces of tears.

"It's OK to cry, you know." His deep, calming voice enveloped the room. "You won't be condemned."

I stayed put. My heavy breathing calmed. I felt inner warmth. Strangely I didn't feel threatened or as though he was invading my boundaries. Although, I was surprised by his sudden kindness. His exposure to my diary didn't lead him to condemn me. His relaxed presence and gentle smile made me feel as though he understood my frustration and inner turmoil. I looked up, face slightly dampened, and didn't even feel ashamed anymore. For once, I didn't feel that urge to roll my eyes, kiss my teeth, or express any disgust towards him, my jarring mathematics teacher. I gazed at him, and we experienced organic mutual respect for one another. His face was soft. With suited arms crossed, he stared down at me. A beam sprawled across his face and mine alike. Then he offered me his right arm, which I grabbed hold of and pulled myself up.

"What are you like, eh?" he said patting my back in a slight circular motion.

"How much did you read?"

"Only to where the page-divider was, but I got the gist of it."

So now Mr. Williams was aware of my feelings toward Mum, the violent things I considered doing, and how much I disliked the context that the Bible was used at home. So now I needed to understand his thoughts on what I said, and so I asked, "What are you finking?"

Mr. Williams looked down at me earnestly, "I think your mum is doing her best, but I think it would help you both to talk more rather than be aggressive to one another or others around you."

"I don't wanna talk to her. What's the point of talking to someone who doesn't listen?" I snapped.

"Stephanie, sometimes it's not what we say but how we say it that will determine how people respond to us."

I sighed. I no longer wanted to talk about my mum or my personal business with him. We walked back to class. I felt in a better place. As I advanced the stairs of the Maths hut, Mr. Ahmed stepped out from the class. "Sorted, Mr. Williams?" he asked.

"Yes." Mr. Williams replied.

"Stephanie!" Mr. Ahmed barked. "I'll be seeing you at lunch—

you're on report! No one…I mean *no one*…gets away with disrupting a class in my school."

I learned that Mr. Ahmed got promoted to Headmaster at the start of my academic year. He ran the school well and executed a zero tolerance mandate. I kissed my teeth neatly and bopped in behind Mr. Williams with a nonchalant flare I possessed.

"Did you just suck your teeth at me?" Mr. Ahmed demanded.

"No," I denied, and entered the class.

*

The rest of the school day breezed past. My diary was returned to me at the end of the day, before I met Safire, Shariece, René and Maria by the benches in the playground. They all wore their uniform in the same way: white shirt untucked over a black or grey pleated skirt, top button undone with tie worn loose. The knot of the tie was thick and its fat tail hung down to breast height whilst the skinny bit was tucked into the slit between the shirt's buttons. Our black blazers had badges that detailed a shepherd with his staff and his sheep. Brown crispy leaves blew about, escorting dust in its movements. I wiped the corners of my eyes. Shariece canerowed Maria's long, dark brown, curly hair. René unplatted her long loose curled shiny hair from its ponytail. As she often did, she was showing off because she was aware most black school girls longed for lengthy, jet-black, loosely curled hair. She looked mixed race, but was black.

"So, where were you at lunch?" Maria queried, zipping up her leather jacket.

"Mr. Ahmed, innit; put me on report and had me eat my lunch in his office true-say I had a little run-in wiv Mr. Williams, but me and him is sweet now." I turned to René. "Stop showing off wiv your hair, man."

"Innit!" Shariece agreed, tying Maria's two loose-plaited ends together with an elastic band.

"I'm not!" René pleaded, baring her teeth while shaking out her hair so the wind could rummage through it like white models did in certain magazines and TV advertisements.

"Look at her! She's showing off for true," Safire confirmed. "Come here, René, let me brush it," and René sat down. Safire brushed her hair with that covetous gaze in her eyes. "Ah, this ain't fair," she said, "I wish I had hair like yours."

I looked at Safire wearing Macy's Click-suit jacket. She had springy coiled, shoulder length, thick, dark brown hair. My family donned an assortment of skin complexions and hair types, from the pale buttercups to the deep dark chocolates, and 4C through to 3B. Unlike Shariece. Her hair was light, short, with tight coiled strands. The 4D hair-type, she managed using Dax waxing products that created ocean waves and worked miraculously to slick down springy afro hair.

"How comes," Safire continued to René, "your hair's so soft when you're not even half-caste?"

"That's what I was gonna ask," I added, picking the bobbles off my tights.

"Oh no!" Maria blurted with widened eyes and flared nostrils. "You shouldn't say dat y'know, Safire. Dat's like...like...not racist, but like... improper, innit."

"Innit!" René added.

"No, it's not," I defended. "How d'you figure dat?"

"Innit, Steph, they're talking rubbish," Safire and I agreed. Thanks to our mutual upbringing we didn't recognise such sayings as offensive.

"I dunno, so I'm staying out of dis," Shariece slipped in, freeing herself of responsibility.

"Trus' me," Maria stressed, "my dad's a social worker, so he's always talking 'bout dese types of like...you know, like... occ...incidences! That's the word."

"So what, is 'half-breed' like improper?" I asked. I just didn't know.

"*Yeah!*" Maria shouted emphatically.

I was shocked...I mean, I was properly shocked.

"So how comes people in our family uses both of dem like unna-not'in," Safire put to her, baffled.

"Innit!" I inserted. My family used these terms in every day language.

They looked at us dismayed. They considered it rude to question our background and why we didn't know the things they'd learned. Shariece's parents were both from Zimbabwe, so she upheld some good African values when it suited her. She lived in a nice four-bed semi-detached house in Catford with a drive and decent-sized garden. The house was privately paid for, not owned by the council like the rest of ours. Her father was a doctor and her mother a primary school teacher. She had many positive influences and choices at home, but like Safire and I, Shariece could also be a rebel when she felt like it. She had run away from home, got into fights, shoplifted, told the teacher to fuck off, and got in late too, but only when she wanted to piss her mum off. Her mother focused on her two younger siblings between the ages of four and seven, and her father worked round the clock and barely acknowledged her at home. She later told me she often called him by his first name.

René grew up with her mum and three younger siblings, under eight in a two-bed house in Brockley. She liked to do right in her mother's eyes, as she'd seen her mother go through a lot of shit. But sometimes, she just got caught out though she would always take time out to make amends with her mum. René would even ground herself.

Maria grew up with both her parents as an only child on a council estate in Turnham. It seemed as though her household was tight. She never came into school complaining about unfair disciplinary methods being executed or bearing scars from the night before. I guessed all was good. I knew her father was a social worker but knew nothing of her mother or what she did, so I assumed she was a stay-at-home mum. We were all different, but we were brethren.

"Anyway, let's get back to the point," Shariece interjected, "which was how comes René's hair's so soft and long when she ain't...you know, directly mixed or anyfing?"

"Girls!!" A voice familiar to me, and my frustration hit us from afar. "Do you not have homes to go to? School has finished; now unless you want to spend your evening in detention, I suggest you leave the premises NOW!" at which point Mr. Ahmed turned and marched away.

We got up to leave. We took the back route home. We cut through Manor Park while René explained that her fair complexion and soft hair was due to a throwback. I asked if it "licks right back to your people-dem's slave master?"

"Nah," She responded, "just my great-grandma."

"What d'you know about slavery?" Maria questioned.

"Just dat Jamaicans and some ovver black people were slaves for a bag of white people. That's why they own nuff t'ings, people's land and dem t'ings, and we don't. And that's why they don't like us, you know, the cultured ones and dat—you know, like people in power."

"Who told you dat, Steph? Mum?" Safire nosed.

"No, I just figured because I never see any black people in Buckingham Palace or in Parliament or any of dat on the TV, plus, remember how Dad would say how da raddy dem used to beat him and his bredrens up for no reason, just coz they were black?"

"What's 'raddy' stand for again?" René asked me. She was scratching her arm and making those annoying scratchy nylon sounds those American Football jackets made.

"I can't 'member what the full word is, but it means 'bull', innit, you know, 'feds', 'bwoy-dem', 'po-po', 'police'," I explained.

"Radication squad," Shariece threw in.

"Yeah, dat's what I wanted to know," René said.

"You know Greeks were slaves too?" Maria added to the plate.

"And Africans!" Shariece attached.

"But ain't black people in the Caribbean, like, from the line of African slaves? Like they brought them there, innit?" Maria questioned, playing with the zip of her leather jacket.

"Yeah, you're right!" said Shariece.

"I dunno, I think so." Shamefully I wasn't sure. Neither was Rene or Safire.

"I didn't know 'bout Greeks," René said, "but remember when they was showing us about African slaves in *Roots*?"

"Yeah, I 'member *Roots*," Safire said getting hyper, recalling the TV series we'd watched. "'Member Kunta Kinte, Steph? 'My name's *Kunta Kin-te*,'" she jested and raised her arms pretending to get whipped, mimicking the scene where the slave master tries to give Kunta Kinte a name not of his tribe.

We all ruptured into a ribcage, muscle-aching laughter.

"Ah, my belly's gonna bus'!" René laughed, fingering the spare tyres around her stomach.

"Nah, dat was taking *lib*erties!" I stressed. "If dat was me, I would've obiahed-up the whole of dem white people; just sent the whole of dem to sleep—permanently, no long-t'ing, like that plague that killed off Pharaoh's people-dem's first born, innit, Safire?"

"Yeah, coz most Africans deal wiv obiah; *pure* blackmagic dey're running," Safire pointed out.

"No we don't, Safire!" Shariece defended.

"Yes you do! Innit, Steph, dey're proper pagans, innit?"

"I dunno, some of dem," I said earnestly.

"Keep me outta dis," René ordered.

"Me too," piped up Maria.

Shariece and Safire argued all the way to our house. That was just what we did. Tomorrow would be another day and all would be forgotten. Mostly.

CHAPTER THREE

BEATING

12th January 1994 – My Gates

Whassup Di? Things ain't looking too rosy and I need someone to talk to as I dunno what to do. I'm due a beating. And having this looming over my head is kinda stressing me out. Plus things were going quite well, you know. We had a nice Christmas and dat, all the family was at Mama's and Papa's house which was really nice because dat's the only time the whole family really get together. There were nuff of us there: me, Safire, Macy, Ricardo and Mum; Aunty Ruth and her kids Stella and Leroy; Aunty Denise and her kids Joanne and Jermaine, and a few other second cousins I didn't know from abroad. Mama cooked up one big-off turkey with stuffin, which was seasoned proper with herbs and spices. We had a roasted leg of lamb, roast potatoes, roasted parsnips and carrots, rice and peas, plain white rice, them nasty brussel sprouts, broccoli, macaroni cheese, salads and proper gravy. Like Mum, Mama uses the juice that comes from the meat to make the gravy. For desert we had trifle, cheesecake, chocolate gateau and ice cream. As I said, there was nuff food, man. Mama set out the glass oval dining table crisp! For real, it properly looked the part. She used her proper china plates with all the gold trimmings and that, cutlery that was polished up like mirrors, plus the twinkling crystal champagne glasses she only takes out for special occasions. Alcohol wasn't running in there though—it was a sparkling non-alcoholic grape juice ting. But it was nice. My aunts helped out in the kitchen chatting away, cracking jokes, whilst me, my sisters and cousins rapped upstairs in one of the bedrooms and on the top stairs. Before you knew it, we were sitting at the table waiting for Mama to finish her big-long-dotty prayer to bless the food and family, sending some of the younger ones into the land of la-la.

But once we'd eaten, everyone quietened down with the dimming lights, spread out on the floor or across the sofas overlapping someone, we watched The Colour Purple which I hadn't seen in a while. That Celie gave me joke. Later, me, my sisters and Ricardo went to Pauline's and Dad's, which was cool until they got into a big argument. Anyway, it was rosy then but it's not rosy now. I'm due a beating.

It was still my first year at secondary school. I continued to diarise my feelings and concerns as I did when I was younger, using Di as a mood board for all my life's events. My sisters and I had only recently returned from the Christmas holidays, so it hadn't really been that long since my last fiasco at school, but still I liked to take chances.

My cousin Stella went to Eltham Secondary School, a short bus ride away from our school. She decided to bunk the afternoon off one day. She came to my school. Safire was in the Isolation Room, so it was up to me to take care of Stella. I did what most trying kids would do. I took Christopher's tie, put it on Stella, and snuck her into my history lesson. I said she was new and Mrs. Mitchell didn't even notice or say anything. She stopped paying me much mind since she'd participated in getting my lip busted by Mum and witnessed my outburst back in October. Guilt must have altered her perception of me, or my indignant stares must have altered her handling of me. Whatever the case, knowing my unsettled frame of mind and Mum's type of parenting, she had enough sense to stay away from me. She understood that violent discipline was implemented both against and by me. So we got through my history lesson without Stella being noticed as a fraud.

After school, Stella, Safire, Shariece, Maria, and I gathered behind the maths hut looking for Charlene. Safire and I wanted to show her that Stella was here, and I especially wanted to tell her of the skilful way in which I snuck Stella into my history class. We were all huddled up in our group with chattering teeth. It was freezing outside! The ground was icy, and the feeling in my toes started to disappear. Icicle raindrops had formed a circumference round the gutter trimmings of the maths hut roof and hung from the tips of branches tempting me to suck them like an ice-lolly. But I knew better than to carry out such thoughts and reap the scornful glares of my people. The lovely Tyrone stood behind the hut with his back leaning against the wall, opposite Sean. He concentrated on what was in his hands.

"Have you seen Charlene?" I got in first before Safire had a chance to exchange words with our nephew's uncle who I was falling for. Tyrone was what some might call 'the dog's bollocks', others 'handsome'. But I called him 'cris'; crisp without the p. And though I had no plans to tell him or anyone else that, I did enjoy whatever attention he put my way.

"She left wiv Donavan," he replied, and continued to sprinkle a green-budded potent herb into Sean's holey gloved hand. Sean was holding the sheet of Rizla. We all knew this weed was potent because the smell violently tickled our nostrils and told us so. The thick, green, furry buds now laid within the crease of the Rizla sheet in Sean's hand waiting either to be rolled or for something else to be added to its potency. Tyrone searched his pockets irritably for something.

"D'you wanna nico?" Stella said. This was totally out of the blue. Safire and I were shocked. For that moment I wanted to be Stella. I wanted to be the one to give Tyrone what he so desperately needed, and give it to him with such familiarity of the process he was indulged in and a cool air that said I dabbled with it too! She backed him a packet of the golden-cased cigarettes, which she'd taken from the inside of her green bomber jacket.

"Rah, fanks!" Tyrone exclaimed, as Safire and I exchanged a glare of surprise. "You're Leroy's sister, innit?" he continued. "You two look alike *bad*!"

Safire and I turned to look at Stella, still surprised that she already smoked and knew about this whole building up spliffs thing. She was only Safire's age, and was so cool about it. I longed even more to swap shoes with Stella and walk her path for those few minutes.

"He's my twin, innit," Stella responded. "Can I get some of dat?"

Tyrone nodded and put a flame to his spliff. Maria then said to Stella, "Let's 'ave a fag?" Stella gave Maria a cigarette, and she smoked it shivering fiercely in the frosty cold. She was underdressed as always. For some crazy reason Maria came out of her house with a shirt and a blazer in the winter. She never wore her leather jacket. She mistakenly thought winter was there to pet her when we all knew winter had mercy on no one.

"It's cutting!" I said and pulled my hands in under my flat puffer coat that I really wasn't feeling as Mum got it from the market, then under my blazer, under my jumper, under my shirt and under my vest wrapping them about my small waist. Back then, my chest was high, trivial things like the cost of clothing would be the deciding factor of whether I would 'feel' it or not.

Shariece initiated cuddling me from behind, her sturdy chin resting on my shoulder. Safire drew for the spliff from Stella and puffed on it erratically. An unrecognisable urge came from within me, and all of a sudden the words: "Let's 'ave some!" left my tongue and my hand found its way from beneath the several layers of clothing and took the spliff from Safire's mouth. I pulled on the spliff and let the smoke roam in my mouth before letting it back out. Stella noticed this and pointed out that I wasn't taking it in properly. Embarrassing. Tyrone's hand was out wanting to redeem the spliff I was so clearly wasting, but I took one final pull of the spliff, sucking it long and hard in the way Stella said it should be done. A heap of smoke bulldozed its way to the back of my throat and attempted to murder me, choking me to what felt like death. My legs started to give way. My vision closed in on me and sound became airy and hollow like the inside of a seashell.

"Ah shit! Let's get her home," Stella panicked.

"I feel nuts too; I'm gonna faint," Safire contributed.

Safire and I got ushered mob-like to our home. Luckily Mum wasn't back from work yet. She now did home deliveries for some company and got a company car out of it, which was good, but even though Mum's car wasn't outside, it was only wise to expect the unexpected with her. I felt fucked. Nevertheless, I was mindful of the repercussions if we got caught. Stella tried to get me to lie down, but I was adamant that I had to wash my hands and brush my teeth before falling asleep. Naturally, they all agreed that that was smart thinking. When Mum got home accompanied by Macy and Ricardo, everyone bar Sean was still at the house. Safire had told Sean the rules: no 'man', boy or otherwise, entered our house. Tyrone was the exception because he was Ricardo's uncle, and Mum had already built a relationship with his brother, Jason, being her only grandchild's father.

I had fallen into a semi-subconscious trance, limbs folded into my chest. I lay within the sunken centre of my bottom bunk. Maria, Shariece, Stella and Tyrone were 'bogling' to 'Wicked Inna Bed' by Shabba Ranks that was playing on my 'bashment' and R&B tape, a dance that was very popular in dancehall videos on TV and throughout Caribbean community. It was at this point when things started to pop off downstairs. Pots and pans crashed against the walls and onto the floor. Safire cursed a range of vulgar swear words after Mum just as we'd do out on the road, if only to illustrate our Jamaican roots and increase the fear that such talk generated. Everyone froze in their dance moves like kids playing Musical Statues. Fear sprung up beneath their feet and held tight to their facial expressions. Realisation settled in and I knew it was on top for us.

Stella and my friends all tailed each other down the stairs to leave as Mum ran them out of the house. Macy politely inquired, "You lot all right?" as they passed, and told Tyrone to come and visit. Ricardo wailed to save 'Aunty 'Fire'. I stayed put. I was pretending to sleep. I subscribed to the concept of 'see no evil, hear no evil'. But that wasn't enough.

It wasn't long before Mum was upstairs dragging me out of my pretend sleep. She smelled my breath whilst pinning me up against a wall where pictures of family and friends were pinned up. She then told me those words that no child in my family wanted to hear: "Today, you ah goh get di beating of ya life," and she said so calmly, which made it all the more formidable and believable. I was placed third in the queue for a beating.

Shortly after, Aunty Ruth arrived at our house seeming hungry to participate in the beating that involved her daughter, Stella. Safire said she removed her coat and rolled up her sleeves upon entry into our home. She calmly expressed to Mum that this visit was convenient as she had just finished a minicab drop-off in the area. To say I was scared would be an understatement. I almost pissed myself at the thought of what I was to undergo. And I was baffled as to how and why we got caught. My breath smelt fresh; I had brushed my teeth three times!

Di, as I said, I'm due a beating right about now and I can't allow myself to go through it. Every way I look at this, this is looking long! I timed Safire's beating for twenty minutes straight; she's with me in my room now and all of her back's looking cake-o; I'm serious, Di, they've drawn blood!

"Look," Safire snivelled, "it's bleeding."

I looked at my sister's exposed bottom, disheartened. I changed into some stretch jeans and a black woolly jumper. I was still trying to figure out how Mum smelt smoke on my breath when I had brushed my teeth so many times. Thick belt marks had split and drawn blood from Safire's honey and cream skin and turned it blood red. Stella was getting dealt with as we spoke. Her screams were desperate pleads for mercy, but the elders weren't giving her any mercy. We didn't get many chances for slip-ups in my family. Macy cried, "Allow it, Mum!" and, "Calm down, Aunty Ruth!"

Mum shouted something about, "In di name of God...!" and I contemplated an escape route. I just couldn't go downstairs and face the same fate as Stella and Safire. I jammed some clothes and my diary into my school rucksack. "Saf, are you coming or not?" I asked my forlorn sister.

She scrunched up her face in pain. "Where're we gonna go?"

"We'll run away to Jermaine's house, and he can hide us from Aunty Denise, den when she goes church tomorrow, we'll be free again. Come on! I'm going now." Jermaine was another cousin of mine. He lived with his sister and his mum not too far from us. I put on my coat and black Nike Air Huarache's that Dad bought me for Christmas. He bought Safire and me a pair of trainers every year, which I thought at the time was his way of compensating for the cheap taste in clothing and footwear that Mum had acquired since her baptism.

Safire grabbed a plastic bag from under my bed and ran into her bedroom across the hallway to get her things. I moved over to the open window, threw my bag out, and then clambered up onto the windowsill and moved one leg gingerly out before carefully pulling my other leg over. I clung onto the window frame with all my might trying to prepare my dangling legs for the fall. Safire threw her bag out of the other window and climb through. I jumped the ten or so feet landeding on my feet. As I scrambled for my bag and stood up, I saw Macy in the kitchen window peering at me. Safire jumped and fell onto her battered behind. She moaned an "owww" through her hand and Macy signalled for us to make moves quick. I picked Safire up, grabbed her bag, and started running through the white sunset, slipping occasionally.

Just as we passed the park, sticking to the back roads through Hither Green, Safire stopped. "I ca... I can't go on; let's turn back and go home."

"Are you mad?!" I shouted at her, the white air licking out on every word. "So I can get double-butted? I don't think so. You can go back if you want, but I'm not, not for at least a couple days. She needs time to calm down, Saf."

"We're just gonna get in worse trouble if we duck out now."

"Look, I'm not going back, Safire! So tell me what you're doing."

"I'm turning back." Her face looked apologetic. Her nostrils flared, her eyelids dropped, her lip hung and her head was bowed for full effect.

"See ya later, den."

I turned and ran swiftly into the night hearing my sister shout, "Be careful!" Once at the bottom of Leahurst Road I turned back to her and waved a brave goodbye.

A few residential roads of terraced and semi-detached houses later, littered with jalopies and a few top-notch cars, I landed outside my cousin Jermaine's house, which was a red-brick, three-bedroom, end of terrace with double glazing. I was sweating from all the running. For a short period I mentally embraced my athleticism and considered running the 400 metre tracks at school. The sweat evaporated quickly and I became cold again, my teeth chattering as I knocked on the door having given the road a once-over in search of Aunty Denise's car. As expected she was at work. Aunty Denise was always at work. She was a single mum who worked twelve to fifteen hours a day to clothe and feed her children, and pay for a mortgage on a property she'd bought from the council at a discounted price. She was one of the smarter elders who reaped and utilised the benefits of the social system, such as the discounts they offered on home purchases, to advance her and her family rather than rely on hand-outs. But she was also extremely heavy-handed on the discipline front. Back then, we would all rather my mum's licks than Aunty Denise's.

"Steph! What're you doing here?" Jermaine questioned. He glanced up and down the road and drew me in hurriedly.

"Madness!" I gushed, rushing in to stretch over a wooden cabinet that housed a TV. I twisted the front room Louvre blinds closed. "Don't think Mum and Aunty Ruth never just found out dat me, Safire and Stella were all bu'ning weed." I dropped onto the sofa and tried to relax a bit. I folded my arms and rubbed down the goose pimples that were still apparent, absorbing the information I just shared.

"Don't lie," Jermaine said relatively calm and unmoved. He tied up an off-white and somewhat tatty dressing gown around his tall, narrow build.

"And don't think Safire didn't get whacked up till blood was pumping from her skin, and Stella was getting dealt wiv as I was dussing out!"

"Don't lie!" Jermaine exclaimed, now gripped by excitement.

I filled him in on what had happened. Sitting before the gas fire, he turned it on while flaring his wide nostrils, thrilled with 'I wish I was there' longing and glee, just as a witness to say he was part of our conundrum. I heard the staircase creak. My heart attempted suicide, trying to tear its way through my chest and into my lap.

"Who's dat?!" I whispered, my eyes darting all over the place in a panic.

"Oh, dat must be Joanne."

Slowly my heart sank back into my chest and softened its beats. My cousin Joanne, a dark chocolate-skinned gal with jet-black kinky hair, entered the room in her nightgown. She was in her late teens, five years older than Jermaine who was fourteen. She had a tall, slim frame with a tiny waist, wide child-bearing hips, a round behind and long, athletic pins that could easily take her onto a high fashion catwalk.

"Oh, what're you doing here?" she put to me in a jarring tone that insinuated she'd rather me not be there.

Again I recited what had happened, this time in a more dramatic way than the first. Joanne's mood perked up.

"And Macy really helped you lot get away?" she asked, appearing to take warmly to the idea that I still had a beating lined up for me.

"Yeah! She stood guard while I leaped out the window onto the tree like a monkey!" I enjoyed embellishing the truth for my cousins and we all had a good laugh.

Jermaine set up a bed for me under his own and we all settled in our rooms to sleep before Aunty Denise was due home.

In the morning, as predicted, Aunty Denise got up to go to church, but unfortunately she forced Jermaine and Joanne to attend church with her, even though they claimed sickness. I was left in the house alone to figure out my next step. Maybe I'll go to Macy's house, I thought. Then again, that's a bit of an easy catch. What about Shariece? They won't find me there, she can hide me in her—

There was a knock at the door. I went to peek out of Jermaine's bedroom window thinking it must be Jehovah's Witnesses. My heart started to dance wildly, licking hard at my chest when I saw Mum pacing the small concrete porch and Safire and Ricardo sitting in her white hatchback company car. As I went to pull my head back, I heard: "Mum! There she is."

Anger boiled over me as I saw Safire's scrawny, bony, yellow-skinned finger pointing my way and I thought of her little grassing-up antics when we were growing up. Grassing was her middle name. She was the one who told Mum that I'd told Dad that Derek had hit me when he never did. She did this so Mum would know whose fault it was that her boyfriend lay in a hospital bed with stitches in his hand and why her children's father slept in HM Prison serving a three-year sentence. Of course the story wasn't so simple, as it was that day that changed my relationship with the household, and subsequently my life.

*

I was six. You could say I knew right from wrong, but I also knew about preferences, stories, how to make sure that you were liked the most by someone even if they were your parent: give them what they want. Safire grassed on Macy and me a lot. She gave Mum what she wanted. I thought she was her favourite. Macy gave Dad updates on us at home, outlining the details of how the house was structured, the fancy goods we had and the excessive amounts of money that rolled through the hands of Derek. Macy gave Dad what he wanted. I followed suit only when Dad asked a lot of questions, but I didn't know much. The expensive clothes, jewellery and furnishings were not unusual for me, and it came from both sides: Mum and Dad.

One day I told Dad I didn't like Derek any more. I knew Dad disliked Derek in a deep, begrudging way. Mainly due to the fact that he was now semi-raising his children, and Dad was anti-drugs (a-class drugs) and aware of Derek's involvement in them. But Derek had really annoyed me that week. He shouted at me for not doing something, which got me a beating from Mum. My backside was stinging for hours afterwards and I felt, even at the age of six, that my punishment did not fit the crime. So I wanted Derek to pay. I told Dad how Derek had shouted at me. But that wasn't enough and Dad prowled for more.

"Did he touch you? Did dat batty-bwoy put his hand on you?" He repeated this two or three times. From my prolonged silence my answer emerged into a 'yes'. The magnitude of the consequence to this answer I was unable to fathom. I just didn't think that far in advance. I did comprehend the possibility of violence, because my father took no prisoners in informing us and the world of his menacing values, but I didn't foresee this violence being directed at us as a family. I just considered my dad as my hero who would beat anyone up who troubled me or my sisters.

The following week it happened. I was standing in the doorway watching Derek stand over the balcony bare-chested with a towel round his waist. He was watching Macy and Charlene roll around on the grass below whilst my cousin Melvin rode his bike behind them. Melvin was Macy's age, which was twelve at the time. Dad suddenly appeared on the communal landing from nowhere. He looked dressed to kill in a crisp suit and tie accessorised with a medallion gold chain that had his initials encrusted with diamonds in the centre. Everything about him was looking sharp. He had a rucksack slung over one shoulder with his left hand fastened tight to its handle. The other hand held a chopper that looked like it belonged in a chef's kitchen or slaughterhouse. I'd seen it many times in Dad's bedroom beside the bible on the bottom glass panel of his bedside table. I knew what was coming but said nothing.

Dad peered at me and put his finger to his lips twinkling brightly with an ostentatious diamond ring. I wasn't saying a word. It didn't take long before words were exchanged. Dad animatedly let Derek know what he thought of him, which was interspersed with the expected 'bombaclaat', 'bloodclaat', 'pussyclaat' and 'raasclaat', you know...for extra effect. Then the glistening steel rose above Dad's head and shaded Derek's eyes before it came down with great speed, murder undoubtedly displaying its intentions. Survival instincts kicked in for Derek. His head ducked low and his hand protected him from the blood-hungry steel. Derek's hand opened up like the belly of a fish and bled profusely. Then it was Mum's turn.

Dad moved on from Derek and entered the house. He headed up the stairs, and it was obvious who he was seeking. That was when the penny dropped and I became immediately remorseful. But I was six. No amount of wishes or prayers were going stop what was happening. Dad was mad that the mother of his three children had settled with a coke dealer, who did coke himself on occasion and was exposing certain things to his eldest daughter, which obviously I didn't know at the time. All I could remember thinking was that my little story had been blown way out of proportion, but over the coming years I realised people didn't always react to one thing.

Derek got chopped right through the middle of his hand and Mum got one of her teeth knocked out and her mouth busted. It was awful, and witnessed in full by Safire. I witnessed Derek's attack and suffering. Macy, Charlene and my unstable cousin Melvin whose father had committed suicide witnessed my dad's arrest after a movie-like chase down the hill of our road. And then the following week in church the pastor asked if he could get a witness!

*

So again I was about to deal with the repercussions of Safire's grassing tribute. Mum's mouth motored off. My heartbeat slowed. I heaved and slowed my thinking. My hearing became distorted. Livid. I glared at Safire with murderous eyes. Stepping off the single bed, and backing away from the window, Mum was shouting for me to open the door. She probably announced I was due a beating. But this I already knew. I took off Jermaine's T-shirt and dressed. Then I just sat at the top of the stairs with my rucksack and stared down at the wooden front door— the door to my pain and suffering.

"If you soh bad, come an' get your beating!" Mum awkwardly shouted through the black letterbox, which was situated at the bottom of the door.

I wasn't usually one to run right into havoc, but I wasn't one to run away from it either—especially when it was knocking at my door. Am I bad? I asked myself. Course! Can I handle getting whacked up? Course! I felt I was bad and tough enough to dish out licks so I should be bad and tough enough to take some back. I continued debating with myself in this way before deciding my destiny. I got up and trotted down the stairs, opened the door and stepped out into the unknown.

"Get ya backside inna di cyar!"

Ricardo climbed onto me as I clambered into the back of the car. Safire peeped back at me from the front seat like she was about to crack a smile and say something.

"DON'T chat to me, you grass!" I barked at her before she got to grin her teeth wide enough.

When we got home it was on top for me: hoover parts, wires, belts, high-heeled shoes and other household items collided with my body violently as though this woman, my mother, was trying to kill me. I wriggled, trying to break free from her clasp. At the same time I mentally internalised the pain. I forced my brain to capture and hold any potential sound that would have revealed my hurt and therefore empowered Mum with the knowledge that this beating was doing what she intended it to do: hurt me.

But my response to this beating was different to normal. I didn't run around wildly, crying tears. Calm and composed I voiced my hate for Mum. I cited she was a hypocrite, since she'd smoked at my age. I told her that God would see to it that she went to hell for her treatment of me. I also added that her disciplinary skills were useless, as I was still going to smoke if I wanted to.

It was like the beating went on forever...

My body was so hurt I couldn't even feel when her instruments struck me any longer. I was numb – tired and numb. Ricardo was crying. He screamed like a child who had lost his mind and was on the verge of vomiting. Safire was crying too. She must have been regretting her role as the informer (I later repeatedly sung the song 'Informer' by Snow to remind her of this).

Soon enough Mum was crying, hopeless. She stopped beating me.

Tears cascaded down her face as though someone had thrown a cup of water on her.

I fled from her grip and the shadow of her high-heeled shoe. I headed upstairs to my room, closed the door and splashed my tears on my diary in silence. I had to get rid of the horrific thoughts that plagued my mind so I wrote of these in my diary with trembling hands, and later scribbled over them so they were illegible. Beatings were a part of the cultural make-up of my family, but they didn't deter me from the crimes and other wrongdoings I carried out. They only made me more determined to keep them hidden.

CHAPTER FOUR

NON P TERRITORY

20th January 1994 – 47 bus

Whassup, Di? For a solid week me and Mum haven't spoken. Not like I'm bovvered, coz I'm not. Safire and Mum are cool since that drama because Safire apologised for everything: smoking, cussing bad-word and running away. She's still smoking though, so that means the beating was for nothing. All week Safire's been trying to get me to say sorry to Mum so things will go back to normal, but I won't. I'll speak to Safire because I know she was forced to grass on me, but I ain't talking to dat woman...EVER! As I said: I'm not bovvered! Stephanie Johnson doesn't say sorry for nothing she's not sorry for—it doesn't make sense. Mum hasn't given me money for school all week because she wants me to have to ask her, but I won't. I rather take Christopher's money than ask her. I don't think it's up to me to make amends anyway—it was her who bruck me up with licks so it should be her that fixes it with words, ah-lie? Di, I said am I lying? Anyway, as I said, I'm not bovvered. That's why I'm staying at Dad's. I'm on my way to his house now...

"Silwood Estate!" The bus driver pronounced.

I slammed my diary shut and rushed off the 47 bus holding on tightly to my things. I ran through the dark estate as I always did. I was on what we called my Ps and Qs. And it didn't mean 'please and thank-yous'. It denoted being alert, being on your toes or on your guard. On a social housing estate like Silwood, it was common sense to be on your Ps and Qs, to avoid either getting mugged, raped, or attacked for fun. Naturally I had my wits about me. I was always ready for an attacker. I held my door keys in my hand in defence mode should I become someone's prey. It was about survival of the fittest. I let myself into the block relieved to be unscathed.

I'd barely come through the door when Dad started on his 'non-pettance', an expression that described Dad him perfectly. He was a man of zero tolerance, no mercy, and he never over-indulged or gave in; all the things soppy people do to their pets. He didn't give you a centimetre, so there was never a chance in taking an inch let alone a yard. He was simply 'non-p'.

"It's after five, where have you been?"

"I was given an hour's detention, Dad. Sorry."

I shut the front door behind me and locked the four secure locks. Dad was in his living room that resembled the Victorian age, ornately decorated with antiques. He sat on a heavily carved rosewood gentleman's chair. He was slow-burning the head of a spliff with a serene air about him, how I imagined Cuban gentlemen smoked cigars. I stepped outside of his view in the hope of removing myself from his radar. I headed straight for the stairs, trying to be quiet, but knocked Dad's grandfather clock with my bag accidentally. Safire and I called the clock Big Ben. The clock seemed out of place there, right at the foot of the stairs, especially as there was another grandfather clock at the top. I gave Dad an apologetic look and mounted the stairs to my room, smiling at the second Big Ben as I passed it.

"Come back down here when you're done," Dad said some minutes later, "coz I ain't even done with you yet, 'bout ya getting detention. Wha' yuh ah do fi get *bloodclaat* detention?!"

I chucked my bag on the floor of the bedroom. The tightness of my ponytail had rippled the hair at the centre of my head, which was bringing on a headache. I pulled the band loose. For some moments I lay there on the bottom bunk trying to ease my stresses out. Dad continued to let his mouth run over and above the reggae drumbeats of Dennis Brown's 'Stop the Fussing and Fighting'. I blocked out the profanities he was undoubtedly cursing. After a while I took off my uniform and had a wash. Then I dressed into a black tracksuit that Macy had given me, though it was big because she got it when she was pregnant with Ricardo. But I made it work.

By the time I got down the stairs, making gun signs at the historic portraits of the likes of Martin Luther King and Malcolm X on my way—this demonstrated an appreciation of their contribution to history, and something I had copied from Dad—Dad was in the kitchen. He seemed relaxed. He was making tea. The music had moved on to a Bob Marley number: 'Who the Cap Fit'. He offered me a cup, which I gladly accepted. "Horlicks, please," I said. Horlicks was my favourite and all I could get at home with the ban on caffeine Mum introduced at home. I explained why I got a detention that day, "Basically I wasn't really concentrating. Julius Caesar, The Roman Empire and all dat doesn't really interest me," I said earnestly, "Especially the way my teacher, Mrs. Mitchell tells it. She's boring, Dad!"

"Well you know it's important that you know the history of the people that make up the country where you're from," His cockney tone was encouraging. I preferred when he spoke in this dialect. There was usually less rage there.

I told Dad what I told Mrs. Mitchell: "What does Julius Caesar and dem gotta do with me? And I thought Jamaica was my country?" I contended. I was confused.

"It is, but what colour's your passport? Because it's that passport that's gonna get you anywhere in life, so learn what you 'ave to learn and don't be running up ya mout' to no teacher. D'you 'ear me?!"

I was confused. I didn't know if I was Jamaican or British, let alone African, and my parents didn't make this subject any easier for me.

"Yes, Dad." I answered and then changing the subject said, "*Daaad...* can I have £50 for a new pair of trainers, please? It's my birthday coming up soon."

"You ain't gettin' jack-squidly until you learn how to behave yourself in school! And didn't I just get you and Safire trainers for Christmas?"

I didn't respond to that. I drank my tea staring out of the kitchen window through draping net curtains. The night was spotted with lights. A flashing light shined brighter and drew attention away from the others. It was the pyramid point of Canary Wharf. Sitting on a wooden stool at the countertop, both hands cupping a Harrods mug, I wondered if there were any black men in history that operated with the same menace as Julius Caesar in conquering another man's land. I quite liked the idea of this ancient form of gangsterism.

Dad was standing by the sink washing out his cup. He looked at me warmly. "Fix up your hair. We're going out."

"Where're we going?"

"Dada's. Ain't you hungry?"

I didn't reply.

"Stephanie! Are you hearing me or what?"

"Yeah...yeah, I'm hungry." I was hesitant because we always ate at the house of his girlfriend, Pauline. Why weren't we now? It alerted me to there being issues in their relationship, but I didn't dwell on it. I hadn't seen my father's dad in a while, so I was keen to visit, and querying the situation between Dad and Pauline would have only caused a scene.

"Well, let's go." He put out his hand. "Gimme your cup. I'll wash it out."

"Why ain't we going Pauline's?" I just couldn't help myself. I handed him my cup and he washed it after a long pause but didn't respond. Asking again would have been stupid. I grabbed my coat and a hairband before leaving.

On the car journey to my granddad's house, who we called Dada, Dad nosed about me seeing Derek. I hadn't. Not since Mum and him had separated. Mum was living a different religious embroiled lifestyle now. She had left her past behind, Derek included, and that's what I said.

"Yeah, I 'eard the cunt's just come out of rehab and is laying up under one next woman now." Dad said maintaining his cockney vernacular. "Dirty tramp. If he ain't got a woman, he ain't got nuffing – d'you 'ear me!" I remained silent. Dad went on, transcending his tongue into patois, "Dem bwoy-deh ain't got nuffing on me; d'you 'ear me, Stephanie?! DEM BWOY-DEH AIN'T GOT NUFFING ON ME!" By this time I had stopped listening, but he carried on with his soap box delivery of patois and cockney fusion.

"Everyt'ing I buy is in cash or I ain't buying nuffing; no one can chat and say I owe dem nuffing! Fucking crackhead! Recognise when you're playing wiv dem drugs you're playing wiv da *devil*—D'YOU 'EAR ME! Dat's one drug I ain't playing wiv, so if I hear any of you girls get caught up in dat –" he swerved the car looking at me, the thought of it maddening him—"'member seh mi tell yuh, anywhere yuh deh, mi will find you and lick-off di whole ah uno *bloodclaat* head—*MEMBER* seh mi tell yuh dat! D'you 'ear me, Stephanie?"

"Yes, Dad!" I said, somewhat startled, but managing to control the fear that was trying to erupt. I knew Dad's bark was much bigger than his bite, but at times the coarse, heavy-weighted Jamaican tone just got me.

"And make sure you tell your sisters what I said," he said in a suddenly calm manner.

*

We strolled, wet, through the passageway of Dada's house. The sky had wrung its clouds out on us and Nina, my cousin and Melvin's younger sister, took too long to answer the door. And for some reason Dad's key didn't work.

"You all right, Uncle Richard?" Nina's tone was bright and enthusiastic. She led us down the narrow passageway and opened the door into the kitchen.

"Yeah, man, where's ya brovva?" Dad responded whilst nodding at Dada, who was sitting in the corner of the kitchen.

"Upstairs," Nina answered.

Nina and Melvin had lived with Dada since their dad, my father's brother, committed suicide several years ago. Not much was ever said about him. Their mum left around the same time. Unfortunately she just couldn't cope with the concept of raising two black kids in the society she lived in alone. The situation was bad, and resulted in my cousins adopting orphan lifestyles as though both of their parents had departed, but their mother lived somewhere remote on the outskirts of England.

Nina sat back at the kitchen table, covered with a white tablecloth. She got stuck back into her plate of 'currygoat' and rice.

"Dinner deh-deh fi me and Stephanie?" Dad had his brow raised as he lifted the lid of the Dutch pot and faced Dada.

"Yeah, man! Not much rice lef', but see hard-dough bread deh?" Dada responded nodding his head simultaneously.

I was standing between the table and a glass cabinet that housed shot glasses, champagne and wine glasses, plus china crockery sets you could tell were for display purposes only.

"Hi, Dada." I was monotone. I felt shy. I hadn't seen my grandfather in a little while and wasn't sure what had been said about me. I knew the elderly were quick to form opinions. Their tremendous life experience seemed to entitle them to judge others. I assumed he had written me off as 'bad-breed'. Like bad meat that can quickly become rotten and inedible.

"What is dis?" he questioned, shocked by how much I'd grown. "Stephanie? Ah soh big yuh get? Rahted! Com' gi' Dada ah kiss! Mi ah look 'pon you an' ah wonder how dis gal look like ah Johnson soh bad?'"

His warmth blew me away. I was so used to the condemning and overwhelmingly critical mindsets of my grandparents on my mum's side. Plus the grannies in church openly displayed their disapproval when Safire and I attended. I guess having cast my mum's sins onto us, mixed with our own shortcomings, they felt able to condemn us.

I did as Dada requested. I entered his corner and embraced him with vigour as though it were my final breath. I held him. I held him for quite some time until Dad questioned why I was holding up my grandfather in that way, but Dada told him to leave me be. Dada's skin was a dark cocoa brown etched with the engravings of life. His eyes were discoloured, round and protruded with the glare of the womaniser he once was. The bridge of his nose had the flatness of a spade. And his nostrils spread wide like the equator, dominating his entire face. He possessed a blackness that had become slightly washed out in the generations that followed. Nose bridges had started to straighten somewhat and complexions became lighter.

I didn't appreciate Dada's beauty at the time. I didn't see this beauty as a reflection of my roots and heritage, something to be cherished. If anything I had always resented the way it had infiltrated Mum's more European features. "You've got Dada's Blackwall Tunnel nostrils!" Safire would say when we'd have our cussing matches. But I realised now that we'd all been dealt, in however small a way, Dada's unmistakeable facial features. Even Nina, as half white as she was, had inherited his nostrils and the boldness of his eyes. Dad had always said her father, Uncle Donnell, was the spitting image of Dada, but my memory of him is vague so I couldn't comment.

Dad placed my plate of food on the table mat next to his while Dada called for Melvin to "have some manners and come downstairs!" I ate my food. Dad ate his while questioning Dada on why he had changed the locks on the front door. Dada offered him the spare key to make a copy and brushed over the reason for the lock change, which was something to do with Melvin. The details were unsaid, but enough was said to rile Dad upon seeing Melvin's giant build soaring over him as he entered the kitchen with an attitude that he curbed quickly when he saw Dad. Nina took to washing the plates armed with an impish grin.

"You all right, Uncle Richard?" Melvin stretched his arms up exposing his creamy skin belly overpowered by jet-black hair.

"Yeah. What's all dis I've been hearing about you?"

"What?" Melvin was baffled.

Dad got up and escorted Melvin outside of the kitchen where they talked for some time.

"Stephanie?" Dada lit up a cigarette and rested his forearms on a chair before him like a really cool brother. "What a pretty girl you is, don't it?"

I smiled. Nina sat back down turning her attention to *Emmerdale Farm* on the TV, which was parked up on a Calor Gas heater. Nina was in her mid-teens, but much more reserved and well-mannered than my sisters and I were.

"Soh, how's yuh sister dem? Macy an'... wha' di nex' one name?"

"Safire?"

"No. Oh yes, mi know there's Safire, but nut she, di nex' one."

"Macy."

"No, nut she, mi know Macy...di nex' one?"

"Oh, Charlene."

"Yes! Ah she me ah talk. How's she? Yuh see her?" Dada stubbed out the rest of his cigarette with his bare fingers and put the half that was left over back in its box.

"Yeah, all the time; she goes to my school." I got up and brought my plate over to the sink. "Dad!" I called out. He popped his head round the varnished wooden door. "D'you want the rest of ya food or should I throw it away and wash up your plate?"

"Nah waste mi food!" Dada interjected.

"Nah, leave it. I'm gonna eat it, le' me just finish talking to dis yout' because the next time I won't be talking." He turned back to his nephew. "D'you hear dat, Melvin? Next time I won't be talking; next time I'm coming to tear off ya face!" and he closed the door.

Dada shook his head disappointedly. "Why ya farder 'ave fi gwaan soh?"

Nina chuckled without tearing her attention away from the soap opera. I washed my plate hurriedly, eager to be sitting down when *Eastenders* commenced as *Emmerdale* had moved onto an advert break on the other channel. I wiped up the side and around the white cooker that had an open grill at the top. Thirsty, I asked Dada for a drink.

"Tek wha' yuh waan tek. Ah fi yuh house dis. Any time yuh waan come, come; any time yuh you waan eat, eat, and same if yuh waan drink...drink!" he informed me.

Again, this was refreshing to know. It was customary at Mama's and Papa's or Aunty Denise's house to always ask before taking something from the fridge or cupboard—there was always a reprimand for not doing so. I browsed through wooden-slatted cupboards searching for a glass.

"Soh, 'ow is school?" Dada asked.

"All right. I'm in the top class but I get in trouble sometimes." Dada's brow folded, so I went on to explain about the Julius Caesar scenario and the whole lack of attention thing that resulted in a detention.

"Don't lie," Nina voiced, turning away from the adverts. "I don't like history eiver. Dat's why I ain't chosen it for my GCSEs." She tied up a section of her permed hair, the rest sitting on her shoulders, wet looking.

"Yuh must try an' tek in what yuh can at school. God knows how yuh ah goh need it later."

"But Dada, dat kind of history is boring. My man ain't even got not'in' to do wiv me."

"Yuh what?" Dada was taken aback by my hybrid vernacular and slang usage.

"What?" I said. "My man? I mean the man I was just talking about—Julius Caesar; he ain't got nothing to do with me."

Dada's brow maintained its ripple for some time before softening. Humour rose up within him. "Ah where uno pickney get yuh mad talk from? Heee?" He laughed with bouncing shoulders, the strength of his shirt buttons was being tested. "My man!" He tried to mimic me when saying this but just cracked up laughing, holding his belly, apparently in stitches. Calming down, he said, "Stephanie, don't question what dem ah give yuh, jus' tek it; what dem not, goh seek it. History is important all round. Yuh know where yuh come from: Jamaica, an' before dat Africa?"

"How can I come from Africa when I don't know anyfing about it and Dad doesn't even like dem?" I put my argument to him. My parents and other elders in the family members always showed there to be conflict between Jamaicans and the whole African continent.

"But ya farder head noh righted," he tried to whisper but his emotions put volume into the words. "Dat's what 'appen when you nah live good. Life 'ave a way of catching up on you—such ah di rules ah karma. I'm telling yuh, Stephanie, yuh were an African before Jamaican."

"Well, I don't know about that; all I know is that I'm glad to be a Jamaican," I said proudly because being a Jamaican was cool at school in the eighties and nineties, and probably for all the wrong reasons. "When I think of Africans," I continued, "I mean like...proper Africans, innit...straight from the jungle—not like my friends born here but like the proper ones. Yeah, I think of like ribcage-hungry people who run around in jungles with bare feet scuffing lions. They'd walk miles with no shoes and dem t'ings. They don't care. Well, that's what I hear anyway. I watch things like that on TV; some African in the jungle killing wild animals on foot with a spear on some non-p, or the ones with AIDS that are proper starving. I'm not talking like 'I'm hungry' starving, I'm talking like proper skeletal, ribcage-showing, a million flies landing on my face and I don't care starving. Yeah, that can't be where we're from, Dada—"

"Stephanie," Dada interrupted my ignorant discourse, "you 'ave a lot to learn, baybi...a lot!"

Dad came back in at this point, followed by a more relaxed Melvin. The *Eastenders* theme tune kicked in. Dad reheated his food in a brown, decades-old microwave and set himself down on the table. Melvin sat next to me putting a 'I haven't seen you in a long time' arm around me.

"You all right, cuz?" he said.

"Sweet," was my reply.

CHAPTER FIVE

NEW GIRLS ON THE BLOCK

23rd March 1994 – New Cross. Spring has arrived

Oh-my-gosh, Di, you'll never guess what us lot are about to do. Well, you know the Ghetto Boys who Tyrone was talking about at school, yeah? The gang that my cousins Leroy and Jermaine are a part of? Well, there's a girl part as well—the Ghetto Girls—and through Stella, we're all getting recruited! Well, me, Stella and Safire, but we're gonna bring in Maria, Shariece and René once we're in— that's if they want the bring-in. Stella said that the Ghetto Girls heard about us jacking some yout' in Lewisham and some other fights we've had. She said they like the way we flex. Plus, true-say Leroy and Jermaine are already in the bring-in was easy. Basically, what all this means is that we've got an extended family, people that will protect us, help us get paid, understand and accept all aspects of us... well...that's what I heard anyway. Don't get me wrong, Shariece, René and Maria are like that in the sense that us lot are really close and they're quick to defend us should the situation emerge, but they're not that big on jacking people and causing chaos in the streets, especially Maria, her mum and dad's got her on lockdown. We accept our differences. There's supposed to be a little family of the Ghetto Girls, like us. I think only five main ones in total. Two of them aren't family, though, but the ones who are, are called Taniqua, Shannon and Candice. Taniqua and Shannon are...

"Steph!" Stella shouted my name, agitated. I was rested up on her bed conversing with Di. "Come on!" she continued. "We gotta meet dem lot now if we're gonna get recruited."

I slammed my diary shut. I was pumped up with exhilaration that we were really going to do this. I had only spent a couple of weeks living at Dad's and Mum had me return back home. We were back to our incessant arguments, and so another reason to leave the home could only be a good thing. I rolled off her bed clad in my school uniform with bobbled ends of twisted kinky-afro hair clinking as I did this. I almost knocked off her TV from on top of the Calor Gas heater. This was clearly a good spot to house a TV. Safire was on the toilet doing number twos with the bathroom door open. I walked past her, pegging my nostrils with my fingers and cutting my eyes at her to express my disgust of her exposing us to the rot within her belly. I headed downstairs and waited by the front door.

"Hurry up!" Stella told Safire standing in front of the opened door. "And you could've at least shut the door, you nasty!"

I heard jingling keys turn the lock and the front door being pushed open, shocking my system with the fear of being caught. My eyes bulged open. My lips trembled into a prayer hoping it wasn't Aunty Ruth. I'd had too many beatings as of late and the last thing I wanted was to be a recipient of another one before getting recruited into a gang. I was sure that would compromise any stripes I was to gain.

"Thank God it's you!" I exhaled upon seeing Leroy. "I thought it was your mum."

"About you thought it was my mum," he banged the door shut behind him, "you wanna be at school 'bout you jamming in my yard."

"You can talk; why ain't you at school?"

"Because I don't go school, you chief, I go to Centre which is where I'm coming from." He tried to dig his knuckles into my head, which I dodged and bopped past, cool and easy. He was wearing Armani jeans that hung purposely low and exposed a pair of boxers. Stopping at the foot of the stairs, Leroy called out, "Stel!" whilst leaning up against the glossy white banister that was now discoloured to a more magnolia hue.

Stella came to the top of the stairs.

"Where d'you fink you're going?" he demanded.

"Wiv dem lot, innit!" Safire appeared behind her as she said this.

I was becoming jarred by the elongated process of leaving the premises, and communicated this by bouncing my back against the wall. The wall was papered with a mint-green stripe on pinewood cream throughout the passageway and a classic dado rail ran along its length. The carpet was a forest-green colour overpowered by heavy stains that gave a dubious appeal.

"I'm gonna tell Mum if you keep up this bunking off of school t'ing, yanna," Leroy put to his female lookalike as she and Safire trotted down the stairs.

"Go on den, you informer, and I'll tell her about that shop you robbed."

And with that we were finally through the door with a light tumble, a knock-on effect from the push that Leroy gave Stella.

We met the Ghetto Girls in Ghetto, less than five minutes away from Stella's house. Only Taniqua, Shannon and Candice turned up. We were standing outside Spanish Steps, a small pub that was modelled on a type of pub in Jamaica, a kind of den for old locals to socialise, play dominoes, and indulge in 'real talk' and shots of rum. Spanish Steps was on a small square which also held an Indian-run grocery shop, a Chinese takeaway, a fish and chips shop, laundrette and dry cleaner's. Surrounding the square were high-rise tower blocks and lower level blocks of flats that didn't require lifts. This was the place that both Mum and Dad always told us never to visit. The kind of place where people got stabbed, shot and robbed and nobody ever saw a thing. Where crack and heroin were sold by the young and old to the young and old. Neither money nor addiction discriminated.

Hearing some of the stories Stella and Leroy would tell Safire and me when we were younger instilled in us a conspicuous terror about this place. As with most social housing estates, it was built to house the poor with little effort made to look after them. Ultimately ghettos like this were a less than ideal place to raise children. The environment exposed them to excessive negativity. To not develop a tough shell, to be instinctive, assertive and streetwise, was to be vulnerable. It was play or be played. And even though I was terrified of it, terrified of being a recipient of its potential brutality, there was something strangely alluring about it. It felt as though I had the acumen, had experienced enough pain and suffering that would grant me the credibility to not only survive in this environment, but to thrive in it. I wanted to be a part of it.

"...And dis is my cousin Stephanie." Stella initiated the introductions. "She's the one who knocked out dat bredda Christopher you were talking about."

"All right?" I mumbled quietly.

"Rah!" a beige-skinned one voiced. "You don't look nuffing like I imagined..."

"Innit!" a cross-eyed girl slipped in.

"Why, how's she supposed to look, Taniqua?" Stella took the words out of my mouth.

"Nah, it's just dat when we saw dat yout' after you dealt wiv him; we thought you were...not necessarily big, but definitely more tuff-looking, but you look petite, innit...small and simple—that's all," Taniqua explained.

The third one who also looked simple, didn't have the hard shell her cousins had, stepped forward from the wall that skirted the pub, "Hi Stephanie, I'm Candice, their cousin." She swayed a finger past Taniqua. The cross-eyed girl must have been Shannon. "You and her look alike," she continued, now looking at Safire. "Are you two sisters?"

"Yeah," I answered. "I've got two other sisters as well. You can call me Steph by the way. What about you, d'you have any sisters or brovvas?"

"Nah..."

Whilst Candice and I were in conversation, Safire and Taniqua, and Stella and Shannon coupled up in conversation too. Without really realising it we all started walking back towards the park from which we'd come. The sun shone brightly without any cloud interference and the wind blew gently against our crisp white school shirts. The Ghetto Girls said one or two hellos to passing boys in their caps, hoods and low-slung jeans. No one questioned why we weren't at school. More than likely they also should have been at school. Soon enough we were surrounded by the green of the park that stood between Stella's road and Ghetto. Taniqua then touched on the recruitment process. I'd been waiting for this part.

"Yeah, so what we would normally do would be to rush you." This unsettled me. Although I was keen for recruitment, I didn't like the idea of allowing three strangers to punch and kick me all at once without retaliation. Instantaneously my brow heightened sending a discontented rippling effect across my face. Taniqua observed this and said, "But since we know you gal know how to handle yourselves, we'll 'llow dat and find so't'in' else for you to do...like jacking someone, just so we can see you in action, y'get me?"

Her words played on my ego. I was keen to show her the high level of my skill set when it came to fighting. I thought I was a strong contender in that department, and the reputation I started to build for myself reflected this.

Safire, Stella and I looked at each other pleased. My smile beamed wide. We all were swinging animatedly on the swings by now, the Ghetto Girls showing their matching grey, 50 denier tights, when Shannon explained our task and prey. "Now dis girl's a proper eediot— trust! Innit Taniqua, dat's why I had to fight her dat time on the bus? She's a proper bounty."

"Why d'you call her a bounty?" Safire asked dragging her feet on the floor to lessen her swing. "How does she act white?"

"She talks like she's white, all her bredrens are white, her man's white." Shannon jumped off the swing high on energy as the memories flooded back. "Innit Taniqua, remember dat time when we saw her kissing up dat white bredda at the bus stop outside Goldsmiths University?"

"I remember," Candice piped up, but her voice was drowned out by Taniqua's who articulated her memory with assertion.

"Yeah, I remember!" she shouted. "We were on the 36 and you shouted out 'sell-out'. The girl was *prang*!"

"Nah, man," Shannon went on. "I see this girl as the red bounty, because she's proper dark skinned on the outside and just pure white on da inside."

We all started laughing, then Stella asked, "How old is she?"

"About sixteen or seventeen," Taniqua uttered, uncertain. "All I know is that when she was at our school for that short period, she was in the year above me and I'm fifteen. Mary-Anne...yeah, I think her name's Mary-Anne."

I continued to swing back and forth in big sweeps. I was twelve by now and still felt confident I could take on a sixteen-year-old. One of the gold bobbles loosened from the end of one of my twists and fell to the ground. I brought my swing to a stop and carefully picked up my bobble watching Stella, who swung calmly next to me, to avoid her accidentally licking off my head. As I was bending over to pick up my golden bobble, I saw three sets of grey legs jump to their feet. I looked up to see Taniqua, Shannon and Candice staring across the park in disbelief.

"Oh-my-fucking-gosh!" Shannon belted out.

I stood up and looked in the direction they were looking in. Three girls were walking, casual but smartly dressed, across the paved area behind the climbing frame. Two were slim built, with milky-toned complexions and straight sun-kissed hair, one shoulder length and the other halfway down her back. The third girl had deep cocoa-complexioned skin and single-braided hair that came down the centre of her back. "What, is dat her?" I asked.

"Dat's her!" Taniqua bellowed. "Dat's da fuckin' bounty!"

Candice pulled her thick, black hair loose. She tied the soft-textured kinky strands back into a ponytail, but said nothing.

Safire and Stella jumped off the swings and we moved toward our prey. I looked at my cousin and sister. They had on their non-p faces that oozed bad intentions and I knew it was on. As we approached Mary-Anne and her peers, I thought she looked pretty straightforward. For a second or two I was uncertain about carrying out the act of both beating and robbing this girl. My conscience struck me for the first recognisable time in my life. I struggled to control the good and bad angels, which were both fighting to take ownership of the actions I was about to carry out. This girl wasn't like the fools that usually brought out my brutality. This girl probably came from a civilised and educated household, and originally from a neighbourhood that nurtured such traits. But she was in a new neighbourhood now with totally different dynamics. It was now play or be played, and regardless of my hesitations, unfortunately this girl was about to get played.

"Oi! Oi you!" The words just burst from my lips unexpectedly with a volume and weight that threatened violence. I pointed at Mary-Anne who was pointing back at herself confused. "Yeah you! Come 'ere!" I belted.

She stopped. The other girls with her did the same, but none of them moved forward. Adrenalin had risen within me and a cloak of evildoing shielded my conscience.

"So ain't you gonna come forward?" Safire uttered behind me.

The girls looked baffled as we neared them. Mary-Anne looked to her friends for answers but got nothing in return.

"Are you talking to me?" Mary-Anne asked, expressing perplexity with a hand against her chest, her thumb and two fingers resting on her collarbone.

"Yeah, I'm talking to you, Mary-Anne, now come 'ere!" My knowledge of her name visibly shocked her. Her friends were naturally frightened to say the least. I clocked her goods as I neared her, my eyes possessed with ill will.

"How do you know my name?" Her naivety was annoying.

Her fingers twinkled with a range of coloured and white stones. I grabbed her hand by the wrist and ordered, "Take—off—your—rings!"

Stella and Safire initiated robbing the other girls whilst Mary-Anne asked me, "What are you doing?" in a soft voice that troubled me.

I thought about my actions for a moment, shrugged off the second thoughts and replied, "Bitch, I'm jacking you."

"Why, what have I done? I don't even know you." Mary-Anne wasn't accustomed to the jacking drill. And as a twelve-year-old girl from a very different environment, it was quite shocking for me to come up against a person who didn't know that when a stranger asked you to "take off your t'ings", then you were in an unfortunate situation. It was simply the wrong place at the wrong time to me, and seldom was it ever personal.

I got aggressive with Mary-Anne. Her well-spoken tone grated me. She had clenched her fingers shut.

"Open up your hand!" I fired, smashing a firm right fist to her eye.

She unleashed cries of pain as the impact of the blow forced her towards the ground. Her hand opened to hold her eye. As she continued to fall, I hit her with a powerful left hook that collided with her descending jaw. She crumbled into a pile on the floor and then tried to get her hands to hold her up to a sitting position. She was blacking out. I turned to Stella who was pocketing her opponent's jewellery. The girl with the shoulder-length blonde hair looked at Mary-Anne on the floor, regretful that she didn't have the stomach to attempt to help her friend or defend herself. I turned to Safire who was being handed money to a palm already draped with gold chains.

I looked back at Mary-Anne thinking, eediot! Her tan leather bag that was designed to carry big, brain-power books hung twisted up round her neck. I popped off her dainty gold chain as she tried to get to her knees. Calmly I voiced, "Now I'm gonna tell you one more time: take off ya rings...or...I'm gonna...knock...you...out."

"Mary-Anne, just give it to them! It's not worth it, Mary-Anne, it is so not worth it," the lengthy blonde haired one smartly advised in that voice that we street rogues highly despised, but Mary-Anne just wouldn't submit.

I booted her firm and hard in the stomach. I thought I heard something crack. Mary-Anne was holding her stomach and squirming as though she was dying. Oh Shit! Are you all right? I thought. I kept my thoughts to myself for fear of looking pathetic and caring. Her friends started to cry helplessly. I felt resistance, deep concern, but showed no sympathy.

I rolled her over on her back and pulled off the four rings. One of them looked like an engagement ring. I heard sirens and saw Taniqua and the rest of them running off, the dust kicking up from their feet.

"Come, yous lot, let's go," Stella let out.

I gazed down at Mary-Anne. Pity and an overwhelming regret seized my conscience, but it was too late. The deed had been done. I forced the sentiment quickly back down, mentally putting my cloak back on that shielded away any emotion or concern firm and tight. "This could've been nice an' easy," I verbalised, "but you had to play da tuff one."

"Come on, Steph!" Safire yelled as she pulled my arm and started to run.

I breezed in their direction. We cut through an alleyway on Rolt Street. "Where's dem lot?" I asked burning fire with the sole of my Huarache's as we darted through the back roads.

"They ran when they heard da raddy coming, innit, and you're dere telling the girl 'bout 'this could've been nice an' easy'. They'll probably phone us at mine now." Stella breathed heavily. We ran. We ran non-stop until we arrived at Stella's gates. Within minutes they were on the phone.

We were in…we were officially Ghetto Girls.

*

Later on in the day once night fell to disguise us from the watchful eyes of the police, we changed into some of Stella's clothes. Then we made our way over to Taniqua and Shannon's house. They lived in a three-bedroom terraced house about three roads up the road from Stella's yard. Their house had the same layout as Stella's. Taniqua and Shannon's room was old-fashioned. They each had a single metal bedstead that lay side by side. An old chest of drawers was by Shannon's bed with all the drawers opened unevenly. T-shirts draped out of one drawer, whilst polka-dotted knickers hung out of another.

I sat opposite with Safire and Stella on Taniqua's bed. They wouldn't stop bigging us up as we talked them through the specifics of what happened. Taniqua threw in the idea that we should all bleach a section of our hair blonde. It would be our recruitment tribute where black and blonde hair joined force, the day we became Ghetto Girls. A supernatural feeling of joy came upon us as we washed the peroxide out of our hair. We glared at each other in disbelief. We approached the mirror, which was broken and leant up against the window above the sink, in awe. We thought our hair looked first-rate. But our hair became insignificant by the time Safire and I got home. Our minds refocused on other things: how to get past Mum without her seeing our hair. Well, at least for that night.

Slowly and sneakily I turned the key to our front door tiptoeing my way through ahead of Safire. It was after 11 p.m. on a school night. Unfortunately Mum outsmarted us that night, as she did most nights. She sat on the stairs with a belt she tapped gently against her hand, looking like a cartoon sketch of anarchy. Again it was to be on top for us.

"Mi did tell yuh fi bleach ya blasted head?!"

PAP! went the belt.

"If it kills me uno ah goh learn dat dere is *one…head…of…dis…house* an' yuh WILL follow…my…rules!"

BOOF BUP-BUDUP-BUP! PAP!!

The belt lashed over my head while Safire made her way past me somehow and ran upstairs. Mum snatched my door keys from my hand and slashed them against my face repeatedly, enraged. I felt temporarily blind. My vision was blurred and watery. I screamed for her to get off of me, but her grip on my hair was tightening and her knuckles surfaced my mouth with an impact that shook me as I had shook Mary-Anne. I pushed her off me somehow and ran upstairs to my room screaming. Luckily she didn't come for me and went for her attack on Safire. But then I heard Safire laughing, and soon Mum joined in this laughter. The fire she used to discipline me was extinguished. Just like that.

I looked in the mirror initially with admiration of my bleached blonde hair. The longer I gazed at my reflection, the cracks started to appear and I became angry and hostile at the spoiled image that was staring back at me. Both my eyes were bloodshot. I exhaled furiously, trying to steady shaken hands. I could still hear Mum and Safire laughing. *How does she do it?* I wondered. It amazed me that Safire could lessen Mum's wrath in this way by mere laughter. It was incidences like this why I started to think Mum didn't like me.

But things hadn't always been that way. I was once bullied, when I was younger, for being poor. I know. Difficult to grasp. I get it. Kids laughed at me. Singled me out over my poverty and buck teeth. I would bawl my eyes out most days. My confidence shattered, I did what

I was told, go away. But cut the violins. An incident happened that reinstalled my confidence, triggered the combativeness I developed through regular quarrels with Safire. Macy. My big sister. She showed me how to handle bullies. She demonstrated how to instil fear into your opponents by presenting fearlessness and brazenly challenging the figures they feared. And she looked cool when she did it. She was 14 years old at the time and caramel complexioned. This was before she had Ricardo. She rocked the Salt 'n' Pepper look with the leather hat and slanted bob. She had a gold tooth and work Karl Kani suits and Raggas. She was so fearless and cool she had the letters RUDE shaved into the back of her head for fuck sakes. Soon after she showed me the ropes, I became the bully. I was bullying for the same reason I was bullied for: being broke.

Before long, I started to crave the power and the fear of my opponent.

CHAPTER SIX

ALLEVIATE

24th March 1994 – Maths Class. New face

Dear Di', my boat looks fucked! Both my eyes are still bloodshot. I've got bruising and welts all over my face. Dis is long, man. People are looking at me like I got jumped or somef'ing, when I'm the one who jumped someone. I'm the one who delt wiv Mary-Anne, and everyone saw it. I'm not to be messed with. Yesterday, in Ghetto, I was a winner; I'm a bad gyal! But when I got home, fings changed. I became a loser. Mum saw to that. And I let her. But not for long. I can't let her win like dat again…

"OK, class, see you in fifteen minutes. Stephanie! Can I have a word with you, please?" Mr. Williams requested as the school bell chimed and the bulk of the class hurriedly packed up their things for break. The remaining eager learners, or boffins as I called them, stayed seated to study through their break.

"Yeah, Mr. Williams?" I said in a flat tone, keeping my face down so he wouldn't see too much.

"Stephanie, what an earth happened to your face?" He was startled; showed deep concern.

"I had a fight," again my voice was flat.

"When will you learn that fighting is not the answer? You're a bright young lady. You got top marks in your maths exercise last week and this week you come in looking like you've been beaten to a pulp, and I fear to think what your adversary looks like."

"What does dat mean?"

"What does what mean?"

"Adversary."

"Your opponent, Stephanie, the person you had a fight with." I didn't want to tell him that he was talking about my mother.

"Oh. It wasn't my fault, sir," I lied. "Some girls were trying it wiv me and my sister—'

"My sister and me."

"What?" I looked up and squinched my eyes together leaving them open just enough to see Mr. Williams' head shoot back in disarray at the sight of my eyes.

"'Some girls were trying it with my sister and me.' You must really try a bit more with your grammar, Stephanie; you have much potential."

I felt an urge to bust his lip.

"Look," Mr. Williams continued. His legs were crossed and his tweed-suited arms folded. "I was thinking that it would help if you could find a way to alleviate—"

"What does that mean?"

"What?"

"Leviate."

"A-lleviate means lessen. Look, how would you feel about your mother and me sourcing some professional help for you? Nothing too serious, just a talk with a counsellor of some kind, huh? How would you feel about that?"

"I think you should do your job, sir, and that is to teach me maths. I don't want you talking to my mum about nuffing..." Mr. Williams was about to interpose with the word 'anything', but I didn't penny him and talked over his grammar correction attempt, "...so just keep out of my business, yeah!" and I turned to walk away.

He ran up behind me and pulled on my shoulder. I flinched. I was bruised. He brought his thick lips to my ears and his patted afro lightly sprung against my face. "Stephanie, you're not as hard as you make out," he said. "I really think that we need to get to the bottom of this and start finding answers to that anger problem of yours, and sooner rather than later. I know you're only my pupil but I care about your future. I've seen it so many times, Stephanie, young children like yourself with so much potential who get caught up in a spiral of hatred and frustration, and pay with their lives for something that, at heart, they're not."

I looked at him thinking, How did 'I' become 'we', but didn't say anything. I smiled somehow and left. When I emerged from the maths hut, Shariece, Maria, René and Safire were all waiting by the benches. Donavan and Sean were there too, busy engraving their names into the bench.

"*Oh my Gosh*! Steph, what 'appened to your face?" Shariece asked.

"Innit man, who got hold of you?" René circled me with shaken eyes. She held onto her loose blow-dried hair to keep it off her face in the wind.

Their voices attracted Donavan and Sean from their art exercise. I ignored the girls' questions, and asked the boys instead about Tyrone's whereabouts. I hadn't seen him in a while. But their focus was on my face.

"Uh-uh, you got dealt wiv, Steph!" Donavan informed me.

I wanted to tell him about his mum in that insolent '*yo' mum got dealt with by the milkman*' kind of way. I wanted to burn his soul with the fact that he didn't know who his father was, which was probably where his shortness came from because his mother was tall. But all I came up with was, "Shut ya mout' you bonehead!"

"Oh-my-giddy-giddy-gosh, Steph got dealt wiv, got her eye bus." Sean sung this to my enragement. I chased him desperately so I could put my fist in his back and attempt to break his spine, but like Donavan he ran, dodging me and laughing.

I walked back to where the girls were standing. Vexed. I told Sean I was going to punch the drip from his curly hair and send his skinny arse back to the eighties if he came near me. He mimicked my outrage and laughed in hysterics. Maria came over with an embrace to soothe my fury. She told me not to "watch dem eediots" and that I still looked pretty. She always knew how to say the right things. We neared Safire and the rest of the girls. Safire explained to Shariece and René what Mum did to us because we dyed our hair blonde.

"Rah!" René blared. "Your mum doesn't pet! Your hair looks nice, doh—both of you."

"So how come your face looks all right, Safire?" Shariece was puzzled.

"Innit doh, dat's what I was gonna say," René added. "If me and my brovver did something dat would cause us to get licks, we would definitely have similar bruising and he's four years younger than me!"

"I was blocking my face, innit," Safire lied.

"Whatever, Mum never brucks you up as much as she does me and you know it." It was the first time I had ever voiced such an accusation, but it was what I believed. Plus the aches screaming from my body were in no way ready to let this lie. Being beaten was something I accepted, but the idea that my mother unleashed more violence on me than my sibling because she favoured the other was extremely painful.

"How do I know it?" Safire fired back. "Just coz you made her bus' your lip and mash up your eye—"

"How did I *make* her do anything, you fucking idiot?!" I roared, puffing up my chest, preparing to smash my sister's skull with my clenched fist.

At that moment I spotted Mr. Williams peering our way through an upstairs window. I looked up at him thinking: Alleviate, alleviate my anger, but I couldn't. My face exposed my bad intentions.

Safire mumbled, "What?" bouncing her shoulders like she was ready to go toe-to-toe. I made for her.

Maria and Shariece grabbed my arms uttering, "Allow it, Steph!" René made an attempt to stand in front of Safire. But why should I allow her to lie and torment me, I thought.

"Get off me!" I shouted. I wanted my limbs free to attack her from every angle. I was keen to give Safire the beating she missed out on the night before.

"Oi!" a familiar voice propelled from behind the school gate distracting us. "Oi, yous lot!"

Two caramel figures in clashing school uniforms waved at us from behind bars. I recognised Stella's voice and the lanky silhouette of our cousin, Jermaine. We approached them.

"Stella, whassappenin'?" Safire screeched theatrically.

"You all right, Saf, you all right, Steph?"

"*Shit*, what 'appened to your face, Steph?" Jermaine probed, a spliff blazing in his mouth.

"Ah, not'in' major. My mum, innit." I turned to Stella. "Did Aunty Ruth say anything about your hair, Stella?"

"Nah, not really. My brovver try t'ump me up, but we just wrestled a bit." Stella waved at Shariece and the rest as they neared the gate. "Ya all right, yous lot?" she said.

"Yeah, you all right Stella…Jay?" Shariece responded.

"You all right?" René and Maria voiced in unison.

"So didn't you get bruck-up as well, Saf?" Stella questioned.

"Why's everyone keep asking me dat? I just blocked my face, innit. It's not my fault that Steph got dealt wiv."

I looked at my sister devilishly, still wanting to give her the black eye or two that she missed out on yesterday, if only to shut her up and tear that smug look off her face. *Alleviate, alleviate anger…*

"Aunty Sonya's being biased again, innit," Jermaine murmured to Stella, flaring his big nostrils.

"Whatever," Safire defended.

"Anyway, I never come 'ere for yous lot's bickering," Stella said as she brandished a tired hand between Safire and I. "I came to get yous lot to go and meet the ovver Ghetto Girls…the older ones, you know, Nicky and Lakiesha—so you coming?"

"Yeah, I'm ready," I replied before turning to my friends. "You lot wanna come?" I then turned back to Jermaine requesting a pull of his spliff.

"Yeah, I'll come," René said enthusiastically.

Safire was already climbing over the gate.

"Nah, I'm gonna allow it dis time and just cover for yous lot," Shariece said. "After all, we ain't even Ghetto Girls. Plus you're already grounded René."

"Yeah, for real, I didn't even think about dat." René changed her mind. Shariece was always able to influence her in that way.

"Yeah, but if you come you can probably get recruited today," I cajoled, turning to Stella. "Is Taniqua and dat gonna be there?"

"I dunno; she's the one dat gave me Nicky's number and told me to make arrangements to meet them. They might be there, but what you lot doing, man—just hurry up!"

I looked back at Shariece who said, "Yeah, I'm gonna 'llow it. I don't wanna seem like I'm eggs-up."

Shariece's reasoning was understandable. To be eggs-up meant to be over-zealous about a relationship or a situation; it meant going against the grain just to be a part of the hype, and it was a negative perception for others to have. Maria said no too. Her father was her reason. He was very strict and she feared him.

"Is Tyrone in today?" Jermaine asked.

"I dunno," Shariece mused, "I ain't—"

"Oi!" Another familiar voice hit me from behind. "Where yous lot going?"

"Oh, you all right, Charlene?" Jermaine exclaimed as she ran our way.

"You all right, Jermaine...Stella? So where're yous lot going?"

"We're going Ghetto to meet the other Ghetto Girls. Nicky and dat," Safire detailed.

"I'm coming."

*

Two free bus journeys later and we were in the heart of Ghetto. In the early nineties when public transport wasn't free for children, we used skilfully plotted measures to get us from A to B for free. There were three options to choose from depending on the situation and number of people involved. Option one was organised well in advance; it was fraud. Those were the days when you had to scratch off the date on a one-day bus pass. I, like everyone else, would merely cut the unused dates out of previous passes and stick them on current ones.

Option two was plotted on the day and only really worked in groups of three when the other two had legal photo bus passes. Shariece, René and I would usually work this one together because our skin complexions made it much more likely to work. Shariece would board the bus first because she was dark complexioned, followed by René who was light complexioned. Then I would come on board and go through the dramatics of someone searching for their pass and not finding it. Then I would call to René and ask if she had my pass. She would return to the front of the bus with her own pass in her mouth and hand me Shariece's. I was a shade lighter than Shariece, but that wasn't a difference any bus conductor noticed—it worked every single time.

Option three was very last minute and what we considered gully-style. One person would have a pass and upon showing it to the bus driver, they would pass it back and it would continue to be passed back through the trail of five or ten sets of hands. Sometimes this worked, most times it didn't and we'd all be thrown off the bus. But that day it did.

We were standing grouped along the wall of the pub, Spanish Steps. Charlene was the first to notice the loudly dressed Nicola and Lakiesha sauntering exotically up a pathway that had green bushes spilling over it. Upon seeing us, Nicola, who was golden skinned and had curves she accentuated, opened up her arms in a masculine hip hop fashion. Lakiesha did the same. She also had the same curvaceous sex appeal. She had deep coffee-brown skin with full lips and false eyelashes. She had a tiny waist, a 'I can see you from the front' behind and huge breasts that would be the envy of any topless model. Her hair was a long, jet-black weave, which she wore with a centre parting all the way down to her bottom. Their clothes were tight...really tight, but they seemed all right.

"How old are they, Charlene?" I asked, thinking they looked older than us. "Macy's age?"

Charlene peered down at me like I was confused. I was.

"Why, they look like big women, innit?" Stella threw my thoughts into words.

"Nicky's fifteen and Lakiesha's fourteen." Nicky was the same age as Charlene and Lakiesha the same as Jermaine. Them being our age group was odd. Charlene jumped off the wall to greet the hip hop bopping Nicola. "You all right, Nicky, what's happening?"

"Oh my god, Charlene! Wha' gwaan?" They hugged as though they were long lost sisters before Nicola stepped back and eyed up Charlene's garments.

"What you looking at me up and down for?" Charlene put to her.

Whilst Nicola checked out Charlene I checked out her. She was kitted out from head to toe in designer clothing. She wore skin-tight patterned Versace jeans, a fitted white top with Giorgio Armani sprawled across the front, a Moschino belt with the gold block lettering and flat black Gucci loafers with the Gucci link. Plus a black bomber jacket that had the Versace logo engraved on the back. Her hair was dyed a platinum blonde and cut short like T-Boz from TLC. As an impressionable twelve-year-old girl I idolised her dress and outlandishness. I gazed down at my flat puffer jacket and well-polished shoes I was still rocking from primary school because Mum had bought them too big. Shame stifled me and I wished I'd worn my Huaraches that day. At least Charlene looked cool in her brand new navy blue Kickers, I thought.

"I'm just checking you out, true-say I ain't seen you in time," Nicola explained.

"Well, as you can see I'm in my school uniform." Charlene had a feisty air about her as we all did.

In the meantime, Stella and Lakiesha delved into conversation. Stella introduced her to Safire and Jermaine. I was standing there watching Nicola because she looked interesting. She had six hole piercings in one ear. Each of them was filled with gold hoop earrings that declined in size as they progressed up her ear lobe. Plus she had two gold stud piercings in the bony part of her other ear. Her eyes were really round and big, like the ones in my family. Her mouth was like her eyes, so when she spoke she appeared to invite you into her mouth.

"...Nah, I didn't know it was your people-dem dat dem lot recruited," Nicola continued. "Dis isn't Stephanie, is it? Oh my god..."

I wondered if I knew her. I glanced at Charlene questioningly.

"Don't you remember Nicky from some kids parties we went to when we were young?" Charlene asked.

I didn't. I had seen her around the way, though. I continued to look at Charlene baffled.

"Don't you remember me from when you were all seven-eight?"

"No," I answered. "I have seen you on the ends, doh." A long lost hug came my way anyway, which I reciprocated. I found Nicola interesting. Even the way everyone called her Nicky as though she were familiar to everyone was enchanting.

Stepping back, Nicola glared at me up and down as she did Charlene, and then asked, "What happened to your face?"

"My mum."

"Your mum's Sonya, innit?" I nodded. "My mum's stories about her must be true den." Her words fell into sniggers that dug at me.

"And what's dat?" Charlene got in quick before me.

"Not'in' major. My mum just said how she used to fight nuts when she was younger...she all nearly kill off one man dat told her to 'suck out her mudder' or so't'in' like dat."

Her story played well in my ears. I loved the notion that my notoriety was an identifiable trait of my mother's. I relaxed while she conversed and made vague recognitions of Safire, Stella and Jermaine, questioning him about his sister Joanne, who she also knew.

"She's cool," Jermaine replied. "She said she saw you a little while ago."

"Yeah, tell her I said hello."

"Me too," Lakiesha slipped in. "Tell Joanne dat Lakiesha said 'wha' gwaan.'"

Jermaine did a fake grin while Lakiesha eyed him up. She then circled my way as though it was her first time seeing me in the five or ten minutes that we'd all been standing there. "Oh my god, Steph," she exclaimed, "look at you! Look how big you are. I didn't even see you there." She hugged me, squeezing tight. She pressed my face against her 34GGs or whatever they were… all I knew was that those breasts were huge.

Smiling, I pulled back. "You all right, Lakiesha?" Though I didn't remember her either, this time I couldn't be bothered to go down memory lane.

"Who did that to your face, man?" she pretended she hadn't heard me just explain that to Nicola.

"My mum. You know how it goes."

"Yeah, I know." She came up close with a tilted head, examining me. "Uh-uh—you better hide from Social Services."

Like Jermaine, I chuckled bogusly. But it wasn't funny.

"So," Nicola continued, "how's Macy den, Safire?"

"She's all right, just tryna cope with Ricardo, innit."

"Oh yeah. Is she still wiv Jason?"

"Yeah, they're tight," Safire confirmed.

Nicola turned to Stella. "And how's your brovva?"

"He's cool, yanna."

"Tell him to phone me; I ain't seen him in a while." Nicola bared her teeth, gums and everything, as she said this.

"Yeah, I will." Stella seemed uncomfortable with this mission.

"Yous lot, what's happenin'?" Jermaine asked.

I shrugged my shoulders at Jermaine and searched faces for answers.

"Well, we were gonna go to Peckham and link up wid some of dem man deh, but I didn't know you lot were coming wiv Jermaine," Nicola said.

"What man, and meet dem for what?" Charlene questioned.

"You know? Typo and dem man deh...from Peckham."

"Yeah, long time he ain't given me not'in'. Looking forward to seeing him...yeah, just a little," Lakiesha said with a lilting tone and a facial expression of a page-three model.

Safire's face lit up and then fell. "Steph's too young to be meeting man," she said.

"You're too young as well, you eediot, like I wanna link man," I barked, still ready to give her that black eye.

"Well, don't come den!" she cheeked.

I kissed my teeth.

"Steph, d'you wanna come road wid me? True-say I'm bruck I just feel like licking a tek," Jermaine proposed.

"Chuh," I voiced resentfully. The idea of stealing someone's purse seemed more appealing now, "yeah, might as well. See yous lot later, man."

"You all right, Steph?" Charlene asked, concerned.

"Yeah, see you, man."

Jermaine and I went our separate way from them, wandering around the estate and then the green area of Moonshot, a community centre across from Ghetto. Noticing I was upset, choked with frustration and trying desperately to control the tears from escaping, Jermaine said, "Steph, don't watch dem, you know; Safire's just being bad-mind but it's anna-not'in'. We'll just make some loot, go mopping in Bromley after an' get some *garms*."

I liked the idea of making money and shoplifting in Bromley because I needed clothes, but I didn't respond. I was trying to alleviate my rage.

"Steph, you all right?"

"Yeah, I'm just tryna alleviate my anger."

"What?"

"Alleviate my anger." I played like I didn't know what he was 'what'-ing me for.

"Yeah, what does that mean?"

I smiled. It felt good that I had knowledge my fourteen year old cousin didn't. "Alleviate," I said, "to lessen, you know to reduce or release my anger. Dat's what I'm saying, I'm tryna release my frustration. I just feel like punching off that girl's face sometimes."

"Who, Safire?"

"Yeah! Look how she tried to make me get left out on purpose."

"She didn't try, she did."

We continued across the grass, me in silence and Jermaine in sniggers. We crossed the road and entered a tunnel that a train sped over. New Cross train station was on the other side of the tunnel. A middle-aged woman walked before us. She was dressed in a beige suit. A handbag hung limp on her shoulder. I didn't even look at Jermaine. I didn't even give my conscience time to prick or probe at my reasoning. As we went to pass her, the word alleviate alleviated my mind. Without hesitation I snatched her handbag as if it were my own. Just like I would snatch my packet of crisps from the greedy hands of one of my sisters. I shoved it in my puffer and we ran wildly back to where we'd come from—across the grass and into the estate of Ghetto. The woman screamed meekly and chased us with flailing arms. She was engulfed by timidness, as though she didn't really want to catch us, for obvious reasons, just merely wanted to see where we were going so someone else could catch us.

"In here!" Jermaine bellowed.

I followed him into a tower block. The beige leather bag fell from my clenched arm. Sirens were whining already and barely five minutes had passed. My heart was drumming loudly like it was playing in a live band. Jermaine grabbed the bag from the floor. We carried on running, heading for the stairs. We could hear police cars skidding into a parking area within the estate.

"Shit! We're gonna get caught! We're gonna get caught!" The words boomed from my mouth.

A front door slammed on the landing above the stairs we were climbing. Unanimously Jermaine and I slammed our backs against the wall. We listened to the slow steps of the approaching person. I held my breath. My heart persisted in tearing its way at my chest. I wanted to close my eyes and wish it all away, but could only wait for the potential witness to pass and hope that this situation didn't get out of hand.

"Rah! Wha' gwaan, bloods?" said a voice I recognised. It was Tyrone.

"Oh my gosh, hide us, please! Quickly hide us!" My voice was crammed with fear and relief as we hurriedly followed him into his flat.

"Dat was nuts!" Jermaine breathed banging the back of his head on the closed door and clasping his hands together with his eyes up to the ceiling. "Thanks God, dat was a touch."

"Innit," I added. "Thanks God! And please forgive us."

Our lifesaver led us into the living room whilst uttering, "You lot are nuts—you just done rob some poor woman and now you're thanking God like He helped you in some noble act." He laughed slightly over the top parading a set of braces over twisted teeth, but we ignored him and fell onto brown corduroy sofas.

I peeped up at him and liked what I saw. I felt glad that it was him that saved us. "How did you know we robbed some woman?" I quizzed.

"Because he's holding some corporate, business-like woman's handbag and the Boy-dem are outside my yard." His tone held a tad of sarcasm, but I allowed him to continue his mockery because I had to. "And," he went on, "what da *fuck* happened to your face?"

"Ah, don't watch dat; I just had a madness wiv my mum, innit." I tried to change the subject: "So how comes you weren't at school today?"

"Yeah, I was asking about you when I touched dem-lots school earlier," Jermaine said as he opened the handbag before pouring out its contents. "Man ain't seen you in a while."

"I got suspended," Tyrone told us. He picked up the woman's cheque book and flicked through the remaining pages. "True-say I nearly knocked out dat Mr. Ahmed. Man was shouting up his *maaga* self in my face like I'm his yout'. I thought you would've known dat. Macy knows. I stayed at her house last week wiv my brovva because my dad was going nuts."

"Don't lie? You've gotta mind wiv dat Mr. Ahmed, ca, it coming like he rails up to people just to get a reaction unna-mean?"

"Dat's what I'm saying! But they're all talking 'bout expelling me now."

"What!" I was shocked. I didn't want Tyrone to get expelled.

"My dad's all saying dat I might have to go live wiv my mum."

Jermaine picked up the woman's wallet, which refocused our

attention. He opened up the coin compartment and poured out all the loose change onto Tyrone's dad's glass coffee table. It reminded me of my grandfather's. He rummaged through the notes section and withdrew a small stack of papers that licked a beam across my face. While I was counting the loose change, Jermaine counted the paper money and Tyrone removed all the cards form the wallet.

"Eight pounds and change," I confirmed. "How much you got there, Jay?"

"One-ninety."

"An' what you got, Tyrone?"

"Dis woman's nuts!" he replied. "She's got bere ID in her purse like she doesn't know about criminals. Look," he fanned the cards out. Yes, she did have a lot of ID, "a MasterCard, Barclays Visa debit card, a Woolwich card, a library card, National Insurance number card—dis woman's *nuts*—a video rental card, some workplace ID card—"

"Where does she work?" I enquired.

Tyrone looked at the ID again. "J.K. Underwriters."

"What does she do?"

"Does it matter?" Jermaine questioned jarringly.

"I'm just curious."

"She's a...PA to a Mr. John Townsend," Tyrone answered. "What's a PA?"

I looked at him baffled. "I dunno—I thought it had something to do wiv singing live."

Tyrone gestured at what we called the bun and cheese. "The cheque book goes wit' da Barclaycard," he continued, "so dis one could get run nicely."

"All right, you can have the bun and cheese and dat, and Jermaine and me will split the cash. Yeah, Jermaine?"

"All right den."

"Ah, thanks Stephanie; I wasn't even expecting not'in." Tyrone informed me.

"Unna-not'in," I assured him because giving him a share of the goods wasn't a big deal to me. "So, what's dat, ninety quid each, Jermaine?"

"Yeah, plus the change you got, but you might as well keep dat as you lashed the tek."

We split the profit and pocketed our goods. Jermaine collected up the non-valuable stuff, like make-up, a diary, a pen, a phone bill and door keys off the table, wiping it all down with a dust cloth. He put them back in the bag neatly, pocketing the door keys and phone bill, all the while avoiding putting his prints back on the other items. He then dusted the bag down and placed it in a plastic bag that Tyrone had just handed him. As we were about to switch on the TV, there was an ominous knock at the door. Unwanted guests identified themselves.

"Police! Open up!"

Thanking God the TV wasn't on just yet to give us away, Tyrone and I shifted delicately away from the sofa near the opened living-room door that was in line with the front door. We sat softly by Jermaine on the other sofa that was more hidden from the door. We looked at each other opened-mouthed. Our eyes tore out from their sockets. This shook the guys even more as they saw all the blood particles in mine.

"Police! Open up!"

Anxiety breezed through my bloodstream setting fire to its path. My heart was racing, drumming hard against my chest. Still we said nothing; just breathed enough air to stay alive. We heard the tinny letterbox flap up. It stayed up for some moments, but it felt like the longest time.

"Don't fink anyone's dere, guv," one of the police officers said.

"All right," another one voiced, his voice thick and rough, "let's continue round the block. I want all of dese flats checked—someone must 'ave seen somefing!"

And with that, they scuttled away. Our lungs deflated. We sighed in relief, but still remained silent and motionless for the next fifteen minutes. Tyrone broke the silence.

"So how comes you lot bunked off of school, yeah, and come all the way up to New Cross to lash a tek and bait-up my ends?"

I explained to Tyrone about Safire, Stella and me recently getting recruited into the Ghetto Girls. About us meeting the older ones, Safire's self-indulgent antics and me wanting to alleviate my anger.

"What does alleviate mean?"

"Reduce...lessen." I dropped it like this word and I had been rolling for time.

Tyrone gazed at me perplexed. "You lessened your anger by lashing some poor woman's handbag?"

"Yeah, outside of dat mad little moment we had just now I'm feeling pretty good. Well, it was either dat or punch off someone's face." And that was the truth. I did feel relieved, as though I'd eased out my frustration. I was incapable of channelling my negative energy in any other way than making someone else a victim of my own victimhood.

Tyrone bounced in laughter and put out his fist to nudge me. I nudged him back. "You're nuts, Steph, but dat's why I love you."

As he said those freakish words that I didn't hear too often, my oak brown cheeks tinted with a deep red and I giggled like an idiot. I knew he didn't mean it in any way, nevertheless those words made my hands fidgety and my eyes dart in every which way bar Tyrone's. Jermaine sat biting his nails staring at the plastic bag on the sofa containing the handbag. Tyrone went on to enlighten me how glad he was that I hadn't gone with Nicola and Lakiesha. He said that Charlene, Safire, Stella and I as virgins shouldn't be "parring with them-gal-deh". He judged the fact that they had lost their virginities some years ago, irrespective that it was taken by grown men. Nicola lost hers before she was even in her teens.

"They free up their front like you free up a beating, Steph, an' dat's no lie," he concluded.

I scrunched up my face. I found the notion of such young girls having sex as readily as I fought, which was disproportionate to my age, sex and size, very troubling. Even I, an unimpressive product of my own ghastly environment, judged their upbringing, their exposures that would have led them into the arms of full-grown men.

I later found out that Nicola had spent the first six years of her life living with her father in the heart of Ghetto whilst her mother served a six-year jail term for carrying half a kilo of cocaine in her stomach from abroad. She had swallowed several pellets of the meticulously wrapped drugs, which she had planned to pass out when nature called. Unfortunately, her sweating, not eating and other suspicious behaviours resulted in her being identified as a likely drug mule and picked up by customs upon arrival at a London airport. Nicola often later reminded us how her mother could have died if one of the pellets split in her stomach.

Nicola's father was a drug dealer. She later told us how competitive her mother became with her upon her release from prison. "She hated I became my dad's number one girl. Well, it was me and him for six years straight," she told us. This escalated to flirtatious episodes with boys 'from round the way' and at school before Nicola's mum finally slept with her first boyfriend. Nicola was eleven and her boyfriend was eighteen. Her mother fucked him anyway knowing her underaged daughter was already sexually active with him. It was a downward spiral from there as Nicola competed with her mother's promiscuity. Some of the men she slept with were thirty and over. And Charlene believed something may have happened between Nicola and her own father, but this was never confirmed.

Lakiesha was simply a freak. No backstory that tip-toed around child molestation and pedophilia. Just a young woman who seemed constantly moist and visibly yearned the penis.

Back in Tyrone's living room, Jermaine was disgusted. "Urggghh, dat's some joke business; didn't their mum bring dem up wiv any morals?!" he fired. "My mum would murder Joanne if she was going on wiv dem t'ings."

"Dat's what I'm saying, Jermaine," I contributed. "Can you even try to imagine what *my* mum would do to me let alone my dad? Oh-my-gosh." I shuddered at the thought of it and resolved that I would remain a virgin for many years.

There was another knock at the door, which sent us into a panic again. I was what we called *boomed*. The anxiety was overwhelming. Again the letterbox flicked up.

"Tyrone!" an agitated voice detonated through the letterbox circulating the room.

Tyrone got up to see to the door. My heart settled back down for the umpteenth time. "Steph, stop tearing out your eyes like that," Jermaine said having calmed himself. "They're freaking me out; they already look nuts and you're making dem look double nuts."

I did it again just to raise the fear up in him. Jermaine made a show of covering his eyes. Tyrone came back in followed by his brother, Jason, who looked pretty pissed off and reminded me how odd it was for me to have a crush on his brother because he had a child with my sister Macy.

"Steph," he was slightly shocked to see me, "what're you doing 'ere?"

"I just came to check Tyrone wiv my cousin, innit. You all right, doh?"

"Nah, I ain't as it goes." He turned to Jermaine quickly. "Wha' gwaan, Jermaine; yuh safe?" He put his fist out to nudge him. This was the common sign of respect and the manner in which we greeted one another, particularly the boys.

"Yeah," Jermaine responded, nudging him at an angle.

Jason rotated back to me and then Tyrone who was standing behind him trying to get past to sit. "Don't think..." He stopped, noticing something. "Rah, wha'appen to your face?"

I rolled my eyes back. All this attention was becoming grating. "Had a madness with my mum, but it's anna-not'in'."

"Sonya still on dem Rambo moves?" he cracked up a little before realising that it really wasn't a joke. I was seriously hurt. "Anyway, what was I saying? Yeah, don't think I never just got questioned and searched on the estate for some robbery dat took place a little while ago?"

"*Is it?*" I feigned confusion in my butted face. "But you've got cornrows and look nuff older than us; plus we're in uniform."

Finally Tyrone got past him and sat down, Jason following suit. "You mean to tell me it was you yout's that rob the woman in your uniform and they're stopping me that's big twenty nearing twenty-one while I'm in my business suit! And den da bwoy-dem wonder why me an' dem nah frien'." He kissed his teeth. "So wha' did you lot get, den?"

Tyrone drew for the cheque book and card in his jeans pocket and Jermaine pointed to the plastic bag with the handbag in it saying, "There's just rubbish in there," and I didn't budge.

"So what, you just got bun and cheese and no papers, yeah?" Jason asked.

Tyrone looked at us and I said, "Yeah, we got a change as well," to which he smiled and said, "No jewellery?"

The boys shook their head no, but I said, "Yeah, I got somefing from yesterday. I was gonna pawn it but I weren't sure where to go."

"Let's 'ave a look den."

I took out a clear bag with the four rings and chain that I had taken from Mary-Anne. Jason was immediately drawn to the engagement-type ring with a sparkling clear stone. "Where d'you get this from?" He twisted the ring to look at it closely up against the light and we all gathered round him trying to see what he saw.

"I jacked it off one girl."

"If this is what I think it is, Steph, you're looking a small fortune out of this."

I jumped up close to him. "Jason, what d'you think it is, tell me, please!"

"Well...it looks like a European cut..." he twinkled the diamond in the light with sincere observation... "definitely Edwardian style and about half a carat's worth of a stone set in platinum...or maybe white gold." He searched for something on the inside of the band. "Yeah... platinum."

Those words meant nothing to me in terms of figures but they sounded good and my teeth started to skin out into a grin.

"I'd need to take it up Hatton Garden and have one of my sly bredren's operation take a look, but I'm guessing you'd get at least a couple gran'."

"A COUPLE GRAND?!" My teeth were fully on show, gums and all.

"Trust me," Tyrone added, "my brovver knows all about these t'ings; he works up there."

"Is it? So I'm definitely looking a couple grand?" The thought of getting some decent money got my heart racing again.

"Probably. Like I said, I'd need a second opinion; but whatever I can get, fifty-fifty, yeah?"

I paused for a good while browsing over Jermaine and Tyrone's face trying to measure the amount of work put in with the figure proposed. "seventy-thirty, man; I'm the one dat jacked it."

"Sixty-forty, and dat's it." His raised shoulders finalised things. "I'm putting myself on the line! If anything comes back it comes back to me and that's my job...my liberty compromised."

I backed down. "All right, sixty-forty." I looked back at Jermaine and he nodded softly, so I turned back to Jason. "But I didn't know you worked up there, Jason. Macy never said."

"Macy doesn't talk a lot of things, which is why she's my girl and I love her; plus for giving me my cris' yout'." We all looked at Jason like he was an eediot with his flowery words, but you could tell he was the proudest father in the world. Ricardo was absolutely gorgeous. "Anyway, yeah...I've been up there as a sales rep for a good year now, but I wish I could do other things, you know, but I can't."

"Why not?" I flung in.

"'Coz you need education to do other things, and I've got a yout' to support, so retail's ideal for me, coz you can't be a criminal forever yanna. That's why when I hear that you, Tyrone, are joking about getting yourself suspended from school, it vexes me, coz we don't get many chances and you know dis, man. And look at you guys, you should be at school in your uniform and instead you're on road committing crime."

Tyrone moved closer to his brother, affected. I looked away giving them the few seconds they needed without the glare of outsiders. Then I asked Jason if he could drop us home soon and how long he would need with my rings to get me my money. He told me two weeks and to "cool my skin." An hour or so passed and we made moves to leave, boarding Jason's Peugeot 205 vigilantly and escaping Ghetto untouched.

CHAPTER SEVEN

RESPECT

8th April 1994 – The Wrong Place

Wha' gwaan, Di? As usual I've so much to tell you. You'd never guess where I am. Anyway, before that, guess which eediot was in my yard last week? Arrgghhh, it really jars me you can't talk, Di! I just wish you could answer when I ask you something, but you're just a blank-paged book. Even so, I'm grateful for your ears and loyalty. But on the real, guess which eediot was in my yard and stirred up this madness between Mum and me? I know you know.

Anyway, as I said from the off, Di, you'd never guess where I am: Bull Station. All of us lot got nabbed for mopping in Woolworths. Maria and René got a bly true-say they didn't get anything, so it's just Shariece and me still deyah looking to get off with a caution. That's what my duty solicitor said when advising me to accept the charges of theft, which I've done. I gave them Safire's first name though, Mum's surname, Stella's date of birth and Dada's address, which makes me Safire Henry born 26th January

1981, 13 years of age. Where I mopped a few journals and stationery for school, the mixed-race fed allowed me to keep you, Di and a pen in the cell with me. I had to give him props for that, big him up coz I know feds are eediots more time trying to make things extra difficult for us yout's. Right now I'm just in my cell waiting for my people-dem to bail me out.

I was somewhere that I shouldn't have been. All I had was the company of my thoughts and my diary to write them in. A tirade of things had come to pass that I was desperate to share, vent or maybe even just put some perspective on.

Not so long ago, I came in from school. I was alone, which was a rarity as I was usually accompanied by Safire. On that occasion Safire had linked up with Stella and the both of them went trawling the streets with Nicola and the other Ghetto Girls. I wasn't so keen to follow this time around because Safire and I were at our peak of sibling feuds. I had literally just stepped into the house when I heard footsteps. I was frightened to say the least. I later described the experience as being "'fraid like puss". I tackled things head on as I always did, never thinking far enough to understand the consequence. I extracted a big kitchen knife and a rolling pin from the cutlery drawer. I removed the set of headphones from my ears and placed my Walkman on the kitchen table. I thought, some burglar's about to get a surprise co-co in his head. I prayed that I'd surprise him and not the other way round.

A few packets of crisps and a couple of chocolate bars were in a blue plastic bag on the kitchen table alongside unopened red bills from utility providers and others claiming to be Private and Confidential. The sweet goodies played on my carbohydrate cravings and a mass of saliva accumulated at my mouth's corners. I fought the temptation. My home was under threat! I prepared to creep up the stairs and strike the intruder over the head with the rolling pin. Then I saw Mum sauntering in a blasé and contented manner across the landing. She appeared to have emerged from the bathroom, as I heard the toilet flush. She tied up her dressing gown upon passing.

"Steph," she said, surprised to see me looking up at her, "what're you doing down there?"

"I thought you were a burglar. What're you doing up there?"

"How comes you're home from school so early?"

"How comes you're home from work so early?" I was bemused to say the least.

"Don't answer a question with a question."

"But that's what *you* just did two questions ago."

"Look, pickney!" the patois kicked in, "mi nah 'ave fi answer to yuh, so go and sit down inna di front room and goh read yuh bible!"

I rolled my eyes, which had cleared up pretty neatly. To say I was peeved would have been an understatement. I hated the way those lyrics—"go and read your bible"—always came into play when Mum became cornered. I turned to do as she said when I heard a male voice I vaguely recognised.

"Sonya, is everything OK?"

I turned back with knife and rolling pin in hand, and was thrown into a time warp. Derek was standing behind Mum on the landing. Four years had passed since their separation and there he was back in the picture again. He was clad in designer clothing that shouted 'I think I'm slick!' The buttons of his jeans were undone and his belt buckle unfastened. Derek! I could not believe my eyes. Crackhead Derek was back on my mother's radar with the intention of continuing the party. He had brought crisps and chocolates in an attempt to befriend me, as he did when we were kids. I looked at Mum, fuming, but didn't breathe a word. He would have looked the same had it not been for the grey hair spiking out from his close-shaven scalp, which I guess was to disguise the bald patch that centred his head. The grey hair competed against the black hair in his beard.

"You all right, Stephanie; you've grown up big now, innit?" Derek said excitedly as though he had already rejoined our family.

I blanked him and almost kissed my teeth...*almost.*

"Stephanie, don't you hear big people talking to you?" Mum put my manners into check.

"What?"

She made a go for me on the stairs. Derek restrained her, kept her on the landing holding her flexing biceps firm. "Don't worry about it, Sonya, she's just young."

Young your bloodclaat, I thought, and Mum shouted, "And mi ah goh kill her wid licks until she learns some manners!"

Again I thought to kiss my teeth, but my tongue was held by an uncontrollable force. However, my eyes said it all. "I'm fine thanks, Derek," finally came from my tamed tongue.

"Awhoa," she added, her tone with clear intent to patronise. "Next time you better know your place."

I shook off her needling and put the tools back in the kitchen. Then I made for the front room munching on a packet of cheese and onion Golden Wonder crisps with a Twix in hand waiting to be devoured. Though I still found the situation intolerable, when I saw the bible laid open on top of the piano before me, I felt spiritually drawn to its content and endeavoured to read. It only took four verses before I came across this: 'Flee fornication. Every sin that a man doeth is without the body; but he that committeth fornication sinneth against his own body.' 1 Corinthians 6:18

The assumption that Mum had read this recently and had deliberately gone against what she preached time and time again grated me. The word 'hypocrite' broke free from my trembling lips. Despite my rebellion towards Mum's Christian lifestyle, I secretly valued and admired her attempts to do what was right in the eyes of her God and belief system. The thought of my mum wilfully going against her beliefs did not sit well with me at all.

A bit later I heard the front door slam shut and Mum entered my space shortly after. Still in her dressing gown, her hair shaken and stirred, she bent her voluptuous waist to turn off the TV. I stared at her wide behind noticing there was no knicker-line, and I knew she wasn't avant-garde enough to consider wearing a g-string.

"It's the Sabbath now; let's have a Bible study."

She seemed carefree. Her voice possessed no self-questioning undertones. Acid bubbled from the depths of my gut, alarming my body that something was wrong. To contain myself was a priority. To keep my feelings internal was necessary, even if it felt toxic to do so. I tried. I could feel the fire blazing in my eyes and could envisage the fixated, demonic look that had taken over my angelic, big, dark brown eyes. I tried to straighten the area where my eyes dipped, but the weight of the dip was too heavy for me to shift.

Mum ignored this tension and opened back up the bible turning to the book of Job, the book that unearths a God-fearing man best known for his struggles, despair and the many other battles of a man who was continually loved and tested by God. Why did she bring to my attention the story of a righteous man, who continued to love and serve his God even at the brunt of his torment? But then she spun her own perspective on the story—that the gates of heaven would still be open to her even if she temporarily turned her back to God—and I soon realised her objective. Justification can soothe the soul and trick the mind into accepting wrong as right. And as she spoke to me of my own sins and what I needed to do to make it to heaven, hypocrisy morphed into her being and was all I could see.

"You're a hypocrite!" The words burst from my lips.

"What?" She obviously didn't hear me.

"You're—a hypocrite!" I repeated. This was a brave move on my part. I was about to open Pandora's Box. But I was no fool to the likely repercussions of my actions, so upon the opening of this box it was paramount that I was en route to the door when I said what was burning to be said.

"I can't believe you're lying down with that eediot man and you wanna tell me what *I* need to do to make it into the kingdom of heaven? If heaven's packed with hypocrites like you, then I'd rather stay buried here on earth."

The door to safety was within my grasp at this point. But strangely, unlike the attack mode she usually adopted, she started to cry. Face buried between her hands, she sobbed, her shoulders heaving uncontrollably.

"What're you crying for?" This emotional eruption had started to occur often. A sign I measured then as weakness. But her shoulders continued to bounce and she wailed a raw cry, coming from somewhere deep, deep inside. The rawness of this moment would jerk the tears of any spectator, but not me. So deep-set was my emotion that I couldn't see past my own hurt, especially as I saw Mum to be the cause of much of it. I rolled my eyes at her incessant display of weakness and attempted to leave the room to go upstairs and get changed.

"Don't I deserve to be loved?" she drooled to me.

I stepped back. "What, by some crackhead that dresses slick and gives you bun?"

Mum was taken aback but looked confused by the term I'd used as I watched her mime the word 'bun'.

"A crackhead that dresses slick and *cheats* on you, Mum; a man that isn't loyal to you. A man that sells drugs and does the things you are now against."

Infuriated, she rose to her feet. "How dare you! How *dare* you! Like God will forgive yuh lickle renkin-self, He will forgive him. And he's nut noh friggin' crackhead! He's a recovering addict..."

"A recovering *crack* addict, Mum."

"He's worth ten of your dotty farder!" she barked.

My neck started to stretch as my attitude accelerated: "He bu'ns white, Mum, my dad bu'ns weed; he's a criminal; my dad's an electrician; he depends on woman for a roof to cover his peanut head, my dad depends on himself; and if he tests my dad my dad would finish him... simple-t'ings. So who's worth more than who?"

"Get out of my house!" she screamed. "I'd rather Derek in my life than your rotten self!" Her high-pitched cry rippled throughout the house. This prompted banging on the wall from our neighbour. I snatched my Walkman from the kitchen table, shouting "Hypocriiiiiite!!" as I slammed the front door hoping the glass would shatter, but it didn't.

Bopping heavy-footed down our brightly lit street, I smashed my hand past rebellious plant stems and bushes that hung from neighbouring gardens. I thought about going to Dad's...only for a minute or two whilst my intentions were blatantly bad. I knew what Dad would do to her if I went there. I knew he would come down and beat her up real bad for bringing Derek back into our lives. And I knew that harbouring these thoughts were malicious and wrong. But the temptation was compelling.

Dada didn't live too far away from my mum's house, so I decided on taking my burdens to him, and hoped that he'd welcome them. Headphones on my head, Walkman set to play, I bounced down Lee High Road rocking my head hard, rapping along to Biggie Smalls' 'Juicy'.

I arrived there to a warm welcome. I informed him of my situation. It was self-explanatory, to those who knew my dad, why I didn't want to go to his place. Dada knew his son and understood. Mum was contacted immediately, and as expected she didn't mind me staying there as long as I didn't come back. I looked forward to life at my new home. Once Dada had finished speaking to Mum, he set the ground rules, which was simply to treat him respectfully as he would treat me with the respect I deserved until I showed him otherwise. I was happy with that, and accepted the challenge. I wanted to prove to Mum that I wasn't that bad, that I could be good if the circumstances and people around me were good.

A short time passed before Dada cooked and dished me out some mouth-watering food: steamed fish and 'boil-food'. We also called boiled food 'hard food' sometimes. Foods such as boiled green banana, yam, sweet potato, boiled dumplings and sometimes boiled plantain or chow-chow, all came under that banner. The food sat so nicely in my stomach I was impelled to hug Dada for some time, which he didn't question, only embraced.

Upon Nina's arrival from college, we headed back out to Mum's to collect my things. Safire was home and pretending, seemingly, to be against me leaving. I warned her that if she went into my bedroom then she was to leave it clean and wasn't to dare touch my diaries or she and I would be scuffing when I returned one day.

"Whatever," she phased but understood this not to be a joke. She then asked, "So when are you gonna come back, den?"

"I dunno."

"What did you do, Steph? If I were you, I'd just say sorry and dunnit dere."

I briefed my sister on the day's events. Safire unleashed a torrent of revolt, filthy names and street terminology, all aimed at Mum's ears.

"Allow dat!" I demanded. "I just wanna get of here without a madness."

Safire went to her room and slammed her bedroom door.

Whilst I packed my flannel, toiletries and clothes, Nina and Mum were engaged in conversation downstairs.

"Don't worry about her, Sonya, she'll be in safe hands. I promise," Nina assured.

"Yeah, you're a good girl, Nina," Mum said. "But that girl upstairs is bad bruck and doesn't have any manners, which you need to get through in this world. All I'm saying is don't let her influence you and rotten your core."

I didn't think I was that bad, so bad an apple that I would rotten anyone who got close enough to me. My own mother thinking of me as so horrid was a hard thought to swallow. But I would rather smash my room to pieces or my knuckle blades against my bedroom walls or the face of a passing enemy than show her I was penetrable. That her words pained me so much I could cry a jug of water to quench the thirst of a family of seven. Focusing on my diaries to calm myself down, I moved the stacked pile from the floor behind the bunk bed and hid them on a shelf in the back of my wardrobe. I thought it best to remove the temptation from Safire. I kept my current diary with me at all times. I headed downstairs with my things packed in my rucksack and a doubled-up bin bag packed to the rim. Safire heard me and followed.

"You ready, Steph?" Nina asked.

I nodded yes.

"Bye Aunty Sonya, take care," she turned to Safire. "You all right, I didn't even know you were here. We're just about to make moves now."

"I know, Steph said," Safire replied, looking vexed, ready for war.

"Here you are." Mum handed me a raffle looking book not even looking at me. "Take this and give it to Dada."

It was my Child Benefit Book. I pocketed it and opened the door without saying goodbye to her, just saying "Later" to Safire.

"Yeah, I'll see you at school, yeah," she replied.

Before Nina and I had even reached the gate, we heard: "How can you be going there with Derek and you're supposed to be a Christian?!" Screams and shouts and ba-dup-bap-bups, PAPS and BLAPS followed, but we didn't hang around to see the results.

*

I spent the weekend and the Bank Holiday Monday moving with Nina. I realised then how different she was from my sisters and others. She wasn't easily riled. She was a peacemaker rather than a violence instigator. These were the traits that I learned to love. Trouble deserted me in her presence. She wasn't a robber, a fighter or a thief, but she'd defend herself if necessary. She wasn't all that I was, and this I found appealing and even inspiring. She liked my passion about things and my honesty though. As a direct family unit Nina only had Melvin and Dada, and now me. We had a mutual respect for one another, and unlike Mum expected, Nina influenced me more than I ever could have influenced her.

Some days later Mr. Ahmed was going to town on his praising of me. We had beaten Eltham Secondary School in a game of football and I had scored a hat-trick. I loved the game.

"That's the motivation I want to see from you, Stephanie," Mr. Ahmed informed me as we all were standing outside the changing room after the game. "Some game you played, Stephanie; we sure showed them! You should know that your peers owe this victory to your undeniable efforts."

His acknowledgment of my triumph thrilled me. Mr. Ahmed went to put an unwanted arm round my shoulder as I waved to some of the girls leaving the changing room. "Extremely proud of you, Stephanie. Keep this up and I'll be personally removing you from report." He grinned with an eyebrow raised like he was giving me heaven and earth. I guess he was overwhelmed by having something positive to say about me. Whilst I wished it were Mr. Williams rather than him who took over coaching our football game in the absence of our PE teacher, I was comforted by his revised approach to me.

I gave him a fake smile. His words meant everything to me, but I would play it down as though it meant nothing. I broke loose from Mr. Ahmed's grip and met up with Shariece, Maria and René in the school playground.

"Where's Safire?" I asked.

"She bunked our last class, innit," Maria said. "Went to meet Nicky and dem lot."

"Who with? On her jacks?"

"Nah, Stella came for her," Shariece added.

We forged a free bus ride to Lewisham in our usual fashion. I needed a new diary, plus I wanted to treat myself to stationery. I planned to shoplift these items as I didn't have any money and, although two weeks had passed, I still hadn't received my money from Jason for the rings.

*

It wasn't long before I was vacating the cell I had inhabited for over four hours. Dada was waiting for me and he was disappointed. He appeared out of place in the police station's bright but dingy space, and was confused when he saw me. He was expecting Safire. At that point, Shariece's mum entered the station, escorted in by a female officer in uniform. Shariece's mum's loud African dress quietened my menacing attitude. I was overcome by shame and couldn't bring my head up to meet her gaze.

"Safire, I thought you were Stephanie as I came in." I was still too ashamed to look up to see what expression her face was displaying. "I'm disappointed in you, Safire. I can't believe you and Shariece would do something like this!"

I didn't say a word. I noticed Shariece materialise from the door that led to the corridor of cells. I wanted to break a smile at her for the sheer novelty of us getting arrested for the first time, but it wasn't a good idea in front of our elders, so I reconsidered and we turned away from each other, suppressing any rising laughter.

Dada was not interested in standing around and loitering within the premises; he grunted customary Caribbean sounds to hasten the process. He and I signed the paperwork that granted my bail and I mumbled goodbye to Shariece and her mum.

CHAPTER EIGHT

BASHMENT TIME!

24th June 1994 – 181 bus

Wah' gwaan Di, tonight's gonna be da bomb! I can't wait. I'm going Moonshot. It's like a rave or dance, or whatever. I fink Saxon's playing tonight. Dey're like a bashment sound system playing dem tunes dat big people wil' out and skank to. I've got my outfit together, I just need to get my papers together, which is why I'm on my way to Macy's....

The dancehall music scene in Jamaica is renowned for inventing words. One of the words that has been adopted internationally is 'bashment'. Bashment is more representative of a community, culture, lifestyle and dress, and is a term that denotes flamboyance, eccentricity and hype. For dancehall lovers, which we were by tradition rather than by choice, bashment time was a time for excitement, soca-type dancing with cool, gangster undertones, and explicit dance moves. When a bashment party was on the horizon, preparations were extensive.

That summer of 1994, I knocked on my big sister's front door with aggression. No one was answering. I think I had been impatient from birth, even at the point of leaving my mother's womb. I smashed the knocker down so that it reverberated back and forth like a ping-pong machine. The pitter-patter of small feet approached down a floor-boarded staircase.

"'Oo is it?" Ricardo's little voice echoed from behind the door.

I pressed my thumb against the letterbox so I could see Ricardo's cute face and said, "Aunty Stephanie, Ric, open up!"

My nephew was adorable. He got excited upon hearing my voice and fumbled at the door, stretching awkwardly to reach the Yale lock. He couldn't open it. Hearing him clunk his way back up the stairs, I folded my arms and sighed irritably. For the second time he clunked back down the stairs.

"Aunty Steph, Mummy said wait coz she's on toilet."

I kissed my teeth. "I thought you was a big boy, Ricardo," I said. "Why can't you open the door?"

"Coz I'm little," he replied.

"D'you wet your bed?"

"No!" He giggled sheepishly with an air of 'I'm a big boy' as two-year-olds do.

"Because you're big; you're a big boy now," I said and pressed hard on the stiff letterbox flap so it would stay up.

"But I can't reach!"

"Then get a chair," I said with a hint of sarcasm. "That's what big boys do, Ricardo, you have to use your head."

His chubby little beige legs that dangled out of Y-fronts ran down the remaining three steps and through the living-room door, into the kitchen. It was an old Victorian house with an odd layout. The heat from the sun was frying the back of my neck, which was peeping out of a tight white cotton T-shirt. Hot and bothered, I turned to sit on the front doorstep with my chin wedged between my palms. I didn't move until I heard Ricardo dragging the chair through the house. When I got up to check on his progress, the chair was up against the front door with Ricardo determinedly climbing up on it.

"Oi!" Macy's voice boomed over Ricardo who was so shocked that he shook nervously and gripped the chair frantically to avoid falling off.

"What're you doing up there?" she barked. "Mind you bus' open your head, 'bout you're climbing up chair to open door!"

Macy ran down the stairs and pulled Ricardo up with one hand. She opened the door, at which point I freed the flap of the letterbox. A bad stench pervaded the air and clung mercilessly onto my nostril hairs. I looked at my sister in condemnation.

"Sorry, I had rotten belly," was her simple response.

I passed through the passageway hurriedly to get away from the smell. I noticed disappointment etched on Ricardo's face as he sat on the sofa with a "humph". I was about to comfort him, but observed Jason's face in a polished silver frame, and quickly remembered why I was there.

"Where's Jason?"

"It's a Friday, Steph; he's at work—why?"

I dropped onto one of the navy blue, leather sofas as though I was at my wits end. "Because he still hasn't given me my money for the jewellery I gave him, and it's been nearly two months now. I'm supposed to be going out tonight and I ain't got no money." My rant was illustrated with dramatic hand movements that informed my sister of the edge I was on.

"All right, Steph—calm down, man!" From the other sofa, she

picked up Ricardo and cuddled him on her lap. "I dunno about the ovver stuff, but Jason—'

"Daddy!" Ricardo interrupted. "I want Daddy!"

"You'll see your daddy later, Ric, be quiet." She turned back to me. "What was I saying? Yeah, he told me about the diamond ring; he said it was put up for sale in one of the shops and he's waiting for it to be sold, so once dat's done you'll be paid."

"So why didn't he phone me and let me know?" I still felt that some wool was trying to creep over my eyes here.

"He did, a couple weeks ago, but you're not at Mum's any more are ya? So I thought I might as well just wait until it comes before doing all this chasing up and down trying to find you. It's not like I'm gonna let Jason bump my little sister now, am I?"

I didn't say anything, which in turn said a lot.

"What," Macy went on, "you think I'd let him bump you? D'you know what, Steph, next time don't do business with my man coz den we won't be in this situation."

"I didn't say you would let him bump me, now, did I?" I said before breaking a smile to ease the tension.

She followed my lead and her gold, misaligned tooth twinkled. "I'm cooking dinner, you hungry?"

Ricardo beamed his eyes and I bared my teeth, and my sister understood that there were hungry-belly-yout's up in her home.

"Where're you going tonight anyway?" she breathed as she walked into a pasty, grey-walled kitchen with a linoleum floor.

"Moonshot," I replied, referring to a hall based in Ghetto that housed community work in the week days and raves at the weekend.

She removed seasoned meat in a plastic bowl from the fridge. She set ablaze the hob, where she placed the black, burnt Dutch pot, which was something to be secretly proud of as it showed the age of the pot and cooking prowess of its owner. She poured oil into the pot, which gradually let off steam.

Ricardo and I watched soundlessly, our mouths drooling, waiting for the succulent lamb chops to touch the oil and release their tasty, steamy scent.

A digital clock on top of the marble mantelpiece told me it was now 18:48. Ricardo and I watched MTV, which was more amplified and enjoyable to watch on a widescreen television. We rocked our heads to Biggie Smalls, who was my favourite rapper at the time, and Junior M.A.F.I.A.'s 'Player's Anthem' track. I loved the rapper's storytelling and his 'fuck the world' attitude that I too possessed.

Macy entered with a plate of food and a glass of Tango on a tray in one hand and a small bowl of food in the other. She handed the tray to me whilst asking, "So, are you still writing all your business in dat diary of yours?"

I took the tray, carefully trying to steady the swaying Tango from spilling over the rim of the glass. "My diary? *Yeeaaahh.*" My voice was tinged with sarcasm to hide my embarrassment. "Ain't dat the whole reason why you started getting me them?" I began tearing into the meat. Ricardo looked up to Macy from the floor like a hungry dog might do.

Sitting down to feed him she said, "Not necessarily. You was only a little yout' when I started getting you them—you're still a yout' now…" I hated it when my sister called me that. "How old are you…thirteen?"

I munched the food in my mouth quickly and swallowed. "Twelve and a bit."

"See. When I started getting you them you were all…six, I only did it to give you an escape from reality really. I used to hate it when I was young growing up with Mum, Dad and all dat madness. Who wants to see their mum getting beaten up by their dad? I would daydream a lot and fantasise about things and try to get away from all of dat. D'you remember dem bedtime stories I used to write about?"

"Yeah. Course!" I exclaimed.

"Yeah all dem fairytale stories, like *The Girl with the Magic Ring*, used to be my fantasy world. I would retreat to them when trying to escape the screams coming from Mum's mouth when Dad would batter her, or when Mum would shout and bruck me up for no proper reason. And when I looked at you I saw the same little girl that I was, someone who needed something...somewhere to escape from the madness."

I stared at her. My eyes were questioning. She continued, "Safire was different. Her and Mum were close for whatever reason; whether it was her lookalike thing or that she favoured Safire's character or the fact dat Mum planned for her and not us—'

"How d'you know dat?" I interjected.

"Mum told me. I was about eight or nine. I remember it was Safire's fifth birthday and she just started going out wiv Derek, and she said...I remember, she said that she was so happy and that she wished she had met him after she'd had Safire. And when I asked her why not after she'd had me, because I remember what Dad used to do to her, she said because she had planned for Safire and was planning to leave Dad but then she found out she was pregnant with you." Macy's voice dropped and bore sympathy. She wiped Ricardo's mouth with a piece of kitchen towel she had crumpled in her hand, then she got up to scrape the leftover food into a grocery plastic bag that hung on the door of the kitchen.

"So what about you?"

"Of course she didn't plan for me. She was barely sixteen. She didn't know what she wanted. It's not like she wanted to get beaten up by her babyfather now, did she?"

"So she stayed with him because of me, then?" I gulped down some Tango to flush down my food. I was trying not to penny this on any sensitive level.

"Yeah," she confirmed from the kitchen sink. "Only for about a year and a half though because she couldn't really leave." She came back into the living room. Ricardo had crashed out asleep on the sofa already.

"You know Mum's back with him now; some joke t'ing, ah-lie?"

"She's just lonely, that's all; you gotta let her get on with it, Steph."

"I am! Dat's why I come out of her stupid house!"

"Allow all dat, Steph, Mum's been through nuff, you know. It wasn't easy for her leaving the man she loved for her religious beliefs despite the fact that he bu'ned white. He used to bring in a lot of money, y'know...trust! We were bade."

I went to fling in how much I cared not about his wealth. So he was bade! Who cares? I thought. Then Macy switched it: "So how do you escape by writing about your business and not things that you fantasise about?"

I thought about her question as I walked into the kitchen where I scraped my plate out. I placed it in the sink noticing some flee-bitten, black cat through the small kitchen window, sitting on the terrace in Macy's nicely kept garden. I banged on the window to scare the puss. Those animals just didn't agree with me. They made the hairs stand up on the back of my neck. "I dunno," I said finally.

"You don't know why you write your business on a daily basis?"

Why is she asking me what I just gave the answer to? I wondered.

"No. I don't," I said. "And I don't necessarily write about events daily... it's more generally that I write...you know, like when there's a madness, which at the moment is on the reg's. Plus, when I think about it, I don't even think I'm tryna escape from reality—that's why

I don't fantasise—I think I'm more tryna understand my reality, coz when I read back on fings I think, Why did I do or say dat? Y'get me? And true-say, Di doesn't talk back or question anyfing, I can tell her anyfing. Dat's a proper bredren, ah-lie?"

"Steph, why're you talking like your diary's a person? It's a book." Macy looked slightly baffled.

"*I know*, dat's just da way I talk about it. Anyway, how did you know I write my business in her...my diary?"

Macy appeared distracted all of a sudden. She flicked through the TV channels pointlessly.

"Macy! How'd you know?"

"All right, Steph, keep your voice down before you wake up Ric!" She sighed, reluctant to let the truth be known. "Safire must've read one of dem and told me."

Resentment bubbled up in me. I pondered deeply on how I would smash my fist in Safire's face when I saw her. Just then the front door slammed shut. I looked up and saw a smiling Jason, who was either mocking me or glad to see me.

"Just the person I wanna see," he uttered and dropped his bag to the floor, leant over my sister and kissed her whilst muttering, "You all right, babe?" He turned back to me. "So wha' gwaan, Steph? What, you come for your papers, little gangsta?" He rubbed his hands together melodramatically and bared his teeth like he had something for me.

A smile broke across my face and those internal bubbles started to simmer down and turned into guilt as the thought of Mary-Anne crossed my mind. I forced that thought to the back of my head. Macy got up and headed to the kitchen. "Babes, you hungry?"

"Starving, babes." Jason rubbed his belly.

I looked at Jason and then at my sister, rolling my eyes at all the excessive 'babes' exchange.

"So what brings you here, gangsta?" Sitting next to the sleeping Ricardo, Jason continued to rub his hands together, shrugging his shoulders.

"What I've been waiting two months for, blood." I wasn't in the mood any more. My tone was blunt and I didn't intend to sharpen it.

He popped open his bag and loosened his tie. "Let me see what I've got here then." He rustled through the bag exaggeratedly. "I'm sure I had something in here for this little facety yout'!"

"Who you calling a yout'?" I defended.

"The only yout' in here besides my son who's sleeping."

I wasn't digging the mockery. As my mouth went to run off the rails, he dashed down stacks of banded-up money, which both silenced and warmed me at the same time.

"You should find two and half grand there, and if I'm not mistaken, my cut of that should total a grand, but by all means get a calculator and confirm the figure."

My teeth were again on show. I counted up the money that totalled at £2,500 and made a quick calculation in my head. I counted out a thousand pounds and handed it to him.

"Glad to see your maths is on point," he said, taking the papers with a wide smile.

"Thanks for that, Jason, glad to see you come through." I looked up at Macy as she entered with a tray of food. "Can you call me a cab please, Mace?"

She handed him the tray and made the call from Jason's mobile phone.

"They said ten minutes. So what you got planned for the summer holidays with all dat money?"

I laughed forcedly and counted my money again. "I dunno." I handed her £150. "Fifty is for Ricardo, yeah?"

"Thanks Steph." She looked at Jason, signalling me with her head. "Jason, Steph's going Moonshot tonight."

"Is it? You fink you're big enough to rave now, Steph?"

I rolled my eyes.

"She thinks she's a big woman now, Macy. You wanna mind man don't soon start take set 'pon you."

"I can handle man, you know; I'm not an eediot." I simultaneously tutted and cut my eye.

"All right, Jason; leave her now," Macy told him.

"She knows I'm only ramping, innit, Steph?"

I didn't respond.

"Anyway," he persisted, "I might see you at Moonshot later; Stonelove's playing, so I'll be looking out for you and your little friend-dem."

I looked at the digital clock on the mantelpiece again. It was now 19:57. I couldn't wait to touch the night ahead.

*

By 22:10 I was at home, bathed and dressed in the kitchen snacking on a pear and wondering when Dada would go to his bed so I could make moves. He was watching Trevor McDonald on the *Ten O'clock News*...and me.

"Where're yuh going tonight?"

The off-the-cuff question shocked me. My eyes darted around before they settled on him and I looked at him, wondering what could have given me away. "Why would you say that?"

"Don't insult my intelligence, Stephanie Johnson, mi nah ah insult yours." He got up from his chair and leaned on the radiator, rustling in his pocket. He removed a gold box of cigarettes and lit one up. I smelt the aroma, longing for the days when I would be able to just simply ask for a cigarette, set a flame to its bush, and inhale the exotic flowing vapour...

"So where it is you ah plan fi goh tonight?"

I was tempted to lie, as I would do to Mum—by any means necessary I couldn't tell her the truth—but I didn't. "Moonshot," I admitted, sighing disappointedly. I knew I would still go out no matter what he said, but I also knew that this could be the point when I disrespected Dada. I didn't want to do that to him, not with all that he'd done for me and the way he respected me, but I had to go out—tonight was bashment time!

"Wid who?" he asked.

"My mates: Shariece, René and Maria. I'm supposed to be meeting my sisters and some ovver friend's dere as well." My attitude showcased my determination to go.

"And what time was you looking to reach back home?"

I was stunned by these questions. Why wasn't he dictating to me instead? I looked at him in hopeful surprise. "Errmmm...about two?"

He drew on the cigarette again and it fogged his view as he voiced, "One."

"Half past one, Dada," I pleaded with a minor whine, clocking on to the negotiation game we were playing. "By the time my mates get here and we get there it'll be eleven."

The doorbell rang.

"Dat must be dem now," I said getting up from the table across from Dada.

"Stephanie," he called as I entered the hallway. I stopped and turned to face him. "Tek off ya dressing gown mek ah see wha' you ah wear."

I untied the dressing gown and hung it up on the door.

"But what a way yuh skirt shart," he expressed as I spun round for his viewing.

"It's not dat short, Dada, it's just above my knee, plus these denim A-line skirts are the lick right now!" and with that I rushed to the door.

I opened the front door excitedly to see my giggling friends 'bogling', a current dance move from the dancehall scene. "You lot are nuts, man, come in," I said in greeting.

They were surprised when they saw my grandfather kicking back in the kitchen puffing on a cigarette, as they knew I'd been planning to sneak out tonight like I knew Shariece had done.

Pointing at them individually and at the same time trying to untie my silk headscarf that I would later wear to bed, I introduced them one by one. "Dada, dat's my bredren Shariece, Maria and René; dis is Dada, yous lot."

Bunched up in the doorway, they waved at him shamefacedly and stumbled over each other to say, "Good evening."

"So wha' di whole ah yuh ah 'quash up yuhself inna di door for?" Dada put to them. "Tek ah seat, nuh! It's nice to meet uno."

My headscarf was off and I was ready to hit the road, so made a gesture for my friends not to sit and get caught up in Dada's stories. Dada looked at us peculiarly, standing together before the glass cabinet. We were all clad the same in cream-coloured A-line skirts, red short-sleeved tops and red Kangaroo pumps with the shell toe. Plus we'd all slicked back our hair flush into a ponytail.

"Ah soh di yout' dem run it now?" He laughed animatedly, his shoulders recoiling.

"Dada, we gotta go now, can I call a cab?" This was me ignoring his humour.

His heaving body settled down. "Wait a while so Nina can goh wid uno."

I sighed as though my world was crashing down on me. "*Ahh*, but she could be ages, Dada; it's probably gonna be finished by the time she comes!"

"'Top yuh foolish talk! Hee," he handed me a white cordless phone, "call Lewisham Cars, by di time di cab comes Nina should be here."

"But how do you know?" I whined, dialling the cab number. I looked at my friends, namely Maria, who was looking uncomfortable by the door, her eyes circling the ceiling.

"Because di gal tell mi seh she ah come in at ten-thirty," he looked to Maria, "an' wha' di time?"

"Ten...thirty," Maria got out hesitantly.

"So 'top yuh foolish noise."

The cab was coming in ten minutes. Nina rolled in within five minutes and rolled back out with us in ten. I picked up some cigarettes on the way to feed my pretend habit. By 22:55 we were in New Cross on Pagnell Street. Moonshot was in sight, just across the grass area used as a sports ground for the local community and the youths who came through Moonshot when it operated as a Youth Centre by day. Nina went to pay the cab with the £10 Dada had given her as we were leaving, but I told her I had money and I paid the cab.

"How much?" Nina asked as we walked across the grass.

Four sets of glares fixed on me at once. I flashed them the rest of the £200 that I came out with, which was now £194 and change. They all clustered around me, Maria took it a step further and walked backwards in front of me.

"Where d'you get all dat from," she asked.

"Some girl I jacked for recruiting into da Ghetto Girls?"

"*Yeeaah*?" they all sung bar Nina.

I looked at Nina who wasn't impressed, her discomfort playing out on her face, "Well, this is what I got for one of da rings, but whatever, it's no biggie."

"Is it?" Shariece was joyful. "What, you got two bills for dat one diamond?"

"Five," I corrected.

René drew for my shoulder to stop me in my tracts as we neared the vibrating walls of the Moonshot Community Centre. "You got a *monkey* for dat ring?"

"£500?!" Maria shouted.

"Yup," I said then trying to play it down at the sight of Nina added, "but it wasn't that bigga deal–"

"What about the girl? Was she all right?" Nina interrupted.

"Nah. I robbed her Nina, I didn't start a girls club with her. She was fucked, but that's just how it goes sometimes, innit?" I tried to make the situation seem blasé like I never gave a fuck! Whether I did or not I thought was irrelevant. The deed was done. Mary-Anne probably visited the hospital, was on medication or had internal injuries. I really didn't know, but I secretly hoped she was OK.

They all stared at me and shook their heads with a seed of budding envy. All apart from Nina. I handed my mates £20 each and Nina £30. "I'll give you some more a next time," I told them.

"Do you know what, I'm good, Steph," Nina said, "Really, I'm just not comfortable taking it. But don't worry, let's just have a good night yeah?" And the rest tumbled "thanks" on me as they tried to suffocate me with hugs.

We queued outside Moonshot. High end and jalopy cars blared out dancehall anthems by artists like Supercat, Nicodemus, Tippa Irie and others of that nature. A group of women dressed in tight, revealing, bright-coloured garments, some with bleached skin and rainbow-coloured wigs, were sprawled out across the bonnets of some of the fancy cars. The Mercedes, Lexus, BMWs and the like. They rocked to the baseline that waved through the air like smoke vapour. They formed shapes that exposed areas of their bodies and told stories of their promiscuity.

I saw my cousins Leroy and Jermaine walking aimlessly with Sean greeting passersby. I cried out to them. They bopped over, all coincidentally wearing Armani Jeans. I laughed to myself. Naively I thought only girls dressed to coordinate! I looked at Sean and his closely spaced eyes thinking he was nowhere near as good looking as Tyrone. He didn't have the height, the smooth dark complexion, the plump lips, albeit cracked, or the crisp oval eyes with long lashes. Sean was medium height, fairer-skinned with rubber pink lips and gelled, curly hair. Nevertheless he was a cool guy.

"How comes you lot ain't queuing up to go in?" I asked.

"I'm waiting to see if I can see Trevor Sax," Leroy said. "True-say my dad knows him I'm gonna try to see if I can speech a freebie. They're charging fivas in dere!"

"What, ain't you got no dough?"

"Nah, man."

I turned to Jermaine who was in conversation with Nina. "Ain't you got dough, Jay?"

"Just a blue."

"There's a fiva between us all, man. Joke t'ing, ah-lie?" Leroy confirmed.

I glanced at Sean conversing with Shariece. "I'll pay for yous lot, innit." It felt good to be in this position of having and not needing. Plus it felt good to be able to give to my family and friends. In a community where most people are out for themselves, these moments counted.

It wasn't long before we were all getting frisked at the door. This was a comprehensive process. We paid our £5 each at the window booth to a sandy-skinned lady with a finger-wave hairstyle (a Marilyn Monroe-type wave except that it was gelled down and rock hard). She smiled sharply and beckoned for us to keep moving. We were then in front of double doors with a small steamed-up window. I could vaguely make out heads bobbing up and down beyond it. The baseline's vibration made my teeth chatter and sent ripples down my spine.

Smoke engulfed us as we entered through the double doors into the dark community hall. Multicoloured lights slashed through the darkness and the many bodies within it. The dance was jam! Jam-packed with bubblers, wall-grinders, one-foot skankers and waistline-rotators. The sound system was set up on a lit-up stage. A deep, melodious-toned MC spoke over the reggae and dancehall beats that were put on by the DJ, who measured the beat with the pace of the MC's patter. At the MC's command, the DJ would stop, rewind, scratch and play notorious tunes. These were prepped up for glamorous introductions that would whip up the crowd into a frenzy. The hoarse Jamaican vocals resonated from eight humungous speakers and drew everyone into captivated submission. We moved through the crowd, passing walls of men and women slow grinding. We walked past a few old-timers skanking wildly with swinging locks.

Getting through the crowd was a challenge. Finally we arrived at the bar, which too was overcrowded. This would take any punter some decent effort to get served.

"Here, Leroy," I said, handing him £20, "get everyone a drink, please."

In reverence to our homogeny, we all opted for a brandy and Coke, except Nina who went for an Archers and lemonade. I rocked my head somewhat tryingly. I desperately wanted to get the bashment's vibe up in me, yet every time I looked across at my friends, I saw in them what I felt myself: uncomfortable and stiff and outside of our comfort zone.

"Safire's coming tonight, innit?" Shariece shouted to me.

"Yeah. Tell me when you see her; I got a bone to pick with her!"

"What's she done now?" Shariece asked. "I hope you ain't gonna start a madness!"

I just about grasped what she had said over the thumping bashment rhythms. "I'm not. I just wanna ask her somefing," I said. Shariece knew me too well.

René uncrossed her arms, picking up on our conversation and moved closer to me. "What's wrong?!"

"Nuffing really, just wondering where Safire is."

"WHAT?"

"Nuffing!" I shouted back taking my drink from Leroy's outstretched hand.

Nina took her drink and leant into my ear. "Come on, let's go over in that corner over there! I swear I just saw your sister!"

"Who, Safire?"

"Nah, Charlene!"

I bellowed in Shariece's ear relaying what Nina had said. She then passed it on to Maria and René. Just as I was about to inform Leroy and Jermaine that we were moving, Leroy made it be known that he and the boys were moving and would catch up with us later. Nina led the way and we parted company. We passed the middle of the dance floor where girls were 'butterflying', a dancehall move where you rotate your knees together in opposite directions, but these girls were doing it on their backs. I hadn't seen this dance live before, only in music videos on MTV. Men surrounded them, hollering gunshot noises of approval and appreciation, rating their performance. The ratings were high. Video cameras focused on explicit, gyratory, bum-flicking moves that didn't shy away from the exposure. Nina stopped. She saw Charlene standing just outside the circle of people that made room for the girls to 'skin-out' on the floor.

"Charlene!" I yelped. She couldn't hear me.

Once we were close enough Nina tapped her on the shoulder and they greeted one another with an embrace.

Charlene saw me over Nina's shoulder. "Rah, Steph; what're you doing here wiv all dese lot?!"

"Raving, innit!"

She uttered hello to the gang who returned the greeting. "I know Sonya ain't letting you out to these places; did you sneak out?"

"Nah, I'm staying at Dada's now, innit. Who you wiv?!" I looked around her hoping to see Safire.

"Donavan, Nicky and Lakiesha!"

"Where're they?"

"Donavan's gone to get drinks and the ovver two are there." Charlene pointed to the centre of the dancehall where Nicola and Lakiesha were getting up off their backs. Nicola did a bum flick with one leg up on Lakiesha's shoulder while she butterflied for the masses.

"*Rah!*" was all I could muster.

The clock ticked on. Another round of brandies had both warmed and excited us all. Dance moves flowed between us. Maria now did the butterfly. René's waist was tick-tocking. Charlene executed finely the heal & toe dance move, and Shariece and I did the boggle.

Not before long I heard "bo-bo-bo-bo-bo-bo!!!" to the intro of General Levy's 'Incredible' jungle remix. Stella, Safire, Taniqua, Shannon and Candice abruptly materialised within our dance area, gunning their hand into the air on every outburst of "bo!" The jungle baseline kicked in and all the young people emerged from their corners and took centre stage. The older people receded to the outskirts or the bar. We were all fully engrossed in the jungle baseline sound, bordering on possessed. We were 'bo!'-ing and 'buoe!'-ing and 'buoyaka!'-ing as much for the excitement of seeing each other as for the passion we shared for this tune. I skipped from one foot to the other in time with General Levy rapping about being the 'incredible general'. The atmosphere was electric. We were having an incredible time, I for sure felt on top of the world.

Candice danced in front of me. I skipped in front of her drawing off her energy. She was wearing a navy blue A-line skirt, a white cotton vest with a navy blue string vest over it and navy blue Kangaroo's. Her hair was slicked up into a ponytail with the top bushing out. We all had the same look.

"Why ain't you been on the ends much lately with Safire and Stella?" Candice belted.

This interruption annoyed me. "That's just the way it goes sometimes," I yelled to save me explaining that Safire and I were in contention more often than we were in harmony.

She added, "Nah coz I thought you two were close."

"We are!"

"Oh, but I thought...I mean, from what I read in your diary—"

"You read my diary?!" I snapped, stopping dancing mid-flow.

"Nah, it was just a small amount when we came to your house and Safire was looking for so't'in' to wear in your closet and accidentally found..."

I stepped away from her as the selector rewound the jungle track and echoed energetic sounds through the mike, feeding the crowd's hype. I approached Safire.

"What you looking at me like dat for?" she challenged.

"Why're you making people, strangers at dat, read my fuckin' t'ings?!" My eyes were boring holes into her, my nostrils flared and my top lip kinked. There was no denying that my intention was contention.

She giggled. In the way that she did with Mum, perhaps to try to lessen the wrath directed at her.

"Why're you bringing people into *my* fuckin' room and den got dem reading my private t'ings dat not even you're supposed to be reading?!" I was all up in her face.

She repressed her smile. "ALL RIGHT! Stop running ya mout' and coming up in my bolt!"

"After you're the one troubling my t'ings!" My fist was clenched. I was ready to roll.

"GOOD! What you leaving your t'ings dere for? You don't even live there, plus Mum don't even want you dere..."

I threw a mighty punch that busted her lip instantly and sent her to the ground. I heaved as I loomed over her. Shariece and Nina stepped in to disconnect our brawl, but I did not budge. With one hand back to hold her up from the floor, Safire touched her lip and gazed at the blood puddled on her fingertips. She jumped to her feet with purpose. Charlene, Stella and René grabbed after her, but I'd already run into her with fists prepped up for the collision. We collided. I jabbed. Safire grabbed, scratched and peeled off small parts of my skin. I heard them all shout "Allow it!" at different paces and depths. But I was too pent up; too ready and willing to roll.

From nowhere Jason emerged between my sister and me tearing each other up with blows and scrapes. He threatened us with my dad if we didn't behave. I heard another voice that was familiar to me.

"Steph," he cried, "Steph, you little gangsta, you're nuts, man! You shouldn't be messing up your pretty little face!" He tugged at my waist some more and finally I let go of my sister.

As I was being pulled somewhere I saw Donavan's puzzled face enter the space with the drinks he had got for Charlene and her entourage. The next thing I knew I was in the brightly lit corridor, blinded by the light. Standing in front of the toilets, Tyrone held my arms rigidly before him, almost shaking me. "Steph!" he yelled, "you need to calm down, blood. Look at your face!"

I breathed passionately. I wanted to curse, but was too exasperated to put the obscenities in my head into any words. Shariece and Nina burst through the double doors and I got a glimpse of Safire explaining something to Charlene.

"You all right?" Shariece's voice was soft and concerned.

"No, I'm fucking not! Safire's gone clean into my room and drawn out my private t'ings...MY DIARY! And making dem-gal-deh read my t'ings. Not even you've read my diary, Shariece! So how's she gonna let people we've known a few shady months read my t'ings...MY DIARY, yanna!"

"Steph, come," Nina uttered sympathetically. "Let's go in the toilet so we can clean you up and calm you down."

"Why should I calm down?! She's taking the PISS!" I followed Nina into the toilet and Shariece followed behind me.

There were a few scratches on my face that oozed blood. Shariece wetted some tissues and handed me them, which I dabbed on my grazes.

"Have you got lip balm?" I enquired.

Shariece rummaged through her leather bumbag and handed me a tiny green tub of Vaseline. I greased my lips and the wounds, and then we left the ladies' room. Tyrone was waiting outside, one foot up on the wall, arms crossed.

"Are you coming back in?" Nina urged.

"Let her cool off with me for a bit," Tyrone suggested, "then I'll bring her back in."

Candice burst through the double doors and I heard one of my favourite tunes playing, 'Weak' by SWV, with all the bashment sound effects. "You all right, Steph? I'm sorry. I didn't mean to cause a madness," she offered.

"Don't worry about it; I'm glad you told me."

Shariece looked at Candice queerly, then back at Tyrone. "All right, Ty, we're going back in. Steph, make sure you don't start another madness if you see Safire, all right?"

I didn't respond because I didn't like lying to my friends.

"Keep your eye on her, Ty."

"I will, Shariece."

Candice touched my shoulder and Nina hugged me. "Don't think about it too much and you'll start to release this tension."

"I'll try," I mumbled and watched them go back in.

Tyrone put his arm round my neck teasingly as though prompting a headlock, but then turned it into a full cuddle. And though I punched him softly in the ribs, I actually liked it.

"Gangsta, d'wanna go for a walk outside?"

"OK." I followed his lead outside once we got our hands stamped at the entrance.

We walked across the grassy area in the warm air of the night. We walked circular motions for some time before heading onto Ghetto. We came to a halt at the bench near the shops by Spanish Steps. He spoke about his expulsion from school and commented on his dad giving up on him by sending him to Brixton to live back with his mum. I talked about living at Dada's and why I had to bust my sister's lip. He sympathised. He spoke about the ghetto, how challenging life was there, how the environment forced him to go down roads he didn't really want to pursue. I talked about my version of the ghetto, my house on a residential road amidst doctors, nurses and teachers. It was more the mindsets, and that was what I tried to express as best as I could. The ghetto mindsets that meant I couldn't have contentment at home with my family. There was always rage, violence and pain. This was ghetto love. And even if we didn't like it, none of us knew how to change it. He spoke about loose girls from our area and the type of ghetto girl that he wanted to make his wife, someone with morals and decency. I quivered at what my dad would do to me if he found out I had a boyfriend.

"I wouldn't even know what to do with a boyfriend.".

"Just be a good friend like you are and kiss him every once in a while."

"But most boys want more than dat, you know dat, Tyrone!"

"I wouldn't. Not while you're so young anyway."

I rolled my eyes. "When would you? When would you think was the right time for a girl to...you know...break her...you know...bus' her...:

"Virginity. You can say it, Steph, it's anna-not'in."

"OK, *virginity*, when do you fink is the right time to bruck a girl's virginity?"

He turned my face to his and looked at me earnestly. "When she's of age, and feels that she's ready to take it there. My brovva always says that he wished he waited longer until Macy was of age, so Ricardo would never have to explain to anyone that his mum was only fifteen when he was conceived. But at the time he wasn't thinking. And now 'not thinking' stares him in the face every day."

I hummed in agreement and smiled. Still holding my face he looked at me up and down and I wondered for a split second why he was 'screwing' me. "What?" I whined.

He held my face, thumbing one of the grazes lightly. His stare was freaking me out. I was about to say something again but then he kissed me. He kissed me on my lips! I was flabbergasted, and yet strangely I didn't move. I didn't punch him or anything. I felt warm, seen and understood. I didn't understand love, unconditional love. To receive and give love based on acceptance of who a person is, irrespective of how they behave. No, the love I was used to was conditional, and even under the conditions granted was barricaded under a pretentious, archaic, non-verbally expressive love. I was a girlish tomboy with violent tendencies, a firecracker, who was equally sensitive, vulnerable, morally grounded and deeply loyal. He seemed to see all of that in me and still liked me and wanted to love me. Not just for sex, which was most of these guys wanted. But not Tyrone. He wanted to show me a different love. I didn't know how to take or what to do that type of love. I just sat there with my mouth and eyes closed as though I'd been schooled on what to do. He pulled away for a breather and then kissed me again for longer. His arm came over my back to edge me forward. I turned away.

"Sorry, Steph. I didn't mean to—"

"I liked it," I reassured, and got up with my hand outstretched to him, "so let's just go back now and not talk about it, yeah?"

He took my hand and we walked back through Ghetto on to Moonshot in silence. I deliberated on what Macy might say about this, and then I tried not to think at all.

Shariece, Nina, René and Maria were outside with a cab when we arrived. Jason and Charlene waited by the doors to question me and say goodbye. Bashment tunes rang through the hallway. We boarded the cab. I stared at Tyrone, and he at me, unblinkingly as the car set off.

CHAPTER NINE

EXPOSED

2nd July 1994 – Dada's gates

Whassapenin, Di? I think I'm in love! And I don't know what to do. I haven't seen Tyrone and I haven't told anyone about the kiss. To be honest Di it shouldn't of happened and my sister would kill me if she knew. What should I do? To be honest I just need to forget about all dat for now because anytime I fink about it I start to feel all sick and my head hurts.

Anyway, guess what? I saw Mum when I went to collect all my diaries from her house the other day, a couple weeks after I busted Safire's lip. I was gonna say hello, but...the way she looked at me like...like...she proper hated me, like what Safire said was true. True to the look I bopped past her. She didn't say a word. I pretended I didn't care and I really tried not to feel anything but I couldn't stop that feeling in my throat. I just couldn't swallow and couldn't stop the tears from falling. I didn't let her see this though. She was long gone by the time I had to hold my mouth to keep the cry in.

Whatever...I've got Dada now, we're really cool. Plus I've got most of my money still, which helps... Don't. Seriously Di, don't. Please don't ask about Mary-Anne. That saga's closed now. We got away with the crime, but the money still makes it linger. She musta decided not to go to the bull dem. Smart move really. It just jars me she still remains in my thoughts. I hate the guilt, but it's not like I had a choice now, did I Di? That was our recruitment job—it had to be done.

Anyway, I'm leaving out soon to link up with Stella. I haven't really rolled with her, Charlene or Safire much since the school summer holidays started. Safire and I were just about on talking terms since our fight. There was an air of unease between us like when meeting new friends for the first time. This was always the case after a fracas, and would naturally sort itself after a period of time. I told Stella I would pass through Ghetto later when I was ready. She phoned in the morning when Dada was giving me a maths and English test—my man's on point. He keeps me on my toes, plus I enjoy the one to one time with my granddad. Nina's on the road already; she left for work at some sick hour this morning. She works at Tesco's in the summer holidays and on weekends now on some raggo tip. I rate her even doh I couldn't see myself doing that job. A bit embarrassing, don't you think? My cousin Melvin's been away for a little while and to be honest I shouldn't really talk about it. But it's you, Di, and I know you won't tell my secrets as long as no eediot picks you up and tries to meddle with you.

I realise how them tings must of bun you, someone else's

grubby hands all up on you. I feel the frustration from your pages. I'm gonna tell you anyway: Melvin's been birded for an armed bank robbery. He's looking ten years. I know, I can't believe it but on the other hand I can. The kind of crime that he does it's only a matter of time before the raddy took him in, plus it's not like he's a juvenile. Anyway, Di, I've gotta go now, but I promise never to leave you or the rest outside of my yard.

Boredom hammered through me. I grabbed a light jacket, left the premises and headed towards Ghetto where I hoped to find some kind of action. The 36 bus let me off at the top of the hill. I bopped down Clifton Rise with nonchalant flare. As I crossed over the road into Ghetto territory I saw the vague figures of Stella, Taniqua and Shannon, who slowly came into focus as I approached them. They were loafing on the wall in front of Spanish Steps.

"Stella! What's gwaaning?!" I yelled.

She turned to me. "Steph, what's 'appening? How comes you took so long? I thought you weren't coming." Stella sounded congested. She was burning a spliff and had just drawn in thick, heavily scented smoke from the spliff that was crookedly balanced between her left index and middle finger. The smell alone told me that the weed was high grade—a high-quality and extremely potent form of cannabis.

"I was rapping with my diary, innit." I turned to the other girls. "Taniqua…Shannon! You lot all right?"

"Yeah, I'm cool y'know, Steph. Just chilling, getting high," Shannon informed me in her cross-eyed way, looking more or less directly at Stella, whilst widely smiling at me.

I tried not to look too hard directly at her with eye contact being difficult.

"Yeah, that's about it," Taniqua added.

"One minute, Taniqua. Let me just get two blaze off of dis *sclit* before Stella dones it. Puff puff pass, Stella, puff puff pass," I withdrew the spliff from her mouth.

"You and dat bloody diary," Stella muttered.

"Nah, I'm just saying," Taniqua continued, "mi-deyah."

"So where's your cousin?" I asked.

"Who?" Shannon interjected.

"Candice, innit, who else?" I jumped up onto the wall next to Stella, trying not to dirty my new pink Versace jeans that Macy had given me recently.

"She's in doors," Taniqua answered.

"Why didn't you lot knock for her?"

"Coz we didn't want to, you fool!" Shannon gave me attitude she hadn't given to me before.

Subconsciously my brow dipped at the centre and I stared at the one eye that was facing me, the other one bobbing up and down to her left somewhere in Stella's direction. I felt the urge to laugh but the vexation held me stern.

Stella recognised the tension and proposed a diversion. "Allow all this long-t'ing, yous lot. Let's do somefing coz dis weed's starting to have me up and I'm getting bored." She swung her legs and banged her heels against the wall.

I allowed it by allowing the situation not to escalate. I sucked heavily on the spliff and then passed it onto Taniqua. Shannon turned to her for another taste of the high-grade spliff. I locked my jaw, rounded my lips and blew out circular hoops of smoke before jumping off the wall animatedly to shake off any antagonism that would have me sending a backhand in Shannon's direction. She passed me the spliff that was now near the butt. This gesture diminished my antagonism. I broke a smile and nodded in acceptance of her peace offering, blazed the final toke before outing it beneath my Nike Air Huarache sole.

"Let's go road or somefing," Shannon announced.

"Yeah, let's lash a tek." I suggested.

"I would do dat, coz I could do wiv some papers. But ain't you got money, Steph?"

"Yeah, a change." My tone was of someone who didn't want to be probed. "But I'll still lash a tek."

"I need money," Stella went on, "but I'm too buzzing now to be doing any kind of big running up and down right about now."

"Well let's go mopping then," Taniqua put to the table.

We agreed unanimously. We needed shopping bags. We advanced through Ghetto toward Stella's house. An unnatural vibe arose between us, Stella and me verses the two sisters, physically splitting us apart with ten metres in between.

"Stella?" I let out, "are they whispering?"

"I dunno."

"Why're they walking slowly on purpose?"

"I dunno, Steph; stop being paranoid. They're on a long t'ing anyway, coz I'm rushing to get in before my mum does in case she stops me from coming back out. You lot better wait on the corner in case my mum sees you."

"For reeaaal!"

"OK, wait 'ere, I'll be back in a sec."

Cautiously I waited outside a boarded-up pub on the corner of Stella's road. Taniqua and Shannon soon came into view.

"There you are. You took your time," I voiced, leaning back with a foot up against the wall.

"Why're you waiting out here?" Shannon asked.

"Her mum might be in, innit."

"Well, I need to go toilet, so I'm gonna knock the door." Shannon walked towards Stella's.

A thought came to mind that I quickly considered and reconsidered as Shannon veered in Stella's direction. My diary. I didn't want to go shoplifting with it like I did before. I had to think about the notion of being arrested. It was feasible as it happened to me before. Last time I got lucky with the police actually allowing me to keep my diary in my cell. I had incriminating info in this diary, so didn't want to take the chance this time. I called her back, gave her my diary to hand to Stella and soon she was off again. Taniqua and I watched Shannon run down the street, swerving dog mess and uprooted trees.

"Was the money you made the other day from that robbery wiv Mary-Anne?" Taniqua questioned.

"Yeah, why?"

"Nah, I was just wondering how much you made?"

"I already said: a change."

"But what's a change, doh?"

"A couple hundred; why, what's da deal?" My brain opened up to rampaging thoughts, and already I regretted the move I'd just made.

"Nah coz when you fink about it, since it was us lot that hooked you lot up wiv the girls to rob, half of dat shoulda been ours."

I looked at her considering her proposition, but concluded I didn't know them long enough to be so generous, it didn't seem reasonable. "Yeah but no one mentioned splitting the goods in the beginning... we all got jewellery. I know Safire and Stella got a change too from pawning their goods. Plus, if you really think about it, it was us-lot that took the risk and did the robbery—we can still get nabbed for that. But it's not'n' Taniqua, yous-lot are doing robberies all the time, you'll get your own papers soon."

Stella and Shannon's approaching put an end to that discussion. "'Ere you are, Steph," Stella said, handing me a large Selfridges plastic bag that she'd stuffed with other shopping bags.

I took it feeling a bad air about the whole situation and asked, "Did Shannon give you my diary to put up?"

"Yeah, I hid it in my bedroom."

*

We caught the 47 bus to Lewisham then boarded the 208. This journey divulged a significant difference in our taste of clothes and brands alike. Taniqua and Shannon opted for stores and brands that Stella and I didn't feel were up to the times. We agreed to separate once we reached the Glades shopping centre.

Two hours later we reunited inside the toilets of Bromley McDonalds. Shannon and Taniqua's eyes became fixated on the crisp Ravel shoe shop bags that Stella and I each had. I put the Ravel bags of the new shoes we just bought aside and attempted a diversion by eagerly showing off the items of clothing from Levi's, Benetton and Morgan that I'd stolen. Simultaneously, Stella removed Levi's jeans, a Benetton tank-top and mohair belly-top from her bag. Taniqua and Shannon gave a sudden smirk that puffed out their cheeks in a mass of flesh, and broadened their nostrils consecutively. Their similarities became overwhelmingly perceptible at that point.

"So what did you get?" Stella questioned when the silence grew too long.

Shannon turned to Taniqua who rotated her head 360 degrees. There was no one else in the toilets.

"Just show us, man, why're you on a long t'ing for?" Stella probed.

Shannon was the first to pull out a massive grey Fruit of the Loom jumper that I imagined being worn by Dad on a job wiring lights in the dusty attic of some council flat.

"Is that it?" I queried.

"Yeah."

"What about you, Taniqua?" Stella pushed.

She withdrew a pair of unflattering cut jeans that didn't appear to have a recognisable name. Silence. Stella and I looked at each other. Sympathy ran through our expression.

"So what did you buy, then?" Taniqua asked Stella.

"Just some Kickers."

"But I thought you never had any money," Shannon flung in.

"Steph bought dem for me."

"So let's see what you bought, Steph." Taniqua tugged on the Ravel bag.

Reluctantly I took out the box and revealed the black square-toe, two inch-heel court shoes. "There all right, innit?"

Taniqua glanced at the box and said, "You spent £40 on your pair of shoes and about £50 on Stella's, so that's nearly £100 you've spent."

"Why're you watching my money for?" I snapped, "I earned it. It was me dat did all dem tings to dat girl, not you-lot!"

"Yeah, but we're the ones that hooked you up, Steph, and don't forget dat." Shannon dashed in.

My temper had been nurtured to be quick to rise. Although I was a part of this girl gang, they weren't my genuine friends. And it was moments like this that reinforced that fact and made me question my alliance with this girl gang. I could feel my tongue swing back, ready to lash out words of heated momentum when we heard the external door swing open. In a hurried and panicked state, we all mustered up our belongings and threw them into our bags just before the inner door swung open to reveal a thirty-something woman with deep olive skin and tufts of mousey bristled curls, alongside a little seven or eight-year-old girl. The woman's head shot back and eyes widened upon seeing us.

"Look, have we got a problem here?!" I challenged Shannon.

"Dis is long. Let's blow," Stella finalised.

We left. I stared at Shannon fiercely in one of her eyes as we parted company. A bold move that informed her I was ready to go toe-to-toe with her. I wasn't threatened by her reputation or gangmates. I would fight her if the situation called for it.

*

Upon entering Stella's house, we tried to sneak past Aunty Ruth who was in the living room. She was watching *Coronation Street*, puffing on a cigarette.

"Stella!" she shouted as I was about to tiptoe up the stairs.

"Yes Mum."

"Who you deh wid?!"

"Steph."

I wondered why Stella had exposed me that way, but sighed in relief when Aunty Ruth called for us to come in a welcoming voice. Stella handed me her bags, which I left with one of mine at the foot of the stairs.

"Oh, you've been shopping, then?" Aunty Ruth asked.

"Yeah, Dada gave me money to buy shoes for school." It was the first thing that came to my head.

She said no more on the subject and instead questioned me how I was getting on at Dada's. I told her the truth, how much I enjoyed being there. She cursed about Mum, considered her choice to allow me to move out so that "idyat Derek can set back 'pon her". Derek hadn't moved back in as far as I knew, he was just staying there a lot these days. She enlightened me that I could come round when I wanted as long as I was behaving myself. She shoved a blue five-pound note into my hand. I smiled expressively, temporarily forgetting what I was there for as I sat down with Aunty Ruth to watch the rest of *Coronation Street*, £5 richer.

"Oh yeah, Stella, let me get my diary before I forget," I said some fifteen minutes later.

Stella got up off the worn black leather sofa, opposite the one Aunty Ruth and I were sitting on. "C'mon 'en; it's up in my room."

I followed her up passing Leroy in the bathtub packed with bubble bath. "You all right?" I said.

"Wha' gwaan, Steph?" he said pushing the bathroom door shut.

"Stella!"

"What?" she snapped.

"Get me a towel, about 'what', before I come out dere and slap you wiv my flannel!"

I put my bags down near Stella's rail of clothes, which was packed with designer clothes, and had a backdrop of posters of 90s R&B and hip-hop music icons across the wall.

"Whassup?" I asked her.

She turned back to me baffled. "I can't find your diary. I hid it in the bottom of my drawer and no one ain't gonna come in here and go through my knickers drawer."

"Stella!" Leroy shouted. "A towel, please!"

She grabbed a towel from the airing cupboard to the left of her room and took it next door.

When she came back having questioned Leroy, I asked her, "What are you saying?"

"I'm saying when Shannon handed me the diary, I put it in the bottom of my knickers drawer."

"Then what did you do?"

"I went up to my brother's room to get some plastic bags."

"Where was Shannon?"

"I thought she was in the bathroom."

"Could she've seen where you put it?"

"Nah, coz she weren't in my room. But she could've heard I guess? Listen. You can hear Leroy in the bath now, innit?"

I turned the TV down and heard Leroy splashing and sliding in the bath.

Silence.

"What are you thinking?" Stella queried.

"It's on." My voice was monotone, grave. "This is beef."

CHAPTER TEN

BEEF

16th July 1994 – Dada's gates

Di' what can I say? It's on. It's so fucking on! Dey shoulda never fucked wiv me – wha did dey fink would happen? Don't dey know I'm a bad gyal? Don't dey know I would smash dey're face in for less than dis. It's on, man. Dis is beef. And the fing about it, it has to be beef. How can I not move to dem after dey've come to my family's yard and stolen from me? If I let dem get away wiv dis, den what's next? Y'get me, Di'? What's next? I don't have a choice wiv dis, Di'. Dey need to be taught a lesson. Dey need to know what time it is! You can't come an' teef from me, a Johnson, and get away wiv it. Dat can't happen to a Johnson. You get your lip bus' and your face smashed in for dem t'ings. Ah lie, Di'? And if you didn't know, you're gonna get to know, coz it's beef now, Di', for sure—it's beef!

'Beef' was a term that was popularised through hip hop. It denoted something far greater than a verbal dispute. In the nineties, when rappers mentioned they were in beef with another rapper…you knew what time it was. They weren't going to have a dance-off or DJ spin-off like they did in the eighties—things had evolved since then.

We were only in our early teens. And though we were still pent up with our own tumult and peer pressure, we still hadn't peaked our violent potential. We didn't really know how far we could actually go, though death was never the objective. In later years when Biggie Smalls released his tune 'What's Beef?' on the *Life After Death* album, which skilfully outlined the catastrophic outcome of what he perceived beef to be (denoting the parents of beef opponent to be unsafe in the street, requiring guns to sleep and rolling no less than with thirty companions because there was likely to be shots fired), this set the benchmark for what was to be adhered to if seriously beefing. Thankfully, we were nowhere near there yet.

*

As pent up as I was, threatening all sorts to my diary, I spent two weeks in negotiation with Shannon through my cousin Leroy for the return of my diary. I knew she cared for him somewhat more than a friend, so thought he may influence her. For two weeks Leroy pushed and stressed this would avoid unnecessary beef, but both sisters were dead set on getting £200 from me for the exchange. It wasn't going to happen. Even Sean stepped in on the negotiation.

I offered him £50 for his part in it if he were to befriend them and retrieve my personal belongings somehow. I didn't think it would be too difficult since Sean knew both sisters very well and it transpired in Leroy's negotiation with her that Shannon favoured Sean more over Leroy. He accepted, but I still wasn't sure if this were the most effective route to take. I had a conversation with Shariece about it, about how best to go about things. Her suggestion was for us to all run up in their house, find the diary and 'deal' with the two of them. I thought about that. I thought about that long and hard, and even asked Dada for his input on how to approach warfare. He was a war veteran.

"Dada, if the decision was yours, would you move in on your enemy's territory even if you were ten men-strong?" I asked.

"Only if yuh know what you ah face and you ah attack heavily from di top."

"What d'you mean, Dada? How can you attack from the top?"

"Pass dat, mek I show yuh." He reached for the notepad I was scribbling thoughts on.

I tore pages from the back and handed them to him. He drew a steep hill with men at the top and men at the bottom. "Now, if dem ah goh war," he pointed to the stick men on the page, "who's more likely to win?"

"Easy, the men up top."

"Why?"

"Because dey're running down on dem-man-deh, and would've picked up speed to greater the blow, innit? Plus, them man-deh coming up from the bottom are likely to be more tired because dat hill you've drawn is a madness!"

"Exactly! Di man up top has di advantage! A warrior going in to war will not attack solely from di bottom so di enemy will have di advantage of di natural force on his side when running down to batter di upcoming warrior who has the force against him. Why yuh ask?"

"Nothing. Just wondering."

It all made sense. I mentally pieced together the layout of Shannon and Taniqua's house. They were likely to come from their bedroom upstairs. Their family was big. It would be hard to know who was in the house and what we'd be up against. Plus they had the upstairs advantage. I cogitated what I would have done then if some crazy fool came to war with me in my house; what tools I would use to defend my territory.

"Stephanie, what yuh t'inking 'bout?"

The house phone rang and paused my tongue.

Dada picked the phone up. "'Ello? ... Yes, 'oo's speaking, please? ... Wollan one minute." He looked at me across the table. "Stephanie, yuh give mi number to a bwoy call Sean?"

"Yeah, that's my bredren, Dada."

"Tell him, him not to call fi mi yard after ten o'clock at night!"

Dada passed me the white cordless phone. "Hello, Sean? Did you hear that? Whassup?" I got up and walked into the living room.

Sean informed me he had my diary and I was to meet him at Leroy's house first thing in the morning.

*

At 10:00 I released my index finger from Aunty Ruth's doorbell and patiently waited. A tabby cat poked its head through the slim black rails that divided the strip of terraced houses. I jumped and frantically shooed for it to leave, but the cat remained.

Leroy opened the door whilst on the phone to see me compressed into the corner of the doorway with eyes fixed on the cat. He looked at the cat and then back at me and laughed, directing me into the front room where Sean was sitting with a self-satisfied grimace. As I closed the front-room door I heard Leroy say, "Come Si-Si," and the furry animal ran past the glass door.

My diary was lying on the coffee table, in his possession, as he had said. A wide beam shot across my face. I counted £50 and handed it to him. "Thanks," I said taking back my personal property.

"Just letting you know," he added, "man had to all kiss dat girl to find out where your t'ings were."

I bared my teeth even more so and left it as that. Cautiously I visited the kitchen, where Stella was making breakfast. There was no sign of the cat. I took out a plate from the draining rack and placed it next to hers on top of the washing machine.

"What you putting the plate there for?" she asked. Her face still looked under the influence of morning puffiness. "Here you are, make your own." She handed me a loaf of bread from a surface that was littered with plates, breadcrumbs and dried spillages, and opened the fridge to reach for a tray of eggs. She then left the kitchen with her own egg sandwich.

I made mine and went up to Leroy's bedroom. He and Sean were playing Playstation, Ridge Racer. "I'm next," I announced, parking one of the kitchen chairs next to his bed.

"Did anyone say you could even come in here?" Leroy mouthed, sitting cross-legged and bare-chested with tracksuit bottoms on. I blanked him and rolled my eyes. "Only joking," he added.

I raced Leroy for a few rounds. I was winning 3-2 until Sean stepped into the driver's seat. That's when the tables dramatically turned. Losing every round became boring. Stella entered the room, dressed and ready to hit the road. "I'm going to meet Charlene and Safire in Brockley, you coming?"

"Yeah, man." I was done with getting my arse kicked on the racetracks.

I took up my diary and dropped it into the inside pocket of the black denim blazer I'd stolen from Next on our most recent shoplifting mission. It gave me a sleek and formal appeal. I fixed it up flush so that it lay flat next to the screwdriver in my pocket. I got it from Dada's toolbox and had kept it in my possession since there were talks of beef. I didn't necessarily intend to use it. I just thought it was always better to be prepared than not. We made our way through the park that led onto Ghetto.

I was wearing those new court shoes from Ravel so was trying to walk like a lady and ease the bop in my step that I had purposely developed over the few of years. Stella was generally very neutral in her approach to this. She walked like most thirteen-year-olds would… normally. That day she wore red Kickers that balanced her well-fitting Levi's jeans and a red French Connection T-shirt with a blue ribbed cardigan.

"So what's happening at Charlene's?" I asked.

"Not'in."

"So what're we going there for?"

Stella sighed.

"What?"

"Why d'you always have to ask questions?"

What kind of a question is that, I thought but responded, "So I know what I'm doing, innit!"

"But does it matter?"

"Why wouldn't it matter?"

"Because it's not like you got anyfing else to do."

"How would you know what I gotta do?"

"So if you've got fings to do what're you coming for?"

As we entered Ghetto and I was about to fill the silence with an answer to her question, Stella uttered slowly, "Oh my gosh, there's Shannon."

I quickly caught the distasteful words that were about to leap from my tongue and looked ahead in disbelief to see the vague silhouette of Shannon bopping towards us. Butterflies materialised in my stomach and I quickly recognised the extent of my antagonism.

"What're you gonna do?" I heard Stella say, but I didn't respond.

I clocked Shannon clocking me clocking her. She continued

towards us, livening her stride and smiling to dismiss her fear. I stopped. A train ran over the bridge a few yards behind us. Shannon was roughly four yards perpendicular to me. I handed Stella my diary and started toward her. My heart rate accelerated and embraced the chaotic butterflies. This was the adrenalin rush I enjoyed.

'No long talking, just knock it; no long talking, just knock it; no long talking, just knock it,' I told myself repeatedly.

"What?" she belted with raised shoulders and open arms that were effectively offering me out to fight.

Once we were within striking distance, my fist landed a blow to her temple, sending devastating waves of pain into her brain. She held onto that area with her left hand self-effacingly, then sent a free-spirited blow with her right hand that ended up wrapped around my neck. With my forehead I bucked her in the lip, but she still managed to get me into a headlock. It became difficult to breathe. I tore at her arm wrapped around my neck, scratching, pinching and digging at the flesh, fighting for a breath of fresh air.

"Get off her neck!" Stella bellowed and made our way.

"So you can't even fight me one on one?" Shannon cajoled.

"Don't...join...in, Stella," I managed to squeeze out of my mouth.

I jabbed a hefty elbow into her ribs three times. She buckled over. I booted her in the ribs too. With the free range to breathe, I took my time to remove one of my shoes. The heel collided with the centre of her forehead. Instantly a lump arose on her head to parade itself. She kicked out at me. I screamed for a long period holding onto my shins whilst hopping on one leg with my knee brought up to my chest to suppress the pain. Stella mouthed, "Are you all right?" and I nodded dishonestly trying to shake off the discomfort.

Shannon got to her feet. I reached into my inside pocket. The butterflies fluttered wildly in my stomach. The battle of wills commenced in my head. My ready hand had already gripped the ridged handle of the screwdriver. I veered towards her. She knew my intentions were bad from the look in my eyes, but was too caught up in the idea of us fighting to comprehend the full potential of my intentions. Otherwise she would have run by now.

I approached her, calm and focused. Thinking through the potential outcome of my intentions, but neither having the desire nor will power to stop myself. As though I'd been resigned to this behaviour by my parents from birth, environment and the expectations of my peers, my reputation. My hand tightly gripped my weapon, still inside my pocket. Upon contact she swung a punch, and though it clipped my chin, clinking my teeth together, I hardly felt its effects. I was pumped up on adrenalin. The screwdriver came into view and hastily made its way into the flesh of her left thigh until my arm began to ache. I stepped back. Both time and pain began to register. Shannon was in shock. I felt numb. Unsure if I had done something good or bad, my memories of our former friendship were absent and without sentiment. I was standing there, unbalanced, with arms by my side, staring at Shannon and my missing shoe behind her. Her blood started to clear from the metal edge of the screwdriver still pressed against my palm.

"Rah! Steph, you all right?" Stella asked.

Shannon turned to her leg. The pierced flesh eased out blood and a clear gooey liquid. She turned back to me. I could see the pain registering on her face. I could see the event, what had just happened, lodging in her mind and advising her of what this now meant. I had taken our level of beef up a notch and now anything could go. Finally, she turned back to her wounded limb. She tried to stem the blood that was running down into her Kangaroos. Then she started to back up, tears filling her eyes. The backward steps turned into full hops as she limped away shaking her head hysterically and screaming, "WATCH!!"

Stella grabbed hold of my arm holding the weapon and I looked at her for the first time since I'd bored a hole into Shannon's leg. "Come, Steph, let's get out of here before someone comes."

Stella handed me my diary and I snapped out of my shell shock, slipping my foot into my shoe that lay on its side by the wall stained with piss and dirt and graffiti. We breezed back through the park where Stella filled me in on her spectator experience. I laughed, but still hadn't deciphered whether what I had done was good or bad. One part of me felt good for teaching her a lesson—she should have known what time it was—and the other part of me worried that I had opened up a can of worms. But my attitude then was always *whatever*, which unfortunately made the odds for the repercussions far greater.

Back at Stella's, I washed the blood off the screwdriver, buried it in the garden and then made a hot cup of Horlicks. When I arrived upstairs Stella was informing Leroy and Sean of the dilemma. Sean called me a "gangsta". Leroy was not too pleased.

"How can you be boring up people when they know where you live and they live around the corner?! It's not like they're gonna be coming back to *your* house, is it? It's my yard they're gonna be licking down." He turned to Stella. "And you're laughing like it's not you that's gonna be getting butted when they can't find Steph."

"Whatever, Leroy," Stella voiced, "I'll just fight dem off, innit. You fink I business if they wanna beef wiv me?" She turned to me. "What's 'at?"

"Horlicks."

"Let's have a sip."

I passed Stella the mug and advanced to the bathroom where I cleaned the minor scratches on my face and neck with wet tissues and a bit of Dettol. I pulled my hair loose and brushed it back neatly into a ponytail with a brush I took from a mug on the bathroom windowsill.

Some of the blonde ends of hair broke off in my hands. I plaited the loose hair, tucking the ends into the root of the plait.

The doorbell rang, rattling my nerves. I craned my neck round the bathroom door to see Leroy running down the stairs. He opened the front door and I heard Shannon and two other big women trying to burst in. I ran up the three steps to inform Stella of the situation. Sean ran downstairs to help hold back these angry women. I stepped back down the three steps and sat at the top of the main stairs above the front door. I clapped eyes on Shannon's mum. Naturally, she was fuming.

"Which one of you focking idiots come stab me pickney?!" she blasted, froth gathering in the corners of what looked like a sour mouth.

I peered down at her and pointed to myself. "I did." My tone was unapologetic.

She cursed some more, hitting out hard on the patois but I didn't really hear her.

Shannon tried to fight Leroy off but she couldn't get past. The old woman, Shannon's grandmother, was trying to have words with Stella behind me, informing her she was to know better since they were supposed to be neighbours and friends.

"Good neighbours don't t'ief from one another, let alone friends!" I belted out.

"Innit! What's she coming in my house and t'iefing people's t'ings for?"

Misinformed, the old woman, dressed middle-aged in denim jeans and a Jamaican T-shirt, rotated to Shannon with her brow dipped while fixing her stylish wig that was cocked front ways to the side. "Shannon, yuh did t'ief people t'ings from dem yard?"

Shannon wouldn't let go of the bad words, she cursed tirelessly.

Her running mouth was gagging to be filled with my fist. But with the old lady there I remained seated and silent. Shannon had another go at trying to reach me at the top of the stairs, but Leroy had a firm grip of her. The sweat under her armpits was becoming visible through the fabric of her grey sweatshirt. I smiled patronisingly.

"You BITCH!! It's ON!!" Shannon screeched. She screamed some other stuff that questioned how bad I was and put it to me that me and my people were to meet her and her people in Ghetto at six where we could war it out once and for all.

"It's on," I whispered back.

At that point Shannon kicked her leg out, screamed louder than before, wriggled and fought frantically to get to me, her self-applied bandage unravelling in the process. Sean assisted Leroy in taming her flailing arms. Even her mother pressed for her to calm down. Her grandmother had already stepped back outside to avoid getting kicked over by her granddaughter. Shannon was buck-wild. I had certainly pushed a button that I was going to have to contend with later! It was only when Sean accidentally touched her breast in the restraint and Shannon sent a packing fist his way, drawing blood from his upper lip, that the boys upped their manpower and forced the mad girl outside. Finally the door closed on them.

"My girl's nuts!" Stella's face was startled.

"Hmmm."

Leroy and Sean looked up at us wearily with their backs against the door.

"See!" Leroy blasted. "I fucking told you! Look what you've brought to my door! Wait till Mum comes in from work, Stella."

"Tell Mum den, you informer."

Leroy went for Stella but she ran into her room and locked the door. He then made for me. "Leroy, 'llow it, man," Sean said, but he still felt the need to push me. I sensed his frustration so didn't respond, just firmed the hefty push. They both headed to Leroy's room. I ran downstairs for the house-phone, which I carried up with its extension lead into Stella's room. We gathered a variety of tools and made what seemed like the most important calls of our lives.

We left the house with confidence knowing that Stella's rucksack was brimming with an olio of tools gathered over time from her brother, from various bus journeys (bus emergency tools were really quite useful weapons) and from our design and technology room at school. I also had a few things tucked into the waistband of my trousers as well. We journeyed through Ghetto raggo, as we would say. This meant without a care in the world for the current circumstance. Not much was said.

In less than ten minutes we were at the top of the hill of Clifton Rise where we met Safire and Charlene. They were stirred up by what had happened. The fact that I went as far as to draw for blood using a weapon, and placing Shannon in her current mad state, was seen as a good thing. I had brought our level of beefing to another stage, broken through another barrier of fearlessness and readiness for war. And, as stripe-relishing gang members, this was something to be held in high regard.

We all practised our upper-cut combinations on the 36 bus to Lewisham where we met Shariece and René. They too were ready to rumble, rummaging through Stella's bag and choosing tools. Lastly, we went on to Brockley Train Station and met Maria. Once again I described the saga, slightly less enthusiastically than the first time. Maria didn't share the same excitement, but she took her tool from the sack that Stella offered. And that was that. It was on.

*

At 18:00 we were in Ghetto and waiting. One by one and two by two, the Ghetto Boys started to accumulate. Dwayne, Donavan, Sean, Tyrone, my cousin Jermaine and a few others. Messages were sent out by a couple of the Ghetto Boys that we were there ready for war. Nevertheless, we waited. Charlene pointed out Tyrone and Jason's dad, Joseph, to me who was standing behind the back of Spanish Steps with a man who looked like your stereotypical yardie, as did Joseph himself. People called him Killer Man Joe.

I hadn't pictured Tyrone's and Jason's dad looking the way he did. I hadn't imagined him in a white string vest pulled taut by his protruding, solid stomach, with a frayed denim shirt hanging unbuttoned over the vest. His jeans were baggy, bleached and slashed horizontally across the thighs so there were strips of clustered white thread. He wore a bandanna over his hair, which was either cornrowed or braided—whatever the case, small, one-inch plaits hung from the nape of his neck. The colours red, gold, green and black—the Rastafarian colours that symbolise the blood that was shed (red), the vegetation of the motherland, Africa (green), the wealth that was stolen (gold) and the beauty of the people (black)—called for my attention from his feet. He was wearing the alternative, and much cheaper, version to the suede, lace-up shoes that Bally brought out in the late eighties. These were called raggas. Each plane of the shoe was one of the Rastafarian colours, and the shoelaces were black. All in all, I was surprised by his look.

Charlene waved at him and he came over. She introduced Safire and me and then Stella. He asked us about Macy and Ricardo, and if we'd seen Jason. Tyrone watched. I wondered why he hadn't come over to say something or at least acknowledge his father. Joseph asked us what we were all doing there and Charlene told him we were going to war, just blatant like that. He livened up with a little skank, rubbed his hands together and waved shoulders in a way that reminded me of Jason. He even encouraged us to do a good job before stepping back behind the pub where his brethren was pulling perverted faces at us.

Charlene told me he was a proper yardie, which I naturally assumed to be the drug-dealing gangster, and that's exactly what he was—a coke-smuggling crack dealer, however he was from Ghana and not Jamaica. Tyrone looked sombre across the square…

At 19:00, upon a falling sun, a nippy wind chilled the steel tucked into my waistband. I took out the chopper, penknife and chisel and placed them in Stella's rucksack except for the penknife, which I put in my inside pocket.

"Tyrone!" I called out, waving him over whilst the others chatted amongst themselves.

He approached me seeming burdened. "What's up?" he asked nonchalantly.

"I didn't know *he* was Killer Man Joe." I didn't know what else to say. I hadn't spoken to him since we kissed and wanted to make it seem as though everything was normal between us.

"Well, you know now. Is that it?"

"No it's not." I frowned. "Why're you being like that with me for?"

"Because I don't want you to be fighting dem girls like dis."

"What do you care? I haven't even heard from you these last few weeks. So what is it? Are you now siding wiv dem, Tyrone?"

"Innit!" Safire dropped in, stumbling into the conversation. "*Are you siding wiv dem, Tyrone?*" she sung.

He sighed and pulled me aside. "Look, you already know how I feel about you, Steph –" I looked around me childishly to make sure my sisters didn't just hear that—"but you warring like dis is some joke t'ing. What if she's looking to bore you up?"

"Den she's to do it. Furvermore, can you go and knock on their door and tell dem they've got five minutes to back their talk otherwise we'll leave it as it is, which proves dey're the jokers I thought they were."

"Get some ovver eediot to run around for you!"

"Well go home den, Tyrone, if you're gonna be like dat." I bopped away from him and him me. I didn't want to leave it like that, leave us like that. I wanted to tell him how much I love him and attempt to address our situation, but I had my war head on. I couldn't deal with his or mines personal sentiment for one another right then. Shariece came over to me as I called out to Jermaine.

"You all right?" she asked.

I nodded as Jermaine approached. I repeated what I had requested of Tyrone. He called for Sean and they headed in the direction of Candice's house where they were all thought to be.

Jermaine and Sean came back moments later. The message was delivered. We waited.

Fifteen minutes then passed with no sign of anyone, so we decided to leave. We bopped away triumphantly from Ghetto and headed to Stella's home. Suddenly, as though they wanted to wake the dead, furious chants of: "What, what, who wants beef?!" pierced through the night. I snapped a look at the agitated and stunned faces surrounding me before peering into the darkness to make out a herd of boys, girls, men and women running ferociously towards us like bulls to red rags. I was suddenly gripped by trepidation.

Things moved in slow motion, but came to pass rapidly, and before I knew it, a bottle had been snatched out of the hands of René by a grown man who looked liked he must be Shannon and Taniqua's father. Taniqua took that opportunity to slip a right hook into the side of René's face. Maria jumped in on that, then Shariece, then Shannon's mum, then Charlene, then Candice's mum, and lastly Safire.

I was standing there, almost frozen, watching this multi-bodied fight when I heard Stella's voice shout, "Steph! Look out!"

I turned to see Shannon's fist heading for my nose, but I managed to duck in time and when I arose, I arose with a mighty dragon punch (as I'd admired in the film *Street Fighter!*) that connected with her chin from beneath, lifting her off the floor. A little boy with an afro, of about nine or ten, attacked me throwing punches and kicks to my back and shouting for me to leave his cousin. I backhanded him to the floor to join his cousin.

I heard Candice's mum mutter something about her pickney and she came for me with a shoe, licked it in my head several times. I threw a combo her way, blooding her nose, as Shannon got me into a headlock from behind. The mum was coming back for my exposed face, but Stella got to her before she got to me and they rolled across the concrete. Shannon unleashed a tornado of blows into my head. I became dizzy and started to lose consciousness. I did try to throw bent punches aimed for her head, but the headlock made this impossible.

The little boy came for me again with little punches to my stomach. I kicked him somewhere and found strength to twist my body round to face downwards in the head grip. Silly move. She kneed me in the face, my lip catching my teeth. I spat out blood, now bursting with rage and searching desperately inside myself for the strength to unleash it. Through a blurry gaze I saw her well-bandaged leg and I knew what to do. I grabbed hold of her bandaged leg, put all my weight and strength on to it, and smashed weighty, knuckle-exposed blows into the bandaged wound. Blood erupted beneath the fabric dressing and seeped through its air holes. She wailed like a hunted beast falling from the blow of a spear, but I couldn't and wouldn't stop. My clenched fist continued to inflict pain and damage onto her injury. A powerful hand grabbed hold of my hair and slammed my head against the side of a parked car. I moaned in pain, brought my hands up to my head to steady the rotating birds that had blurred my vision.

"Fox!" Killer Man Joe cried. "'Llow di yout' dem; ah Richie pickney dat!" he tried restraining Fox who was Shannon's and Taniqua's father.

I was now sitting on the concrete ground rocking back and forth trying to protect my head from Fox with my arms. The birds were pounding through my skull. Joseph continued to calm and physically restrain Fox who was reaching after me. With squinted eyes and a curled, angled upper lip Shannon marched my way. I leaned up against a car and started to panic. I couldn't see any free bodies to come to my rescue. Everyone was so heavily involved in their own one to one fight, and my vision was diminishing, my head swaying from side to side.

"Safire!" I mustered. She had just thrown a collection of blows onto the head of a woman who in turn was attacking Charlene.

Safire turned to me but at that moment Candice's mum's fist smashed against her jaw, which Safire then retaliated by imbedding her nails into the woman's face, drawing flesh and blood. Meanwhile, Candice was in tears, roaring pleas of, "Stop! Please, you lot, STOP FIGHTING!"

Blood spattered from my nose as I realised Shannon had made contact with me and was punching my lights out. Suddenly however she went flying off somehow with an arched back and when I turned my bloody face I saw Shariece's foot outstretched, having kicked my assailant. She went for her again stamping out the air from Shannon's lungs.

I shuffled back against the car, then sat on the kerb to steady the birds and dizziness. As Taniqua went for Shariece who in turn was attacked by René and Maria, Fox broke free from Joseph, grabbed Shariece and threw her over a parked car. That move vexed me. I fought to shake off my dizziness, found a big rock and served it into

Fox's head, as I would serve a ball into a wicket, and ran back behind the car at a crouch to help Shariece up, and hide.

"You all right?" I asked leaning her up against the car.

"My back's hurting, man, and my hands are a little grazed."

I looked up, peeping over the car to see Joseph trying to help Fox by keeping a white flannel to the back of his head which was surging blood. Yes! I thought and scanned the car park to see the Ghetto Boys gathering again; Stella scuffing Taniqua and Shannon's mum; Charlene rocking another big woman who I didn't know; Safire going toe-to-toe with Candice's mum, her brother and a shoe; René going all out with Taniqua; Maria getting her hair pulled out by Shannon, and then Jermaine running over to where we were.

"Is she all right, Steph?" He looked down at Shariece.

I looked up. "Yeah, I think—"

"Rah! Look at your face! Your nose is all bleeding!"

"I know." I wiped the blood with my sleeve and pinpointed Shannon. "Where's Tyrone?"

"He went home after you lot..."

I got up, leaving Jermaine mid-sentence, ran in Shannon's direction with rage stampeding through my limbs bringing my adrenalin rush to its peak. I pounced on her back, the wind lifting me like a wave. I was tempted to bite her but didn't; instead I landed my fist about her face like chickenpox. She let go of Maria's long curly hair. Fox broke from Killer Man Joe's grasp and made for me as I tightened the grip on Shannon's neck, trying to cut off her air supply, squeezing and squeezing…

Blue lights flashed from out of nowhere and everyone scattered in various directions before the police pulled into the car park. I jumped off Shannon and swiftly followed Jermaine, Shariece, Stella and Charlene, dashing my penknife into a bush as I sprinted.

"Gotcha!" The tail of my jacket was gripped by the hands of an officer. "You're nicked!"

I was arrested for Grievous Bodily Harm, using an offensive weapon and causing an affray. Worn out and feeling the come down of my adrenalin, my body, limbs and head started to ache.

I was secretly glad the fight had come to an end.

Handcuffed, I was carefully guided into a police van. I felt neither victorious nor defeated when seated upright mulling over the previous events. A male officer sat next to me. He shook his head as he took in the true state of me. Stella, Charlene, Shannon and Taniqua soon joined me in the police van. We looked at one another with a silent respect for our fighting efforts. Our friendship was concluded, we were no longer Ghetto Girls.

As we drove en route to Deptford Police Station, I noticed Fox face down in the gravel with his hands on his head and a police officer hovered over him with a baton in hand prepared for the strike. Candice, her mum, little cousin and aunty were all standing in an animated confrontation with a female and male officer. It wasn't clear if they were being arrested or not. I didn't see any of the Ghetto Boys, Safire, Maria, Shariece or Renè, and hoped that they had got away.

*

The next day, although my right eye felt heavy and burdened, I attempted to crack it open and take in some of the morning light. Jarred at my failed attempt, I felt the fluid around my eye and accepted that I probably looked like Rocky after the fight he had with Dolph Lundgren in *Rocky IV.*

I stood up off the bench and struggled to lick my bottom lip that seemed to have tripled in size. I frightened the officer who pulled the flap back to see my messed-up face—right there, looking at him like it was no big deal, and like I was unaware anything was wrong with me. He slammed the flap back, flabbergasted, and took a moment or two to open my cell door.

"Stephanie Johnson."

I looked up surprised he knew my name. My memory was a haze of blows to the head and renascent birds, but it was very likely that I gave fake personal details. It was just what I did in these situations.

"We've got your grandfather and cousin here waiting to take you home." He continued. "And don't worry, since none of you will press charges, we've decided to ignore the fact that you gave false personal information, which is an offence I hasten to add, and let you off with a caution. The rest have already been taken home."

I smiled at the officer somehow.

He seemed shaken and turned away. Again, I pictured Rocky after that militant fight and understood his repulsion.

Dada nearly dropped down flat on his face when I emerged through a door into the waiting area. Nina's eyes widened but she still just embraced me.

"What kin' of war yuh been in fi yuh face fi look like it get blow up by grenade?!"

He loved to exaggerate.

"Sorry, Dada," I said wearily, "but can you just take me home, please?"

CHAPTER ELEVEN

AREA CHANGE

15th September 1995 – My Yard

Oh my gosh, Di, I've so much to tell you. Mum finally kicked Derek to the kerb and now I'm living at home again. She finally realised he weren't ever going to change. Plus she got all maternal when she saw me after that beef us lot had last year. I looked messed up for several days after that beef. Every time I looked at my swollen right eye, felt the cut beneath my top lip, saw the bruising above my cheekbone, felt mad aches in my neck and body the moment I moved, I appreciated my true bredrens and family. We all defended it till the end. And we woulda done so till our dying breath. Dat's true, real friendship...real love. Y'get me Di?

Anyway, right about now I'm getting ready to leave my yard to go to Peckham. Stella, my sisters and I have been parring with dem man-deh since we blew up that ghetto gal t'ing. Charlene had to bring me up there to introduce me to them coz Safire was going on like she didn't want me to meet Typo and dem man-deh, saying that I'm too young to be parring with dem man like she ain't young too. My sisters and Ella already met dem over a year ago when my cousin Jermaine and me lashed dat woman's tek. But now I just wanna make sure I meet them, see what they see, and have the option to taste the hype if I choose to. I've chosen to do this today. I'm bunking the rest of the day off of school to meet them. They've asked me to come in on a robbery— just a little Post Office or somefing. I know what you're thinking, Di but dis is different. It's not like when I robbed Mary-Anne. This ain't someone's personal possessions, plus no-one should get hurt.

It should be an easy job...anyway, bottom line is I need to get paid.

The past year held me hostage to a barrage of feelings and uncertainties. I missed Tyrone deeply. But I pushed the thoughts, the moistness that would populate between my legs informing me of my puberty and the hormonal changes I was undergoing, right back inside me. My relationship with Mum was up and down. Sometimes we were good, more often we were not. And when I tested her authority, gave her reason to believe that we were stealing or acquiring material things outside of the law, she cascaded a wave of beatings in her usual style. Until she tired from throwing the blows. Sometimes I left, ran away to Dada's or Macy's for a few days, but I always returned and our cycle would continue.

I changed out of my uniform feeling more confident now that I'd had a word with my diary. I slid into a pair of black jeans, a black hooded jumper and my black Huaraches. I grabbed a black DKNY cap Macy had given me, adjusted it nicely on my head and pressed stop on the cassette player that was playing Method Man & Mary J's 'I'll Be

There for You/You're All I Need'. Downstairs I flung on Safire's black silk bomber jacket, found a pair of gloves in the pockets, and headed through the front door.

At 14:00 I had disembarked from a 36 bus and was strolling up a garbage-littered road that cried poverty. It was the frontline of Peckham high street, populated mainly by the black and Asian ethnic minority groups. I eased to a stop outside Crackerjack's, an all in one broken down off-licence and grocery shop. The shop's exterior, the graffitied shutters and market hustle and bustle, was very much the appeal of the road and the Rye Lane that broke off from it. I hung out beneath the shelter of a derelict bus stop, littered, dirty, and graffitied like everywhere else. I waited. There were many black-owned businesses as there were Asian.

Soon I noticed Killer Man Joe who I hadn't seen since that day we fought the Ghetto Girls. I was reminded about Tyrone upon clasping eyes on him. Both Jason and Tyrone favoured their father. He was standing outside a Caribbean takeaway called Aunties. He looked suspicious, and by his very presence outside of Aunties, I knew he was selling drugs. I knew he was 'shotting' like they do in that film *Shottas* with Kymani Marley. And despite 'Yardie' being that stereotype assigned to both Jamaicans and British Jamaicans in the late eighties and nineties who adopted the 'bashy' dress from the bashment dance scene and were associated with drugs and crime, Killer Man Joe had the label. Originally the word yardie was in reference to any Jamaican because yard was how they referenced their home. However, negative connotations of the word would align the term with people like Killer Joe despite him being Ghanaian.

Switch was the first one of the Peckham Boys I saw. He was eighteen, slim built, almond skinned and certainly someone I'd place on the 'crisp list'. I was only thirteen but quite happily and inaudibly revelled in his beauty. He had that whole afro thing going on, which then wasn't a fashion statement, more of a demonstration of individual flare. He skipped energetically across the road and was followed by his brother, Darren. They looked nothing alike. Darren was twenty-one and of a darker tone, but his features—both facially and bodily—were much bigger, or better yet, broader. Plus he never smiled and hardly talked. He was a serious guy that you'd rather not bump into at night in a dark alley on your own. Switch had one of those model faces with very commercial features, which he often bragged about. His real name was Damien, but because he was originally from East London, then moved to North London, then West London and now lived in South London. His friends thought it appropriate to call him Switch.

"Wha' gwaan, babe?" Switch attempted to hug me but I put my fist out to nudge him. I wanted to make sure I was seen as one of the boys, and not eye-candy for the day's event. I was young, but certainly aware of the advances guys like him would happily make to adolescents like myself. He stopped in his tracks, changed course and nudged me. "Sorry, Steph, I keep forgetting you're wanna be one of da mans-dem."

Darren nodded his head at me, and I nodded back before continuing conversations with Switch. He always wanted to know something about my sisters, cousins, Nicola or Lakiesha's whereabouts. Or when I was planning to bring some of my decent school friends up here so they could all attempt to have their wicked ways with them? These guys were forward. And a lot of the girls from their way, who were supposed to be our equivalent in the girl gang sector, were extreme versions of Nicola and Lakiesha. Many of them had countless sexual partners, some were open prostitutes or strippers and others were regular crack cocaine users or all of the above. And all of them were between the ages of thirteen and nineteen. But my school friends weren't those types of girls. Violence was their only thing, and only when it was called for.

Soon enough I clapped eyes on Typo and Manic, the final two we were waiting for. We made our way in their direction. Typo had quite a stocky build. His head was shaven at the back and sides. On top he wore rusty plaits that were nearing dreadlocks, but he claimed no Rastafarian intention and boasted strictly of his Nigerian roots. Manic had my complexion, tall bodied and slightly manic. He would have crazy obsessions that would last the day, like pinching your nose, slapping your bum animatedly, ringing tunes on your bottom lip, running and leaping wildly in an attempt to touch the sky, unexpected headlocks—that sort of thing. That day his thing was a balletic 360 degree rotation on one leg, a pirouette, and that was what he did when I went to greet him with a nudge.

We walked up the frontline further passing the Killer Man Joe outside of Aunties, who'd just neatly exchanged a package for money with a shabby-looking female who was clearly a crackhead. He nodded at me miming "Johnson!" and I nodded back to validate my name, not mentioning to the guys I was with that he was the grandfather of my nephew Ricardo. As we veered closer toward our target, Typo went over a few points.

"...and Stephanie, you're gonna wait outside by da door—be our eyes for feds and dem t'ings. You man already know dat when I say 'collect' dat's when man's ready to collect da papers. So really and truly it's you, Steph, who needs to be on point for dis. Make sure the door's open for us to make a quick exit, y'get me?" I got him, so nodded."All right, so we all meet up in Red Brick, yeah?"

Manic, Switch, Darren and I sounded our own interpretations of 'yeah', and Manic did a pirouette as Typo craned his head round the wall of the petrol station. I pulled down my cap, pulled up my hood, drawing the strings tight, and slipped on my gloves.

"Come, you lot, let's go," ordered Typo, and Darren looked at him strangely.

Four black-clad figures appeared from the side of the wall. No doubt we looked shifty with our shoulders held high and dipped eyes that apprehensively peered left and right. Following behind, I watched them enter the petrol station calmly. As the door softly closed behind them, I turned and rested my back against the door to keep it ajar. I rustled through my pockets for a box of cigarettes and put a flame to the white stick. Only two wisps of smoke had entered my lungs before that word sounded out and hastened everything up.

"Collect!" Typo's vocals had boomed throughout the store, reverberating off the door and frightening me. I almost dropped my cigarette, which I quickly put out on the wall and peered through the glass door. Though this wasn't the first robbery I had taken part in, the feeling at the time was foreign to previous experiences. Excitement, as opposed to anxiety, came over me. We were robbing a petrol station and I was excited. Things ran smoothly. Whilst Switch forced staff members to the ground, Typo and Manic were bagging up money at the back. Then Darren, to my surprise, started pointing a gun and blaring orders at the two staff members. Rah! I thought, right there and then. I didn't realise we had guns.

When I turned back everything seemed fine on my side. People wandered about their business as usual. But then a split second after my satisfactory browse, I clapped eyes on a blue Vectra indicating right for the petrol station. I burst open the door, pushing it back as far as possible and shouted, "Feds! Come on, we gotta blow, we gotta blow!"

The guys fled the store like mad men. Manic leapt over the steps with a balletic spin. They ran wildly. Money escaped from the bags and waists of Typo and Manic and floated in the air angelically as though part of the gentle wind. The blue Vectra pulled up at a pump. The boys ran sloppily, tripping each other over. I ran behind them trying not to enter the sloppy chaos that was ahead. As I passed the pump where the Vectra owner, a forty-something man, attempted to fill up his car, I heard a CLANK! and his heroic arms made an unexpected effort to stop me. I coiled between his arms like a belly dancer.

"Oi, you! Stop, you thieves!"

We were being chased by a middle-aged man who came into a petrol station to fill up his tank. His efforts were exemplary. I was forced to split from the guys to get him off our trail. I turned right into an alleyway, breezed through the needles, the burnt tinfoil, cling film and trash that infested it, and jumped over the back of a garden fence. He was still behind me when I flashed a look behind me.

"Oi, you waste of space! Stop! Stop I said!" he shouted authoritatively.

I just kept on running. I was huffing and puffing, but running all the same. It was only a matter of time before the police would be on our tails. I ran into North Peckham Estate, sprinted up and down flights of stairs, along several balconies where I finally lost my pursuer. I filled my lungs with desperate gasps for air on the urine-stinking stairway. Then I removed my cap, pulled the band loose that held my hair in a ponytail and tucked my hood into my collar. I turned my sister's reversible silk jacket inside out and the bright orange instantly fragmented the black. I made for Red Brick estate, a social housing estate in Peckham built with red bricks. When I arrived no one was there. Four small blocks of flats surrounded me. I rotated in a full circle. They're not here. How could they leave me? I thought.

Moments later, "Psssst!" echoed into the square, and then again: "Psssssssst!"

"Who's dat?" I said clearly, but not shouting, walking cautiously towards the voice whilst I sought an escape route.

"It's me…quickly, come here."

I recognised the voice and approached the block where it came from. Manic and Darren were sitting on the lookout.

"Where're Typo and Switch? Who's got the papers?" I hastily questioned.

"Dem man, innit. They've gone to dump it at Typo's yard because you were on some long t'ing. What happened to you, doh? You were off. You're so ghetto, you little gangsta." Manic nudged me.

Darren nodded at me and I felt good—like I was gaining additional stripes—that they acknowledged and approved of the stance I had taken with this. I shared with them how far I ran, the lengths I went through to divert the heroic man on our trail from them and our meeting place.

"Yeah?" Manic's neck snapped to the side and I got a double dosage of his approval, a personal gratification of my thoughtful actions. Darren didn't pay me any more mind. Manic went on to inform me that Switch had taken a liking for me, that he was "bang on your case" as he put it. As I said, these guys were very forward. Any opportunity to ignite conversations of attraction, leading to sexual innuendo, flirtatious bodily contact and ultimately sex, they would incite and grab with both hands…and feet! All I had in my defence was my age, which I used time and time again.

"Well, I've only just turned thirteen, so what are telling me that for?" I said. So when Manic did his version of the pirouette to express his supposed shock, I had to kiss my teeth because as young as I was, I knew for sure what these guys were about. That was when Darren looked at me up and down at the humps and bumps that bulged through my loosely hung sweats. I hunched my back to lessen the visibility of my breasts and said with my usual attitude, "What?"

He cocked up his lip that was imbedded with a centimetre-long scar and demonised his eyes. "I'm just checking you out, innit!"

"Darren, allow it man, she's thirteen," Manic informed him, clocking his moves were those of a deranged paedophile.

I looked at Darren sickened by his move. He totally creeped me out. I sensed he was the type of guy that would commit rape by the way that he would stare at my private parts regardless of how uncomfortable it clearly made me feel. A rusty black Fiesta XR2 Turbo skidded on the pebbles diverting attention from the uncomfortable situation. Typo was alone. Manic and Darren climbed into the back of the car and I into the front.

"Where's Switch?" Manic questioned.

"I left him at my yard with the papers, innit. Steph, you little gangsta, ya all right?" Typo's tone danced towards the end of his sentence.

"I'm fine," I said, "but can everyone stop calling me a gangsta, please?" I pretended to be annoyed, but I secretly enjoyed this gangster persona they put on me. That's what stripes were for: face. To create a façade through acts of defiance that would lead to a formidable reputation.

"But I never know you could handle yourself like dat; dussing like ya on the tracks." He bowed over in hysterics licking his head accidentally against the steering wheel.

I looked at him. He rubbed his head, started up the engine and burned rubber pulling out of the estate. As we were about to pass the estate where I had not so long ago burnt a decent amount of calories, we came to a stop at a zebra crossing. An elderly woman slowly hobbled across, hands clasped upon a Zimmerframe. We patiently waited. Manic mentioned she could be somebody's grandmother. Darren suggested we ran her over. I looked at him. I thought he was nuts and looked at him thus, noticing a deep inch scar in his head where he had two shaven lines to the top right of his short back and sides. Typo laughed off the fact that his brethren weren't quite right in the head, a bit further afield than we were.

Suddenly, out of the corner of my eye a familiar figure loomed towards the car barking, "Oi! You little shit!" it was the man who had chased me. "Thieves, stop 'em!" he continued.

He pulled out a pen from his shirt pocket and strode hastily towards us, noting down what must have been the car registration number on the palm of his hand. The old lady pushed on... With a prompt from Darren, Typo panicked. He hurriedly shifted the gearstick into reverse, reversed back, then into first gear, up on the pavement and straight into the man. He was knocked violently to the ground where he lay screaming. With his pain ringing in our ears Typo hastily reversed back onto the road and sped off. I turned to look behind us and saw the old lady seeing to the hurt man and Manic, sitting on the backseat, bowing with dainty horizontal arms as though holding up a tutu.

"*Voilà!*" he said.

Darren just nodded, soft and solemn though somewhat pleased, whilst Typo drove off in a panic at high speed with erratic control of the steering wheel. Me? I sat there bulge-eyed and silent. I thought, Please God don't let us get arrested for this...I really don't want to get locked up for this. It didn't occur to me we had left an innocent man to die. I refused to think of it like that. No! How could I consider him when I had so many of my own issues to think about at that moment.

I was even a little bit scared.

"Where's da car?" Switch queried as we ascended the staircase to the flat we were meeting him at.

"We had to dump it down da road, t'ings got a little messy. It's all nuts right now! Call a cab, we gotta blow, man!" Typo looked around with paranoia.

"What 'appened Typo man? Man ain't flexing right." Switch asserted looking to his brother for answers.

"No biggie Switch," Darren clarified, "Man just had to lick over man wid da car innit. It was da same man dat was chasing us, so he had to get dealt wiv or he'd be calling da boy-dem for us." He was as calm as a feather.

"Rah! Don't lie?" Switch queried.

Typo paced quickly to the window, looked down either ends of the road and then closed the living room curtains. "Feds are circling da area; dey're gonna send helicopters for us soon and you're talking 'bout no biggie." He stated this a little manically showing clear signs of hysteria about the turn of events.

I moved out of Typo's way as he started to undress and head into his bedroom, and sat down on a single leather chair.

"It *is* no biggie, man!" Darren continued. "What else was man to do? Let dat brudder take down man's number plate? He should dead! Man ain't no pussy! Man ain't 'fraid of jail and dem places, yannah!"

Switch smiled at his brother with an unusual look as though part of him was in awe and the other part was taken aback by his disturbing comments. I felt the same. One part of me wanted to not give a shit about going to jail and justified our actions for knocking him over as a reason to save ourselves. The other side of me was sickened by his disregard, and afraid of his mental state. This side of me I could not show.

"Let man borrow some of your clothes, Typo, till I reach my yard?" Manic asked following him. You could see he too was uncertain about what had just occurred and needed some guidance from Typo, who wasn't in a calm state himself.

Switch watched me watching a blank television screen behind

a coffee table where the bags of money lay. Darren sat on a brown leather sofa to the left of me. Sirens whined in the distance. I wondered if we'd really get away with this and if the man was OK. Shit, what have we done? I thought

"You all right, Steph?"

"*Yeeeaah*?" I snapped. I needed to appear cool, unphased, like I was able to deal with these types of situations. And whilst I knew how to block sentiment from what I physically displayed, internally my head and conscience played pingpong with my emotions.

Switch dipped his brow. "Look, what's just happened is nuts. But like you, I don't give a fuck if the man dies. Do you know how many people I've seen die in my life? Fifteen...sixteen...eighteen year olds. My friends...family. Death don't mean much to me, Steph. Neiver does jail."

I turned my head taken aback, wondering what murder and jail meant to me. Would I intentionally kill someone? I thought. The answer was yes. I mean, if it were my life or someone else's then I think I would intentionally kill. But this was different. This was an innocent man trying to be a good citizen. If he died, I guess I would deal with it as I've dealt with most things, force away the sentiment and attempt to move on. But it's not something that I want or am prepared to deal with. Unfortunately, these guys had lived and were living lives much more heinous than mine. I was outside my comfort zone. All I had was my attitude and ability to hide emotion from physical display. I kissed my teeth as he rolled the jumper down over his body. I glanced at Darren who wore a perverted smirk that was unsettling my stomach.

A car horn blew.

Typo stepped out much more reserved and relaxed. He was clad in jeans and a white roll-neck. "Dat's da cab."

I walked out first, boarding a seven-seater Space Cruiser. Once I was sure things were clear, I nodded for Switch to come out followed by Typo, Darren and Manic with the money.

The journey to Nunhead was silent and grave. Once inside Manic's fourth-floor flat, he grabbed some Rizlas and a box filled with weed. I neatened a space on Manic's crumpled bed sheet, then dropped my weight onto it. I wanted to leave. I was in a flat with three young men who had a different level of exposure to life than I had. I wasn't sure where their limits were. But at the same time I was here to get paid, and that's what I had to keep as my focus point. Manic and Typo took to the floor. Switch found a space next to me. He handed me two sheets of small Rizla papers and a couple buds of potent skunk. I licked and stuck the wafer-thin sheets together and crumbled the buds into the palm of my hand before sprinkling it into the L-shaped Rizla. I was keen to feel buzzing, relaxed and carefree again.

"Give us a nico, please," I asked.

"A what?"

"Nico."

Switch showed me a pack of Silk Cuts questioningly. "A *blem*?"

"A what?"

"Blem."

I squinched my eyes at him puzzled. "The fags I'm talking about, what you talking about?"

"I'm talking about the cigarettes, what're you talking about? Nico? What's dat?"

I heard the toilet flush and soon saw Darren's dipped head enter the room just missing the top of the door frame.

"It's an abbreviation for nicotine," I replied. "What's blem?"

Darren sat adjacent to Switch snatching Rizlas and the cigarettes from his lap. Typo looked up at us jarringly. You could see the unease in him still. He switched on the television, all the while continuing to count the money up with Manic.

"Whatever," Switch mouthed handing me a cigarette, which I chipped off and sprinkled onto the greens. "All I know is dat people from your ends talk nuts."

"People from *your* ends talk nuts," I defended. "Wait a minute, what ends are you from, *Switch*? Nort', Sout', East or West?"

He drew out the gun that was in his brother's waist, knocking the tobacco from the Rizla sheet, and rested it up against my face, the barrel pointing north. "Say dat again...*gangsta*."

"Get dat out my face, Damien, I ain't even playing." I used his real name to show I was serious and mask my fear. I knew his actions were playful. It's the type of games that these guys were renowned for playing, but at the same time I knew these guys were from a completely different walk of life to me, and so couldn't judge what could make things go serious. Plus the look on his brother's face suggested he wanted Switch to be serious.

Switch laughed...or rather guffawed. He went to put the gun back behind his brother's trouser waist, but Darren took the gun reluctantly and replaced it himself. I was clearly uncertain by the set of friendship rules these guys lived by.

"Don't ever do dat to me again," I warned, putting my fear aside.

"Yeah, dat wasn't called for, Switch; 'llow doing dem t'ings around me in future," Typo told him.

"But she's too facety, Typo." Switch looked at me and kissed the air as though it were my lips. I wondered what his mum thought when she named her child Damien and what hell-ground Darren emerged from. "If you weren't so cute I'd slap you for half the t'ings you say."

I was about to lay into him again when he dashed in: "I'm only joking! Before you start running up dat mouth of yours."

I licked and rolled my spliff, then lit its fat head and burned its potency. Typo and manic stopped counting.

"How much?" I asked remembering what today's event should have been totally about.

"Just under six Gs—fifty-nine and change." Typo pushed a pile my way.

I did the maths in my head and worked out I was owed £1,180. I slid the fat bundle of cash into my jeans pocket. Darren looked at me grudgingly but I didn't penny it. A sweet feeling clasped onto my body and I reclined. This encouraged the potent weed to marinate my brain cells, infuse its way into my bloodstream and semi paralyse me. Strange thoughts of the Care Bears entered my mellow, airy brain. I smiled at the spectacle of Good Luck Bear and Grumpy Bear going toe to toe...

"Look!" Switch barked. "Turn up the TV! Turn up the TV!"

I fought the urge to pull myself up, and then the urge to widen my eyes. ITN *London local news* was on. I didn't get the big deal, but then heard:

> ... *John Brown, a father of two, was run down earlier on this afternoon after he tried to catch the criminals behind a petrol station robbery. The incident took place on Sumner Road's North Peckham Estate where one of the robbers was believed to have run to from the scene of the crime. Mr. Brown was taken to King's College Hospital and is believed to be in a critical condition. CCTV captured footage of four black males and one believed to be of mixed heritage at the scene of the robbery. Police are appealing to the public with any information to call Crime Stoppers anonymously...*

"Man try call man mixed race, yanna," Damien blurted out ignoring all the other details of the news report, "after man's a black man," he continued.

Fuck. Father of two in a critical condition, I thought. I lay back down submitting to my high. I could see John Brown's face just before we drove into him. I wanted to change the subject in my head.

I looked at my walnut-brown hands and for a moment I felt uncertain about my identity, angry about the scarce history I knew of myself and how it made me feel: confused. It was at that point, after everything that had happened that day, that I felt compelled to leave.

"Manic, call me a cab, please. I wanna go home."

CHAPTER TWELVE

HELLO AGAIN

29th November 1995 – Maths Class

Hey Di, guess what's happened? Seriously, guess? It's a karma ting. And to be honest, I expected somefing to happen. After running over dat John Brown brer, I had that same feeling I had after I robbed Mary-Anne. Just dat wrong feeling like somefing could happen.

Well, somefing did. Switch and Darren got shifted for the robbery. I don't even know all the facts yet, but I heard Mr. Brown's alive and kicking, thank God, and picked them out of a line-up after they got arrested for robbing their local shop. I know—some joke ting, ah-lie? I feel so bad for Switch. Even though he got on my nerves at times, he was all right. Seemed as though he was influenced nuff by Darren, who you done know was off of his rockers. But I guess he was cool too at times. They're on remand now in Her Majesty's Young Offenders, Feltham Prison. Damien's looking three to five years and Darren six to ten because of the gun.

Dat, on top of the bad feelings I've been having with

these robberies, has totally put me off doing it. I don't want to go to jail. The thought of prison is quite scary, and as hard as I appear to be, dem places aren't for me. Plus they're handing out heavy birds for robbery now! I think I'm gonna just stick to shoplifting if anyfing. Last week Nicola and Lakiesha brought Safire, Charlene, Stella and me to a few big department stores with designer garments galore. All the clothes were tagged up with red ink cartridges that don't even set the alarms off and can be burned off. We cleaned the stores out. That day was cool...

"Stephanie!" Mr. Williams shouted. "To the front please—and bring that book!"

I slammed my diary shut and approached the dude with the afro. "Yes, sir?"

Mr. Williams sighed, crossing his legs and arms simultaneously. "Stephanie, you know the drill. There will be no diary documenting while in this classroom or any other classroom for that matter. Now hand it over." He showed me the palm of his hand, and as always the thought of slapping his hand tempted me.

"When will I get it back, sir?"

"When class is over."

I handed him my diary, which he put in his top drawer. The class looked up at me as I walked back. "What?" I said matter-of-factly and they turned back to their books except for Geoffrey who was one of the classroom boffins, the eager learners, the intelligent ones. He smiled at me pushing his taped glasses back as if to get the frame to sit nicely on the bone that circled his eyes. I smiled back for the sake of it and his eyes widened with glee; my brow dipped and his face normalised. Sitting down, I started back on the percentages:

Q. What is 7.8 as a percentage of 143 rounded to the nearest decimal point?

I battled with my brains for a bit dividing 143 by 100 and then multiplying it by 7.8 but it didn't look quite right. I tried dividing 143 by 7.8 and multiplying that by 100, but that looked more wrong than my first try. I put my hand up.

Mr Williams strode over. "Yes, Stephanie, how can I help?"

"I can't remember how to do this percentage, sir."

He knelt down to my level. "If you came to class regularly then there would be no opportunity for you to forget!"

"Now that's just speculation, sir, but I see your point. Percentages for homework?"

"Too right you will, plus the 'means and averages' you failed to hand in last week."

"OK, sir, I'll bring them in on Monday."

He showed me the formula to convert figures into a percentage of the mass figure.

A. 7.8 / 143 x 100 = 5.5%

I breezed through the remaining questions with ease. After class I collected my diary and waited by the benches for my sisters and friends. I waved goodbye to Geoffrey and a few other people in my class as they walked past. The main building was busy with people buzzing around to leave school. I clocked Donavan and Dwayne who made their way over.

"Wha' gwaan, Steph?" Dwayne asked with a fist poised for nudging.

I nudged him and then Donavan and they sat on either side of me.

"Where're my sisters and Shariece and dem?"

"I think Maria's been given a detention with Mrs. Mitchell—innit, Dwayne?" Donavan turned back to me. "And dem lot must be waiting for her."

I got up to look for them but Dwayne stopped me by asking after his rapping spar, Tyrone, but like the rest of his mates, I hadn't seen him. Probably longer than they hadn't. For me it had been almost eighteen months. The two of them had started freestyling when they used to roll, and getting a record deal had always been their goal. Feeling his lyrics, Donavan started to beatbox and I rapped my knuckles on the bench to the beat...

"Steph!" my sister called to me from afar.

I stopped rapping my knuckle on the bench and saw Safire waving me over with René and Shariece. I jumped up to tell Dwayne and Donavan "later", but they followed. On the way to the bus stop, they told me that Maria had got an hour's detention and her mum was coming for her.

We boarded the 21 bus after seeing Stella's head hanging out of the window on the upper deck of the bus. As usual we backed bus passes to one another. We disembarked at Lewisham, when the day was beginning to surrender to night, and changed onto a 136 bus.

*

"Wha' gwaan, Stella," Typo packed volume into his words as we strolled towards him and Manic north of Peckham's frontline. "Safire...Steph! You little gangsta, whassappenin'?"

Stella and Safire got their hellos in before Typo noosed a playful arm around my neck. I noticed Manic bow melodramatically as he greeted Stella and Safire. I laughed to myself, then introduced Shariece and René to Typo, and then Manic. This was the first time they had met. Manic forwardly kissed them both on their hands. We were sheltered by the bus stop outside of Crackerjack's. Manic sat on the narrow strip of red plastic that protruded from the shelter purporting to be a seat. He built a spliff.

"Steph," he called, "d'you wanna bill up?"

I skipped over and freed the Rizla sheets, nico and *gunja* from his hands. I built the spliff and set the head ablaze. Shariece manoeuvred my way, René following. I passed the spliff to Shariece. Safire wandered across the road from Stella and Typo.

"Manic, bill me a spliff," Safire demanded.

He looked up at her and wedged his head in an L-shaped hand, his thumb placed horizontally beneath his chin.

"Please," Safire added, but Manic didn't move.

Moments later he said, "Safire, if you can't bill it, you shouldn't blaze it."

"Who says?" she snapped.

"I said," he drew on his spliff like a sultry woman wearing exquisite silk gloves, "the owner of that which you seek."

Shariece, René, Safire and I looked at one another and then at Manic. We were taken aback and amused by his pompous use of words and choice of posture. He certainly was manic, eccentric even.

"Give us some of dat spliff, René," Safire asked.

René passed Safire what was left of the spliff I'd made, which was literally two pulls.

"Manic!"

Manic turned, peered through the clear plastic wall of the bus shelter. Typo waved him over.

He got up. "Blood...whassup?!"

"Dem man just lan'—they're on Sumner," Typo bellowed over the road.

We followed Manic across the road, Shariece and René querying with Safire if he was OK...still had all of his screws kind of thing. We bopped through the alley onto Sumner Road where a herd of guys beamed moped lights that pierced the night like needles through black wool. Fists were nudged, shoulders collided and words exchanged between Manic, Typo and the other brothers that had just rolled in. We girls all were standing huddled in our own corner afraid or unwilling to interact without an introduction. Sleet-type rain broke loose from the sky, lit up by the moped lights to look like confetti. We huddled closer shielding our gelled-up hair trying to maintain a look of confidence, roughness and maturity while glaring at the light-distorted faces of the brothers from out of town.

"Steph?" Shariece called, "who're dem brudders?"

"I dunno, I fink they're from Brixton."

"Yeah, dey are," Stella threw in. "My brovva had a fight wiv dat one in the white hoody."

I tried to make out the face of the guy in the white, but the night and lights had joined forces in making that task difficult. Their faces were blurred with explosions of light.

"Steph!" a voice partially familiar to me called out.

I looked in the direction of the voice, then at Stella, Shariece and then at René.

"Ain't dat yous lot...?" Stella started.

"Steph!" the voice called out again and by then I knew who it was. "Steph, is dat you? Rah! Shariece, René...Safire!" The face started to materialise in the light and take visible shape. I felt tingly, timid, 'eediot'-like and embarrassed, unsure of what to do. My head dropped searching the floor for answers. I wiped the sleet off my brow. Stella's brow ridged. I raised my shoulders to say 'I don't know' because I didn't. I didn't know why I was pretending I didn't know who this person was. I didn't know why I was looking at the floor like it was my diary and I could put my questions out there. I really didn't know why I was feeling like an absolute idiot, and probably looking like one too.

"Oh my god!" came from Shariece's mouth, then the same from René's and then Safire's.

He clocked Stella last and she went over to him adding to the four-way conversation, rapping about what he was up to these days, where he lived and how good he looked. Tyrone looked so good.

I stayed put. Typo came over to me. He wanted to know what was wrong, but I couldn't answer.

"You're bang on my man's case, innit?"

A demented look steamed through my eyes and I retorted, "No I ain't!"

"All right, blood!" Typo took a step back. "If you ain't, then you ain't."

I sat on the wall in front of the estate alone, trying to look nonchalant. I hit the back of my heels against the wall and concluded that must be the reason why my shoes had got so lean. Manic suddenly appeared before me, did a theatrical bow like I was the Queen, and then kneeled down on the moist ground. "Steph, will you marry me?"

The seriousness in his face frightened me. "Blood, are you sure you're all right?" I asked.

Seeing this spectacle, Tyrone hurried over.

"Manic, what are you on, blood?!" Tyrone was heated. "Move from her!"

"Cool yuh skin, Tyrone, me and Stephanie's long time bredrens y'know, I was just tryna get your attention, blood." Manic got up off the floor and brushed my chin softly with the back of his fingers.

I smiled, shaking my head and lightly cracking up. The mad boy had sense! Tyrone nudged Manic as he passed him to sit next to me. I looked at him. All my emotions started to run around, and right there and then I felt I loved him, but I was also angry, worried that he didn't feel the same, otherwise he would have called. He looked older, but he looked good! He had a slight moustache, was taller and had lost the braces. His teeth were dead straight now. One of his eyebrows had two shaven lines, and he had his right ear pierced. What a difference eighteen months makes.

"Steph."

I heard him call my name but my brain wouldn't signal a response and I just sat there thinking my hair must be getting frizzy in the sleety rain.

"Steph, I've missed you," he said.

"Then why didn't you call?"

"Let me explain."

"On the real, Ty, I ain't up for hearing no long-t'ing story from someone I don't even get. You get bang on my case, try kiss me and tell me you would want to be with someone like me; den when I'm warring wid people, big man is all licking me unconscious, you disappear without even checking on me!" He was shocked by how animated I was. So was I. I didn't get emotional about men. I didn't know them intimately enough to get emotional. I was always one of the mans-dem. But right then I cared, I felt the loss from his absence and I couldn't disguise it.

He put a wet, leather Avirex jacketed arm around me. My throat became clogged. I could feel the tears nearing but I strained, I fought to keep them inside my eye sockets and tilted my head back.

The sleet had stopped. Safire, Stella, Shariece and René were mingling with Typo, Manic and the other guys Tyrone had come with, though their ears were cocked our way.

"Steph, please, let me explain."

"What's there to explain?"

"I told my brovva how I felt about you and that you felt the same way too but were worried about Macy and him not approving..." I gawped at him stunned, my eyes leapt out. What exactly did my sister know? "...and he just went loops," Tyrone continued, "calling me a nasty, wo'tless boy. Saying I shouldn't be looking at Macy's little sister like dat and I should be checking girls my age."

"But you're only two years above me and we're not doing anyfing."

"I know, but he wasn't 'aving it. Said if I got wiv you he'd never chat to me again, and that's my brovva who's been like a dad to me. Dat hurt, man, trus' me, it hurt man when he said that." His eyes filled with tears, but unlike me he didn't restrain them from falling and they spilled over his lengthy lashes, clogging them together.

I quickly wiped them. I didn't know what else to do. "Did my sister say anyfing?" I was unsure if that question was appropriate but needed to know what my sister thought of me. I needed to know that I had her respect and love as I'd always had, but he seemed lost in a gaze. He was lost in a moment that I too began to join. A moment that excluded all that surrounded us: people, sound, buildings, colour, day/night...all except the temperature...the temperature was warm. That was a special moment, and though I didn't know it, I didn't want to lose it. Our watery eyes did not lose contact. The distance between our faces shortened. The temperature of his breath increased as the distance between us became non-existent. His lips touched mine. My eyelids fell to a close. I didn't move. His mouth inched open and my heart drummed fast, smashing against my chest. I was going through a door that I was never to return from. But I didn't want to lose that moment. That moment felt so good…so alive!

Something wet touched my lips and my instant reaction was to close up my mouth, which I did. His pursed lips continued to smooch at mine and I inched my mouth back open. His tongue felt wet and unusual to me. It came powerfully at me, and our teeth accidentally clunk one another's. I drew my tongue back to lessen the attack by his tongue. When I tried again, bringing my inexperienced tongue back into the playing field, I focused on following his repetitive rhythm: up…down; up…down; up…down. I thought I did OK. His hands clasped hold of my face, but I decided not to complicate things and left my hands in my lap. With so much concentration going into getting my kiss right, I drizzled away from the moment and noticed bewildered faces enter our space. I stopped kissing. Sound kicked in and words formed clarity from Safire's motoring mouth.

"…what kind of joke business is dis?! How can you be kissing Ricardo's uncle?! Watch when I tell Macy and Mum, they're gonna go MAD!"

I didn't care what Mum thought, though I did care what Macy thought. I thought she'd understand, though. I hoped she'd understand… she had to. I wouldn't be able to enter into a relationship with Tyrone if she didn't and I really wanted to…

Shariece and Typo had corner to corner smiles on their faces. I heard Stella make a "Rah!" noise and Manic mouthed "Seeeeen!" at the sight of us. I looked at Tyrone questioningly.

"Steph, we're gonna do this, yeah?" he said.

I nodded yes without hesitation.

CHAPTER THIRTEEN

APPROVAL

2nd December 1995 – My Yard

Today's the day. I'm just gonna talk to my sis, tell her how I feel and what the situation is—what's the worst that can happen? So, she doesn't approve, then what? Butt me up; not chat to me? Nah...never! I'm in love and want to remain in love in the person who loves and respects me for me. Everyone's worried about my virginity and the complication of someone so close to our family having the potential to hurt me. But I'm willing to take that risk. I love him. I have to take dat risk. Macy will understand dat. Dat's my big sis, she'll always be there, innit Di?

My bedroom door cracked open to reveal Safire's jarring face and the sound of 'His Eye is on the Sparrow' ringing through my room with Mum's warped vocals ruining it.

"What?" I asked crossly.

"Mum said are you coming church today?"

"Nah, I'm staying in, I got homework to do."

"Mum!" Safire bellowed over the banister. "Steph said she's staying in to do her homework!"

I heard the thunderstorm Mum made as she mounted the stairs and then turned for my bedroom. My sister stepped out the way and entered the bathroom next door. As she did this I noticed her tatty nightdress pinched up in the crease of her bottom. I closed my diary and slid it under my pillow. Mum was standing in my doorway watching me.

"What, Mum?"

"Don't 'what' me, where yuh manners deh?"

I sighed heavily not knowing what else to do. I'd come to realise and accept since moving back home that our relationship was what it was: fucked, at the best of times. It had been that way since I was old enough to understand what 'fucked' meant. I accepted that I just didn't come from a wholesome home and I'd stopped trying to figure out why.

"Why aren't you coming church?"

"Didn't Safire just tell you, Mum?"

"Don't tell mi' 'bout Safire, I'm asking you!"

I rolled my eyes at the wall then looked back at Mum. "Because I've got homework to do, Mum, plus I just don't feel like it."

"Why not?"

"Why're you questioning me on it, Mum?" I rolled off the bed to my feet. "You said you was gonna stop tryna force us to go church when I moved back in and now look what you're doing!" I bypassed Mum and pushed open the door to the bathroom. Safire was soaking in the bath.

"I'm not forcing you to do anyt'ing, I'm just asking why you don't wanna come," Mum said, now standing in the bathroom doorway.

I sat on the toilet seat shifting Safire's nightie and knickers across moist floorboards with my foot while I urinated into the toilet bowl. "Why don't you wash out your knickers in the bucket?"

"I *will*," Safire squealed, "when I'm done."

"Steph!"

"Yes, Mum?!" I got up and wiped myself dry. "I already told you, I'm not coming—I've got homework to do." I closed the toilet seat, pushed down on the gold lever to flush the chain and washed my hands noticing my headscarf hanging from the back of my hair from the reflection in the gold taps. I dried my hands and tied my scarf back on my head.

"But wait!" Mum stretched her neck out at me with folded arms. "Just coz I'm giving you the choice to come to church, dat nah mean yuh can brock my rules and run dis pen. Dere's only one bull inna dis pen!"

"What rules?!" I bared both hands questioningly. "How am I running dis pen by doing my homework? What are you talking about?!" I walked past her agitatedly.

"I'm talking about the Sabbath. And calm yuhself when you ah pass me!"

"Mum, what are you on about?" Safire questioned, soap suds gliding down the side of her face.

"Safire, shut your mouth when I'm talking," Mum shouted.

Safire slammed the bathroom door shut and I rested back on my bed trying to pretend Mum wasn't there.

"Stephanie, buttum line is dat today is a day of rest, so there will be no homework doing under this roof until sunset unless it's di Bible you ah goh study!"

"OK, I'll come out of your house and do it somewhere else, then." I turned my head away from her to face the wall again and she stormed out of my room. I turned back to catch her floral, frilly, calf-length dress taking the shape of her voluptuous and fiercely moving body. At the same time her thick, shoulder-length hair bounced its big curls.

I lay there in a navy blue Reebok tracksuit tired by the conversation. I was tired by most conversations with Mum. Half an hour or so ticked by and Safire popped her head into my room while I was slicking my hair back into a ponytail with some Jam brand hair glaze and Dax. I then tied the headscarf back on. She was dressed like a child of the Virgin Mary, the sister of Christ himself. She looked nice in an unusually innocent and sweet way. Her hair was ringletted. The bleached blonde section of her hair made her look a bit like Goldilocks.

"Did you tell Macy?" she asked in a furtive way.

"I haven't had a chance to speak to her yet. I will do it today, so for the record: don't open your mouth to Mum or anyone—OK?"

"All right, but you better hurry up and tell her, coz dat's nuts what you're doing."

"How is it nuts, you eediot, he's liked me for ages and I've liked him for ages; it's not like we're gonna do anyfing."

"You better not. And you're da eediot, falling for your nephew's uncle; what kind of joke business is dat?"

"Shut up and get out of my room!"

Safire cut her eye as she turned to leave and I kissed my teeth. A few minutes later, Mum was back upstairs, cloaked in a floor-length overcoat and carrying bibles, a hymnal and her church bag, which was a semi-circled black leather clutch bag. She placed one of the bibles on the floor, opened it before my bed and told me goodbye in a soft and humble tone, which staggered me though I didn't move from my lying position on my bed. Then she left.

I heard the front door slam and the car drive off. I glanced down at the opened book only to close it, but noticed parts of the text had been highlighted in green, probably especially for my reading, and I was strangely lured in, by a force outside of my own, to read it.

Remember the Sabbath day to keep it holy. Six days shalt thou labour, and do all thy work: But the seventh day is the Sabbath of the Lord thy God: in it thou shalt not do any work, thou, nor thy son, nor thy daughter, thy manservant, nor thy maidservant, nor thy cattle, nor thy stranger that is within thy gates. For in six days the Lord made heaven and earth, the sea, and all that in them is, and rested the seventh day: wherefore the Lord blessed the Sabbath, and hallowed it.
Exodus 20:8-11

There was a knock at the door which interrupted my reading. I jumped to my feet to see to it.

"You all right?"

"Yeah," I said looking into the street behind his shoulder and then slamming the door shut behind him. "Were you waiting long?"

"About twenty minutes or so, nothing major. Your mum looked vex when she was leaving; did you tell her about us?" Tyrone removed his blood red Moschino puffer jacket and hung it on the banister.

I looked at him lost. "No! She was just trying to Bible-bash me into going church."

"All right, don't look so surprised, it's not like you're not gonna be telling her soon."

He followed behind me up to my bedroom and sat on my made-up but crumpled bed, ducking his head to avoid hitting it against the railing of the top bunk.

I stood and faced the mirror beneath the netted window when I unravelled my headscarf to reveal ocean-waved hair that went into my ponytail. "I'm not," I voiced after some delayed thought.

"You're not?"

"No, I'm not."

"Why not? I thought we were going to do this. I thought you wanted to be with me like I want to be with you." Tyrone dropped his head to the pillow, his hand laid across his brow.

"I do. We're gonna tell Macy today like we said we would, but I didn't say I'd tell my mum. I don't flex like dat with her. I don't want her knowing my business. She'll just disapprove and try to stop us from seeing each other. You don't want that now, do you?"

"Of course I don't," he felt for something obstructive beneath the pillow, "but I don't wanna go behind your mum's back or against her wishes either—I like your mum."

I rolled my eyes noticing my diary appear in his hands. "Give me that, please." I reached for my things but Tyrone recoiled his hand not comprehending that I would clap him for playing games with my diary. "Tyrone, give me back my t'ings!"

My stern voice shook him slightly and he handed it over. "Steph, you don't need to get so serious when I'm playing wiv you, yanna. If you're gonna be my girl you can't be tryna boy me up like you did when you was my bredren. You can't try and handle me like how you bad up dem brers in your school and dat. Let me know from now if that's how you're looking to run it."

"No, I'm not…" I paused, getting to grips with this new emotion of humility. "I'm sorry; I just don't like people messing with Di." I knelt in front of him with a sincerely apologetic face.

He sat up. "Di?"

"My diary."

He handed it to me and cuddled me warmly, soft, but protective. I stayed there for some moments. I glanced down at his feet and clocked the bible's illuminated text staring right back at me, the words being dictated in my mind by Mum. "Tyrone, let's go."

*

Thank God Jason was not there; that in itself was a blessing. Macy seemed in a cool mood. Chicken limbs were roasting in the oven. We had only been there for fifteen minutes and I was frying plantain while Macy washed basmati rice. Tyrone and Ricardo played and conversed in the front room whilst watching MTV. The hot oil sizzled the plantain's exterior, browning and crisping it up nicely. A sweet aroma filled the kitchen and taunted nostrils with the food that was to come.

Ricardo's head appeared around the white door frame of the kitchen door. His face was still cute as a pressing four year old. The puppy-dog eyes were getting bigger and more beautiful by the day. He had eyelashes that curled 270 degrees, plump cheeks that bore a hint of rose and deep, round dimples. His little white milk teeth clenched together to force a smile.

"Aunty Stephanie," his voice was so sweet and mischievous, "can I have one...*pleeeaase?*"

Macy went to tell him no while struggling to ignite a hob on the stove, but I pleaded with her and got a tasty plantain over to his salivating lips. He brushed his curly hair, woven into several plaits, away from his face to fully appreciate the flavour without distraction.

Soon enough the rice came to a boil. The plantain slices were layered on a plate into a mountain-like heap, which I placed at the centre of the kitchen table. As well as the tantalising aroma that filled the room there was a vibe that I couldn't quite place.

Macy sat down in the front room. Ricardo continued to climb over Tyrone, using his limbs as branches from a tree. She offered him a drink, which he accepted and then she asked me if I could make it. She then questioned him on his happiness now he'd moved away; how his mum was keeping; if he'd seen his dad and how long he'd been looking to have something with her little sister? I froze. I couldn't believe what I'd just heard so I replayed the words back in my head whilst trying to steady the drink spilling onto my hand. *So, how long have you been looking to have something with my little sister for*? Yep, I was sure that was what I had just heard.

"Steph," she called.

"Yeah?"

"Come in here; let's talk."

Uneasily I entered the front room. I felt shame. And not necessarily because I'd fallen for Jason's brother, but more so the fact that she'd found out and it wasn't through me as I had intended. I was vexed by that.

I sat next to Tyrone and handed him his drink, the cup drenched from the spillage. He took it carefully, flicked off the excess liquid and passed me a questioning look. Ricardo climbed onto me. I used him to shield my embarrassment.

"So?" she questioned. "Tell me wha' gwaan."

She looked at me and I passed the look onto Tyrone who sunk into the leather sofa, making rubbing sounds like he was passing wind.

"We didn't plan for dis, seriously, Mace. Just over a long period of time, since I started school really, feelings just started growing. I tried to fight them off at first..."

"Me too!" Tyrone slipped in.

"...but they just kept growing stronger."

Macy was nodding her head but her face didn't suggest she was agreeing with me. "Tyrone, my little sister is thirteen, underage and a virgin; you're nearly sixteen, underage but are already having sex."

"But dem girls were different, Macy, I don't just want Steph for sex. I already told her I wanna wait till she's of age and ready to go there."

"But what if she tells you she's ready now, what you gonna do, say 'No, I'm waiting'?"

"But I wouldn't say that, Macy!" I piped up. What was my sister trying to say? How could she think of me like that? "I wouldn't want to end up like—"

"What, like me?" she challenged. The gold-detailed headscarf Macy had on was tied low on her head, almost covering her eyebrows, which emphasised her frown.

I upset my sister. The last thing I wanted to do was upset her. I loved and respected her too much for that. I cast my mind back to the times when she would cradle my head in her lap whilst cornrowing my hair and allowing me to listen to Salt 'n' Pepa's 'Tramp' on her Walkman. The times when she would regularly come to my defence if she felt Mum, Mama or anyone was treating me unfairly.

Tyrone broke the silence. "Macy, I think what Steph's tryna say is—'

"I know exactly what she's tryna say, Tyrone." Macy turned to me. "And the joke is, I don't want you to end up like me either, Steph. You fink it's easy having a child at fifteen? Me and Jason have been bredrens since we were all ten and eleven, then he became my boyfriend when I was your age, Steph, nearly fourteen. D'you fink I planned to break my virginity before I was of age?"

I went to answer but realised the question was rhetorical.

"No," she continued, "but shit happens when you're in the moment, and because of that moment when everything felt so nice and nothing else mattered, I'm an eighteen-year-old mum with a three-year-old. And that's the bottom line. Don't get me wrong, I love Ricardo and I wouldn't change him for the world, but if I could do things again I would've done them different."

Ricardo looked at his mummy and planted a wet, slobbery kiss on her cheek. She wiped her cheek along with his mouth holding a humble smile, and then pressed her lips against his with a loud kissing noise. She hugged his body and rocked him from side to side in her lap. He giggled hysterically. The music video for Whitney Houston's 'I Will Always Love You' onto the TV set. I glanced at Tyrone, turned back to the TV and peered at it blankly. I didn't know what to say or do; this wasn't what I planned, this wasn't what I wanted.

"Not only that," Macy went on, "it's just too close to home. What if you broke up and weren't on talking grounds? What if you really hurt my little sister, Tyrone, or *you* hurt Jason's little brother, Steph? Have you thought about how this can affect both our families?"

"Macy," Tyrone spoke, "I hear and respect what you're saying... trust me, I do; but, what d'you expect us to do right now? Are you saying that I should just walk away and just pretend to be friends with someone that I love because of 'ifs' and 'maybes'?"

I twisted round to look at him, my eyes wide with shock.

"Yeah, that's right, Steph, I love you. I've loved you since that walk we took in Ghetto when I told you certain things and you didn't judge me, you just listened. Do you love me?"

I looked at him loving what I saw, "yeah, of course I do," was set free from my mouth instinctively and we gazed at each other sick with unearthed love.

"You two!" Macy's words tore through our moment like lightning through a tree, splitting, dividing and breaking the moment in two. "OK, I can clearly see that you've fallen for one another, so it doesn't even make sense me telling you to allow it. But I'd say this: I'm putting my trust in you both that you won't rush into things because of these *moments* that come up, and you will wait until Steph's of age and the time's right before you even consider sex. You're both young, you've got all the time in the world to start having sex, so why not wait till you have a little more sense, huh?"

"Macy, I promise," I said. And I meant it.

Tyrone glared at me with glee and an 'I just got a new bike' type of happiness. He said solemnly: "Macy, just so you know, I've bere respect for you, Steph and your family, and I wouldn't do anything to jeopardise dat."

"Good." Macy said, "And I know you've got a lot of respect for me and my family Tyrone, but at the same time you're still very young.

"So, you gonna talk to my brovva, tell him dat we spoke to you and sorted things out?"

The front door opened and slammed shut. "That's him now," Macy got up with a corner to corner smile and Ricardo in her arms, "you can tell him yourself."

The trepidation that came over Tyrone divulged the love and respect he had for his brother, Jason. This was certainly going to be a difficult conversation and I was glad I didn't have to lead it.

CHAPTER FOURTEEN

BLISS

....

19ᵗʰ May 1996 – Dada's House, Lewisham

Oh Di...I'm in love! Dis shit just feels nuts, man, but I know for sure I'm in love. You know like when someone's your last thought at night and your first thought in the morning? You know like when you have a constant warm feeling, like your constantly full up and... I dunno; it just takes me to a place dat feels so nice and affectionate...outside of the crazy and painful thoughts that I have sometimes. I don't feel all that bad stuff when I think of him. I've never felt like this before, and on the real, I'm not even sure if I'm supposed to. My feelings jump the line of love and hate like I jump a rope when skipping.

It's crazy, I know, but it's like I'm losing the urge to want to break people's noses or whatever to rid the tension that races my heartbeat and pounds on my nerves. Now, more time, I just need a hug from Tyrone, or to hear his soothing voice on the phone. I feel so protected and loved and prioritised when I'm around him. He likes to keep me happy and smiling, and for the first time in my life outside of when dealing with my nephew, so do I.

In the beginning, not knowing what I should do to keep a smile on his face, I would tief a lot of things for him: toiletries, aftershaves, underpants, socks, pyjamas...things that he wouldn't always get himself. And that was mainly because he was always buying me stuff and taking me out to eat or to the cinema or whatever and I wanted to give back to him in some way. But now I know he's happy when he sees me happy, and I'm happy when I see him happy, so when we're together we're just happy. We talk about any and everything, we coming like you and me, Di, best friends.

It was now just under six months since Tyrone and I had officially been together as boyfriend and girlfriend, and I was happier than I ever could have imagined. I was fourteen by this time, and having his professed love and continuous affection, helped shape out a softer side to me. I giggled childishly a lot, learned to welcome his warm embrace instead of stiffening upon his touch. With him being in a tuition centre instead of school, he received two hours schooling per day and I got to see a good amount of him. He visited my school often to both see me and check in on his old brethrens, Donavan and Sean. I often wanted to bunk the rest of the day off to spend with him. I loved the time we shared and the feeling that came with it, but Tyrone encouraged me to remain at school and frankly wouldn't have a bar of it. He didn't want me to get expelled and end up like him, but from where I was standing, being like him didn't seem that bad.

I was at Dada's house on a Sunday afternoon, resting on his bed in his room when I was penning my thoughts in my diary. I visited

Dada's most Sundays as he would always do a big Sunday dinner cook up, and I considered this home my second home.

"Stephanie!" Dada's voice spiralled up the staircase, pushed open his bedroom door and tapped my eardrum from where I lay on the bed.

"Yeah!" I sent a wave of vibrant vocals right back at him.

"Goh get di door for Nina!"

I jumped to my bare feet, jumped down several flights of stairs like a youth and opened the door. "How comes you took so long?" I asked and took one of the carrier bags from her.

She managed to get the remaining two bags through the door, bouncing them against its frame upon entering, "I had to go all the way to Lewisham shopping centre because the shop around the corner was closed."

I led the way into the kitchen. Dada was stirring a big pot of boiling kidney beans over a low fire. "How yuh tek soh lung?" he queried.

I passed the table area and started to unpack the bag on the counter. Nina sighed as she came up beside me, not because she was jarred by the question Dada asked her, more so because she was jarred by the answer it prompted. "I had to walk all the way to Lewisham and back with these bags because the shop around the corner decided to close early."

"Yuh did 'member di coconut cream?" Dada drew for a black flannel spotted with bleached patches from the back of his jeans pocket and wiped the sweat across his brow and down his hairline.

Nina handed him the boxed coconut cream block from one of the bags. I reached for a glass from the cupboard and poured myself a glass of Sarsaparilla before packing away the shopping. Nina sat at the glass table with Dada. He was smoking a cigarette coolly in his usual corner position. She was opposite the TV set where the *Eastenders* omnibus was showing. The aroma of sweet rice 'n' peas and chicken stew was pleasing to the nose.

Nina began to quiz me on my relationship with Tyrone: how long we'd been going out? Where he was from? Where he lived? How old he was? What he looked like? Was he still in school? What school did he go to? Why was he excluded? Was he going to college? What did he do for me on my birthday? She had many questions that wanted answering and I answered. Dada went out the back door to finish his cigarette, catch some air, silently encouraging our conversation and cocking his ears our way to hear.

I told her Tyrone's story. About his troubled relationship with his dad. The fact that his father is a drug dealer who doesn't really invest much in Tyrone's development. They just exist day by day. Tyrone doesn't respect him for that, but at the same time understands his life choices to make a living. That's what he himself has to do: make choices about the type of income he makes to support his material wants and needs. He has an odd relationship with his mum. I'm unclear of the details, just know that she wasn't around much when he was younger. Since his mother and father separated when he was a toddler, he's lived with his father Killer Man Joe and had an intermittent relationship with his mother. His brother Jason has filled a lot of parental gaps in terms of guidance and general life's reappraisal. He respects his brother to the core. I told her about the six months we'd been together and what it had done to me. I told her about my birthday several weeks ago; how he took me clothes shopping, bought me Versace, Moschino, Cerruti 1881 and Iceberg jeans; how he took me to the cinema to watch *Scream*, then later on in the night took Safire, Charlene, Stella and me out raving to the Voodoo Magic at Equinox in the West End. How we met up with Nicola and Lakiesha and raved until the early hours of the morning.

"...you should've been there, Nina."

"I know, it sounds like you lot had a wicked time! Nah, he seems like a cool guy, just don't rush into anyfing."

I shook my head discreetly. Dada came back in from out the back. He sat down next to me, withdrew another cigarette from the golden pack laid out in front of him and tapped the head on the table before setting it alight. He blew out the smoke smoothly, steering it away from my face, but I could already taste the fumes at the back of my throat and my desire for a cigarette came on. I looked at Nina with questioning eyes, and she returned my look with a nod. She got up to lead the way outside. I got up to follow but...

"Stephanie?" Dada's voice was calm and monotone, yet stern and slightly threatening.

"Yeah?"

"Dis bwoy, Tyrone."

"Yeah?"

"Soh wha' him do to buy yuh di t'ings him deh ah buy yuh?"

I paused. The question came so suddenly it threw me off course. I went to speak but nothing came out. Nina turned and sat back down respectfully knowing her father wanted to address me.

"Wha'appen, yuh tongue-tie?" His face was relaxed and emotion free.

"What d'you mean, Dada?" I said to give me time to gather my thoughts. He attempted to answer but I came back with, "He works part-time with his brother up Hatton Garden, plus his mum and dad support him," I lied.

"Fi buy you an' yuh sister dem ticket fi go an' rave?"

"Well, he spends it on what he wants to spend it on; it's his money, Dada." I tried to play confused by Dada's confusion, so he would check his own thinking instead of checking mine.

Dada laughed mightily, purely for dramatic effect (an affectation that ran through my family). "Bwoy, Stephanie, yuh must t'ink seh mi ah fool. Gi' me more credit dan dat; lie a lickle better, hee!"

"I'm not lying!"

His face straightened and he just looked at me. Nina's too like I should stop the lying, but what could I say? *The truth.* I hated it when my conscience took over.

"Dad, maybe Stephanie's not ready to tell you what he really does."

I looked at Nina like she'd lost her mind.

"Den she fi tell mi soh instead of ah lie like monkey."

"OK," I got out, "so he robs the occasional bank." Dada's eyes widened, his large pupils hastened my heartbeat. "But he won't be doing it for long! Just until he's got enough money to pay for the music equipment he'll need for his course and to set up his own thing after."

"And den what?" Dada's voice was solemn and I started to see where my dad got his non-p persona from. "Live good? Live like ah honest citizen? Yuh t'ink life soh easy? Yuh t'ink anyt'ing in life is for free? Stephanie, hear wha' mi ah tell yuh when mi tell yuh seh deh is a price fi everyt'ing man put here 'pon dis ya eart'. Not'ing in this world is for free. What you tek from di world, di world ah goh tek from you. Same way when yuh ah give, yuh ah goh get it back somehow, some way. But ah debt always needs to be paid, and whether yuh pay it wid cash or wid a life, di debt will get paid. So next time yuh see yuh lickle bwoyfriend, tell him yuh granddaddy sai': him inna debt to society and society 'im ah goh 'ave fi pay."

CHAPTER FIFTEEN

THE REVELATION

6th July 1996 – My Yard

Oh-my-gosh, Di, I got dat feeling again. Somefing doesn't feel right. I dunno what it is, but I got dis bad, bad feeling, and I can't shift it. It's Tyrone. I know it's Tyrone. I just don't want to fink it's Tyrone. You know like when you have to put good energy out into the universe, just be positive. Believe in good things for the people you love and care about. Like when Mum prays for people or when the church prays and fasts for its sick members and they miraculously come back to full health. Yeah, dat's what I'm doing now. I'm praying for Tyrone, I'm putting good energy out there for Tyrone. Somefing doesn't feel good, but I'm thinking all that is good for Tyrone...

I peered up at the clock wondering, Wha' gwaan? It was coming up to seven and Tyrone should have been at mine from four. Where is he? I checked the connection of the telephone line and whether there was a dialling tone. There was. Our phone was working, but it wasn't ringing. Wha' gwaan? I strolled up to my bedroom window pushing the net curtain aside and gazed up and down the street through gaps in the fresh, plump, green leaves of the mighty tree in our front garden.

It was a beautiful summer's day, the summer of 1996, the air was warm and the sound of insects and birds became prominent in the air. All should have been perfect, however something wasn't right. *Wha' gwaan*? I muttered a quick and meaningful prayer. With nothing left to do I opened my wardrobe door and reached in deep for some clothes I'd hidden from Mum at the back. I tried on each designer item, from Escada jeans to Trussardi, Cerruti suits to Christian Lacroix, and a few other random designer bits and bobs, mixing and matching them with each other to create looks I'd one day carry off. The chime of the clock in the passageway informed me that yet another hour had passed.

There was a heavy knock at the door. I took two frightened steps away from the mirror and turned to the window. Looking out, I searched the road for Mum's car. It wasn't there so I bolted down the stairs grateful that my prayers had been answered.

"What you standing up there looking at me like that for?" Safire said after I'd opened the door.

My eyes welled up with tears of frustration and anxiety. I knew something wasn't right. I was overwhelmed standing in the doorway lost in a train of thought.

"Steph, whassup?" Safire looked at me concerned, rapidly entering my personal space.

My thoughts moved onto other things as I closed the door behind her. "Why didn't you use your key?"

"I lost my bag," she replied, "I left it on the bus. What's wrong with you? Why d'you look like you're gonna cry?"

I climbed the stairs, Safire following behind. "It's Tyrone; I think so't'in's happened to him. He was supposed to come and get me at four;

we were supposed to be going to get so't'in' to eat and then cinemas but…he ain't come and he ain't even called." I flared my nostrils, fought hard to hold down the tears.

"Check out the new *It Was Written* album by Nas that I got on CD… this will cheer you up." Safire put in the CD and selected the 'Street Dreams' track. I bounced my head lightly. I was feeling the song but then I remembered the situation. I sat down on the bed and eased the price-tagged jeans off my waist.

"They're my knickers!" Safire blurted out, taking the conversation down a road I hadn't considered.

"No they're not, you joker, I got these from Marks 'n' Sparks, your ones are from BHS."

"Oh." Safire sat next to me as I pulled a new DKNY vest top up over my head. Her chin rested on her fists. "Are they the clothes you got with Nicky?"

I nodded unhappily and lay on the bed in my bra and knickers. Safire looked at my breasts oddly; I mimicked her look back at her and questioned, "What?" An outstretched hand suddenly shadowed my right breast and squeezed pryingly.

"What?" I tried to wriggle from her clasp.

"How comes your tits have gone so big? They're bigger than mine!" She pulled out a breast to compare. "Nah, Steph, what's going on?"

"What you talking about? My tits have been this size for ages now, true-say I don't show off on you, you must've got it twisted." I pushed her hand off me at the point where she started to squeeze them really hard, poking at my lumps of breast tissue.

The phone rang. Safire got up to see to it but I scrabbled to the floor to get ahead of her, knocking the receiver off its base clumsily. "Tyrone?"

"Steph? It's Macy."

"Mace, have you seen Tyrone?"

"One minute, Jason wants to talk to you." I heard the phone being passed over. "Steph, you all right?" Something wasn't right in Jason's tone but I waited silently for him to fill me in with what I already knew… "Tyrone's been arrested for bank robbery. To tell you the truth, Steph, it looks like he's gonna be looking at least five to six."

"Years!?"

Jason went silent, as though reluctant to confirm a question I already knew the answer to. I just wanted it clarified. I just wanted to know the facts. Him being arrested I kind of expected, felt it itching on the surface of my bones, but five to six years? Oh my gosh… That amount of time without him seemed unthinkable. A weight gripped my heart and I felt the pressure building within me. I swallowed to get the phlegm over the swollen tissue that blocked my throat. I toiled to breathe. Each breath down that phone became heavier and heavier as my lungs became desperate for air. I was kneeling on the floor, bent over trying to find a breathing rhythm that would let me speak.

Safire threw questions over me: "What's wrong? Who's there? What's happened?" But I couldn't process her tumbling questions. There was a shuffling sound down the phone. I heard Macy's soft, apologetic voice return, telling me she knew the pain I was suffering. I terminated the call with haste.

Safire was still in my space awaiting answers to questions I wish didn't exist. "Steph, what's happened?"

"Tyrone's been arrested…for bank robbery. He's going jail." As I completed these words, a force tugged at my emotions, triggering an outburst of emotion I'd never known before. My face was quickly soaked by tears as though water had been thrown from a cup. Safire stared at me. She didn't know what to do or say. She had never seen me cry apart from when I was about to receive a beating from Mum, and even then it was rare. Her eyes welled up. I held my heart like it was wounded and torn. Safire joined me on her knees moving forward to comfort me, but she didn't understand. I didn't want her hugs, her voice, her presence, or her scent; I wanted Tyrone's.

I turned my back on her affection and asked for her to give me some time alone. She got to her feet, her face tearful and distorted, reminding me of that extreme cry-face she often displayed when we were little kids. She couldn't understand why I didn't want her near me to comfort me; couldn't understand why I'd rather face the pain alone as I'd done many other times until Tyrone had entered my life to share the burden. She left my room wailing like it was her loved one that had gone to prison.

I closed the door behind her, blocked out her torment and brooded on my own. Dada's words climbed over to where I now lay on the bottom bunk and showed itself up like the alphabet over clouds in a dream: 'Him inna debt to society and society 'im ah goh 'ave fi pay.'

*

The next morning when my eyes first broke open, they were overwhelmed by beaming sunlight. Dried tears and matter had crusted the corners of both eyes. I picked at it for some time. Recollection of the night before came quickly to me, as did the tears. They drew a few dehydrated drip lines down my face before I smeared them over with my fingertips.

The door was pushed open to the usual sounds of 'His Eye is on the Sparrow'. Mum was standing there with her hand on her hip. She appeared ready to have a go at me. She didn't know how to talk to me, address me properly when there was clearly something wrong. She didn't gel well with words like sensitivity and consideration. I wondered then where her manners were, whether it ever occurred to her that it was about time she started respecting my privacy and knocking on my door before she entered my room. I was a fourteen-year-old teenager who needed space. My thoughts grew into my face and it displayed a jarring expression.

"Who you looking at like that?" she asked.

I really wanted to say 'you' but had other things on my mind. I couldn't be bothered to fight that morning despite Mum's intentions. A tear was about to spill onto my face so I turned my back to her to wipe it away.

"I heard you crying when I came in from Bible study last night." Her tone changed, was now slightly more sympathetic, more regretful. "You was crying all night; what for?"

Silence echoed through the room as I processed my reason for the tears, the pain I felt. I capped the emotion quickly. It was the wrong time and place. I turned back to her with my voice as it would stand on any other morning and said, "No reason." I noticed a page in my diary folded and slightly torn—I must have rolled onto it in the night—I straightened it up and shoved it beneath my pillow.

I got to my feet and headed for the bathroom, passing Mum without making eye contact, though her head followed me as I passed. I ran the taps for a bath then moved over to the sink to brush my teeth. Safire entered in a pair of red shorts and a Wonderbra, rubbing her eyes. She sat on the toilet to pass urine and looked up at me. "You all right?"

I nodded, gargling mouthwash for thirty seconds. I set a cleaned sink in shallow water to wash my face before washing my knickers in a bucket of soapy water and jumped into the bath. It was a Caribbean tradition that addressed hygiene, particularly amongst girls of a certain age, to hand wash personal items such as knickers before machine washing. Strangely this didn't apply to boys' pants. Whilst Safire washed her hands and face in the sink, I asked her to pass me a towel, which she grabbed from the airing cupboard. I told her not to tell Mum about Tyrone until I was ready, in a tone low enough it was practically silent.

Mum appeared from nowhere, most probably from my bedroom. "Don't tell me what about Tyrone?"

Safire peeked at me, scratching her neck and making her cream complexion red with risen flesh. I was silent. Mum strode the boards of the bathroom floor. Safire exited the bathroom, and Mum relayed the question to me. I raised my shoulders and washed my body with a soapy flannel as if she wasn't there. She snatched the wet flannel and repeated the question again: "Don't tell me what about Tyrone?" Her hand was in a position of threat. I recalled episodes of beatings that included a wet flannel and a slippery bathtub—a painful circus show.

"*What*?" I said in a defensive, high-pitched tone. "He's been arrested that's all."

"For what?" Mum lowered the flannel and I lowered my hands that were ready to protect myself from the lashing flannel.

"Robbery. He was arrested for bank robbery and now he's going jail." I took the flannel from Mum's hands and rinsed out the suds.

"Oh Gud!" Mum looked up to the ceiling as though it was the sky and shook her head.

I rinsed off my body and pulled the plug. "Where's my towel?" I was looking at Mum but not necessarily asking her the question, just merely thinking out loud.

A skinny, long-fingered hand appeared from behind the door. I took the towel realising that Safire had been there listening, watching all the time. I was drying off my foot bottom to get out of the bath, when the question I'd been dreading came: "So why are you crying all night because Tyrone's been arrested? What's going on between you two?"

Silence penetrated the room whilst I sat on the lid of the toilet seat with my towel wrapped round me.

"Steph, you might as well tell her." Rah! Safire was still there.

"Safire, are Stephanie and Tyrone boyfriend and girlfriend?"

I glared at Safire with pleading eyes as I moved back towards Mum standing in the doorway, Safire on the other side of her, and bent over to wash out the bath with Jiff. My spine straightened with the shock of hearing what was reeling from Safire's rubber lips: "They've been going out for about eight months, Mum, but as far as I know they haven't done anyfing."

My eyes fired up and I blazed them upon her, staring at her hard, silently mouthing 'Informer' as I passed her to go into my bedroom.

"Stephanie!" Mum called out.

"Mum, I don't want to talk about it," I asserted as I closed my door.

"What d'you mean you don't want to talk about it?"

Mum and I repeated this back-and-forth about four times.

I rushed to dress for school and purposely left Safire behind.

CHAPTER SIXTEEN

THE DAY AFTER IT WAS REVEALED

23rd July 1996 – My Gates

Oh, Di, what've I done? I'm doing it again. I'm asking you questions I already know the answers to. What've I done? I've butted up Geoffrey, blooded up his nose and granted him a need for stitches in his bottom lip. Why have I done this? Well, I came into my maths class as usual, Mr Williams doing his usual, checking on me as usual, claiming he can sense something's wrong with me like usual. Something was wrong and still is, so I told him to "'llow me, sir" coz I was proper vex yesterday morning. Then Geoffrey kept asking me what was wrong, getting all up in my space, all sitting next to me and skinning out his teet'. I told him "'llow me, Geoffrey, I'm not in the mood!" But true-say I've been giving him blies as of late, well...really since the beginning of year nine, since the beginning of me and Ty...I mean Ty and me, he's been growing some balls. He grew enough balls to tell me he liked me. Yesterday he must've grew some more when he came and sat next to me...all put his arm around me after I told him to "'llow me, I'm not in the mood!" So I'm thinking now, Does dis boy want me to punch off his face for him to take what I'm saying serious? And even though I'm thinking that, I'm not thinking I'm really gonna have to do that because outside of the little stupidness he was keeping up yesterday, he's all right. He doesn't bovver me too tuff so I don't bovver him. I learn from him if anyfing true-say I get on well with his dad, Mr Williams—yeah, I know it was a shock to me too. So when he's putting his arm around me I knew the boy must've lost his mind, lost the route on his natural way of thinking, lost his instinct on the likely repercussions, lost his judgement of character, lost his way back home to reality, the route that I had to provide him with.

"Geoffrey, take your hand off me or it's on," I said.

Now, I know Geoffrey's not too clued up on street slang and dem t'ings with a dad like Mr. Williams, but common sense would've told him that 'on' is likely to mean 'on and popping', 'toe-to-toe', 'let's take it to the streets', 'I will bruck you up!' type of fing, especially with the look on my face and the deadness in my tone. But Di, guess what Geoffrey took it to mean? Guess what this eediot yout' went and done having lost all of the above? Come on, guess? He kissed me. The punk slapped his wet, pink, rubber lips on my lips and then didn't even run. He sat there. Right in the middle of our maths class he sat there looking at me like I was gonna give him a hug. I gave him a beating. Yeah, I did! I stood up and clapped the tick maths exercise book around his head making it collide with the table and bounce back up. The rest of the class spiralled outwards. Like a drop of water on still water. Mr Williams rushed over to us from the front of the class, the distance of which I couldn't work out as I was too busy punching his son's lights out.

And then I spent the rest of the day in isolation thinking hard about my actions and regretting every minute of it. But that wasn't enough. I had to stay behind at school for a further half an hour, and then Mr Ahmed suspends me until further notice. Mum's going nuts. Not only is she disappointed and condemning me for falling in love with my nephew's uncle, she's lost hope in me in actually getting through school. But I ain't bovvered. I really couldn't give a shit what she thinks.

Now, I'm just sat at home having to write out some scriptures Mum's given me to do a thousand times like I'm still in year seven.

775. Wherefore, my beloved brethren, let every man be swift to hear, slow to speak, slow to wrath: For the wrath of man worketh not the righteousness of God.

776. Wherefore, my beloved brethren, let every man be swift to hear, slow to speak, slow to wrath: For the wrath of man worketh not the righteousness of God.

(James 1:19-20)

It's only true-say I'm still waiting for Tyrone to call why I'm even here, or I would've ducked out from time.

There was a knock at the front door as I wrote, "Wherefore, my beloved brethren, let every man be swift to hear, slow to speak, slow to wrath: For the wrath of man worketh not the righteousness of God" for the 807th time.

I'd taken some time out from repeating that biblical sentence to get down my version of events whilst I was still annoyed. I had lost the love of my life to the prison system, had Mum's judgement and condemnation casted upon me. She was embarrassed about the relationship more than the fact that he had been jailed. She had already concluded me as promiscuous and likely to be having sex, though I was still a virgin.

All I could do now was feel regret for the cruelty and violence I had imparted on Geoffrey, and indirectly on Mr. Williams. I knew it was unlikely that I would stimulate his forgiveness after what I had done to his son. If given a chance I would apologise to Geoffrey and Mr. Williams. I would inform him of my suffering and pray that it fell on understanding ears as previous events had. There was another knock at the door. The reverberations of the repetitive bang frightened me. I was caught up in my diary and writing lines I had totally forgotten I heard the knock the first time around.

"Who is it?" I shouted as I bounced down the stairs to open the door. Mum and Safire were out.

"Shariece."

I swung open the door and greeted her with a bright smile and a cool forward and backward head movement. She followed me into the kitchen where I made us both a hot cup of Horlicks. We then advanced up to my bedroom. She sat on the bottom bunk and I took to the floor in my white Reebok tracksuit after I'd pressed play on my cassette player. The strong scent of Joop! radiated from her white shirt collar, which was dirtied by the hair grease and gel used to slick her hair into a ponytail where a curly piece of weave hung from. The hairs in my nostrils were tickled by the aroma and I pinched my nose for relief.

We conversed whilst our heads rocked to Snoop Doggy Dogg's 'Gin 'n' Juice' from his debut album *Doggy Style*, which was a big tune then and heading for classic status. I explained to Shariece the childish things that my mum had set for me to do as punishment and her bad judgement of me and my relationship with Tyrone.

"Your Mum's alms', man," she agreed.

"I know! It's not like we're related," I defended.

It wasn't long before Shariece's eyes were all over my diary, but my attention was drawn away when Biggie Smalls' 'Suicidal Thoughts' played into my eardrums. I rapped and bopped along. I was up on my feet, rocking my head in time with each knee raised to the baseline's rhythm. I emphasised the ordeal of this track with outstretched arms that expressed appreciation for the hip hop beat and lyrical content that fantasised about death and a realisation of self-loathing. I was fully immersed into the song and what it represented. Feeling swallowed up in self-pity, worthlessness and at a total loss without Tyrone. Shariece's arms were outstretched and jamming to the rhythm too.

I rapped along, word for word, until the end when Biggie Smalls committed suicide with a bullet to the head. I sat down and neither of us uttered a word.

"It will be alright, you know," Shariece eventually said. "Tyrone won't be gone that long. He may come out much sooner."

I hoped she wouldn't mention his name, and as she did my throat immediately started to block and tears filled my eyes.

I tried to smile to confuse the brain of what I was feeling, but the tears spilled over nevertheless. "Sorry," I added. "It just hurts so much. I really can't believe he's not here....and won't be..." I couldn't finish my sentence. The sniffles overwhelmed my breathing control and took hostage of my voice.

Shariece's arms circled me and again she rubbed my back, "Ah babe, don't cry. I'm here for you."

I stifled my cry into the crevice of her neck and the collar of her school shirt. We stayed like that for some time in silence.

"D'you feel better now?" she asked breaking the silence.

"Yeah. Don't worry about me. I'm fine." I forced a smile. "I promise you Shariece, I'm fine."

Shariece took that as her cue to leave. Once she had left, I turned over the hip hop tape and revelled to Busta Rhymes' 'Woo Haa! Got Ya All in Check'. Laid upon my bottom bunk, sunk into the springs of my mattress, I made shapes out of many plastic bags and coloured pamphlets that peeped through the wired base above me which supported the top bunk mattress Safire owned before she moved into Macy's old room.

Briiinngg briiinnnggg!! Briiinngg briiinnnggg!! I dropped off the bed to see to the phone.

"Hello?"

"Steph?"

"Yeah?"

"It's me."

"Oh my gosh, I've been so worried—are you all right?" My lips trembled.

"Yeah, I'm fine, man. The only thing that's damaged right about now is my heart. I can't bear the thought of losing you."

"You won't! Jason already told me how many years you're looking, and I'll be here waiting for you right the way through. Five years, ten years, I'll be here."

"Promise me, Steph. Your word is all I've got to hold on to."

"I promise. I swear."

I began to sob down the phone. I felt pathetic, idiotic, which I even said so there and then as I became a blubbering mess, wailing like a five-year-old, exposing myself and my love for him like I'd never done to anyone before. I wanted to stop. For the sheer embarrassment and risk to my hard-fought reputation I wanted to stop, but I could not. He begged for me to calm down, but the palpitating squeals kept scratching at my throat in time with my heaving chest. It took a prison officer to interject with "five minutes" for me to calm down enough so I could find out a thing or two about what was going on in the new world of Tyrone.

He was into his second day at Feltham Young Offenders Institution on remand. Disliked his food, but relished the opportunity to be able to work out regularly in the gym. There wasn't much else to do. He was with friends and family also serving time and claimed the only thing he was truly missing was me. That was nice to know. He'd written me a love letter and rhyme verse that was on its way to me.

And he hadn't taken three days to call me; he'd actually called me the day before, however Mum had a go at him and decided not to pass on the message. I was furious about that. After the phone call with Tyrone, I had to uncover my soul tape with 'I Miss you like Crazy' by Natalie Cole to compose my temperament and stop me from destroying Mum's room in the heat of the moment.

CHAPTER SEVENTEEN

A DIFFERENT KIND OF DAY OUT

17ᵗʰ August 1996 – Journey to Feltham

Oh-my-gosh, Di, I'm nervous. Today's the day I get to see my baby, Tyrone. I've missed him so much. Been really worried about how he's coping in there. I know he's got a strong head on him and he ain't gonna let anyone take liberties wiv him, but I still worry. Dere's bare man in pen. All from different ends, so you never know who has beef wiv who just on the basis of where you live, your postcode, and nuffing else. But as I say, Tyrone ain't no eediot. Plus I've been praying for him. Yeah, I fink about God sometimes. Why he took Tyrone from me. I fink about what Dada said about having a debt to society, and dat's what Tyrone's doing. He's paying his debt. And when he comes out, fings will be different. I will be different. He will be different, and we'll both make better choices in life…

The door knocker resonated. I was waiting for a response.

"Who is it?!" boomed from inside some seconds later. Macy's

distorted face appeared from behind the rippled glass of the front door.

"It's me," I replied.

She drew the net curtain that draped over the glass back in its place and opened the door. Ricardo poked his plaited head between her legs, and then squeezed his body through to cuddle his Aunty Stephanie. I carried the cute little bundle of joy inside the house, planting kisses on his face, and took a seat in the front room.

"Mace, you ready?"

"Yeah, let me just get my handbag then we can go."

I glanced at the digital clock on the TV—it was 10:59. By 11:03 we were leaving, about to stroll the hilly roads to Lower Sydenham train station. It was a few weeks after Tyrone's arrest and we were travelling an hour and a half to the shuttle bus that escorted inmates' family, friends and lovers to Feltham prison for young offenders. The journey was bright, the bus well-lit and comfortable.

We disembarked from the shuttle bus, and I stood outside in a sheltered queue. Ricardo swung on the railings watched closely by a prison officer who was monitoring the queue. Macy went into the visitors' waiting room where visitors could purchase confectionary and drinks for the inmates, as well as sit down to fill out a visiting order form.

I moved up in the queue. I thought I looked pretty crisp that day. I had tried my best to. I was sporting a pair of chocolate brown Cerruti jeans, the quality of which was sublime. I paired the chocolate, high-waist jeans with a loose-fitting, white, cotton Mondi shirt that had gold, floral stitching around the collar and on both cuffs that also boasted gorgeous gold buttons with anchors stamped in them. The shirt was tucked into the jeans. Brown patent Shelly shoes Tyrone had bought me completed the look.

"Ricardo!" I called, "Go and get your mum and tell her we're going in soon."

Ricardo happily ran inside the little hut and within minutes his mum came out with a fat, sealed, clear bag brimmed to the top with snacks, confectionary and drinks. She also held the sheet of A5 paper. There were two more families to go in before us. And then we were in.

"Visiting order, please," a sombre-faced prison officer requested. We called them screws. He sat high up behind a bullet-proof windowpane.

Macy slid the visiting slip that we filled in under the window along with her birth certificate. He examined it, flicked through a book and gestured for us to go through. We passed another prison officer on the left. The one on our right sent in the next visitors. We were directed into a cornered area operated by electronic doors. As one door closed, the other door opened to a locker area. We walked down the narrow corridor that had clear planes of glass followed by prison bars on either side. The view past the prison bars were of green fields and building blocks with small gated windows. Some arms and hands clenched on the bars appeared from the gated windows of inmates cells. Macy came to a halt at a set of metal lockers.

"Put all your stuff in here," she said.

"Everything?"

"Yeah, everything."

I tossed my pockets clean. I made sure there weren't any buds of weed in my pockets—a simple mistake I heard many suffered great repercussions from. Once satisfied, I chucked my beige Burberry bag in with Macy's things. Ricardo's hands and face were pressed flat up against the glass, peering out over the fields onto the red brick buildings. Macy pulled him away, gave him that stern look and we walked on to the closed barred door ten yards or so ahead, Ricardo now more subdued.

A door flap was pulled back to reveal a bearded face. He closed the flap promptly. I glanced at Macy thinking, What a facety bwoy. The door opened. He called me in. He pointed at me and gestured for me to come in. I stepped over a high doorstep that nearly tripped me up. Macy and Ricardo followed.

A wooden desk was to the left of the security space. It smelt of fresh polish. Another prison officer sat behind the desk towering over us. He was clean-shaven and had a gut that suggested he might suffer from high cholesterol. Beside the desk were several grey plastic trays.

"'Ave ya got anything on ya?" the meaty prison officer behind the desk asked.

"Nah," I showed him my palms, "I put everyfing in da lockers."

He nodded to the left, an indication that I should move that way to the next point of contact. Now a dark-haired, slim built prison officer with a menacing grimace was standing before me and ran a hand-held metal detector across the lines of my body.

"Keep your arms up and your legs open."

He was close. Barely an inch away from contact, especially the protruding body parts. He signalled for me to move on. Yet another prison officer, mousey haired and long faced, guided me through a self-standing metal detector and out through another door where visitors were seated waiting to see their loved ones. It wasn't long until Ricardo and Macy were out behind me. Nature called me but I held off following the advice of Macy. She said going to the toilet added to their suspicion, and people got strip searched after coming from the bathroom. I held on real strong watching the minutes roll on by. The strain on my bladder became unbearable, and defiantly I surrendered.

"Have they called for us yet?" I questioned when I returned, blotting the remaining moisture from my hands onto my trousers.

Macy didn't look up. She was watching Ricardo playing on a racetrack mat in the kids' play corner. I perched beside her and repeated the question.

"Oh, nah, they 'aven't," she finally said.

We waited in silence, and watched Ricardo. A bashy and familiar voice entered the visitors' waiting room arena. I turned and was faced with Nicola and Lakiesha. They too were dressed up to the nines, having made a serious effort for the recipient of this visit and his fellow inmates. This was the kind of place where details like what your girl was wearing was talked about. These two girls were kitted out in designer trends from head to toe, from Gucci to Dolce & Gabbana. They looked bashy.

"Rah, Steph, you all right?" Nicky said as she bowled up to me with open arms.

"Whassappenin', Nicky, who're yous lot visiting?" I queried and she told me as we were in our embrace.

When we parted, I waved a fleeting hello to Lakiesha, but her arms too came about me and I carried through this charade we often did when greeting one another. I hadn't seen them in a while. I usually only met up with them if I was with Safire or Charlene and either of them was making connections. I didn't get that feeling, that vibe from them that would encourage me to forge a friendship. I didn't have much to say bar, "Wha' gwaan, Lakiesha?" And she spoke using a similar façade. She was always looking out for someone more interesting. She winked flirtatiously at a guy reclined on a chair, his eyes fixed with murderous inclinations. They knew one another as he curled his upper lip menacingly, which was his way of expressing a smile. She was there visiting Darren. Darren?!

"Switch's brovver, Darren?" I exclaimed. She nodded. "What the hell you doing with him?"

"Long story," she said. "Anyway, I hear you're dealing wiv my little Tyrone now—"

"*My* little Tyrone now," I corrected.

"Uh-uhhh! All right, Steph, *your* Tyrone; is that who you're visiting?"

As I was replying yes, another prison officer stepped forward and called out, "Visitors for Tyrone Nana Boateng?"

I put a flickering hand to the ceiling and called on Macy and Ricardo. "I'll see you later, yeah," I cried to Nicky and Lakiesha as we waved goodbye.

The visiting halls looked similar to the interior of a hospital. Everything was structured. Seats and tables numbered. The hall was packed. You could sense the mothers' fear; hear the friends' stories, keeping their allies updated with life on the outside; see the girlfriends huddled up against them, keeping them wanted, loved in a way that they would never experience in there. Their world seemed a hard place, a place that no one would want to come back to, yet many were riding their third and fourth bird.

Macy and I sat on one side of a divided table, Ricardo on my lap snuggling his bony behind into the crest of my thighs. We waited for Tyrone, waited for his unknown state of mind, whether he'd show up happy or sad. Minutes had passed when Tyrone's tall figure appeared. He snaked along the floor towards us with a calm swagger that was captivating. I was overwhelmed by his readily available smile, the glint in his eyes and the confidence of his stride. A luminous orange overtop numbered 421 hung over a light blue T-shirt from where defined limbs dangled loose. His hair was overgrown and uncombed. Almost two weeks since I'd last seen the love of my life and I didn't know whether to laugh or cry.

"Ty, ya all right?" Macy stood to embrace him.

"Yeah I'm cool, man. Just tryna keep my head down in dis place so I can get outta here wivout a long-t'ing. Where's my brovva, couldn't he make it?"

Macy was seated. "Nah, he had to work; he said to say he'll see you weekend."

Tyrone mumbled, "Ah…hmmm," and looked at Ricardo, who was sucking his thumb, and then at me who was sucking my bottom lip. "You all right, Steph?"

"Uh-huh," I hummed nodding my head. My eyes unexpectedly fell into my lap.

"Ricardo!" he cried. "How comes you haven't even said anyfing to your Uncle Ty? What, ain't I your friend anymore? Come here."

Ricardo scrabbled over the table to grasp a hold of him. He gave Tyrone one of his 'pat your back' hugs. That was when Tyrone lost something in his eyes. That usual spark disappeared like stars from the night. It was as though something had just dawned on him.

"You all right?" Macy asked.

The water glazed over his eyes and thickened. "Mace, I don't fink I'm cut out for dis, yanna; I swear…dis place ain't for me." A teardrop swung from left to right within the bottom rim of his eye.

"Oh, Tyrone," Macy oozed a motherly tone, "don't worry, you're gonna be out of here in no time." She got up and wrapped her arms round him, Ricardo beneath, his shoulders jolting whilst his tearful face wedged in the crease of her neck. "Ty, you're gonna get through this but you gotta be strong, you can't let people see your weakness or they'll use it against you."

Ricardo poked his hot head out from beneath his mother's arms. He was sweating and looking at me. Tears gushed down my face. He then looked back at his uncle whose shoulders bounced uncontrollably. He looked as though he was wandering into some far place beyond the general knowledge that his scant years on earth had provided.

I wiped the tears from my eyes as I looked across at his puzzled face. Macy eased up off Tyrone and I gazed at his flushed and dampened face, and he at mine. We entered a moment that we'd entered many times before. Macy reached into our moment taking a bewildered Ricardo from Tyrone. She kissed him on the cheek saying, "I'm gonna leave you lot to have some time together. Steph, I'll be waiting outside," at which Ricardo started to ball his eyes out. I watched, but didn't say much. I wasn't sure what I was thinking or why I was crying.

As Macy and Ricardo took off, a part of me wished for them to stay. I didn't know what to say and felt as though I should. Our eyes locked into an embrace and I was held firm by his gaze. The palm of his hands clasped with mine into the prayer position, our fingers gravitated and locked with such comfort and precision they become as one. Nothing had been said since Macy's departure.

"Did you get my letter?" he asked some time later.

I thought about the letter, his cry for my companionship, presence and love; his expression of his frustration and irritation of being in there, the resentment he had for the place and the regret he had for his crimes. The more I thought about the letter, the more I became besieged by a sadness I'd come to know and detest. I wept and nodded my head.

"If I'm to have strength at all in this place, I need to know that you're all right and not crying because of me."

I didn't know how to reassure him of that, so didn't. I couldn't lie bare-faced. I sat down and we shared smiles. We fell into conversations of life outside those walls, my schooling situation sitting tightly on a question mark, and how much we loved each other. Then a prison officer walked by at a pace that seemed musically in tune with a wedding song whistled for effect, and tapped Tyrone on the shoulder.

He then moved onto the next table and disappointed that inmate and visitor with a blunt indication of 'time's up'.

Tyrone and I stared at each other knowing it was time to part but not ready to make that move. He held my hand, massaged my palms and stroked my fingers. He stared intensely into my watery eyes.

"You're gonna be all right," he insisted.

"So are you," I reciprocated.

Lunging forward he kissed me unexpectedly, holding me tight though his kiss was soft; lips of tender care, tongue of patience—bliss. Simultaneously our eyes opened. I cradled his head like a baby. He was my Tyrone and I didn't want to let him go. Another prison officer, or maybe the same one, came over and patted Tyrone's shoulder a second time and spoke in his ear. "All right, sonny boy, say your goodbyes."

We did as he said. Reluctantly we disconnected as I stepped away. He pulled me back by my arm and whispered, "I love you more than life, please don't let me down."

I told him what I knew to be true, deep in all the chambers of my heart. "I won't." I turned for the exit and heard my name bellowed from the other side of the room turning the heads of all the remaining prisoners and visitors. It was Damien. He looked different, bearing long thick locks of curly black hair. I waved to him reminded of the petrol station robbery that we all part-took in, and the petty local shop robbery that they were both serving time for. He was sitting next to his brother opposite Lakiesha and Nicola. I looked back at Tyrone, waved and left.

"You ready for that journey back home?" Macy checked.

"Ready as I'll ever be."

And we journeyed back home almost in silence.

CHAPTER EIGHTEEN

MOVING ON

19th July 1998 – My New Home

Hey Di, how're you doing? I know it's been a long time, and to tell you the truth I did forget about you for a little bit. I hope that doesn't make you feel bad, but like…I've just had too much to deal with over the past couple of years. I know, I know…what's new? But on the real, the kind of shake-ups I was dealing with this time round, I hadn't dealt with before. So I've had to learn to move on from a lot of things and people to limit the drama because I wanna be different. I think I have to be different if I'm to survive this. I can't really deal with the despair any more. I feel like I've only got two roads open to me now and I know I'm taking the right one, but God willing I'll continue to take the right one coz there's a lot of crossroads on this path I'm realising.

I'm sixteen now and I've decided I wanna go to college. Well, I decided that a little while ago when Mum told me I wasn't gonna amount to anything because they expelled me from Lee High School after two weeks of 'careful consideration' after the incident with Mr Williams' son. I was happy anyway because that school wasn't doing me any favours. My reputation meant that I had too much peer pressure to fight unnecessarily. I was living up to other people's expectation of me and drawing blood in the process. It's this kind of reputation and hype that keep rappers in war with one another; and now I've lost one of my favourite rappers, Biggie Smalls. He got smoked early last year by some west-coast brer during that whole east vs. west-coast hip hop warfare. It's all long.

In my tuition centre, which is where they've put me (they ruled out trying me for another school after two schools refused to accept me), there're only two other pupils in my class. And they're cool, not inna the hype, just there to learn. I'm not in the mix again. We barely talk to one another in class, let alone argue, let alone fight—that's how I like it these days. I'm starting to understand myself a bit: when I argue I feel like I wanna fight, when I fight I feel like I wanna do some serious damage to my opponent, so therefore I don't wanna fight, and to avoid that I need to avoid intense arguments. I guess it was Mum that made me see that...

A year before I had spent my last night under Mum's roof, I was working night shifts, getting paid cash in hand at a factory in Deptford packing envelopes. I was trying to get paid the right way, without robbery or thievery. Of course I was earning peanuts, less than the minimum wage, but I was earning my keep and that I valued immensely.

It was one of those nights when I'd finally earned the right to say 'I've had a long day'. I had been at the tuition centre prepping for my GCSEs from 11 a.m. to 4 p.m., then started my night shift at 5 p.m., clocking out at midnight. The day had been long, though my temperament short. I peered out the window of the bus on my way home looking forward to entering my own space, having no one to talk at me but the TV as it watched my eyelids flutter to a close. The entire week had zapped my energy, the world had been set to mourn the death of Princess Diana, and I too mourned with most of the world's population. My mood was contaminated.

"Manor Road!" the bus driver announced.

I stepped off the bus. Shattered. My hands cried pangs from paper cuts that opened up to reveal the inside of my flesh dare I clenched on to something. Paper-cuts were a bitch! I stumbled through the rotting wooden gate. The grass in the front garden had sprouted up to the proportions of a corn field, as it often did in the summer.

Inside the house, I closed the door almost silently, dragging my feet up the stairs with obvious intentions for my bed. Opening my bedroom door to find Mum sprawled across the bottom bunk watching TV wasn't amusing.

"Your dad called," she said.

"Fanks. Mum, do you mind coming out now? I'm tired and want my bed." I was held up by the door frame, my eyes practically closing right there where I leant.

"I'll come out when I'm good and ready. This is my house."

I was a rogue fifteen year old. It wasn't often that someone took the piss with me, but what was I to do? More importantly, what did she expect me to do? I was intolerable, violent and a short-tempered teenager who had stabbed, sliced, punched, baseball-batted, kicked and smashed people's heads in. And there I was being treated like what we sometimes called a 'chief', a 'bone-head', a damn-right folly.

I sat on the floor in silence trying to manage my disposition. I knew she sensed I was feeling cantankerous. She noticed my dipped brow, weary posture and overall distress and yet she remained obtuse. I rose to my feet, ignoring my conscience that warned me to settle down and refrain from any actions that might provoke Mum. But I was a teenage delinquent with zero tolerance and I no longer feared my mum; I had long become immune to her violence.

I turned off the TV as she lay there looking at me. I wondered if she'd make her attack as I grabbed hold of it, but even the thought wasn't enough to stop me. I carried the TV downstairs and waited. I knew my actions would cause a stir and a stir I intended to cause. How else could I express my torment? Verbal communication tended to end in one way with Mum if she disliked what you said. It was actions that spoke volumes in our house. It was actions that communicated anguish, desire and frustration. I waited…

"*Stephaniiee!*" she screeched. "Bring that television back in here NOW!"

I did nothing. Just sat. And waited. Then I heard: BOOFF! BUP! BADUP! BUP!!!

She smashed my room into pieces. I didn't care. I felt the grounds for my actions were justified, as Mum felt with hers. Knowing she was being fired up fired me up even more.

I headed for the passageway leaving my TV on the bottom stair. All I needed was my school bag with my books and a few clothes and underwear to get me through the week. All I needed was to get past her, get my things and go. But hesitation held me on the bottom stair as I heard Mum cuss aloud. Finally her pace softened and she began to calm down, which I took as my cue to get my things and leave. I crept up the stairs soon reaching the landing where I gingerly peeked round the white banister. She sat on the edge of my bed, her bowed head resting in her hands.

"Mum, I'm just getting my fings and then I'm leaving."

I was about to get up from the stairs when she set her eyes on me and made a dash in my direction. She was so quick I didn't quite see her coming. I mean, I saw her move from her position on the bed, and then all of a sudden I felt her hands in my hair pulling me up from where I knelt on my hands and knees. I gripped onto her wrists, scrambled up to my feet trying to ease her grip on my hair, which was slicked into a ponytail, the ends bushed out like the curled leaves of parsley with stems gathered by an elastic band.

She propelled me around the room by my hair and managed to land sporadic blows into my head at the same time. I fought to keep a grip of her wrists, to stop her fingers becoming tangled in my hair and her blows knocking me unconscious. I fought to suppress the urge to reach into my bottom drawer for my penknife and end this circus show. I was a bit wobbly but when I saw my school bag scrunched up at the side of my bed, I went for it. I tore my hair away from her grip screaming, "Get off my hair!"

She replied, "You t'ink you is dis bad somebuddy, huh?!"

"Get off my hair!" I continued to scream.

She too screamed, and threw blows into my head advising me I should have just gone to bed. Her eyes were furious. I was familiar with those detached set of eyes. I had worn them myself many times before. I tried my best not to look at her and focused on getting out of there. I grabbed my school bag and packed the necessary things from the tall chest of drawers next to my bed as quickly as I could. Though her hands were free from my hair, her voice still fought me. Whilst I was bent over my task, she cursed for the world to hear. I wanted to request that she 'shut the fuck up!' but the sight of her stopped me from doing so. She looked almost demonic.

A heavy blow struck the back of my head taking me down and off my feet. An old-school JVC stereo system with two tape decks and a record player dismantled from her throw and landed by my feet. I held the back of my head screaming for the devil to take her back to the hell from where she came. Blood ran down my hand that held the wound. Mum screamed 'bloodclaats' and 'bombaclaats' and all told me about my 'pussyclaat'. She told me about my 'puppa' and how she wished she weren't my 'mumma'...Soon her voice fizzled out.

The pain at the back of my head alleviated but I was experiencing a rage I'd rarely felt before. And it was all for my mother. The person who had brought me into the world, whom I was supposed to love unconditionally. Something erupted. My conscience turned bitter, begged me to kill, begged me to go all out and have no mercy, directed me to the six-inch penknife in my bottom drawer, told me it was OK to do so.

I leaped up and like a bull I raged into her, taking her off her feet, but something guided me and, forgetting the penknife, my hands brought machine-like blows into her legs. And though her clenched fist came at my head from above, I couldn't feel or hear a thing. Tiredness eventually stopped the detached repetition of my blows to her legs. I heaved to the demand of my thumping heart. She panted pathetically beneath my hovering body. I looked at her. Her lips quivered and mouthed words. Still I heard nothing. A single tear scrolled down my face and floated at the opening of my lips. I wiped away the rebellious runaway tear.

Realisation settled in. I had hit my mum. After all the beatings I had incurred from her throughout my life, I had finally hit her back. I had heard stories at school from English counterparts of them swearing and hitting out at their mum, but that was something you just didn't do in the Caribbean culture. But right then it felt so right and I knew I wouldn't allow her to lay her hands on me again. I left that day knowing I'd never return.

I moved in with Charlene, and shared the small bedroom she occupied in a hostel with another seven occupants. Unemployed and kicked out of education, life's prospects were limited. She tried a few times to get on board the system and get through college, but the challenges of submitting to authority were too great for her to adhere. When I called that night from a telephone box with my TV and rucksack in hand, she welcomed me like most sisters would. We grew closer in the time I lived with her. We shared a single bed, split the food bill, shopped together, raved together, visited Feltham Prison together, fought together and laughed together.

I moved on again after seven months at Charlene's and this time I went back to Dada's house because things weren't too bad there before. Nina was doing her last year at college, Melvin still had a good few years to go in prison and Dada was just, well, cool. We addressed the outcome of my boyfriend, and I accepted he was right. Dada respected my acceptance and we were back to normal, but after two months there my dad stepped in, giving me the choice of going to live with him or go back to Mum's. No way was I going back there, and Dad's didn't seem too appealing either—too regimented, too strict. I turned to Macy and she was receptive to me living with her. I shared Ricardo's room, which was cool for me and fun for him.

Things were back on track at the tuition centre I attended. I got sacked from my factory work for bad attendance, but Macy had lined up a few of her friends for me to do their hair because I was good at it and it was a good little earner for me. During this period, Safire and Mum's relationship further dismantled and Safire too left home off the back of a violent exchange of words and physical exertion. Safire spent a short stint at Charlene's hostel before being housed in her own hostel accommodation.

Four months into my stay at Macy's, Tyrone was released after serving sixteen months in prison. We were still together, had communicated regularly through letters, phone calls and visits. I had remained loyal and a virgin as I said I would. Nothing had really changed between us, though everything had changed around us.

It was two weeks after my sixteenth birthday when Tyrone and I were babysitting whilst Macy and Jason went out for dinner and a movie in the West End. Once Ricardo had eaten his dinner and had a bath, we put him to bed. Cuddling up on the sofa, we watched Love Jones, kissed, watched the movie and kissed some more folded into each other's arms and caress. I didn't want it to end. Even when Tyrone started touching me in places he'd never touched me before, I still didn't want it to end. I knew where it was going and I didn't mind. He told me how much he loved me, how he'd never leave me, how much he appreciated my loyalty and that he would never be disloyal to me, that he would do anything for me, which meant never going back to jail.

"Should I get a condom?" he asked.

Why not? I was ready to do it with him, I wanted to do it with him, only him, I loved him and knew then that he would be the one I'd marry and have kids with in the future when I had graduated and he would be settled into a good job. The next place I would rest my head needed to be permanent.

"Yeah," I replied.

My answer sent a beam across his face and he held me tightly against his chest, and kissed me softly but with intense love as though it was our last kiss.

After a difficult initiation we made passionate and sensitive love for the next half hour. I felt happy, glad that the deed had been done, especially as he was going away again. His mum and dad had planned a trip for him to go to New York for a month to stay with family, get away and get his head around things. He didn't want to go, didn't want to go without me, but I convinced him it was a good thing, that it would do him good. Though I'd miss him greatly, I had missed him greatly for sixteen months, so one more wasn't going to hurt anyone. Or so I thought.

It turned out that his parents and Jason didn't plan for Tyrone to return, were providing just a one-way ticket into the land of opportunities. Macy didn't tell me until a week after his departure. I was heartbroken. The muscle tissue around my heart felt torn and bruised. How could my sister do that to me? Sit there with silent lips whilst Jason and his family plotted to take away the only person who had ever loved me back in the same way that I had loved him?

I had to leave. I couldn't live there any longer with Jason, seeing Tyrone in him and knowing that he wasn't coming back and he didn't even know it yet. But I didn't know where to go, and went to social services with a black bag and told them of my homelessness, telling them in no uncertain terms that I couldn't go back to Mum's.

*

It felt good to know I had a permanent abode. My new home was in Woolwich. The house was relatively big with a basement converted into a living area where I resided. My bedroom was a decent size, homely and comfortable.

Right then, it was a Sunday afternoon in the summer of ninety-eight, two months since I'd left Macy's. I was chilling, reclined across my new bedspread which matched my curtains. I had set my clothes rail that was packed with designer gear parallel to my bed. Resting on one of the bedside tables, a wooden lamp beamed light over my head and onto my diary. The other bedside table held my TV and stood across the room by a chest of drawers where I had laid out all my perfumes and toiletries. I shared the living room and bathroom with Daniel, the other child that lived there with me. His bedroom was down the hall. He was all right.

I was now a foster child. And though eerie to me, and embarrassing for my family, as a new identity I was as cool as can be about it.

...Everyting's cris now. I'm feeling good about this experience because I can sense the change, the difference that has been made. I've spent a lot of time away from my family and friends figuring out this change; why I feel it coming and what I feel I need to do. Yeah, it is a bit blurred, but I know I just gotta follow my instincts on this coz that's what my instincts are telling me. I pray a lot these days...you know, for Tyrone's safety, happiness and to make sure that he remembers me. I haven't heard from him, so have no idea what the deal is, but yeah, I pray for him anyway...I pray for him nuff, my peop's and me. I haven't even seen Shariece, Maria or René in a little while... I miss my bredrens at times. But I know I can't concentrate properly on what I need to do when I see people, my bredrens and that. But Claudia, my foster carer, is the nicest person you'd ever meet. She's got one of them auras that just warm to you instantly. I loved her vibe the moment I set eyes on her. We've had the deep conversations that I usually reserve for you, Di, but the way she made me feel so comfortable, interesting and loved, I couldn't help but relay my life stories.

She's told me a lot of stuff about herself as well. How her mum left her and went to Jamaica when she was like only 13 and she had to fend for herself. We've got a lot in common, Claudia and me. She tells me things like I can be anything I wanna be, which I've always felt, but at times doubted myself because I didn't really get the reassurance I needed. Dad would always say 'make sure you graduate from university' but he wouldn't really know how to best go about it apart from just telling me to go to school. Claudia really listens to me. When I want to cry but my pride doesn't let me, she holds me tight and rubs my back we both stand in silence. I tell of her of my violent ways and she tells me she understands and I don't need to explain. I don't understand where this woman has come from; I didn't know human beings could be this way. I didn't know people loved like this, gave like this to people like me outside of family parameters. I wish I'd had this from the start. I wonder what type of person I would be if I had...

"Steph!" Claudia's voice propelled down the stairs, pushing open my bedroom door and broke through the sound of 2Pac's 'Dear Mama' song that resonated from my speakers. "Your dinner's ready!" She cried.

I closed my diary and went up the stairs. Claudia was sitting across a lace dressed, mahogany table serving a mixed salad on to her plate with a variation of Caribbean food.

"Where's Daniel?" I asked.

"He's spending time with his family today so won't be back till late," she replied lifting her heavy dreadlocks that hung at her front so that it lay flat across her back down to her buttocks. "Come on, sit down and eat," she urged, "whilst you're beautiful as you are, a few more pounds on you will make you look healthier." She often highlighted my slender frame as both an admirable trait and a cause for concern. Neither of which I minded as I was content with my 26 inch waist.

With the salad clasped between two wooden spoons, she gestured for me to have some salad. "Yes please," I said taking my seat opposite her and settling down to eat.

CHAPTER NINETEEN

TRIAL AND ERROR

25th September 1998 – South-east London, 54 bus on way home

Hey Di, guess what? I passed all my GCSEs—only got to take 5 but hey-ho—and Claudia has agreed to pay for ten driving lessons for me! I know...that's proper cool, right? My start at college has been nuts, still. Obviously I had to choose to go to a college outside of my manor if I'm to avoid living up to that little rep of mine. But as per usual, it's like no matter where I go, Di, trouble seems to send a search party out for me and at some point find me. There's me trying to keep my head down, going to class and avoiding hanging out in the corridors as most students do in my college at breaks an' before class, and some eediot girls start staring me down like they wanna move to me. I say eediot because whenever I saw them without one another neither of them would look at me. Di, you of people know what I'm like. So I'm there thinking how the hell am I gonna avoid this situation getting violent. Because the first thing I thought of doing was going straight up to them and asking 'what?' as in like 'what the fuck are you looking at?' but then I thought that they're likely to respond 'what' back, as in like 'what the fuck are you looking at?' and my response thereafter was likely to be a beating, and I didn't wanna do that. I don't wanna get angry and out of control like I used to. I don't wanna compromise my education, let myself down. And Claudia, coz she believes in me right now. So I turned to Claudia. I told her exactly how I was feeling and this is what I said:

"These girls are tryna threaten my position and I feel to tear them all down to make 'em know that I'm not the one they're gonna try and have like dat." I told her exactly how I was gonna bowl up to them questioning what their problems were, and if their attitudes weren't right then it would be 'on'.

"Where's the change?" Claudia asked, and I explained that it's in the chances. I explained that me not moving to them straight away demonstrated some change but Claudia explained differently. She said: "Change comes from you, not what you expect from others. Try and deal with how you respond to your emotions before you think about how other people should respond to you."

I was trying. But these girls came to disrespect me, not the other way round. So why should I hold back from giving them a beating and teaching them the lesson? Which is what I said to her, and she replied: "Well, who are you trying to save, you or them?" Well me of course! I thought, and she continued, "Well, focus on you, and let God deal with them."

And only then did it make any sense. I mean...

suddenly my instincts came alive again and I felt as though God was reaching out to me, teaching me and I felt open to it. I went to my room, opened my bible and came across this: "Do not ye yet understand, that whatsoever entereth in at the mouth goeth into the belly, and is cast out into the draught? But those things which proceed out of the mouth come forth from the heart, and they defile the man. For out of the heart proceed evil thoughts, murders, adulteries, fornications, thefts, false witness, blasphemies: These are the things which defile a man, but to eat with unwashen hands defileth not a man." Matthew 15:17-20

I thought about it and what I had just said to Claudia, the things my mind cooked up for my hands to follow. I thought about one of the Bible verses Mum had me write a million times: "Wherefore, my beloved brethren, let every man be swift to hear, slow to speak, slow to wrath: For the wrath of man worketh not the righteousness of God..." James 1:19-20

I'm not tryna be righteous, but I do wanna feel at ease and just not so angry. I don't wanna think as devilish in harming people as I do at times. I cried myself to sleep with little understanding as to why, probably due to the frustration, but I felt better after. The next day and days that followed I tried this new tactic of steady breathing and counting in my head, then I started reminding myself that their issues aren't mine, as I have too many of my own to focus on. Slowly I started to realise that they weren't even watching me anymore.

An impulse prompted me to look up from where I sat at the back of the bus. I looked out of the window to see that my two hour bus journey had nearly come to an end and the next stop would be mine. Gathering up my things, I jumped off the bus in Woolwich's centre and strolled up Burrage Road to the place I now considered my home. I entered the white, semi-detached, bay-windowed house where Claudia and Daniel were chilling in the living-room, each sprawled out on a sofa.

"Evening!" I cried.

"Hello sweetheart," Claudia replied.

"You all right?" Daniel said, not really wanting to know if I was OK but resorting to the mechanical way of greeting.

"Steph," Claudia called, "your dad phoned."

"Is it? What did he say?" I took off my grey Calvin Klein boots I had bought in the sale at Pied à Terre, followed by a grey and white Armani sports cardigan, which I hung up on the banister, and entered the living room.

"He said just call him when you get the message." I wondered why he didn't just call me on my mobile and stop being a cheapskate.

The TV displayed white and blue lights across the small living room area. The side of Daniel's face highlighted highly defined bone structure. His cheekbones barked character and pinpointed a strong African lineage. The other side of his face was absorbed into the darkness. The TV showed the scene of an eighties London setting, a cockney white woman cussing after a white bloke hanging out with a crowd of black guys, some of whom wore dreadlocks.

"What's this?" I queried. I perched my behind on the sofa Claudia was laying across and rested my head on her belly.

"*Babylon*," Daniel said, his tone ringing with patois. "Yuh see it yet?"

"When I was young, but I can't 'member much of it." I snuggled up closer with Claudia, playing with the tips of her crinkled dreadlocks, which had shells and other gold accessories embedded in it.

"Do you mind? You're taking up the whole chair, missus," she teased.

I snuggled up closer. My mobile chimed. "Pass my bag please, Daniel?"

Daniel rose to grab my black Ralph Lauren bag, pausing at the sight of the label as he did with most of my designer gear. I hadn't lost the desire for designer things despite the end of my criminal affairs that acquired much of them. Now I saved my monthly allowance and the money I earned through my private hairdressing work to buy a new item every now and then. Finally he handed the bag over after Claudia pressed on him to do so.

"Hello?"

"Hey babes..." It was Shariece. As with most Fridays, she wanted to know if I was up for hitting the clubs. I was a raver; one of the youngest on the raving scene that incorporated jungle music, house, garage, and drum and base, and drug use. And although I had made the decision to give it a miss for a while, I missed it all tremendously and relished the opportunity of getting back into it, though I had made a decision not to mess around with Ecstasy again. Friday meant the Coliseum down in Vauxhall, which, with my girl, equalled unparalleled fun.

At 22:35 I was dressed and ready entering the living room clad in a floor-length, black, body-hugging Karen Millen dress and square, black, open-toed Roberto Cavalli mules. My hair was tied up into a ponytail with ringlets hanging loose from its centre. My make-up was neutral and sparse.

"Well, look at Miss Johnson," Claudia voiced musically. She got to her feet and requested that I gave her a twirl. I did so theatrically. "Steph, you look so ravishing."

"Ravishing?" I repeated.

"Yes, ravishing...delicately beautiful—doesn't she, Daniel?"

Daniel looked up at me in awe with his seventeen year old eyes from where he lay immersed in the darkness of the room. "Yes, yuh is looking fine, Steph, truly like a fine princess—trus'!"

"Ah, thanks Daniel. That's very sweet. Claudia, do you think I could get my allowance money now instead of tomorrow?"

She gave me an indulgent look and then rummaged through her huge handbag at the side of the chair muttering, "I thought we agreed I would write you a cheque monthly." She pulled her purse out. "Here, I've only got fifty, I'll write the rest out in the cheque I'm to give you."

"Thanks." My phone rang. The curtain lit up. The lights of a car pierced through the night. I quickly pursed the £50. "That must be Shariece, I'll see you guys in the morning. Clauds, I'll probably stay at Shariece's house."

"As long as that's OK with her mum, but make sure you phone me when you get there and first thing in the morning, please?"

"Yeah, I will."

"And, Steph?"

I paused, my brow raised and neck extended. "Yeah?"

"Are we going to sort out your CV this weekend so you can start handing it out to retailers?"

I peeped down at the missed call on my phone. "OK, we'll do it tomorrow—thanks." I placed a kiss on her soft mahogany cheek, said goodbye and then made an exit clutching onto my small handbag and overnight bag.

Shariece was standing at the back of her relatively new R-registration Renault Clio, popping open the boot as I stepped down onto the pavement. Claudia and Daniel peeked out at us from behind the drawn curtain. I could hear them muttering. Shariece waved animatedly to them, her many bangles, dangling earrings and draping gold necklace jingling in the process.

That night she wore a stunning hot pink Versace dress with the signature safety pin and a fuchsia pink pair of Jimmy Choo shoes. As always, she looked striking. Like a million dollars.

Daniel and Claudia continued to watch us from the window. I could tell that Daniel was fixated by the vision of Shariece. I slammed the boot shut and climbed into the front of the Clio where Shariece joined me.

"Hey babe," she said kissing my cheek with excessive gloss coated lips, "you ready to rave?"

"'Course!" I bared my teeth with excitement.

"Safire called," Shariece informed me. "I have to pick her and Stella up from her hostel." She reversed hastily round a corner almost licking over a lamppost.

"Shariece! Take it easy, man."

"I'm cool, I'm cool."

Nervous about the car ride I tried to change the subject: "Is Charlene going by the way?"

"Yeah," she hooked a lock of hair over her ear, "she's coming with Nicky—"

"She's out?"

"Yeah, didn't your sister tell you?"

"I haven't really spoken to any of them except Macy in a little while." I didn't realise how long it had been since I'd spoken to my sisters. At least a couple of months. And I certainly didn't know that Nicky was out of prison.

"Oh, OK. Well, Nicky should be coming, Lakiesha and I think your cousin Joanne, but they're making their own way—Nicky's driving now."

"What's she driving?" I asked and mentally retracted the question for fear of appearing covetous, but it was too late.

"A Puma; she drives a Ford Puma."

We raced down the South Circular on the way to Safire's hostel in Lewisham.

*

The rave was jamming. All my people were in there: my sisters Charlene and Safire, cousins Joanne, Jermaine, Leroy, and Stella, and brethrens Shariece, René and Maria who I hadn't seen in a little while. As Shariece had informed me Nicky was there too having been released from prison. She was with Lakiesha who it was also nice to see. I saw Sean and Donavan—I hadn't seen them much since I left Lee High School.

"It's so good to see you, Steph, man" Sean said as he embraced me ruggedly so that I would almost fall over from my heels.

Donavan put out his fist to nudge me as though I was still the boisterous twelve year old they considered as one of the man-dem. Though I had grown up somewhat since then and carried a look of sophistication, I nudged him with a childish grin and my neck leant to the side. These moments I embraced because of the memories I attached to them that though were filled with pain, were also filled with fun and laughter. MJ Cole's Sincere track filled the room and arms flew up in the air as the crowd got down on dance floor. White, blue and green lights spiked through the dark space and I grabbed Shariece's hand as we swung our hips and shoulders to the rhythm.

Later in the night when I was dancing wildly with Stella to Kelly Le Roc's My Love, a pair of hands grabbed my waist from behind. It was Typo accompanied by Manic. "What's happening gangsta, man?" Typo said hanging his arm around my shoulder.

"Hey Typo! What's happening man?" I replied continuing my wild dance in front of him. We caught up briefly in motion, Typo informing me of Switch coming out of prison soon before moving on to dance and catch up with Stella. I embraced Manic who appeared unusually indifferent to me. We danced for a bit anyhow, though I noted that something had changed with him and he was reserved about it.

The night projected good vibes. The late nineties garage tunes had us raving hard. Cristal and Courvoisier were being drunk in great quantities. Drugs were circulating, though I'd made the decision to not take E's anymore. I was content with a spliff and my drink. The experience of the rush E's gave people didn't appeal to me as it had done in the past. A couple of hours had past when Charlene and I were at the bar, Shannon and Taniqua bounced past almost bouncing into me. This move would have been purposeful, and though I felt the urge to respond, I held onto my lip fast and held my hand to calm my nerve.

"What, Steph, is it on?" Charlene asked.

I didn't want it to be on, and certainly not by my starting. I looked at Shannon who seemed open for confrontation, but not so keen to initiate anything. "Nah, 'llow it man," I responded, "Let's just enjoy ourselves. I'm not even pandering to these eediots. It's long, Charlene." And with that I took my glass of wine and walked back to where our people were. I was defining my own path now, thinking through the aftermath of the choices I was faced with and choosing the path that served me best.

*

The following day I laid across the sofa at home in deep thought, reliving the night before through my hazy recollection and enjoying every minute of it. Later on I would call Shariece and live through it again, hearing her perspective on the night and planning when we'd do it all again.

"Steph!" Claudia's voice frightened me.

"Yeah!" I said trying to collect myself and slow down my racing heart.

"It's twelve o'clock, are you ready?" She was looking at me with my headscarf on sprawled on her sofa.

"Give me ten minutes, Clauds. Let me get my shoes and neaten my hair" I got up and went downstairs to my basement room.

"Please hurry up because I've got things to do after, you know."

"Ten minutes," I repeated flashing both hands with pointed fingers that counted ten, and then bolted down the stairs.

I pulled my headscarf off my head. My hair was slicked neatly into a ponytail with loosely hung curls, which was the aftermath of last night's affair. I then grabbed my CV's that Claudia was going to accompany me to hand out in retail stores in Woolwich. Despite the fact I was hung over, I felt confident and good about the prospect of securing a weekend job off the back of today. I materialised at the top of the stairs to see Claudia leaning up against the lilac wall in the hallway. She was draped in African fabric and had an African headwrap around her waist-length dreadlocked hair.

"Have you got your CVs—are you ready to do this?" she queried.

"Yes."

"OK, let's go so you can get back in time for your driving lesson." And with that we were off.

CHAPTER TWENTY

POSSIBILITIES

18th June 1999 – 54 bus

Hey Di. I hope you're well. I'm cool, just thinking about the possibilities. I think I'm dating again. It's a bit too soon to say, but I like him and I'm conscious you probably won't approve, but if you knew him like I do, you'd know he tries. We're all on our own journeys. I get dat now more than ever. My journey is one about ownership and choices. I'm trying to own my choices in life so I can steer my own ship to the destiny of my choosing, y'get me? He's still trying to figure out his interests and who he is, but I think I can help him do that...

Woolwich was only a bus ride away from the manor where I grew up and where most my family and friends were still based. I was close enough to see them when I wanted, and far enough to detach myself if necessary, meditate longer on establishing who I was and who I wanted to be. I could allow my character to flourish without the peer pressure from before. Plus the long bus journeys provided me with ample amounts of time to document and evaluate my thoughts and experiences.

It was the entering of summer in 1999. I had boarded the 54 bus at Woolwich en route to my sister Macy's house due to babysit my nephew Ricardo who I hadn't spent quality time with in a little while. Seventeen years old and finally starting to enjoy the day to day living of life. I did well on my art course at college, creativity served my energy well, and I secured a weekend job in retail. First I started at a small fashion store in Woolwich and quickly moved to a larger outlet in the West End. It was only the week before that I had broken up for the summer holidays and met up with Shariece. She picked me up outside my college surprising me with her new car. The fact that she also looked eye-pleasingly hot and sophisticated only added to her appeal. That day she rocked her fuchsia pink Jimmy Choos with three-quarter length grey trousers and a pink and grey twin set. She also wore a pair of Versace sun shades that carried off the whole look. I looked good too. I wore a fitted floral dress that came just above the knee. I had on my Kurt Geiger baby blue strappy kitten heels, which matched the base colour in my dress. Upon seeing Shariece roll up on my college street in a silver MG that was only a year old, I pulled my Prada shades from my bag and added lip-gloss to my lips. Impressed. Shariece exuded swagger. I circled the car like the authority.

"Where did you get this from? It's cris'?" I exerted.

"Do you really like it, babe?"

"Yes!" I said, feeling a glint of the green eye, "I like your whole look today. You're looking fly, Shy."

She smiled wildly as she popped open the boot so I could put my portfolios in. "I sold the Clio and got a top-up from my man."

"Man?! What man? How comes I don't know about him? Are you keeping secrets from me, Shariece?" I said with both arms up in the air in a questioning way.

Her giggle fell into a full throaty laughter as she couldn't retain her joy. She opened the driver's seat door. "Get in babe."

"Come on, tell me. I'm your best-friend you have to tell me...come on Shariece, tell me!"

"Get in Steph and I'll tell you but you promise not to laugh."

"OK, I promise," I smiled and boarded the car.

"It's Sean."

"Who's Sean?"

"Sean Sean. Like Donavan and Sean from School."

My eyes widened. Shariece was dealing with bean head Sean from our secondary school. This was too funny, but I promised I wouldn't laugh. "Oh my gosh...how did that happen?"

"I don't know, Steph. We exchanged numbers when we saw each other at Coliseum ages ago...you know that time when all of us were there. It was only supposed to be a bredren thing, but we just get on so well. We talked and talked for hours, laughed till we were crying.

"Oh my days... Well, what can I say babe? I'm happy for you. If you're happy, I'm happy. Seriously, I'm really pleased for you."

"Yeah Steph, we just talk about so many things..."

I gazed out at the scenery as we drove through Streatham with the roof down. My mind started to wonder off into thoughts of Tyrone, wondering what he was doing, whether he had thought of me, still felt anything for me...that kind of thing. I still held feelings for him, still loved him dearly and prayed that he would contact me one day and things would go back to how it was. At that point Shariece noticed I had stopped listening.

"Steph! Keep up with me. Yeah, so because I work in an estate agency now and he's studying business, I was advising him to invest his money in property and things like that. Then I found we kept talking about business opportunities, exploring how much we wanted the same things, but we still were more like bredrens until I met his mum at that same yard in Ghetto, a couple blocks from Tyrone's, and she like proper loved me off, Steph, you know like how my mum would cook you dinner or how your mum would cook me up soup if I were sick?"

"Don't even talk about my mum." The thought of her just jarred my head. I would have just preferred to pretend I didn't have a mother.

"What, you two still not talking? That's just silly, Steph, that's your mother." I hated it when Shariece got all serious on me.

We were driving through Brixton when Shariece added, "...it was only a few months ago that we had our first open proper kiss and since then he's been calling me his girl and I've been calling him my man."

I was truly happy for her but just couldn't stop thinking about Ty. Shariece gauged this and said, "Steph, I know you're still in love with Tyrone, but I'm sorry, it's been over a year and he hasn't contacted you—you've gotta move on now, consider other possibilities. Look how cris' you are! You're a beautiful seventeen-year-old girl who hasn't even properly looked at another man, let alone kissed another man since your one love, Tyrone. Do you think he hasn't looked at another girl, kissed another girl and slammed another girl since you?" I gulped. I didn't think of that as a possibility. The idea of Ty being with another girl was just too hurtful. "I just don't want you to waste your time on something that may never happen." She continued, "You're my best friend, man, I don't like seeing you hurt."

I smiled. I got her point and wanted to know where we were going. She blushed, and let spill. "For a drink up at Alexandra Palace. Meet some interesting skeety-ballers, and then take it from there."

"But I thought you're loved up with Sean?"

"I am. The skeety-ballers are for you, my dear."

I liked the idea of meeting a good looking, tall, athletic man. I exposed my mercury fillings to her, so great was my beam...

A drunken man sat beside me on the 54 bus. My thoughts were distracted. The stench of his odour sickened me. I got up from the back seat of the bus with my overnight bag, handbag and diary wedged under my arm. I headed upstairs, exhaled deeply and found a seat right at the front. Rah, I'm in Lewisham already, I thought. I made a mental note that I needed to get off the bus after five stops, then took my thoughts back to the scenes of my most recent event with Shariece.

...So there I was thinking about skeety ballers as we proceeded up the hill on approach to 'Ally Pally' where top-notch glistening cars had assembled. And it was there that we saw the skeety-ballers. Well at least in looks. The sun was scorching. My skin had darkened on the ride up there. Upon parking, it appeared the show began. We strutted up the stairs as though we were on a catwalk, conversed for the sake of it. Scratch that, more so for the scene. We made ourselves visibly noticeable, confidence emanating from us like a halo. We enjoyed the attention. We headed towards the bar atop a platform of concrete at the roof of the stairs. Heads turned. Some called out to us others just stared.

We entered the bar where a sweet pub aroma lingered. I raised my arm to the bar tender. She was underweight and had brown straggly hair tied up by a blue biro. "Can I have some help, please!" I called out, and she made her way towards me. "Yes, can I have two glasses of your house white wine, please?"

Shariece sat on a stool beside me topping up on her Mac lipgloss, watching people. "Steph, ain't that wha's his name from Peckham?"

I scanned across the bar tables...

I looked out of the window and realised we'd arrived at my stop. I drummed down the stairs of the bus almost falling on my face. I crossed a busy road in Catford, part of the gyratory system, and headed for the 202 bus stop outside of Laurence House, the local council office. Just as I was about to take a breath having noticed that the bus driver had seen me and knew I wanted to board his bus, he pulled off again. The imbecile had barely stopped to let a granny get off the bus and even nearly took her handbag with him. Peeved.

I sprinted toward the next bus stop like my life depended on it, praying for the Lord to strike lightning through the roof of the bus and down the spinal cord of the driver to bring his journey to a halt. Instead, electricity ran through the traffic lights ahead which turned from a green to a bright red. The driver eyeballed me as I breezed across the road ahead of his stationary bus, my bags swinging wildly from my arms. I panted like a wild cat, sprinting uphill, to the bus stop opposite Catford Bridge Station where a small group of people awaited the bus.

When I got on the bus, the driver looked like a dweeb. His large ears were at odds with one another. His hair a see-through arch journeying from front to back. I couldn't disguise my fury even if I wanted to once I came face to face with him. Only a transparent screen separated us. He bleeped me through without the confidence he'd had when he'd been ahead of me, without looking at my face or pass. I counted to ten quickly in my head to calm myself down and made the choice to move on. I took a seat behind the exit doors next to a butter-skinned female in her twenties. She had a young toddler on her lap munching through a packet of crisps. I relaxed my shoulders and eased myself back into my rekindled thoughts.

...I couldn't see anyone.

"I can't see anyone," I told Shariece as I snaked around the wooden tables to an area of comfy chairs at the corner of the bar.

We had barely started our small talk before a figure was standing before me that had me baffled and then double-baffled at my being baffled.

"Wha' gwaan, Steph?" he said with a pleasant smile that suggested he was very happy to see me. "I've been hoping I would bump into you."

"Oh my gosh! I forgot you were out, how have you been?" I asked, bewilderment spreading through me infectiously. He looked good. His brown eyes had the slant of a boat and depth of the ocean. Skin, a soft clear oak brown, hair a low-cut fade. I smiled.

"I'm all right, you know, just doing a business access course at university now, trying to keep on the straight path, need a good woman to support me." He sat down beside me.

Shariece's eyes at this point fixed my way and she smiled with deeply hidden agendas. "You all right?" She turned to him with her arm stretched out. "I know I know you from Peckham days, but for the life of me I can't remember your name."

He took her hand shaking it, his head faintly nodding as though he approved of the handshake gesture. "Damien, but you probably remember me as Switch. I definitely remember you, doh, what's your name again?"

"Shariece," she answered freeing his hand, her corner to corner smile still imprinted across her mouth.

He sat with us for a while before inviting his two friends over who I'd never met before, though there was a familiarity. We exchanged numbers, or rather I took his number—I wasn't too sure of the lifestyle he was keeping up with and I didn't want to get caught up in the politics of street living. Didn't think much into it in terms of him being a possibility, just thought this might be interesting...nothing more, nothing less. Shariece thought a lot more into it than that, though. By the time we left she sprinkled so many possibility seeds in my head, plants started to grow but I had to weed them out. We headed back to my house where another surprise sat waiting for me...

I pressed the red 'stop' button as I prepared to get off the bus. I had my diary open, browsing over pages that helped me recall the events I was relaying in my head. As I went to close my diary shut, crisp flakes landed on it and I crushed them between the pages by mistake. I looked up at the child next to me whose face indicated that he'd done it on purpose. Opening my diary once again, I brushed the crumbs onto the dim, grainy floor of the bus and stood up just as another crisp propelled through the air and skimmed across my face only to tumble onto the ground.

Within moments the bus stopped. The door opened and I stepped off coolly. Briskly walking down the end of Perry Hill, I withdrew my phone from my handbag, a silver DKNY number with the logo printed repeatedly across it. I looked at the time on my phone. It was almost 18:00—I'll still be on time, I thought. I turned off the main road onto a side road just past a small estate. Rowdy-looking teenagers hung out on the corner talking loudly about someone.

Once at Macy's house, I banged on her door and heard Ricardo call out "Daddy!" A cat poked its head out from behind one of the black bags filled with grass by the bin in front of the house.

Macy pulled back the door seconds later. "Do you have to bang the door so hard?" she questioned.

I blanked the question. "What time are you lot going out?" I said instead, stepping in behind her, placing my bag at the side of the three-seater sofa that was to be my home for the evening.

"Six-thirty," Macy replied.

She sat beside me. She looked stunning beyond belief. She seldom dressed up. However, when she did she made up for it tenfold. She wore a fitted cream satin dress with embroidery detail around the bodice. I think it was a Karen Millen number or Whistles. Her eyes were accentuated with mascara and eyeliner, plus a creamy silvery eyeshadow. Her lips held a shimmering gloss coat that enhanced the upward curve of her top lip. Her hair dangled loose ringlets.

"Just waiting for Jason to get ready," she said,

Swift footsteps crashed down the stairs and Ricardo's face, filled with glee and excitement, soon appeared. He ran at me. I got up in preparation of the weight I was about to receive—he was nearly eight years old and almost as tall as me! He jumped up with no comprehension of his increasing size shouting, "Aunty Stephanie, where you been?!" I caught him and swung him as best I could before planting kisses all over his face. I'd missed Ricardo tremendously. I hooped my arm round his head and playfully scruffed his newly shaven head.

"Mace," I called to my sister who seemed saddened, "whassup?"

"Nothing, just a bit tired that's all, but as we don't go out often I don't wanna put it off."

"Where're you going again?"

"Some restaurant Jason's been telling me about in Fulham, and then probably to a bar."

"You look proper cris' today, so make sure you go somewhere nice after."

"Jason's working tomorrow anyway, so can't stay out too late anyway. I'm glad he's got next Saturday off, though."

"Hmmm…" I paused for a bit, hesitant about the question I was about to ask. "Mace?"

"What?"

"Have you heard anything from Tyrone?"

She looked at me as if to say, "Why are you going there?" especially with Jason upstairs, but I wanted know.

"Well, have you?"

"Steph, I know this is hurtful for you but you're gonna have to move on from that one."

"I asked if you've heard from him, that's all."

"Yes, I've spoken to him once, but as you know Jason speaks to him all the time. He's doing really well out there. He's getting really good marks at high school…college or whatever, and already has sponsorship for university. In his spare time he's focused on his music."

My nostrils flared. "Hasn't he asked for me?"

"Yeah, he has. Trust me, Steph, if this was my way I wouldn't be dealing with it like this, but Tyrone's family doesn't want him getting distracted in any way right now, and unfortunately they think you will be a big distraction for him."

Swallowing the knot in my throat, I turned round to hug my nephew because the sight of my sister wasn't sitting well with me.

"Aunty Stephanie, what's wrong?"

"Nothing, Ricardo, certain people are just getting on my nerves. Have you had your bath yet?"

"Do I have to go bed already?" A whining eased through his tone.

"No. We'll watch TV and I'll read you a book after. OK?"

He smiled nodding his head and went upstairs to run the bath while I absorbed myself back into my thoughts once more.

*

…The surprise that sat waiting for me was Dad. As Shariece and I entered my home, Claudia was busy in the kitchen cooking dinner. Dad sat formally on the sofa behind the coffee table in the living room, as though he was waiting to be interviewed. He was wearing a dark tailored suit and bow tie, his legs crossed and hands wrapped together in his lap. He had his glasses on, the square ones with the gold frame that made him look a bit like Malcolm X.

"Dad?" I said, genuinely shocked. Though my dad called to check on me occasionally, he didn't make an effort to visit. I think there was some resentment of me choosing to go into a foster home instead of going to live with him, and so since Dad insisted I left Dada's house I only saw him when I visited him occasionally.

He got up with ease and lightly pressed his lips against my cheek. "You all right? I just thought I'd come down here and check on you but you weren't in." His voice was innocent and full of concern for me. "I was gonna leave, but Claudia insisted I stay. Who's this?" he looked past my shoulder, "René?"

"Shariece," I corrected.

Shariece came from behind me and squeezed in between the coffee table and sofa. "Hi Uncle Richard," she said kissing him, "you look really smart, are you going out somewhere nice?"

"Nah, just coming straight from work."

"Dressed in a suit?" Shariece knew the work Dad did, which was why she was perplexed.

"Just because I do a labourer's job doesn't mean I have to look like one."

I giggled lightly and took off my shoes, advising Shariece to do the same, before I went out to the kitchen where Claudia was rummaging in the cupboard for plates. "Can I help, Clauds?"

She stopped and tilted her head slightly, her mass of locks falling over her face. She kissed me on the corner of my mouth. "Yeah, wash your hands and carry these plates into the dining room for me and lay them out...please."

I washed my hands in the kitchen sink and took the plates noticing something in Claudia's eye that I couldn't quite put my finger on. It was just a different, more serious attitude to serving dinner, much more pressure laid on herself than she normally would. I gathered it was my father's presence. I was unclear whether her nerves and intensity was because the father of her foster child had visited, or whether it was my dad, a good looking slim built man that had visited. For now I would set aside my observations. I laid the plates out in the dining room, while Shariece sat in the adjoining living room explaining to Dad what she did in her job. Dad looked up at me through the arch in the wall and asked whether I had a job as yet.

"Yes," I said, my proudness tinting the 'es' of 'yes', "Didn't I tell you I got a job working in Oasis?

"Oh yeah! Where's that then?"

"Regent Street."

"And what is it exactly that you do?"

"I sell clothes, customer service...that kind of t'ing." I found my dad amusing when he asked me things he already knew the answer to. I guess it just made him feel proud, especially when he learnt about what others did my age. It was important that he could reference his children in the same positive light.

Despite my embarrassment, I warmed to Dad noticing my attempt to make a difference in my life and his belief in my ability. It was the softer side he didn't often show, but when he did, it was soothing. At that point Claudia arrived. White furry slippers peeped out the bottom of her floral skirt. She wore a matching waistcoat over a black long-sleeved top. One by one she brought in dishes of rice, oxtail with butter beans, fried fish and vegetables. I went out to help her bring in a dish or two.

"Shariece, you staying for dinner?" Claudia asked.

Shariece smiled and answered, "Yes please."

Claudia called to Daniel. We heard him climb the stairs with long strides as though he missed a stair or two with each stride. "Good evening, Sir," he said to my dad in his Jamaican accent, "Nice fi finally meet you." He shook Dad's hand.

"Yeah man," Dad replied keeping in tone with the Jamaican patois, "yuh safe. Nice fi meet yuh too."

"Stephanie, Shariece...good evening everybuddy."

"You all right, Daniel?" We said in unison, moving so he could be seated.

We all tucked in, everyone helping themselves to the selection of food. It was notable that Claudia kept offering each dish to Dad first, as he would do to her. I couldn't stop the questions that had started to stampede its way through my brain at that point: is there a flame of interest between Dad and Claudia igniting here? A jarring sensation troubled me. I wondered, but since I couldn't answer that question, I couldn't ease how much their cordiality to one another started to grate me.

Daniel diverted my attention with his interest in Shariece, "So wha' yuh ah do wid your life, Shariece?"

Shariece delved into the day-to-day going on of her day job, and

Daniel, totally enchanted, continued to throw questions: "Is it now! And where you is from den? What school yuh goh?"

Once Shariece answered to Daniel's inquisition, Dad moved the spotlight to Daniel. "Soh Daniel, which part of Jamaica yuh from? Yuh accent 'trong like yuh just lan'—how long yuh de-deh ah England?"

"Ten years now. Mi mudder carry me over when mi was seven. But it's Spanish Town me come from."

"Spanish Town?!" Dad repeated, noting the rough area in Jamaica that Daniel was from.

It was at that point Claudia took control of the spot light and shined it up Dad, "I think it's my turn to ask questions," Claudia interjected, "Richard. Stephanie speaks about you all the time, but I have no idea what you do and what your interests are?"

Dad smiled and toothy smile. "I'm an electrician Claudia, but there's no handiwork I won't have a go at. I'm a fixer." He was back to his standard cockney English, "But my main interests are my kids. I love the sax, antiques—I've got a bit of an antique collection, and vinyl—but apart from that it's just football and my family and friends."

Claudia swallowed her smile, and then asked, "How do you feel about Steph being in care?"

Dad took some time to mull over the question and muster up some words whilst sucking on an oxtail bone. He glanced at me, turned back to Claudia and said: "To be honest, I feel sad." He paused for a long time, then: "Since that day in May last year when Stephanie went into care, not a day goes by when I don't ask myself why? Why didn't my little girl come to me first?"

Claudia turned her eyes to me but I didn't say a thing. It wasn't the right time for my explanation, nor was it the right time for him to express his feelings or for Claudia's psychology questions...

*

"Aunty Stephanie, I've finished." Ricardo was standing naked in the centre of the front room drenched in bath water and suds.

"Where's your towel?"

"In my room."

I followed him back upstairs to his room, towelled him dry, creamed his body down with cocoa butter and powdered his chest, neck, armpits and private area. He put on his Spiderman pyjamas and followed me back downstairs. I flicked the channel over to MTV Base. The thought of Horlicks tickled my taste buds. I headed into the kitchen and made Ricardo and myself a hot drink. Once seated, another thought came to mind and I headed back upstairs to act on it. I didn't know kids could produce so much dirt, I thought scrubbing the black ring left in the bath.

I gathered Ricardo's clothes up off the bathroom floor and shoved them in a wicker laundry basket under the sink. I rinsed out his flannel and hung it on the radiator. All of a sudden, there was a knock at the front door. The clank ricocheted through the house, frightening me. I heard Ricardo making his way to the front door. I called to him from the top of the stairs: "Ricardo, who's there?"

He froze right where he was standing, looking through the peephole. "Aunty Safire and Aunty Charlene."

I indicated for him to open the door. Safire, Charlene and Stella toppled in full of energy like they'd just committed a crime. "Wha' gwaan?" I asked.

I got: "Shocked to see you", "Hello" and "You all right?" from all of them and then Safire asked how come I was there.

"Babysitting," I replied. I followed them into the front room, grabbed my cup of Horlicks from the mantelpiece. "What are you lot doing here?" I dropped lightly onto the sofa next to Ricardo and looked to Charlene for the answer.

"Oh, we're supposed to be going Ministry of Sound tonight but Safire ain't got nuffing to wear. We thought Macy could borrow her somefing. Where is she?" Charlene put her foot up on the chair and picked at her big toenail, the bottom of her foot resting on Stella's thigh who seemed too distant to pay any attention.

"Jason's taken her out to some restaurant in Fulham." I heard Missy Elliot's 'Supa Dupa Fly' track come on and I turned to the TV. Safire was standing in the way. "Come out my way, Safire."

"The Blue Elephant?" Charlene queried while Safire nudged forward making little difference to my obstructed view. Ricardo jumped up off the sofa and did some robotic move, emulating Missy in the video.

We all turned to Ricardo, except Stella, cheering him on. Charlene changed feet, a small gathering of toenail clippings piled neatly on the arm of the chair, and picked at the other foot. "So did Macy go Blue Elephant?"

"I dunno, Charlene, I fink so. What's wrong with Stella?" I was looking at Stella's weird disposition whilst talking to Charlene.

"I'm tired," Stella uttered, monotone, her head flung back against the backrest of the chair, eyes closed as though she were dead.

Charlene tittered to herself trying not to knock over the neat pile of toenail clippings and pickings. Ricardo glanced around the room on a musical spin, wanting the attention of his audience back. He soon sat back down beside me and watched Safire pick at her face.

"So what're you lot gonna do then?"

"I dunno," Charlene didn't raise her head from her toes as she said this, "Macy would go mad if Safire borrowed her clothes without asking, innit?"

"No she wouldn't, Charlene," Safire disagreed. As she said this I was drawn to the blood bubbling out of the spot in the middle of her forehead.

"Yes she would, Safire." My face was distorted, brow ridged from the sight of my sister.

"What?" Safire asked.

"Sort out your face, it looks nuts," I told her sipping on my Horlicks.

Having looked in the mirror, she rushed upstairs to the bathroom and returned with cotton wool and the smell of antiseptic.

"D'you wanna come out tonight?" Charlene asked.

"I'm babysitting."

"Oh yeah."

"Plus, I got a hairdresser appointment in the morning."

"Just you?" Safire asked.

"Nah, me, Shariece, and maybe René and Maria. We're supposed to be going Coliseum tomorrow night."

"Is it?" Safire squashed up beside me. "I wanna come."

"Come, den."

"So what, ain't we going out tonight den?" Charlene said disappointedly as she gathered her nail pickings and binned them.

"Allow tonight, Charlene," Stella still looked dead though she was speaking, "tonight's proving too long."

I felt for the remote under Ricardo and flicked through the movie channels. "Turn the light off, Stella." I waited a few seconds but she didn't move. "Turn the light off, Charlene." Huffing her disappointment, Charlene saw to the light above Stella's slicked back head and switched it off, cosying up next to Stella, as Safire did with me and me with Ricardo.

We all fell asleep watching The Usual Suspects.

CHAPTER TWENTY-ONE

THINGS CHANGE

27th June 1999 – My Gates

Hey Di, a couple of things have come to light. Things I didn't know and now know but still can't shift the fucking surprise it gives me. Before I fill you in though, I need to tell you first that Damien and I have started linking. Well it's been since we saw each other last week. I know, I know, I didn't expect it either. But what can I say, I'm feeling him. And like Shariece said, it's highly unlikely Tyrone's thinking about me and holding out on relationships!

It was another one of those Sunday afternoons where I was chilling in my bedroom listening to music and diarising my life's most recent events. It all started a few weeks prior at the Coliseum the following night after Charlene, Safire and Stella had gate crashed Macy's house where I was babysitting. That was when I met Damien. He came over, accompanied by Typo, to where we were standing with my cousins Leroy, Joanne and Jermaine. He was dressed casually smart in dark trousers and a crisp white shirt with his top three buttons undone revealing a light wool of black chest hair. Typo seemed his usual female-loving and energetic self. He'd cut his rusty top heavy plaits off rocking a cool short back and sides with a number two on top. Shariece's now boyfriend Sean, and Donavan from school were around us as well seeming slightly discomforted by Damien and Typo's presence. No one showed signs of potential beefing, though. Strangely, Stella bopped off in a strop when they came over. Typo reached out for her but missed. Maria bubbled closely with Donavan as though in a world of absolute bliss. I wondered what were going on between them!

The crowd was sweaty and the air was moist and heavy with smoke. Men dressed in tight costumes with the fabric around the bottom area cut out, wandered around nonchalantly having a break from dancing in cages. As you would expect, men and women alike noted their firm brown behinds as they passed. When classic garage tracks like 'The Boy is Mine' by Brandy and Monica came on, the crowd roared in appreciation, as did we. Safire was bubbling down with Charlene to the rhythm making boi! boi! noises.

Having said his hellos, Damien pulled me aside by my wrist, which soon fell into a tender and gentle grasp of my hand. I followed his lead trying not to spill the brandy and Coke that swayed over rocks in my other hand. We left the room and went into a spacious corridor between that and another floor downstairs. We stayed in the corridor and settled on a big leather sofa.

"So can I get you a drink?" he questioned softly biting his bottom lip, which made him look all the more sexy.

I was mindful of his bad and troublesome ways, so focused hard on not getting caught up in his spellbinding looks. "I've already got a drink," I said some moments later swirling the ice in my tumbler glass.

He took my hand once more and guided me away from the bar tenderly, stroking the centre of my hand with his middle finger until we reached the sofa area. My hormones started to play ping pong and I felt my insides palpitate. When we sat he just stared at me and I blushed with sniggers like I did with Tyrone.

"What?" I offered, having nothing else to say just wanting him to take the attention off me for fear that he could see I was starting to fancy him more than I imagined.

"I just like looking at you that's all. You're so pretty, I could stare at you for hours. You make me wanna give up all the girls in my phone and dedicate myself to you."

He took my hand again and I gulped on my drink to relax me a little. "Look Steph, you know I like you. You've known I've had feelings for you from the day you strolled into Peckham with your little bad-bruck self. If it wasn't for your age I would've made you my girl then. I'm a different person now, Steph. Jail's changed me. I wanna do something with my life."

Just then I noticed Stella come from one of the fire exit doors looking slightly off-balance. I called out to her but she couldn't hear me. I got up pulling down my one-armed Karen Millen black number and click-clacked over to her in my Roberto Cavalli four-inch heels. I felt Damien watching me from behind and I felt uber sexy.

"Stella," I pulled on the sleeve of her denim jacket as she was about to open the door to go back into the house and garage room, "you all right?"

She looked at me like she wanted to cry, and shook her head. I had Shariece's car keys in my bag so steered Stella to the exit and waved an apologetic goodbye to Damien who sat waiting for my return on the sofa. He mouthed: 'I see you in a bit'. He was cool.

As soon as we got to the car Stella blurted out, "I'm pregnant. I'm fucking pregnant Steph!"

My eyes bulged. Clearly I was in shock. I wanted to know by whom, when, where? Everything...I wanted to know everything that had led Stella into that predicament as it was so far outside of her make-up. However, "How come?" is what I mouthed.

Her shoulder rose as though she had asked herself that questions many times before, no answer lifting the burdening of her shoulders. Her face longed with sorrow. "Steph," she said, "You have to promise me...I mean it! You have to promise me not to tell a soul!"

"I promise, I promise."

"Typo's the father. We've been parring as bredrens, nothing sexual or anyfing. One occasion we went to a rave, went back to his, which I had done before so wasn't a biggie. But we were smashed, and one thing just led to another. Before I knew it, he broke my virginity. It was a one-off. And...now...I'm...pregnant.." she started to heave uncontrollably, and the tears came tumbling down.

I couldn't believe my ears. Stella had broken her virginity in a one-off, and now she was pregnant! I was hugging her and trying to calm her down. "Don't worry about it Ella, man. It's done now, and there's nothing you can do to change what's happened. But whatever you decide to do in the future, I'll support you. Have you thought about what you're going to do?"

"Abort it," was her response. Her face solemn and resentful of the words she'd spoken.

"Ok, if that's what you want. Is that what Typo wants too?"

"He doesn't know, Steph, but my minds made up. I've booked my appointment and that's that, I'm aborting it."

I heard her loud and clear. We were all running from the same negative expectations we thought society expected of us.

The following Monday I was sitting in an abortion clinic in Brixton waiting for Stella to return from surgery. Regret, disbelief...reality clung close to her and she cried for some time, even when we got back to her house where Aunty Ruth sat puffing on a cigarette watching *Coronation Street* none the wiser.

*

Back to my Sunday afternoon I lay in my bedroom engrossed in my music, my thoughts, my diary. A soft knock rapped at my bedroom door.

"Yeah?"

Claudia pushed open the door. "Couldn't you hear me calling you? Turn down your music, please."

I lowered the vocals of Timbaland rapping on the 'Clock Strikes' track whilst I explained to Claudia that I couldn't hear her.

"Is that rapper rapping over *Knight Rider* music?"

"Yeah, it's sampled. The track's heavy, ah-lie?"

Claudia stared at me queerly. "Your mum's on the phone."

"Oh." I headed to the living room, Claudia following behind, and plonked myself on the sofa where a crumpled blanket lay. She shuffled me over as I picked up the phone. "Hello?"

"Why d'you take so long to come to the phone?" Mum asked.

"I was in my room."

There was a long uncomfortable silence that I wasn't too keen to fill like in most of our conversations.

"So, how're you?" she forced out at the point the silence became unbearable.

"Fine."

"How's things going with your foster carer—what's her name again?"

"Claudia."

"That's it; how're things going with her?"

"Fine."

"How're things going at college? I've been hearing you're doing well."

"Well, I get support from Claudia and my dad, which helps."

"Well, you would get it from me if you weren't so blasted facety—"

"Is that it?" I cut in. "Is that all you wanted? Coz I've got to go to my dad's now."

Unable to conceal her thoughts, she raged. Containment of her anger was never her forte, "Your farder is di scum of the eart," she barked, "And if you think any more of him, what do you think dat makes you?"

By now, Mum's venomous tongue just sounded like 'blah blah blah'. Her poisonous words had no impact, as though they just fell upon deaf ears. I was about to hand her over to the dialling tone, when she cut off. I heard scuffling with the phone before the delicate, chiming tones of my grandma came down the line.

"Steph?" she called.

"Yes, Mama."

Claudia was lying across from me, flicking through the cable channels, her feet almost upon my lap. She passed a quick look my way, which I didn't acknowledge.

"Oh. Yuh all right?" Mama continued.

"Yeah."

"Oh, that's good. Well, yuh know yuh mudder is having a tough time at di moment wid her Christianity and separating from Derek and everyt'ing. Right now, she needs the love and support of her children, so try not to be so hard on her, yuh hear?"

She passed the phone back over to Mum who had calmed down somewhat. "Steph, I just want to say that no matter what happens I want you to know that I love you whether you see it or not—I love all my children; I love you lot to the bone, man. I love mi kids until mi inside ah bu'n me wid pain..." Her words trailed off as she transcended into a blubbering, hearty cry.

I hated this. No matter how angry I was with her, no matter how I rationalised her treatment of me, her brokenness and how dysfunctional our relationship was, it always hurt profoundly to see or hear Mum cry and utter her love for her children. My throat clogged up and solitary tears lined my face. It was emotional torture. The repetitive cycle was just too much.

"Steph?" Mama broke into my reverie. "Try not to hol' up t'ings inna yuh heart fi yuh mudder, God knows how she been hell and back fi uno. I know it hard fi yuh, but open up and let God work 'pon yuh heart fi show yuh mercy so yuh can have mercy."

"I've already opened up to God."

"OK, but try and learn forgiveness."

"How can I forgive someone for what they're not aware of?" I demanded.

"Steph, seek in God and he will give you answers. Read Luke 6:37. Just remember, you have already been blessed. Tell Claudia mi sai' bye—see yuh later."

Claudia's arm encircled me. "Are you OK?"

"Yeah." My voice shook. My eyes brandished woeful suffering. My heart made an attempt at forgiveness. But I wasn't a saint. I was not a fucking saint! I was just a seventeen-year-old trying to figure all that bullshit out.

"Do you want to talk?"

"Nah, I'm all right. Anyway, I wanna leave out to go to my dad's before it gets too late."

"Well, get ready and I'll drop you."

"Are you sure?"

"Yeah." She pecked me on the cheek.

I headed back to my room, gathered my things to leave and turned off the music. Out of nowhere, I noticed the gold script on my Bible's spine in the bottom compartment of the side table. It freaked me out how the Bible always came into view and drew my attention at poignant moments. Of course, I was tempted to read the verse Mama had suggested. I was curious to learn how she'd imagined I'd interpret it. She knew I was no saint. I turned to Luke 6:37: "Judge not, and ye shall not be judged; condemn not, and ye shall not be condemned; forgive, and ye shall be forgiven..."

I rolled my eyes. I'd heard those words a thousand times before. The message was simple, but as I embarked on the car journey to Dad's, my digestion of the words became different; it permeated through the soul rather than the mechanics of my mind. The air was still warm. A sunset breeze bit me beneath a pink cotton Ralph Lauren shirt. I shivered outside the metal door to a block of flats on Silwood Estate waiting for Dad's response on the intercom. The intercom appeared to be broken. I called Dad's landline. Whilst we were in conversation about the situation, Claudia called out from the car.

"Steph! Is everything OK?"

I went to reply, but Dad's voice kicked in with a question of his own: "Is that Claudia?"

I looked at my handset, confused. "Yeah, why?"

I could hear Bushman's 'Fire Bu'n a Weak Heart' playing in the background. I could tell he was having one of those self-righteous moments.

"Steph?" Claudia called, "is he in?"

"Yeah, thanks for the lift. You can go now!"

"What you doing?" Dad persisted. "Tell her I said to come in—go on!"

As Claudia dropped the handbrake to roll on, I reluctantly waved for her attention. "Claudia! My dad invited you up," I called out.

Her face revealed she was pleased about this. It was clear to see that Claudia was interested in my dad and my dad in Claudia. As we disembarked the cranky, urine-soaked lift and walked along the ninth-floor balcony, I made my feelings visible, "My dad's not for you, Claudia. Please put a stop to whatever these feelings you guys are developing for each other. Please trust me when I say it will all end in tears."

CHAPTER TWENTY-TWO

DUPED

9th December 2000 – South London, South-Eastern train service home to Forest Hill

Don't ask me how I got to this place, Di, this dismal place that I've entered, but here I am again. I wouldn't blame you if you were becoming tired of the erratic turns my life seems to take. Never simple, peaceful, and just somewhat normal for a long enough period. You must think I'm doomed to failure...that me living a life of misery is inevitable! I must be cursed with my mum's woes. The apple never falls far from the tree.

Things turned an odd shape once I left care. Claudia gave me no option... Lies! I'm telling lies. She gave me an option. She told me how intelligent and graceful she thought I was and that she'd always support me in every way possible. I was about to start uni, so I needed all the support I could get. She just couldn't help what she felt. I wanted her to help it. I needed her to help it so for once, I could feel prioritised. But she couldn't. She couldn't help it, not even for the sake of my feelings...or her own, as knowing how I felt hurt her to the bones, but this feeling didn't come often, she said.

She was falling for my dad, and nothing could stop that, except me, I guess. Well, so I thought. But how could I accept it? I couldn't. Claudia and Richard together...an item...a couple—hell no! She wanted me to, though. She badly wanted me to accept it because she knew as well as I did Dad would not lose me for her, but I couldn't...that was something I just couldn't accept. Claudia was mine. She was my special friend and mother figure who had shown me the light from the dark cave I'd come from. She was my inspirer, my understanding of trust, mercy and love. This I could not share or give up.

I visited Dad one day. He was sitting in his chair, playing his saxophone along to Ella Fitzgerald and Louis Armstrong's 'Summertime' as if entertaining a sea of fans. I listened for a bit, reeled in by the sorrowful combination of vocal and instrumental brilliance. I turned my mind back to the reason I was there and told him: "I dunno what's going on between you and Claudia, but Dad...please, you gotta make it stop."

He stopped playing his saxophone and his musically spellbound demeanour changed. "But look how long I've been single for, Steph?!" Agitatedly he put the saxophone back on its stand, brushing down the front of his deep red polyester round-neck top and positioning his diamond-encrusted medallion so that it lay centred and flat.

I could see that I had messed up his vibe, messed up a world of harmony that he was currently tuning in to. He tried again: "How can you get upset when finally I meet someone who's down to earth, decent and has her own

wivout a million an' one pickney wrap aroun' her foot,
huh?! What, yuh raader mi get wid one ah dem dotty
gangre gal dat deh 'bout New Cross?"

I moaned some kind of bottomless, intonated and
instantaneous "Nooooo..."

My phone rang.

"Hello?"

"Babes, where are you?"

His tone sent an unnerving twitch down my spine, but I answered him anyway. "I'm on the train, where are you?"

"I'm outside your house."

"Why? You knew I was working today."

"It's five o'clock; I thought you finished at four."

"I did, but I didn't get out until twenty past. Anyway I was gonna meet Nina tonight."

"Well, I'm here now so you might as well just come here."

"But I'll be still meeting her."

"OK, I'll just spend a small amount of time with you then."

As the call ended, I dialled Dada's number and requested he get Nina.

"Hello, Steph...you there?" Nina belted out.

"Yeah. I need you to do me a favour. Damien's randomly come to my house, so I'm gonna have to come to yours instead of us meeting at mine. I should be home by about five-thirty, so could you call me at about five-forty in case he tries it?" I needed to cover my back. I had entered a relationship with Damien, which had developed into a possessive one. Nothing I didn't think I could handle, just something I needed to carefully manage at times.

"Yeah, yeah, I'll call you then."

"Thanks."

I opened back my diary to the page where Dad was cussing me.

"...So what foolishness you going on wiv, Steph?" he continued.

I wasn't going on with foolishness, Di. I just didn't understand why her. Of all the women in London...in the world—why her?! But as he said: "I already told you why her, so you tell me why not her?" And this I could not do. I shrugged my shoulders trying to procure words—the right words—from my limited vocabulary. He probed further. He wanted an immediate answer.

"What, you don't think I deserve that kind of woman?" I didn't say that. I wasn't sure what I thought, but he pushed, Di. He pressed on for an answer: "So what is it? Come on! You go to college; you've got the brains and the courage to say what's on your mind!"

I sat down across from him, the onyx and brass-trimmed coffee table between us, and gazed at the many pictures on the wall. "I just don't want you to compromise what we've got. I've never had a mother figure treat me the way she's treated me, and I don't want you to compromise it—simple."

"And how am I gonna do that?"

My eyes darted around the room—looking at the memories on the wall—and came back to him. "I dunno, beat her like you did Mum."

As soon as I said it I regretted it. Claudia wasn't the kind of women who would put up with any type of aggressive behaviour. Even though I considered my dad an aggressive man perhaps she hadn't seen that side of him. She just saw the soft, kind, warm-hearted side of him, which not many people got to see. It was there, just barricaded behind steel weaponry.

An array of 'bombaclaats', 'rasclaats' and 'bloodclaats' tumbled down upon me like an avalanche. He was enraged, as I'd never quite seen him before. Bubbles of froth appeared at the corners of his mouth. I took that as my cue to leave…

We soon arrived at my stop. I disembarked from the train and walked briskly in an attempt to stave off the cold lurking beneath my golden fake fur jacket. Damien was sitting on the wall outside my rented flat with folded arms.

"You took your time," he said as I passed him to walk through the bush-infested front garden to open the front door.

"Well, I wasn't planning on seeing you now, was I?"

He poked at my waist playfully. I picked up my mail from a pile on the floor and we bypassed Mr. and Mrs. Bailey, an elderly couple who lived below me. I waved at them meekly as we entered my flat and closed the door behind us. I felt ashamed. I knew they had heard our raucous arguments.

We took off our shoes and went up the stairs, which were springy and padded with deep pile carpet. Every time I sunk my toes into the deep pile of my carpet, felt its softness, its undoubted good quality, I felt an accomplishment.

I heard a muffled ring and dug deep into my brown leather Louis Vuitton handbag for my mobile. It was Nina. Right on cue. I informed her I'd shortly be leaving and jumped up to inform Damien.

"I just got here, and you're leaving out already?"

I sat down next to him on one of the three giant cushions I had as temporary seating whilst I saved for my leather suite. "I already made plans with Nina and didn't know you were coming," I explained for the second time.

He twisted up his face like he was going to cry and wrapped his arms about my waist tightly. "Babes, I just want to spend some time with you."

"I spent time with you yesterday."

"I wanna spend time with you every day."

I cuddled him; stroked the back of his head, which was now short and faded, in a tender way before I balanced up onto my knees. "I wanna spend time with you too but I need my own space as well, OK?"

I was impacted by a sudden force, which threw me against the wall. My eyes bulged open with shock. I couldn't believe it was happening. "Ah!" I screamed.

"There, you can have your fucking space!" he exclaimed and made for the stairs.

"Why are you pushing me and I already told you what my plans are?"

God knows I wanted to run after him. I was desperate to push, punch...hit him back in some way as I would deal with any attack. But I had spent the last few years learning how to control my temper and my violent tendencies. And here I was, the victim once again of unwarranted aggression.

I tried to get up from my folded position on the floor. I needed to show him that pushing a girl down may have cut it in Peckham, but it wasn't going to go that way with me. Slowly I folded my legs back out and massaged my knees. I was really hurting. He knew I still had my own violent traits, and I would always fight back. That's why he ran. But I didn't chase him out the flat, just descended the stairs to slam my front door behind him. I didn't say another word—I didn't have the energy for it.

I sat on the bottom step in an attempt to calm down and gather my thoughts so I could at least still my trembling hands. Several minutes later I ascended the stairs, called Nina and told her I'd decided to remain at home. I collapsed on one of the big cushions in front of the TV. A musical sound informed me that I'd received a text message.

> I'M SORRY 4 PUSHIN U, I PROMISE IT WON'T HAPPEN AGAIN N I'LL MAKE IT UP 2 U. I LUV U 4EVER! DX

I didn't reply. Just watched the TV from where I lay in hope that it would all go away.

*

I first noticed the change in Damien during the spring of two-thousand. Safire, Charlene, my dad, and I had returned from a holiday to Jamaica. Dad had suggested the trip away as an opportunity to rebuild our fractured relationship and spend some quality time with his girls. And it did just that, plus it enhanced my relationship with my sisters that had started to deteriorate with the different paths we were taking in life. Safire had just started college to pursue her passion for poetry and creative writing, and Charlene had secured a job as a young person's advisor at a local youth centre. We all still very much had our flaws but were all making an effort to advance ourselves in society. For much of our entire holiday, we giggled childishly on the beach, reciting memories from our childhood, the good and the bad.

Or Dad went through all lengths to facilitate the introductions of his daughters to key family members and friends. He was very proud.

The insecurities in Damien didn't materialise until when I returned from holiday. Damien had got it into his head that I had cheated when I was on holiday. I was confused. It had taken him several months to enter my rose garden, and there he was accusing me like I was a floosy. I quietly blushed at his jealousy. What can I say, I was young. We managed to get back on track, but he couldn't get over his jealousy.

The second notable event that followed wasn't until the summer of two-thousand, just a couple of months since my return from Jamaica. I had arranged with Damien to attend the interview for a photography course with me at a major Arts Institution in the west end as my moral support. He had offered his support when I mentioned I would get Macy to come with me. I was grateful to him for offering. However, his enthusiasm seemed to wane the moment we got up the morning of the interview. His attitude was unbecoming—grumpy and belligerent. For the life of me, I couldn't figure out why so I ignored it.

On the way to the station he dragged my larger portfolio on the floor like a spoiled child. Still I ignored it. I fought with myself to maintain a spirit that was warm and likable. The subject of my attitude had come up many times at work and college. If I were pissed off, then all in my path would know about it, and I wasn't going to let that happen that day. I had to focus hard on what was positive: the interview. And refrain from thinking about what was negative: Damien. On the train journey, I read through my notes about photographers like David Bailey, Patrick Demarchelier, Mario Testino, and Tom Munro. I thought about what I wanted to achieve from life: travel, photograph the world dressed in its best...and worst. Those thoughts carried me into the university's waiting room for the fashion photography course. It wasn't long before I realised I was the only black face in the waiting room. I acknowledged it but wasn't fazed by it. I liked standing out.

The other (mainly white, some Asian) candidates in the room fashioned eccentric looks. They wore bold and daring colours and funky haircuts. I sat away from Damien, but he swaggered over to me with an unflattering deportment. The larger portfolio he carried of mine bounced against the chairs he passed. Heads turned, and presumably their perceptions of me, of him... of us!

"What you sitting over dere for? If you wanna start acting like you don't know me now we're in front of rich white kids, den I'll go," he muttered.

If the floor could open up, I would have happily fallen into it. "Damien," I hissed, "be quiet, *please*, everyone can hear what you're saying."

"So!" he cried, turning heads again. "Do you fink I care what people fink?"

My heart raced. I counted: one, two, three, four... I needed to fight the urge to curse him out. I thought about the Care Bears and other happy infant memories like when Macy would cuddle up with me in my sleep and tell the story about *The Girl with the Magic Ring* or when Mum would take Safire and me to the farm to pick fruit and gawp at the chickens and cows. I tried many things to contain my temper and refrain from confronting the buffoon right there and then in the wrong place at the wrong time. But my blood was boiling; all I could see and feel was the colour red. I closed my eyes tightly in an attempt to squeeze away the anger.

I cracked open an eye and noticed another black girl walking in, looking directly at me. The fact that she was black made all the difference. Now there were two of us representing our entire race. *Shame, did she see me talking to myself?* I thought. *What's wrong with me? Why am I still talking to myself? Wait a minute...I'm not; I'm thinking to myself. I'm allowed to think to myself, that ain't crazy now, is it?*

I said a prayer. It was strange. I began praying more than often these days. The prayers I once mocked when observing my mum, I know relied upon to keep temperament...my sanity at bay. I struggled to keep it together. It would have been so easy just to flip the script and let that fucker have it. Just release a barrage of punches and insults, letting him know exactly how I felt. But I had to be much stronger than that. I had to choose the path that would serve me.

I opened my eyes, saw the rear of Damien disappearing through the door, and breathed a sigh of relief. I had no idea where he was going. I was just glad that he had left. The African girl still peered my way. I could tell she was African by the prominence of her cheekbones, the silky hue of her bourbon brown skin, and an ancestral air of confidence that started to become rife amongst my peer group of Africans in the late nineties and early noughties. It felt like, as a culture, they had a better understanding of the self and true identity dating farther back than any Caribbean's I knew could track of their past. It was this ultimate value of one's self held in the highest regard, that was perceptible.

"You all right?" I asked with a self-conscious smile. She looked at me with surprise.

"Yeah, I'm fine," she said with poise, "just eager to have my interview. How about you—are you OK?"

"I'm fine now; just a little nervous."

Whilst waiting, I read through my notes. Every time I looked up, this African girl was still looking at me. I paid her no mind.

A man in his late thirties materialised through a set of mahogany paneled doors. He held a clipboard and walked with a tortured limp. He sported denim jeans that were fashionably dirty and his black

T-shirt black clung to his frame. Like his jeans, his Adidas trainers were dirty, worn out, and old-school, as was the trend.

"Stephanie Johnson!" he called.

"Yeah, that's me," I replied with a bright smile.

"If you would like to follow me." I got up and followed behind him. Getting my two portfolios with all my artwork through the double doors without a bang proved quite a feat. "Hi, my name's Martin, Martin Davis. I'm the course director." He outstretched his arm, and we shook hands. "We'll have the interview in here; if you'd just like to go through."

I walked into the room with confidence. Even getting this far was an outstanding achievement for me. I could have been in prison, I thought, a crack den, a mental asylum, or buried beneath the ground like other children from my neighbourhood, but here I am at a world-renowned Arts University. I sat where he gestured. Yes, I was nervous, but also excited. I had been given an opportunity to achieve my goals.

The interview went quickly, but I thought it went well. I felt confident and articulate when discussing my art and the photographers who inspired me. Martin responded positively.

As I left the room, I crossed paths with the African girl in the corridor. She stared at me boldly now.

"Is everything OK?" I asked.

"Your name's Stephanie, isn't it?"

My brow dipped. Not because the girl knew my name, Martin had announced my name before the interview, but the tone in which she said it. "*Yeeaah*," I sung, in a defensive manner, gearing up for the fracas she seemed to want to instigate. "Do I know you?" I finally replied.

"My name's Mary-Anne."

Images of the past rushed at me like on a movie reel. I saw myself robbing, kicking, and traumatising Mary-Anne. I saw the mental cloak

I had worn that day that shielded my conscience from my wrongdoing. I saw the retreating figures of her friends. The tanned saddle bag that contained her heavy books and became twisted around her neck as I cracked the base of my foot against her ribcage. The disgruntled faces of my sister and cousin. The laughing and approving Ghetto Girls. The face. The bruised, bloody and questioning face of Mary-Anne, as she lay broken in a heap on the ground.

"I don't know what to say," my eyes welled up, overcome by mortification and disgust. Shame hung its hat on my head, and I dropped my face to peer at the ground, "I'm sorry, Mary-Anne," I said finally, "I don't know what else to say other than I'm sorry." Silence filled the space for a few long moments. "This is probably too much to ask. But I hope that someday you can find it within your heart to forgive me."

Her rounded face gave nothing away. She just looked at me without uttering a word, as if she was working out how she felt.

"Mary-Anne *Eshun*?"

Martin struggled with the pronunciation of her name. She forced a smile onto her face and turned to attend her interview. Relief flooded through me.

Not quite knowing what to do, disturbed by the encounter, I continued down a set of spacious stairs with a portfolio in each hand. I walked past an elaborately decorated reception room with sculptures everywhere, and went through the glass double doors to exit the building. Damien stood leant up against the historic walls of the university, puffing on a cigarette.

"D'you wanna blem?" he joked.

I shook my head and bopped past him. I was still reeling from my past coming back to haunt me.

"Come on, babe, I was joking. I just wanna know how you got on.

I bet they loved you, innit? But they'll never love you as much as I do." He took my portfolios from me.

"You just don't get it, Damien." I walked on ahead of him. Bond Street underground station was in front of me.

"What don't I get? Talk to me, babes! You wanted me to come here with you, and I'm here with you. I could've—"

"You could've what?" I challenged, stopping in my tracks and turning back to him. "You've dropped out of your business course. You ain't working anymore, so what could you have been doing? Besides that anyway, you're missing the point."

He grabbed my hand with affection and caressed the centre of my palm with his middle finger. "Well, tell me it then. I know I was a bit moody this morning, but I've still come. I've still come because I love you, and I want to be here for you."

"If you love me, then why would you stress me and be emotionally unsupportive on one of the most important days of my life? I could've folded in my interview because of the negative energy you were putting around me."

"Because that's what you make me do. You start stressing me and stressing yourself, babe, and then when I react, you don't like it."

"Forget it. It's always my fault. I just need some space right now." As I moved off to get to the Tube station, I heard my name hollered. I spiralled round to see Mary-Anne approaching me.

I waited.

"Who's dat?" Damien enquired.

I shook my head. I couldn't utter a word to him. Adrenaline pumped through me, readying myself for her words of vengeance. Of anger and hurt and resentment for all I had put her through. I was ready for whatever she wanted to get off her chest and throw at me. I deserved to hear that, at least. I gulped. Finally, she stood before me.

"I just wanted to say I have forgiven you," she exhaled, taking me completely by surprise. "I'm not going to lie, what you and your friends put me through back then was difficult to try to understand. I spent years asking myself what I did wrong to make you come at me so violently..."

"Nothing!" I interjected, "It was me. It was all my issues. We all had serious challenges we were dealing with. You were just the unfortunate passer-by. You could have been anyone. I'm just so sorry it happened."

"I know that now. It took a good amount of therapy to get over the anxiety of leaving the house and understanding the potential horrors you would have endured to want to put someone else through that type of pain." She stares at me with such intent, that I feel her eyes amid my soul and I'm drawn to tears. "Look, I know it's weird, but here we are. For whatever reason, our paths have crossed, and since we're the only two black girls trying for the same course, maybe it's worth us being friends instead of enemies?"

"I'd like that. I'd like that a lot...err, thank you," I just about managed, overcome by her kindness.

However bizarre and surreal the situation seemed. It was what it was, and I accepted it with humility and gratitude. We exchanged phone numbers and parted ways.

CHAPTER TWENTY-THREE

NEW YEAR'S DAY

1ˢᵗ January 2001 – Home

Dear Di. It's been a few weeks since the debacle at my flat when Damien pushed me against the wall. I know you're wondering what am I still doing with this guy. It's weird. Really difficult to explain. I love him. And I know that's not all that counts. He's got issues, I'm aware of that, but I almost feel like I can help him sometimes. That he needs me to help him make better choices. He has these rages, which I try to understand. I've had them too, remember. But it feels like his lacks the maturity that I know I've developed over the years. To know that I cannot control everything, and so try not to control or expend my energy on the things I can't control. I am still learning this practice, and so it's weird…difficult to understand some of the areas he places his energy. Literally making shit up sometimes and letting the made-up shit mad him. I'm not gonna lie, sometimes he scares me too. Like he'll hurt me or hurt himself if I leave him. I don't show him I'm scared though. I can't. I know how fear works. How it empowers the perpetrator inciting the fear. When he threatens me, I usually threaten him back with my dad or my cousins. Putting his hands on me just wouldn't be worth it. And he knows that. He knows there'd be consequences if I choose there to be. But like most of the arguments between us, time's a healer, and I've become quite the forgiver. Sometimes I don't know how I'm still standing here, healthy, living a life no one expected of me. I have so much to be grateful for, so at times it feels like my duty to be forgiving and understanding of him because that's what God and society has been to me.

Did I tell you I secured my place at university on the photography course? I got that retail job for a luxury fashion department store in the west end. Did I tell you about Mary-Anne? Ah man, Mary-Anne! What can I say about her? She's so cool, so kind and also very forgiving, Di! I can't imagine not having someone like her to experience this course with me. I'm making significant moves in my life right now Di. I'm both proud of what I've achieved and am humbled by having the opportunity to achieve them.

It was the morning Damien would finally meet Mum and Macy. Macy was particularly interested in meeting him because of the length of time he had been in my life, and that he was the reason I no longer doted on Tyrone. Eighteen months had passed already since we got together. Immersed in hot, steamy water, I felt relaxed. A silky, pink bubble bath and bath oils added a scent to the steam that wafted from the surface of the water. The edge of my silk headscarf wrapped tightly around my head became damp with perspiration. I hoped my hair, which was gripped into a one and pinned into a neat bun, would remain flat and neat. I rapped along to Dead Prez's 'Bigger Than Hip Hop'. It provided a base-heavy backdrop to my serene setting.

I loved this tune. This was the kind of heavy, rugged baseline and lyrical content that got me fired, took me into the zone. Stabbing the air with my two gun fingers in time with the beat, I pondered on the song's lyrics and thought about the culprits rumoured to have murdered Biggie Smalls and 2Pac.

"Steph," Damien's head popped round the bathroom door a while later, "Shariece is on the phone." I was making notes in my diary. I put the diary down on a wooden clothes basket next to the bath and took the phone.

"Shariece?"

"Happy New Year, babes!"

"Ah, thanks. Happy New Year! What you up to today?"

"I'm going to my mum's for dinner with Sean, innit, then going to pass by his mum's later. What about you?"

"I'm doing the same. Damien's coming to my mum's for dinner. Macy and Safire will be there as well, so it should be cool."

"Ah, tell Safire that I'm gonna call her soon, if not later, and check that she's OK. But I spoke to Maria the other day. She said that she sees René and Safire all the time but doesn't see you much."

"You know how it goes, Shariece, sometimes you just get caught up in the turns of life, innit and sometimes friends drift apart. But I did call Maria not too long ago, she said she's still with Donavan, who I haven't seen in ages, but I plan to visit her and René soon or invite them round for dinner or something coz I miss my old bredrens-dem from school, y'know." At that point, I thought of my cousin, Stella, and made a mental note to call her.

"Yeah, me too. Oh yeah, how're fings going wiv... what's that girl's name who you butted-up and now goes to your university?"

"All right! You don't have to say it like that, man...jeez! But anyway, her name's Mary-Anne."

"That's it. How are fings with her?"

"Really good, man. She's an absolute gem! I still find it hard to believe that we're bredrens. If the shoe was on the other foot, I dunno if I could do what she's doing. It's nuts, Shariece, she is just proper safe, and I really respect her for being able to forgive me the way she has without any deep explanation of where I was coming from. I guess she could see the sincerity in my apology."

"You apologised?" Shariece questioned. "You didn't tell me you apologised!"

"*Yeaahh!*" I sung. "Of course I did! What was I supposed to do? What I did was wrong. I'm adult enough to see that now, swallow my pride and attempt to fix it, which is what I did with my apology. It was surprisingly easier than I thought it would be, and I felt better for doing so."

"I'm not knocking what you've done, Steph. I'm just proud of you."

Knuckles rapped against the door. Damien's honey-brown face, beaming with love, appeared at the door once more.

"Babes, can you hurry up, please? It's after eleven, and I ain't even baded my skin yet."

"Yeah, sorry babes," I told him. I remembered what I had to do. "Shariece, I'm gonna have to rap with you a next time. I've gotta get ready and tidy up my house before I go." I pouted my lips at Damien and released a kiss for him to catch. He disregarded the airborne affection, bent down, and snatched a real kiss.

"All right, hun," Shariece mused, "you seem busy now, so I'll catch up with you later. Tell Aunty Sonya and Macy I said hi, and tell Safire

I'll chat to her later, and kiss little Ricardo for me, yeah?"

"Will do. Tell your mum and Sean I said hi and happy New Year, babes."

And with that, we ended the call. I cleaned up the bathroom, ran Damien's bath, and neatened up the place before getting dressed. Soon after, we were ready to leave.

*

The grinning circular face of Ricardo was pressed against the rippled glass of Mum's front door. He steamed it up whilst he made funny faces. I banged the knocker hard and watched it reverberate for some time. I trusted that the noise in Ricardo's ears would teach him a lesson about opening the door when you're supposed to. Ricardo squeezed his eyes closed and slammed his palms to his ears.

"You're evil," Damien said, shaking his head.

I giggled. "Ricardo, open the door," I told him. Ricardo looked at me squarely as I leaned over to kiss him on entering. I passed the family portrait of Mum, my sisters, and me on the passage wall opposite the kitchen. The family portrait made me smile. I was taken back to my earliest memories as a child, some good, some bad. I pointed at me, the one-year-old baby sat on Mum's lap. Damien gazed at the family portrait with pleasure.

I removed my Miu-Miu boots from snug feet and lined them up next to the other shoes. I neatened them so they were all positioned horizontally under gold coat pegs that branched out from a varnished slab of pinewood and drowned in heavy winter coats. My cheeks became warm whilst my nose still had the chill of the cold. I took off my three-quarter length wool and cashmere coat and hung it over a pile of others. I glanced into the kitchen. Laid out on the table was a set of china serving dishes with red and gold floral detailing. Sparkling silver serving spoons peeped out from under the lid of each dish. A large golden, roasted chicken took centre stage in a roasting dish, nestled amongst a pile of roast potatoes. Lured into the kitchen by tempting smells, I raised the lid of one of the serving dishes, which held a vegetarian soya meat stew. I surveyed the food. My mouth watered.

"You're not allowed to eat yet!"

Ricardo's squeaky voice took me unawares, and the lid of the dish plummeted from my grasp. I caught it just in time. Only one side clanked against the base of the chinaware. Thank God it didn't break!

"Who's in the kitchen?!" My mother's booming voice tumbled down the stairs and into the kitchen.

"It's me—everyfing's fine!" I called back. My eyes fixed on Ricardo, sending his shrinking body into retreat.

I stepped away from the table and went back into the passageway where Damien removed his shoes, and left them right there in the middle of the passageway floor. He was ogling the family portrait in awe. "Is that your mum?" he almost whispered. She was stunning. In this picture, as a mother of three young children in her mid-twenties, she was very slender, wore a fitted, leather, camel mini skirt and an off-the-shoulder T-shirt. I nodded, smiling at his showed interest. "She looks stunning," he said. I tidied up his shoes and strolled into the living room. Damien trailed behind.

The living room had gone through a few changes, but generally it was the same as when I had lived there some years ago. The carpet was the same light grey with a few spots of scrubbed-out stains. The set of *Encyclopaedia Britannica* still lined the far wall unused. Safire sat playing Beethoven's Für Elise on the piano opposite new leather sofas to the right of the encyclopedia. They were a soft mahogany brown positioned beneath a set of netted windows framed by gold patterned curtains.

"Happy New Year!" I cried, overpowering the luscious gospel voice bellowing from the speakers. This frightened Ricardo, who was unsure if I were still upset with him. He burrowed his head into the beanbag where his mum sat.

Macy got up and bared her teeth as she approached me with open arms, her gold tooth twinkling. We embraced as though we hadn't seen each other in years, even though we had.

"Why d'you take so long to come in?" she queried.

"I was checking out what was for dinner."

I introduced her to Damien. He nodded and finally got out, "You all right? I've heard a lot about you." This wasn't an enthusiastic 'I've heard a lot about you' but one with a negative intonation that suggested he'd 'heard' about Macy from empty conversations with people I considered to be a part of the 'passa passa'. The idle gossip and bitching.

"Is that right?" Macy's reply was scathing, indicating that she had read into his tone. My tongue was anchored in by shame.

I looked at him. My disappointment played out on my face. I wondered who he'd talked to. I wasn't one to talk about my family's business with lovers or friends. That was rule number one. I would never give him ammunition to use any information on my family against them or me. You just never knew with street guys, whether the street life was their past or present, you just never knew. But I was confused. Damien had assured me he had no interest in that way of life anymore and that he was withdrawing from friends within it.

His look in reply to my scepticism said, '*What have I done?*'

Safire drew my attention. "All right!" she exclaimed from where she perched at the piano. Her head waved musically. Her face brightened and became animated, and her piano-playing progressed into a performance, once she realised she had our attention.

I dropped down onto the sofa and rolled my eyes at her exhibitionist antics.

"I didn't know you could play the piano like that, Safire!" Damien flattered.

The flattery went to my sister's head and upped her performance, even more, exaggerating every move. She pressed harder on the keys, offered more flamboyance to her wrist manoeuvres and poise to her long neck. My eyes rolled clockwise. I threw myself against the wall in an ironic gesture and uttered, "Can someone shrink Safire's head? I can't breathe... this—big—head—is...pressed—against—my chest... killing me..." I fell to the floor as though I was dying, about to take my last breath. Macy cracked up laughing as Ricardo jumped on top of me. It only encouraged Safire even more.

As Safire finished her recital, I moved along the floor towards the stripy beanbag where Macy sat, now cradling her son as though he were a baby. Macy squeezed my left breast.

"Mace!" I screeched. "What're you doing? That hurts, man!"

"They look enormous, man! Why're your breast looking so big?" Her question held weight. I knew what she was insinuating, but she didn't need to worry. I could see Damien tensing up.

"I'm on my p's, that's why, so get whatever else you were thinking out of your head."

Damien relaxed.

"I know this song!" I cried, excited about the fact I was recognising gospel tracks now. "This is one of Kirk Franklin's; 'Why We Sing' or somefing... '*I sing because I'm happy, I sing because I'm free; His eye is on a sparrow, and that's the reason why I sing...*'" I crooned. Safire soon joined in with me before I let it filter out.

At that moment, Mum entered the room, turning my head and body language alike. I was still in an odd place with Mum. I never quite knew what to do or say around her. I always felt awkward. My sisters' sudden silence put pressure on me to act first, speak first, show love first, and do something *first*! Mum's big, voluptuous frame clearly startled Damien. He looked down at me, then up at her, two or three times. He was trying to make sense of her from that picture in her twenties. Mum was wearing white trousers and a white cotton shirt with ruffles on the sleeves and around the button strip. Her hair was naturally streaked with grey and had an inward cornrow straight down the middle from her forehead to the back of her neck. The plait at the back was tucked into the cornrow. Her face bore a smile, and her arms were semi-open, semi-encouraging an embrace.

"You all right, Steph?"

"Yeah. You all right, Mum?"

"Hello," Damien quickly threw in with a slight wave.

"Come and give your mum a kiss, then."

I got up reluctantly and went to her. I didn't want to be reluctant to hug my mum. I didn't want such a simple and natural act to feel weird or fake even. But I could not control my feelings. I did what I thought was right but which felt all wrong. Mum scanned my appearance up and down as I approached. She often did this. Looked me up and down usually before a critique. It only increased the awkwardness and my unease. I tried my hardest not to penny it. My sisters smiled cumbersomely at this somewhat bogus scene.

"So is this Damien?" Mum asked as we finally got to the end of our staged moment.

"Yeah. Damien, Mum; Mum, Damien."

Again, the wave came out. Mum grinned at him, observing his good looks and smart appearance—blue Firetrap denim jeans, a black Ralph Lauren polo-necked jumper, and fresh black socks. The smart-casual look I liked, which is why I'd bought him the outfit for Christmas.

"Is everyone ready to eat?" Mum asked. We all nodded and grunted yes. "OK, can we all stand so we can say our grace and ask God to bless the food?"

Damien peered at me, slightly startled as though he weren't aware of my church upbringing when I had referred to it many times. In the middle of the room, we formed a circle linking hands like Safire and I used to when playing 'Ring a Ring o'Roses' before we grew up to trade blows. Damien stood to my left with his hand linked to mine, which he intermittently squeezed. Damien's other hand linked with Mum, who linked with Ricardo, who linked with Macy, who linked with Safire, who was linked with me.

"Can we bow our heads?" Mum continued. "Dear Heavenly Father, I'd first like to thank you for bringing us all here today as a family and pray that you continue to unify us in a way that we understand the importance of family and support for each other when we're in need. We're gathered here for the consuming of an abundant amount of food; I pray you bless the food, Lord, and allow it to nourish our bodies and purify any ailments known or unknown, as you have the power to do. Lord, I'd like to pray for my children, in particular Steph..."

My ears burned upon hearing my name. Automatically Damien and Safire both increased the pressure on my hands. Their eyes broke open and fixated upon mine, which were open wide beneath a furrowed brow.

Mum went on as I went to look up at her, perplexed by the unsaid "...that she may find you and experience your love in full submission of herself to you, oh Lord! Have mercy on us, oh Lord, as we're all in need of your mercy and grace. Forgive us, Lord, forgive us of our shortcomings, fallacy, and folly, as without your forgiveness, we are worthless. Teach us, Lord, teach us to love one another and not to hold malice up within our hearts that they remain purified to receive your touch—"

A tutt and heavy sigh escaped from Safire's lips as she whispered, "This is taking long; hurry up, man."

Mum carried on determinedly, irritation clouding her face. "Finally... I'd like to take this opportunity to welcome Damien into the family and ask, Lord, that you direct him to the right path so his relationship with my daughter can be based on your values, Lord, and not the temptations of the world. Thank you for the food we're about to receive; in Jesus' name, our Lord and Saviour, amen."

With a chorus of 'amen' the chain broke. I collapsed back onto the sofa, watching Mum stare down on Safire.

"Don't yuh ever interrupt me when mi ah pray! Dis is God's house and if yuh can't respect di Almighty under in dis yuh roof, COME OUT!" Mum's nostrils flared like those of a smoking dragon. Safire didn't take the bait with a verbal response. She did so in body. Her face disgruntled, as she slumped herself to the ground. Mum turned to me. "Steph?" I looked up at her with questioning eyes. Ricardo took cover behind his mother's rear. "D'you wanna help me dish out the food for everyone?"

'No' was about to leap from my tongue. I didn't want to be in the kitchen with her right then. I didn't want to be in a confined space with her and that discontented vibe she was carrying. But Macy interjected, "Nah, Mum, just let everyone dish out their own food, so no one gets what they don't want."

"OK, d'you wanna sort out you and Ricardo first, den Safire can sort hers, and Steph can sort out herself and...Damien."

At that moment, my phone chimed from my black leather and canvas Gucci clutch bag. "Hello?" I answered once I'd retrieved it from the bag.

"Hello Steph, it's Mary-Anne. How are you?"

"Oh, you all right?" My pitch was high. My dimples sunk in deep and my cheeks became taut with delight. Damien perched next to me, mouthing "Who's dat?" He placed his ear against the speaker of the handset. Macy headed to the kitchen. Safire shuffled over to me. She clasped her hands onto my kneecap, willing me to divulge who I was talking. I continued my conversation with the 'five minutes!' hand gesture. This was when I anticipated I'd tell them both who I was trying to have a private conversation with on the phone. At that point, Damien's phone rang. He got up and left the room. The front door opened and closed. Mum was standing in the centre of the living room ogling Safire and me with a curious gaze, still seeming vexed. Safire's hands continued to squeeze at my kneecaps. I brushed her hands off me. "Move!" I told her.

"Who's dat?" she pried again.

"Mary-Anne," I whispered. Her bulbous hazel-brown eyes widened. When I looked up to Mum, the slightly dipped brow that accompanied my eye contact silently informed her I wasn't at one with her observing me, she bared her teeth tryingly and left the room.

Mary-Anne was talking about a project we were undertaking at university. We had to do a dissertation and photoshoot on a subject matter of our choice. Mary-Anne had chosen politics and its relationship with fashion. I decided to focus on beauty and how it was perceived, but hadn't developed my thoughts yet, unlike Mary-Anne.

"Babes," Damien's voice was panic-stricken as he entered the living room, "I've gotta go."

"What?" I frowned. "Mary-Anne, can I talk to you later?"

"Yeah sure," she said. "Speak soon and have a lovely New Year."

"You too." I ended the call and turned back to Damien. "What's going on? Why have you gotta go?"

"I can't explain now. Just trust me. I've gotta go. Nice seeing you again, Safire." Damien blurted fast-paced goodbyes to Mum and Macy and more or less bolted out the door. I followed behind him, questioning him on his departure, his leaving out of the blue before we'd eaten, his leaving without explanation, his blatant rudeness...*my* embarrassment.

I watched his receding back. Fear and panic raced through my body. The front door closed without me noticing. I did a 180-degree turn and walked back past the kitchen where Mum and Macy were more than likely passing judgement on me and the man I had brought back to my family's home as 'my man'. *Please don't say anything, don't ask me no questions, just don't say a word!* I internally begged of them. Just as I was thinking it, Mum's mouth began to move.

"Uh-uhhhhhh. Him nah 'ave no manners! I wonder what kind of lifestyle him ah live... on big New Year's day him just lef' we like soh. Uh-uhhhhhhhh! So where's he going?"

"Didn't you hear me already ask him that?" My tone was flat, grave, and impatient.

"Yeah, but mi didn't hear him answer you."

"Exactly! So why're you asking me for if you know, I don't know? Stop winding me up, Mum."

"But wait!" she started. "Gyal, who yuh t'ink yuh ah talk to? Heee? Don't yuh dare get bright wid me, true-say yuh lickle bwoy-frien' vex yuh. NAH PASS YUH VEXATION 'PON ME! Wid yuh renkin self..."

"Allow it, Mum!" Macy pleaded, neatening the onion rings and finely cut pepper slices on her plate so that they lay balanced on the fried red snapper fish. She continued to serve other foods onto her plate. Ricardo wrapped his arms around her thigh as I shuffled my foot into my boot.

"But how dare she get renk wid me ca her man nah know how fi treat her." Mum turned to me with a jug of liquidised fruit in her hand. "DAT'S WHY YUH NAH FI LAY DOWN WID DOG! Ca you will catch flees!"

"How is he a dog?" I defended.

"Soh where 'im deh?" Mum demanded.

Not having the answer to that question pained me. I felt my glands inflame, and my eyes fill up with tears simultaneously. I found my coat and went into the living room.

I grabbed my bag from beside the fireplace and left without the offering of too much sentiment. Mum cussed me. I was barely through the front door, but she found it imperative to exclaim, "Dat's why yuh nah fi lay down wid dogs!' because of course, she was offering a new piece of parental information that was vital for my consumption, and I probably hadn't heard it before.

"Mace, I'll see you soon," I said on departure.

Safire pulled her big brown suede and fur coat from the peg, and we were off. At the minicab office on Lee High Road, Safire and I conversed about Damien, his brother Darren's recent release from prison and Mary-Anne. I had calmed down. Nicotine gave me stress relief I needed.

The drive home was spent with the investigative mind of Jessica Fletcher from the crime series *Murder She Wrote*, asking all the questions on what, why, where and how? I feared the worst. I spent the remainder of the day in silence and tears, diarising my thoughts and feelings.

Later on, I received calls of seasonal well wishes from Dad, Nina, Charlene, Stella, Safire and Macy, Jermaine, Leroy, René, Shariece, and Claudia.

I heard nothing from Damien.

CHAPTER
TWENTY-FOUR

THE BOOMERANG'S COMING BACK

1ˢᵗ January 2001 – Home

Oh Di, what can I say? I feel shame. I'm embarrassed that as much as I can't stand my mum sometimes, as much as I find her a hypocrite and I don't want to care what she says or thinks. She's probably right. Not that I think Damien's a dog. Well in truth, I dunno. It's just…it's just the way he moves puts me out of sync. Things seem to be going right for me, then he turns up and things go wrong…like I've caught his flees and am scratching alongside him. Today was supposed to be a normal, good day, celebrating New Year's with my family and my boyfriend. People who I love. Instead, I've spent the last few hours in tears, wondering what's wrong with me. Why does he treat me this way? Is this the kind of love someone like me deserves? I want more from love, Di. I need more.

The following night, as I was asleep in bed, the faint sound of my ringing phone stirred me. I groggily reached out for it.

"'Lo?" I croaked in a whisper.

"Babes, it's me…I need to see you… I'm coming now." There were long pauses between his words, doused with alarm.

"My car's 'side…."

"Steph! It's me, wake up! I need you!"

"Hmm…Dam'n…t'morning…see you…hmmm, 'morrow."

"Nah, I need to see you now! Stop chatting shit!! I need to speak to you…I'll be there in ten minutes."

I put the phone down and fell back onto my pillow, sinking into its softness. The land of nod quickly grabbed back hold of me…

RING!

RIINNNGGGG!!

RIIINNNNGGGGG!!!

I sat up in bed and took a moment to assemble my faculties. Once I had differentiated the dream from my reality, I hurried to the front door. Dressed in a white T-shirt and plain black cotton knickers. I swayed like a drunk. "What's so 'portant yat could wait 'morrow?" I burbled, my eyes still closed.

Damien darted in through the door. He was out of breath, chest heaving, body perspiring. He was boomed out of his head—clearly afraid for his life!

"Quick, close the door and come here. Just hold me. Please, I want you to hold me."

"Come upstairs, come upstairs," I repeated, afraid of what the neighbours might hear.

I led him up to the living room by a trembling hand. I wrapped my arms about him. I clasped his neck and the back of his head in the motherly way the situation asked of me.

"What's wrong? Why are you shaking like this?" I asked, locked in his trembling arms, held tight against his vibrating body.

His silence was enough to increase my heart rate and turn my stomach. What the hell has happened to this boy? I thought.

"Damien, let go of me a second, let me get you a drink. Have a seat and try to calm down." He released me. I grabbed a tumbler in the kitchen and quarter filled it with Ray & Nephew's Jamaican white rum, and returned to him. "Here you are, drink that, and then tell me what's wrong."

He downed it in one gulp like his life depended on it. "Get me another one," he said. I got him another, and he did the same. "Steph, you need to promise me that if I tell you this, you won't leave me… promise me!" he cried.

"Damien, what have you done?"

"Promise me!"

"But what have you done? You're frightening me!"

"Babe, I need you to promise me…you have to promise me!"

"OK, I promise, now what is it?"

He got to his feet, circled the room like a cross-examiner in court. "It's Darren—"

"What about him?"

"You know he's out now, innit?"

"Yeah, of course."

"Well, it was him that phoned me yesterday, said he was in a tight situation and needed my help. He reminded me that family have to stick together and said he was sorry for asking me to get involved in this, but he had no one else to turn to. That's all I needed to know, and so I went."

"That's all you needed to *know*?"

"Babes, listen, please! This is really hard for me. What I'm about to tell you ain't no joke."

I gulped. "OK... Go on."

And so his story began...

"...I left your mum's in a mad rush, properly pushing the engine of my 206 jalopy, burning some crazy rubbers on the road as I zung down to Peckham. I was feeling excited, y'know, I wan'ed to see what my brovver had on lockdown for me. He asked me to stop off somewhere to get some black bags and tape, but true-say it was New Year's day; trust me, this was long. I finally found an open petrol station and got them anyway. I get to North Peckham Estate not too long after, an' ring da doorbell on the seventh floor. He opened it blacked off in his tracksuit wearing a balaclava. I'm finking; what da fuck's going on? But he just grabs me inside and leads me down the...like hallway, making up pure noise on da creaking floorboard. He goes down into a small dark room at the back of the flat dragging my arm wiv him, and den stands in front of dis lean-off chair in dis little dusty, empty room with drawn dirty patterned curtains—you know dem old skool ones? Then he said:

"'Ere's what's gonna 'appen now; eiver you're gonna take us to where da belly is... And don't FUCKING shake ya 'ead like you nah know wha' man ah chat 'bout! Ca I done get da full SP on you, blood, an' I done know dat you got two an' a half of ki' of white inna New Cross...an' I know where ya baby-mudder live. So once again what's gonna happen, blood; eiver you're gonna take us to New Cross where da belly is, or, you see my brovver behind you? He's gonna tape up your eyelids by your eyelashes and burn the bottom lashes till you start talking, coz I don't fink you recognise what time dis is, blood. And while my brudder tortures you, blood—An' D, when you done burn off his eyelashes, start on his pubic hairs—I'm gonna go to ya baby-mudder's yard and fuck her. You 'ear what I'm saying, blood? I'm gonna fuck your baby-mudder's brains out, den put one of dese pretty bullets in her head.' He starts loading the barrel of a forty-four magnum, spins it and clips it shut.

"I'm just standing there still asking myself, What da fuck is going on? Wid da plastic bag in my hand, and den he spins the chair round and dere's dis black man dat I've seen on da ends, a man dat I know. His face is all blood-up (busted eyes, fat lip, swollen nose and cheekbones) and cut-up like Darren must've been just carving shapes in his boat and just t'umping him silly. His mouth was gagged wiv a bandanna; hands and feet tied together wiv rope. Instantly I'm finking SHIT! He's seen my face, so whatever happens from here on, I'll always be a part of dis. He knows my face and when he can't get my brovver he'll be coming for me…I'm a dead man!

"Then my brovver says, 'Damien! Hold my t'ing for me while I'm gone,' he pulls out a nine millimetre from the back of his waist, and I'm finking, Shit, he knows my name now too, 'and if dis bredda gets out of hand, pop two inna him. When he's ready to talk, hopefully before I get to his baby-mudder, den bell me on my blower…seen?'

"I don't know where the word came from, I swear, but I said yeah—it just came out my mout'…'yeah', and dat's when I realised I'm properly involved. I am now a part of dis robbery and will have to see it out till the end. So I took da gat and straight away I felt empowered. The control's been passed my way and I'm taking it and at da end of it I'm gonna be rich and when I meet my girl I can do for her like I'm supposed to…"

My stomach churned with revulsion. However, I knew the feeling of empowerment that he referred to. I'd been at the mercy of it in my adolescence when other people's fear only fuelled that feeling of empowerment. But I was older, somewhat wiser and, irrespective of the internal battles I continued to face with managing my anger, I could see how wrong this was and how his involvement could not be justified. I tried to remain silent so he could finish his story. My tongue ached with a desire to be heard. Ached so hard it pressed up against the inside of my teeth rebelling against its caged environment behind clenched teeth.

"You're a man, Damien!" I blurted out. "You're a big...fucking... man! How can you tell me as a man you had no control over getting involved? You had control! You just chose not to take it!"

"Babes, please don't shut me down like this. I know what I've done is wrong—trust me, I *know*! But I'm not you! I don't have the strength you have to turn away from things and certain people...even your family. I don't know if I can do that. I don't know if that's in me. I need my family, Steph...the good and the bad...and they need me. So please, babe, don't judge me on your own merits right now because you can't make me feel any worse than I already do. I nearly committed suicide this evening."

"What? What are you talking about? Why? Why would you wanna do somefing like that?" I raised my eyebrows hands were gesticulating wildly.

"Because I don't think I'm worthy of living!" He paced my front room, teeth clenched, his nose rippled with rage, and his breaths were deep. "LOOK AT ME!" he shouted. "I'm twenty-three, and what have I achieved? Don't answer! I already know—NOTHING! I've been in and out of prison. I can't even finish a business course, and I can't get a job—"

"Yes, you can, Damien!" I stopped him mid-flow. I was standing before him and held each of his arms firmly. "You can be what you wanna be, do what you wanna do—you just have to make a choice! I've come to realise that life is about choices, Damien, nothing more, nothing less. You've just gotta make da right ones, and everything else will fall in place."

"Am I the right choice for you?"

The question caught me off-guard, but I answered it anyway. "If you wanna be. I love you, Damien, but you've just gotta fix-up. Start initiating things and stop waiting for me to tell you what to do. You need to get a job…fast! If you want me to help you, I will, but I'm not gonna do it for you. That won't help you better yourself."

"I'm hearing you, and I will do this properly now, I mean it. Not only for me, but for us, y'get me? But wait, there's more to this story that you're not gonna like."

I exhaled until my air supply was no more. "All right, go on…"

"My brovver takes da keys to my Peugeot and leaves. I'm holding da nine millimetre, feeling out its weight and polishing its silver surface wiv my jumper, and I'm smiling. Don't ask me why I'm smiling but I am, somewhere inside me, I've found contentment, and it feels good. The nerves have already disappeared. I pull open the cartridge to check that it's full…it is, so I slam it back shut and put it in my waist noticing the busted eyes of da kidnapped bredda widen and den him sounding some kind of noise, and I rummage t'rough da plastic bag. I take out da Sellotape t'ing and start to tape up his mout', briefing him on da situation again.

"His eyes just continue to widen. I tape back his eyelashes and he starts to grunt. I mean proper recklessly like he's screaming behind the tape and bandanna. I stand over his fucked-up boat, blood everywhere, and take out a blue clipper from my jeans pocket and ignite a flame…

"'OhmmmmmmMMMMM!' he screams…but he can't.

"The flame singes his bottom lashes and burns da lip of his lid. He's in proper agony. I'm blinding him! I'm blinding dis brer, but can't…won't stop. He stomps his feet on da floor, which I think is him

signalling dat he's prepared to talk, so I strip off da tape from his mout'
and untie da bandanna, and he said: 'Eh bwoy, mi know sa' yuh nah
'pose fi invulve inna dis; but 'ear wha' mi ah tell yuh, if yuh let me go
now, mi gi' yuh mi WORD, mi will let yuh live. But IF, if yuh nah let
me goh NOW t' bloodclaat, yuh an' ya brudder better just KILL MY
BLOODCLAAT NOW! Ca mi ah goh kill di two o' yuh, ya mudder,
ya farder, sista, ya granpuppa, granmudda, every BLOODCLAAT
BUDDY inna ya family, an' every BLOODCLAAT BUDDY dat 'tend
ya funeral...so 'MEMBER dat every BLOODCLAAT time ya bu'n me!'

"His eyes kept tearing out at me like he was possessed and he meant
every last word he just said. I look at him knowing that I know his face
but unable to pinpoint it, but knowing it's close. Just not close enough
for me to let my brovver down, so I tape back up his mouth and he
stares in my eyes informing me I'm a dead man. No joke, dis man was
letting me know dat I'm a walking dead man. I tie da bandanna round
his eyes. Man can't even bear to look at him; can't bear to deal wiv the
f'reat he's putting on man tryna get me vex. MAN AH BAD MAN
TOO, YANNA. I relight da flame by his ears; close enough to frighten
him, but not to burn him...

"He tries to scream again...but he can't. Again, he stomps his feet,
tricked by da sound of da gas and closeness of da flame. I stop. Strip
off da tape.

"'All right, me'll tell yuh where de belly is, just don't bu'n me,
PLEASE!' he says. So I phone my brovver...

"'He's ready to take us to da belly now, where are you?' I say.

"He says, 'I'm wid his baby-mudda like I said; she's lying underneat'
me.'

"'What've you done to her? Is she still alive?' I ask, suddenly worried.

"'Just cool, brov, she's all right; I'll see you in ten...seen?' he replies.
Then my man shouts:

"'If 'im kill mi baby-mudda, mi nah tek uno NOH WHERE!'

"My brovver hears this and says, 'D, gag dat fool back up before he makes me act off of impulse an' blow dis gal 'way.'

"'Just cool, yeah, she's still alive,' I reassure my man and put the phone to his ear so he can hear her voice. But the more I look at this man the more I'm starting to realise that he's someone I know. I let my brovver go trying desperately to figure out where I've seen this face but the face in my head just won't show clear.

"And like my brovver said, he was back in ten. We bag him up in two black bags, punching out two holes for his eyes, and shift him into da back seat of da car, drive up to New Cross, down into Ghetto and park up.

"'So where's da belly now?' Darren asks sitting in front of the man's scrunched-up body, which is lying across the back seat. And now he's got da magnum pointing to his head.

"'It inna ah rucksack underneat' di floorboard under mi bed,' he says all muffled through the bags.

"'Dere's just one bedroom, yeah?' Darren asks.

"'Noh, ah two mi 'ave.'

"'So which one is it?'

"'Di one next to di bat'room.'

"'All right, I'm going in; gi' me da key.' Darren reaches out his hand, but da man can't reach.

"'Mi can' reach, it inna mi pocket.'

"Darren tears da bag around his pocket area digging into his pocket. He takes out the keys wrapped round a bag of weed.

"'Keep da nine milli to his head while I'm gone, back in a sec,' Darren says to me. He takes off his bally and dusses across da road. I just keep da gat in da middle of da two front seats lined up to the centre of his head, watching da road over da steering wheel at da same time.

My man's breathing hard like he's suffocating, so I tear the mouth open some more asking if he's OK. And dat's when the face becomes clear. I've seen this man's face in someone's...in someone's face I properly know...in... Tyrone, Tyrone from Ghetto. I've seen this man's face in Tyrone from Ghetto, a man I was cool with on road and in prison, and all I can fink about now is you, knowing how close you're connected. So I ask him, I had to ask him, 'Is your son's name Tyrone?'

"'How yuh know?' he asks.

"I swear, my heart just sank when I realised we were robbing Tyrone's dad. All when the man's calling my name asking me how I knew he was Tyrone's dad, I couldn't say. I couldn't move, I couldn't speak—I was gobsmacked...proper gobsmacked! All I could do was think of you and what this would do to us..."

My hand clamped round my mouth as I sat stunned. My tongue temporarily paralysed.

"Steph, say something, please. The silence is killing me. I can't bear the look you're giving me. Don't be disgusted with me, please. I didn't mean for this to happen; to get involved in somefing like dis and I'm properly regretting it. That's why I came straight here..."

"Straight here from where? What did you do to Tyrone's father? What did you do to Killer Man Joe? *Oh-my-gosh!*" I screamed. "You're a dead man, Damien. You're a walking dead man!"

"I know! I know!" he cried, falling upon his knees. "I need your help, Steph; I don't know what to do. What should I do?!"

"Where is he?"

"We dropped him in the bushes on the A2."

"*Oh-my-gosh*, is he alive?!"

"Yeah, he was still alive, just badly beaten up."

"We've gotta go and get him..."

"What?"

"We've gotta go and get him! What'd you take from him?"

"Two and a half ki'. My brovva gave me a ki'."

"Where is it?"

"In da car."

"You've gotta give it back."

"What?"

"You've gotta give it back! D'you wanna die?"

"No!"

"I'm tryna prevent your head from getting blown off, and you're questioning me! We've gotta go and get him, and you've gotta give him back his work."

"But how will that stop him from smoking me? He'll still wanna get to my brovver."

"It's a start. You'll have to go missing for a bit; keep your head down until this all blows over." I glanced up at the clock on the wall. It was 5:10 in the morning. "Come, we've gotta go to my sister's."

"Why?" Damien seemed startled.

"Because Joseph's Jason's dad too, y'know! And Jason's the only way we're gonna prevent your head from being blown off your shoulder top."

I wasn't clear on what I was doing or how I felt. My boyfriend, the person who I had chosen to partner with, had robbed, tortured and probably killed my ex-boyfriend's dad, the grandfather of my nephew, Ricardo. How this would impact my family or even my relationship, I wasn't clear. Whether, in respect of all that was happening between us, I wanted to remain with him, support his choices and behaviour as my boyfriend, again, I wasn't clear. I wanted more from life, more from love. And even so, I did not want Damien to die. Plus Killer Man Joe could be still be alive. We could prevent his death. My frustration with Damien and his unconscionable choices served no purpose at this time. All I could focus on was potentially preventing the loss of life.

Within twenty minutes, we had arrived at Macy's front door. It was still pitch black outside. Snowflakes had started to fall, gently landing on our faces. Ricardo opened the front door. He was wide awake wearing navy-blue pants with a picture of Spiderman on the front, and a navy-blue dressing gown tied loosely round his waist. He kissed me with raised shoulders and twinkling fingers. "We'll play soon, bubba," I told him, directing him back to the TV where Floella Benjamin, with her enthralled and energetic face, pranced around a garden with dolls. Soon enough, Macy came downstairs.

"What are you doing here?" she quizzed, naturally puzzled by my early arrival and, based on the frown between her eyebrows, rather pissed off that I'd arrived there with Damien without any warning.

"Macy, I'm sorry for coming out of the blue like this, but something's happened..." I looked at Ricardo with sorrowful eyes, then back at Macy. Damien hung his head in shame.

"Ricardo, go upstairs to your room, please."

Ricardo went upstairs sulking but didn't say anything back to his mum.

"Jason!" Macy called out. "Jason!"

"I'm coming, babes. I'm coming!"

My heart pounded for the thirty seconds or so that it took Jason to enter the living room. He was bare-chested with pyjama bottoms on; his hair neatly cornrowed back. "So what's all the excitement about?" he asked whilst taking a seat.

We all sat down, bar Damien. As considerately and as briefly as possible, I told him what had happened and what we were now trying to do. Jason remained calm throughout, then suddenly realisation kicked in, and he leapt out after Damien, circling his hands about Damien's neck, choking him.

Macy lunged after Jason. Hauled him off Damien by his waist. "Jason, no!" she screamed. "Get off him! Calm down! Come on, our son's upstairs! This isn't going to resolve the situation…"

I pulled Jason's fingers off Damien's neck one by one. Damien held onto Jason's wrist with increasing resistance.

"I'm sorry, man, I'm sorry!" Damien proclaimed to Jason, who he had met for the first time. "I didn't plan for this, trust me, I didn't plan for this to happen to no one, let alone your dad. I just got pulled into this situation unknowingly, and dat's why I'm trying to resolve it, but I feel like I'm a dead man no matter how this goes! C'mon, I know Tyrone man, I used to chat to man on road, in jail—why would I do this to someone I know knowing how easily it can come back on me?"

Jason finally eased his grip. He fell back on the chair, smashed his head back against it, and growled.

"WHY?!" he demanded, his tone full of poison, his eyes full of disbelief and fury. "Why are you road-man so callous and thoughtless? Dat's someone's dad; you must've known dat! But still, you're gonna rob and half kill someone's dad—in this day and age?! What if someone done this to your dad, Damien? Tell me, what if someone done this to your dad—what would you do to that person?"

"I dunno is the truth, Jason. I ain't seen my dad for years, but I'm sure if I had a proper relationship with him, I would respond to fings differently. But you've gotta believe me when I say: this isn't me, I didn't intend for any of this."

"You didn't intend to, but you did, so now your intention becomes invalid. It's times like this when I'm so glad my brovver isn't around to get caught up in some joke t'ings like this. I'm so glad he's got another chance in life to do things right without temptations from his joke bredren-dem and his peers."

Damien glanced at me. Every time Jason or my sister spoke of Tyrone, my throat clammed up. I tried to mask my emotion with words: "If we're to get to your dad, Jason, we need to go now."

And with that, Jason, Damien, and I left.

CHAPTER TWENTY-FIVE

AN EYE FOR AN EYE

10th February 2001 – South-east London, 122 bus to Claudia's

Dear Di, sometimes I wonder when I'll get a break. What more do I personally need to do to earn a break. Irrespective of this mood, this feeling that occasionally occupies my spirit and tampers with my thoughts, I'm enjoying the feeling of excitement that comes with passing your driving test. Time to say goodbye to bus rides. Yup, that's right, I passed my driving test and now have an official driving licence that permits me to drive legally on the roads. Now all I need is a car.

This is likely to be one of my final bus rides. I want to change the way I think and document the negative stuff that impacts my life. In effect, I want to reduce the frequency of having these types of stories to tell. Like today I'm on my way to Claudia's, who I've missed immensely since our fallout. I'm looking forward to seeing her in person. I know she'll have questions about Damien, even though it's been like six weeks since Damien went into hiding and I've not seen him. He's somewhere in the Northern England, which is good for me to be fair. It's given me the space to see the negative effect he's had on me. I know I need to leave the relationship, but I cling onto having loyalty and understanding. The truth is maybe...the likelihood is that weirdly I question if I'm good enough to do better than him since Tyrone left. I know, Macy and Charlene would be having serious words with me if they could hear me. But it's the truth. Maybe this is what I deserve? That's what I hear in my head. Both voices target me late at night when I'm vulnerable. You're all he's got; give him another chance; he's what you deserve! These voices strangely keep me here, against your better judgement Di, waiting for his arrival from his hideout. That's why I continue to talk to him over the phone since that night we rescued Killer Man Joe from the side of a dual carriageway, begging for his leniency as we drove to Queen Elizabeth Hospital in the hope that saving his life might incline him to save Damien's. Man, that day was nuts. That day was cold...

Driving at over one hundred miles an hour made it a short journey to Queen Elizabeth Hospital from where we found Killer Man Joe. Damien and I burst open the double doors to the hospital's Accident & Emergency unit. Jason staggered behind us carrying his father's weight, slumped in his arms, his face swollen and disfigured and bruised and bleeding.

"Help!" I cried, "We need a doctor! Can somebody help?!"

Sky blue overalls and white-jacketed hospital staff rushed from different directions tooled with lights, a stethoscope, and a bed.

Let's get him onto the bed, the female doctor in a white coat said. She looked to her three colleagues, who gently took Killer Man Joe from Jason's arms. She felt his pulse, "it's faint," she said. She turned to Jason, "What's his name?"

"Joseph. Joseph Boateng," he replied.

"What's happened to him?"

I looked to Jason with pleading eyes, "I dunno, I think he was badly beaten up, and this is how we found him."

Whilst I felt relief that Jason decided not to give Damien up to the police, where ultimately his answers to this line of questioning would be going, I knew Jason had also decided to give Damien and Darren up to the streets. That meant there were no rules of law. Anything could go down and be accepted as retaliation against the atrocities received by Killer Man Joe.

"Joseph, can you hear me?" She asked, shining the light in his eye. "Joseph, my name is Dr. Mensah. Do you know where you are?" With no response, Dr. Mensah continued, "You are at Queen Elizabeth's Hospital, and you are badly hurt, so we are going to take care of you. Blink if you can hear me."

We all peered down at Killer Man Joe, waiting eagerly for his response. Several seconds passed before his puffed, singed eye gently moved to attempt a blink.

"And how are you related to Joseph?" Dr. Mensah asked.

"He's my dad."

Dr. Mensah went on to ask a list of medical questions, which Jason answered "no" to, then she wheeled Killer Man Joe away. Damien and I sat waiting on the grey metal seats whilst Jason paced the corridors. It was a busy morning for the start of the year. It was the second of January, aside from A&E staff, most people hadn't yet returned to work. Damien rocked in his seat, biting his nails, spellbound by a surge of nerves. A dark cloud of the unknown lurked over him. I felt his worry and saw the halo of his fear. The mercy required here was out of our hands. Joseph was called Killer Man Joe for a reason.

Barely an hour passed before the police arrived. Dr. Mensah directed the two officers towards Damien and me with a point of her finger.

A tall, slim-framed officer led his shorter and broader counterpart. "Jason Boateng?" he said.

I pointed toward Jason, who was still pacing the corridor.

"And you are?" he queried wide-eyed.

"Is there a reason why you want to know my name, Officer?" I asked.

Surprised by my response, his shorter and broader colleague interjected, "Sorry, Madam. As you know, Joseph Boateng has recently suffered acute grievous bodily harm, so we need to understand as much information as possible from the people around him. Any information, no matter how big or how small, you can provide at this stage will help in finding the perpetrators." At that point, the taller officer walked over to Jason.

"OK, no probs," I confirmed, "My name's Stephanie Johnson."

"And how do you know Joseph?" the shorter officer continued.

"His son Jason," I said, pointing my head at Jason, "Is my sister's boyfriend. They have a son together."

"And before tonight, when was the last time you saw Joseph?"

"Oh my gosh, it's been ages...months...maybe a year plus."

"And can you think of any reason why someone would want to hurt Joseph in this way?"

I raised my shoulders, shaking my head.

"OK." He conceded. "One last question: how did you come to learn of Joseph's situation?"

"My boyfriend received an anonymous tip-off. Of course, he told me, and we told my sister and Jason."

The short officer looked to Damien, who was sitting opposite me, with a renewed interest. "Is he your boyfriend?" I nodded, and he continued, "And his name is?"

"Damien."

He walked over to Damien, who had a sombre disposition. When I glanced over at Jason who the slimmer and taller officer was still questioning, he had an air of frustration. His brow was furrowed, face questioning and his hand gestures seemed to direct questions back at the officer. A man rushed into reception, pushing a woman who was pregnant and screaming in a wheelchair. Nurses came out to see to them and guided them more than likely to the maternity ward.

Finally, Dr. Mensah returned. It had been almost ninety minutes, "You can come through now." She sought out Jason's eye contact to add, "He has a broken jaw, so will find it difficult to talk for a while. Two of his left side ribcage are fractured, and he has a lot of bruising to the body and face. His eyelashes have been burnt, which has caused some damage to the retina, but nothing to cause long-term sight problems. He may still be in some pain, but he's had a good dosage of pain relief that should start to take effect now. Joseph has undoubtedly had a lucky escape. If you hadn't found him when you did, he probably wouldn't have lasted another twenty-four hours.

The officers thanked us all for our cooperation and advised that they would be in touch if they needed anything further. As we discussed in the car, our stories remained the same: Damien received an anonymous tip-off where Killer Man Joe was left badly hurt. He told me, and then we told Jason. Jason and I went to see Killer Man Joe whilst Damien waited in the ward's waiting area. He was asleep.

Jason buried his face into one hand. He peeked through his fingers at his father and heaved himself into a chesty cry.

"I'm so sorry," I expressed, and placed my hand on his back in a circular motion.

At that point, his father stirred, and his eyes opened. His face lit up upon setting eyes on us.

I smiled. "Joseph, are you OK?"

Killer Man Joe squeezed a smile and tried to speak.

"Dad, don't speak. It's OK, just rest. I'm just glad you're still wiv us."

Damien entered. Killer Man Joe's eyes enlarged, and he tried to sit up.

"Lie down, Dad, please. I know what you must be thinking, but really and truly, if it weren't for dis yout' you may not've made it."

"Sir, I'm truly sorry. Dat's all I can say is I'm sorry, man." The plead in Damien's words was prevalent.

"Burial....'ave fi...goh...run..." Killer Man Joe whispered loud enough for us all to hear.

The next steps were clear. Someone would die, and loved ones would partake in a burial ceremony. What was yet to be clarified was whether mercy would be afforded to Damien, and whether Damien would truly accept this without wanting to side with his brother in potential warfare. Time would tell.

*

In the weeks that followed, a series of events occurred. Damien moved to a safe house. A privately rented flat in the north of England. Killer Man Joe made a full recovery. Darren was murdered in cold blood on Peckham High Street by a man in a balaclava on a motorcycle. Two bullets to the head and four into the body finished him. I didn't tend the funeral. Watching this unfold was a sad realisation of how quickly my past life had become part of my present. This was something I had to change. That bus journey en route to Claudia's was just another moment when the urge for change resonated.

CHAPTER TWENTY-SIX

ECLECTIC MOMENTS

15th February 2001 – Home, Forest Hill

Di, it's been weeks since that terrifying night, and yet I still find myself doing a double take, checking my back, blighted by paranoia. Wondering what if someone wants to use me as a comeback for Darren, Damien or even Killer Man Joe. How I allowed myself to get caught up in all of that chaos, I do not know. Since Damien's been gone, it's actually been therapeutic knowing that he's in a safe house, far, far away, and will likely not return for a while. We didn't conclude our relationship was over, but I expect it to fizzle out over time. I'm not quite sure how to end a relationship with someone who's possessive and prone to violence. I will have the proper conversation at some point, and not me simply alluding, but directly informing. I just don't want to get hurt, but neither do I want him to get hurt. Yes Di, I've evolved, but I'm still no shrinking violet...

It was 4.30 p.m. on a weekday afternoon. Stella and I were chilling at my flat. Missy Elliot's 'Higher Ground' played in the background. Stella slumped across the beanbag in the living room. A bobbled cream scarf lassoed around her neck. Looked hand-knitted. Like something a grandmother would make. She stroked the leather of the beanbag deep in thought. I watched her from where I sprawled across a rug. We tackled the ever-growing dilemma of men and love. A subject I usually veered away from. Stella had recently bumped into Typo, now her ex, during her lunch break at college. She hadn't seen him in years.

Stella studied Health and Social Care at Lewisham College. On ambling up to Honey Pot, a Caribbean restaurant off of Lewisham Way, she saw him. Parked outside in a new Alfa Romeo. They rapped about for a short period before her nerves took the best of her, and she hurried back to class without getting any food.

"Why, what was up?" I enquired without thinking.

Stella sat up. Her face subdued. She sighed and exclaimed, confused, "The baby, innit!"

Of course, how could I forget!

"I used to think about it all the time," Stella expressed. "It was only recently I stopped. When I saw him like dat, just out of the blue like dat, I instantly thought of our baby again. And the fact that I knew he didn't know about it just made it worse...made me feel worse. I miss what we had, man. Not like the sex or anyfing, but...like...the friendship, y'get me, Steph?"

"Yeah, I hear dat. It's a shame you guys have lost dat, but...try not to feel guilty...you did what you thought was best for you. Can you imagine trying to raise a child in your teens? I don't think anyone would judge you for what you did." I paused, observing Stella's forced smile. "OK, so tell me what he said then." I continued, rolling onto my tummy like a schoolgirl at a slumber party. "What did you guys talk about?"

"Not'in' much. Time was limited. He said he'd call me Thursday afternoon—today—when he's back on the ends, and maybe we can meet up. But he hasn't called."

I wondered why Typo would be back 'on the ends'. It wasn't often you would see someone like him, once a gang member from the Lambeth borough, would roll freely in the Lewisham borough area where a rival gang resides. It was indicative that we were growing up, I guess. We thought less about the territories that limited our geographic exploration as youths. I propped myself up onto my knees. "Well, it's only just gone five," I offered, "so don't rule his phone call out yet. D'you wanna drink?" I got up to my feet.

"Yeah, can I have a hot drink, please? You got Horlicks?"

"Yeah, course." I made my way down to the kitchen.

I heard her phone ring whilst I mixed the Horlicks powder in with milk and sugar. As I poured the piping hot water over the mixture, Stella strolled into the kitchen beaming like a Cheshire cat.

"What?" I asked knowingly. "Who was that on the phone?"

Stella widened her grin childishly. "Typo."

"*Annnd…*" I showed both palms, "…what did he say?"

"He-said-he-wants-to-meet." The delivery was so fast her words merged into one and I missed most of what she said.

"He said what?" I handed her the Horlicks as she dropped onto a kitchen chair.

Her lips hovered on the rim of the cup, testing its temperature, and she cosied herself in to the chair. She slowed down her pace and repeated: "He said he wants to meet up. That's all…" I lit a cigarette on the gas fire, passed it to Stella, and lit another one for myself. She unwrapped the hand-knitted scarf from round her neck, careful not to knock the cigarette hanging loose from between her lips, and fell deeper into her thoughts.

*

We met Typo at Forest Hill station. He'd aged somewhat since I'd seen him last, only a couple of years ago. He didn't look old, but he looked like an experienced man now with some serious life encounters added to his belt. Manic was there too. The same old Peckham Boy Manic with a heart of gold. I was comforted by his presence and the recollections it brought. He looked well-groomed. When he got out of the car, I wondered if he would do his signature pirouette, but instead he leant over and kissed my hand in an elegant and non-promiscuous way. I blushed self-consciously. His soft hands, obviously well moisturised.

"Steph, wha' gwaan, man? It's been so long!" he said, still hanging onto my hand.

My mind embarked on a question as I turned to see the back of Typo's hand brushing lightly, most would argue intimately, across the side of Stella's face, but the time wasn't right.

Twenty minutes later, after a journey complete with laughs, memories, Biggie Smalls, and total relaxation, we arrived at Brixton's Z Bar on Acre Lane. We were welcomed by a lively DJ booth playing Soul 2 Soul's club classic 'Back to Life', and two massive, empty, deep red leather sofas. Typo and Stella made their way to the bar with our drink orders. Warm faces of soulful couples and friends engaged in deep, meaningful conversations shared the space with us. I lit a cigarette. A few moments had passed before Typo and Stella joined Manic and me on the sofas.

"…Stop lying," Stella said playfully to Typo, "how do I look the same? I know I've put on weight!"

"Yeah you have a little," Typo admitted, "but in all the right places."

He grinned, showing a set of stained teeth as he blatantly checked out her behind.

Stella hit him impishly whilst taking a seat, and I rolled my eyes indulgently, speculating where all the flirtation would lead.

"Two's me," she said, just as I had smoked the cigarette down to halfway. I was trying to cut down, so I willingly passed her the remaining half of the cigarette.

The DJ kept the eighties vibe alive with Kool & The Gang's 'Get Down on it,' and New Editions' 'Candy Girl.' My neck was popping hard, but I remained seated. The dim lighting and overall ambiance created an perturbing desire to dance. No one had touched the dance floor as yet. Bodies simply moved from side to side, necks swaying to the music.

"Steph, you look like you wanna dance," Manic put to me.

"Yeah, I will later."

"Why not now?"

"I just don't feel ready yet. Why don't you dance?"

"Because I ain't got da feeling for da dance floor like you do wiv your neck popping and all that!"

"So, what *have* you got the feeling for?" I asked sincerely.

"What do you mean?" Manic replied with an air of confusion.

"I mean…" I said, getting slightly embarrassed, "I sense you got the feeling for something else like…man?"

Typo and Stella turned to me simultaneously, shock and humour showing on their faces.

"What kind of question is dat, Steph?" Manic seemed surprised but not offended, almost like he welcomed the discussion.

"A serious one." I bared my teeth, though my interest was no joke. I just had to know. "Are you a batty-man?"

Typo and Stella fell into fits of laughter, but I was serious. I was desperate to know, not to offend, but to know how, when, and why. Homosexuality was still new to me. To my generation. And I was curious with the clumsiness curiosity of new, misunderstood, information brings.

"Oh-my-days!" Typo filled in. "Steph, the way you said that was hilarious. Who asks questions like dat wiv your voice? *Are you a batty-man? Dat's just nuts, man.*" He mimicked my accent, which caused Manic to giggle, but I ignored them both and widened my eyes at Manic.

I continued, "You know what I mean. Are you feeling for men now instead of women?"

"Yeah…

"Don't lie!" Stella interjected.

"What, you never knew?" Typo was confounded by our ignorance.

"How the fuck would we have known dat?" Stella had to ask.

"He was pretty blatant back in da day, and once he touched pen and did dat big bird…boy…dat just pushed man over on to the ovver side, innit!" Typo started chortling, holding on to his chest.

Manic took on an austere manner, which simmered Typo's laughter.

I sipped my glass of wine. "Manic, trust me, I had no idea before, just thought you were a little nuts…a little manic. But I get it. It must have been so difficult for you holding that all in and playing a role that lived up to your peers. But it seems more obvious now. Or maybe it's my gay-radar that's sharpened." I paused, noticing Manic retreat inside himself. Stella just sat and observed whilst Typo tried to refrain himself from laughter. "Hey, are you all right?"

"Yeah." Manic replied and took a swig of his glass.

"Sorry," I acknowledged, "Are you cool talking about it? I was just a little stunned, that's all." I was more than stunned. This was the first closet reveal I had personally been exposed to.

"Yeah... I'm fine." His tone was despondent, and though he had removed his grey cashmere coat, his body language was introverted. "Let's just leave it, yeah? All you need to know is that yes, I'm gay, and not everybody knows about it because I'm still coming to terms wiv coming out, but it is what it is, y'get me? You eiver like me, or you don't."

Stella flared her nostrils snootily. It was moments like this when I realised how ingrained our culture and childhood religious learnings were. I recalled the teachings of Leviticus, which condemned homosexuality, and was disturbed by my judgement of him. What am I thinking? I thought. I really adored Manic. Despite the different paths our lives had taken, I had some very fond memories of him from our crazy hay days. My learning of his sexuality hadn't stopped or changed my feelings, my care for him. His lifestyle, his biological state, was something I was brought up to understand was wrong. But knowing how challenging it must have been to finally accept himself fully irrespective of who disagreed with how he legally chose to live his life, earned Manic my greatest respect.

I took to the dance floor dragging Manic with me if only to alleviate the tension.

Suddenly a firm hand placed pressure on my right shoulder. I peered down to see the chipped red nail polish of an unfamiliar hand. I turned and faced a disgruntled, big-breasted, long weave-wearing, mini-skirted Lakiesha. I tried to curb my instinctive distaste for her despite having not seen her in some years.

"Wha' gwaan, Steph?"

"Oh, you all right?"

"Nah, I'm not really. But it comin' like you ain't got no love for me when you know wha' gwaan!" Lakeisha shouted over the thumping music.

I clocked Nicola at the bar and motioned Lakeisha towards the bathroom, where there was less noise. "What're you talking about?"

"Darren. You know he's dead, right?"

"Yeah, I heard. I'm really sorry to hear about dat."

"Well, I was finking you would've at least called, like how your wiv his brovver and dat."

"But how was I to know you guys were still together, Lakiesha? And to be honest, because of his lifestyle, it's difficult to be surprised by it all."

"But he was your brovver-in-law!"

"Whose in-law? I'm not anyone's wife! Come on, Lakeisha, I'm a bigger girl now, I'm done with dat wifey talk. Don't get me wrong; I know a life has gone, and of course, I'm regretful for that, but people like Darren don't last long in this world. It's sad, but it's the truth, he never had the heart for it!"

"Let he who is without sin cast the first stone!"

This quotation from the Bible threw me. Stunned. Jolted into introspection and overwhelmed by guilt. She walked off. Manic met me at the bathroom exit with a glass of wine. I suppressed a gutful of vomit fighting to emerge from the pit of my stomach. Lakeisha had put me in my place, tapped on my conscience and guilty emotions in the process. Let he who is without sin cast the first stone.

CHAPTER
TWENTY-SEVEN

WHAT'S LOVE GOT TO DO WITH IT?

22nd February 2001 – Home, Forest Hill

*Dear Di, some things, some people, just never change.
They can change. I mean they may have the opportunity
to change, but not necessarily the means to. Therefore, they
choose not to. But that's their journey, their choice. And I
must remember that.*

*They say it's a sign of a mad person if you do the same
thing again and again, say bang your head on a wall,
and expect a different response, say your head hurting
afterwards. I feel like the line between sanity and insanity
is very thin. I find myself talking to God, reaching out
to a higher power, more than I'd ever imagine me doing.
It's funny. I thought Mum was nuts when she'd call on
her God. But I get it now. When you experience things
in life that's difficult to make sense of. That's personal
and contains layers of sentimental value you'd rather not
divulge to your friends. Seeking the spiritual guidance*

from a higher force, not only feels natural, but feels necessary for survival.

The doorbell rang.

I rushed from a pot of boiling peas to see who was at the door through the front room window. No one was there. I knocked twice on the window. No one appeared. I skipped back the CD track in the stereo and skipped back to the kitchen. The baseline of Lauren Hill's 'Lost Ones' reverberated through my limbs forcing me to dance and sing.

The doorbell rang.

Lowering the heat on the hob, again I ran to the window. I rapped my knuckles against the window harder than I'd done before. Still, no one showed. Wha' gwaan? I thought, and then I noticed the back of a jean trouser leg and white trainers. "Who's there?" I shouted down through the window.

Damien stepped back from the doorstep and looked up at me at the window. He was smiling oddly. He ran his top front teeth over his bottom lip repeatedly. He paused and shouted, "Surprise! You gonna open up the door, then?"

I opened the window. "Oh-my-gosh! Why didn't you tell me you were coming?"

"Because it wouldn't be a surprise then now, would it? You gonna open the door or what?"

I ran down the stairs as though I were happy, which I should have been. But I wasn't. Upon opening the door, I thought I should hug him, my boyfriend Damien, who I hadn't seen in several weeks, who I believed I loved. Instead, I stood in the communal hallway with a fake smile spread across my face, mentally trying to work out what the hell was going on. He was standing there for some moments, mute, munching heavily on the gum in his mouth. The old couple who lived beneath me stepped out from their flat, greeted me, and left.

"You're looking good. You've put weight back on," he smiled.

"Have I? I didn't notice," I lied. "Are you all right?" My voice displayed concern.

"Yeah, I'm cool, yanna! You? Everyt'ing cool wid you?" He watched the couple slowly make their way out to the street as he stepped in from the cold. "Is it just you here?"

"Yeah."

He walked up the stairs ahead of me and into my kitchen. Something wasn't right. I was unsure how to address the situation, so I pretended there was no situation to be addressed. I passed him to get to the fridge. I took out a box of coconut cream and sliced a block off, adding it to the pot of boiling kidney beans. I increased the heat back under the pot before finely chopping two spring onions and adding them. His nose was tantalised by the flavoursome aroma of the chicken stew. Territorially he lifted the lid off the Dutch pot and tasted its contents using a spoon I'd left on the side.

He licked his lips with his eyes closed as though engaged in a private moment. "So, who you cooking for?" he said, surprising me.

"I always cook on a Sunday! Safire and Charlene are coming down for dinner later, plus Stella said she might pass t'rough." I was trying to sound chirpy, but I felt ill at ease like something was brewing within him.

"So it's not Manic, and dem man deh you're cooking for, den?" He looked at me coldly, and then I thought: What the hell's coming over him?

"*Noooo*! Why would you fink dat?" I got myself a glass from the cupboard and poured myself a glass of water. "D'you wanna drink?"

"Coz I know you're fucking out on me, dat's why!"

I slammed the empty glass onto the side. "*NO!* What are you talking about? I ain't done anyfing, and you're making these accusations—*why*?"

"Accusations. You're gonna look me in my eyes and tell me I'm making FUCKING *ACCUSATIONS*?!!"

I scratched my head, astounded. I couldn't think. I turned my back to him, loomed over the sink, and started washing a heap of brown rice in a plastic bowl. "Look, Damien, I'm not sure what's going on, what you've got in your head about me or why, but I can assure you I'm not cheating on you and never have cheated on you."

"There you go again, with your little posh university accent and your little innocent act. What you tryna tell me? Dat you ain't been seeing anyone behind my back while I've been hiding in the country, mourning my brovver's death?"

"NO!" I cried, turning my neck, "I haven't been seeing anyone!"

"*LIAR!!*" he roared, whacking the glass off the side. It collided with the floor and burst into little pieces.

I paused. A ripple of fear flowed through my nervous system and rattled my bladder. I caught my pee with the cross of my legs reversing the signal.

"I can't do this anymore," I murmured, "This isn't working, Damien. God knows I've tried with this relationship, but it just isn't working."

"So what you saying?" His volume settled.

"I'm saying I sympathise with the loss of your brother…I really do, but I can't mentally manage this kind of volatile relationship, especially while studying! So I guess what I'm saying is…is that I think we should split up."

His nostrils widened as I passed him to get the tall broom and dustpan from the corner. Sweeping the shattered glass into the dustpan, he confirmed what I'd just said. "So me and you are done, yeah?" Fingered his facial stubble as I emptied the glass into some newspaper and then into the bin. I passed him again to see to the fire.

Silence. I stirred both the pots. I turned the knob for the rice and peas onto a very low fire. I heard a thud. It sounded like a metal object placed on the kitchen table behind me. I turned and faced a 9mm semiautomatic pistol, like those you see in the movies. It was lying in the centre of the table. Damien stood beside it with a smug air about him. I felt sick. Couldn't bear the look of him. Inner voices rambled on to one another in trepidation and confusion. *He's not doing anything; he loves you, he wants you, why would he hurt you? He's crazy, that's why…*

I tried to remain on top of the game, to uphold some element of control. I opened the fridge, pretending not to have noticed the gun, and placed the tub of margarine on the top shelf. I casually walked out of the kitchen, passing him and his weapon of obliteration.

"Steph, I asked you somefing." His lips cracked open with a sickly grin. "So me and you are done, yeah?"

Silence. I proceeded to my bedroom… *I need to get out of this house, he's gonna kill me. HE'S GONNA KILL ME! I'll jump out the window and scream…where's my mobile? Ah SHIT it's in the kitchen; I need to call da police. Fuck it, I'm jumping out the window…*

"Steph, what're you doing? I'm talking to you, come back here!" His voice came at me through the passageway and seeped through the cracks of my closed bedroom door…

I could hear him making for my room. *You can't jump now; if you jump, you'll only vex him, and he might kill you by accident. Remain calm; he ain't gonna kill you, he loves you; he ain't gonna kill you. He ain't gonna kill me; I just have to be calm, see no evil, fear no evil. Oh*

God please…I'm begging you, please, spare my life today. Please don't let him…

The door was pushed open. Damien stood before me in a blasé manner. He wore a loose, blue sweatshirt under a denim jacket and a pair of jeans. His hair was in need of razors…face too. Left hand on his hip, right hand hung loosely by his side with grubby fingers clutching the polished silver piece.

"What're you doing?" he asked.

"Nuffing." Finally, I spoke aloud. "I'm just getting my hair bag coz I gotta go and do someone's hair in a minute. I'm just waiting for my rice and peas."

"So I'm not invited for dinner?" He smiled mockingly.

I felt nauseous. I picked up my bag and caught sight of my reflection in the wardrobe mirror: a scared girl in a dark place without knowing what the future held. I greased my lips with Vaseline, turned, and bypassed him with my head dipped down. I progressed to the kitchen.

"Where're you going? And when I ask you a question, stop blanking me!" He grabbed my arm as I neared the kitchen.

I twisted to him vacantly. "Can you let go of my arm, please? I need to check my pot!"

With a gun in hand, he trailed me into the kitchen. I tasted the pot. It needed another fifteen minutes or so. *I gotta get out now; I gotta make my exit.*

"Damien…errrmm, what're you doing now, coz I need to make a move?"

He breathed a heavy sound…a sort of laugh, and treaded backward towards the front door. "Hmm…you ain't going a place. You cheat on me, lie to me in my face and then done wiv me. You really fink I'm gonna let you treat a man like dat after *all* dat I've done for you? I put you before my family. My brovver's lying six foot under because I was trying to do the right fing by you, and you're just gonna try and handle me like I'm some eediot? Me and you are really done, yeah?"

My stomach ached as though barbed wire was being torn through it. Beads of water glided down my skin, and I continued patchily breathing. My bag dropped loose from my trembling hand. Numbness pervaded my body. Strength deserted me...God deserted me.

Damien grew energized by my weakness, empowered by my fear. He grabbed onto my arm, limp and motionless. "What, is mouthy scared now, huh? Are you scared now? You ain't got no mouth now 'ave ya? You ain't denying fucking Manic now! ARE YOU? I KNOW! So don't play stupid like I don't know because Lakeisha told me every *fucking t'ing*! How you was on a date wiv Manic, dancing up on him like a little whore, like you and him are in love..."

He dragged me back into the kitchen. I dropped to my knees. He held my arm up by his waist while he thrust forward with the gun in his other hand. Quickly, I scrabbled back to my feet.

"LET GO OF ME!" I screamed hysterically, bending his fingers back. He let go, backing into the kitchen, the table forcing him to stop, and he circled its edge. "Damien, are you mad?! Have you gone fucking crazy?!" I screamed. "Manic's gay you imbecile! I was with my cousin Stella who wanted me to go with her to meet Typo who brought Manic with him, but he's gay, *he's fucking gay*! And even if he wasn't, how dare you accuse me based on some flimsy argument of what someone's said they've seen? Lakeisha of all people! *Lakeisha of all fucking people!* Get out. *GET OUT!!!*" I shrieked, banging my fists on the table with ferocity. Every breath became an effort, every movement a strain. I was tired.

Silence. Just my breathing. Damien peered at me, despondent. I wiped my mucus-filled nose with the back of my hand and pointed to the door.

"Leave," I sobbed, stepping back into the passageway, but he made no move. "Leave! I said FUCKING leave! HELP! HELP!" I screeched from the top of my lungs.

He dropped the gun onto the table, dived in my direction, forcing me onto the floor, and covered my mouth with his hands. We wrestled on the floor recklessly. I gripped the fleshy palm of his hands between my teeth and used all the muscles of my jaw to bite down. His free arm explored my neck like a snake would do the earth. His meaty biceps inflated under my jawbone. I wriggled...kicked out hysterically; I tried to scream too. Tighter. He squeezed tighter. I squirmed, fighting with my hands. Tighter. I wriggled. Tighter. Blank...

My name echoed in the abyss of my mind: *Steph, Steph, Steph...* Something came alive, and I felt a force to my face.

"Steph...Steph! It's me, wake up," he yelled, slapping me in the face.

"Uh, wha' 'appen?" I murmured. Blood poured from beneath a cut on my jawline.

"Babes, I'm sorry, I had to put you in a sleeper; you were screaming and going crazy, you were gonna make the police come."

I rolled out of his arms in contempt. Queasiness came up within me as recollection came back and vomit strained my throat. The acid cut my taste buds. I held my mouth to hold it in, crawled into the toilet, and let it all out into the bowl.

"Are you all right?" he asked when I came out.

"Damien, jus' get ou' my 'ouse; I don' wanna see you ever again," I whispered, wiping the drool from my mouth.

He shifted to the kitchen upon his hands and knees and picked back up the gun, both hands firmly on the trigger levelling it vertically between his gaped legs, pointing it down to the ground. "Steph, you ain't leaving me alive yanna. Don't make me do this. We can work this out. Just stop sneaking around."

My head was pounding. I felt claustrophobic and sick. I was tired...I was so fucking tired and weak. I couldn't do it anymore. I thought about the warnings Claudia, my mum, and even Macy gave me. What Dada explained about debts to society. My heart sank further upon the realisation that he was ready to take my life with the pull of a trigger. I caught another glance of his eyes: disheartening and ambiguously hollow; beauty not quite diminished.

"Go on then, what you waiting for? Kill me. Blow my fucking brains out...smoke me, I don't care anymore."

I blinked. A mass of droplets raced down my face and hung loose before falling from my jawline. With two thumbs, he pulled the safety back off its hinges, he closed his eyes, and scrunched his face in comprehension.

"Don't fucking close your eyes! Look me in my eye when you take me out. *Damien! YOU FUCKING LOOK ME IN THE EYE WHEN YOU PULL DAT TRIGGER!*"

What was I thinking? I dunno...see no evil, hear no evil? I dunno, I wasn't thinking. I felt it was my time to go, that would be my debt being paid. I'd fought, screamed, and prayed. I could do no more except prepare to die...face my fear. All I knew was I couldn't live in fear like that anymore. I had done a lot of awful things to a lot of people, so maybe this was my payback. This is what was needed to balance things. And if it was my time to go, then I was going to go.

Blood spattered out from the indented opening of my fleshy brow, contrasting against the wall as the shot exploded through my head. The bullet burst through every nerve and blood vessel that sent a signal to my brain. Everything happened so fast and yet so slow. Right before the bullet cracked through the back of my skull, sound evaporated. My vision and stamina followed suit. Blood trickled over my eyes beneath the lids...

The heavy steel knocked my nose as it descended to the floor. The extent of my imagination had been confirmed. Yes, the trigger had not been pulled and I was still alive. Damien followed its lead. He broke down with submission, bawled like a baby. I towered over him and watched. I silently watched. I bled from the chin and wondered why he hadn't pulled the trigger.

"I'm sorry…I'm so sorry," he squirmed, "is that how much you hate me? You really rather be dead than be wiv me?" He carried on bawling, still upon his knees. He looked up at me and bowed his head back down. Blood splashed against my white vest from beneath my jawline. My arms were flat by my side, "I'm so sorry. I can't believe what I've done to you…I'm sorry…I'm so sorry. I love you. I need you to know that I do love you, Steph, and I'm sorry. I'm deeply sorry. I know you might be hurt and angry right now, but if you love or have ever loved me, you'll give me one more chance—that's all I'm asking for, just one more chance."

I watched him impassively as *The Miseducation of Lauren Hill* surreally rolled on to track ten: 'Forgive Them Father'.

"Please leave," I breathed, "this has nothing to do with love."

CHAPTER TWENTY-EIGHT

A SIN FOR A SIN

7th March 2001 – Hospital.

Dear Di, as you know, today's my birthday. I'm nineteen now. And I'm pretty pissed that two weeks since that mad man tried to wreak havoc on my life, I'm spending my birthday in hospital, forlorn and forsaken rubbing my bulge...

Blue patterned curtains outlined and closed off the small space I had to myself. An empty wooden cabinet sat to my left and one to my right. Across from me, Stella sat in an oversized leather chair. My bags and clothes were underneath the chair entwined about her legs. A bright spotlight above me sent hoops and spots of colour through my eyes. "I'm sorry, but it has to be done," I said to my bump of fifteen weeks. I hoped that it or someone would empathise with my choice. Guilt and other disconsolate emotions permeated my heart. The thought of this baby laying undetected for twelve weeks to then be sentenced to death through no fault of its own seemed tragic. Of course, I felt sorry, but it had to be done! I continued to tell myself this. Not to convince, but to remind me why I was doing this. What it was I was up against.

"You don't have to apologise to no one, Steph. You're doing what most would do after what he did to you. He's da son of da devil himself—no lie! And to think how we all used to be bang on his case. You shouldn't let him get away with it, y'know. Leroy would kill him—"

"*You told your brovver*?!" I belted out with eyes popping.

"No, if you let me finish... I was saying Leroy would kill him *if* he knew, but obviously, he doesn't."

The curtain folded open. A white, ginger-haired male with thick square glasses popped his head inside the parted curtain animatedly. "Stephanie Johnson? May I come in?"

I nodded. Even managed a half-smile.

"Hello," he said to Stella, "are you a friend?"

"Family. I'm her cousin."

"Good. I'm Doctor Newton," he turned to me, "I'm the one who'll be doing the termination later. The procedure we're going to use on you today is called a Surgical Dilatation and Evacuation Termination, which we use on pregnancies between fifteen and nineteen weeks. The little implant thing we gave you yesterday is called a laminaria, and basically, what that does once being inserted into the neck of the womb is expand the cervix by three or four millimetres. So if you've been feeling a little cramping, that would be it." He smiled. Keen to provide all the information in relation to my experience. "Soon, you'll go under the general anaesthetic," he continued, "where we'll use forceps and suction to remove the pregnancy. The procedure should take no longer than half an hour." He cleared his throat. "Now, there are a lot of patients who need seeing to today so there might be a bit of a wait...any questions?" His forehead rose, eyes widened, all to ensure that I would see that they were green. He used the bridge of his nose to lift his glasses.

"No."

"Do you have someone to pick you up and monitor you for the next twenty-four hours?"

"Yes."

He patted the bed twice. As he left, he added, "And Happy Birthday."

"Steph, I'm going to call and see where your sisters are—do you want anything whilst I'm out, a magazine or somefing?"

"Yeah, can you get me *Pride* magazine? Do you need some money?"

"Nah, I'm all right."

Stella drew the curtain back to leave. I noticed the clock on the wall above the desk where the nurses were stationed. It read 12:08. My eyelids soon flickered to a close…

"Steph, wake up; I'm here…wake up."

I cracked open my eyes to make out a blurred vision of Damien that slowly came into focus. "Ermmm…mmm, uh? What're you doing here?" I mumbled.

"I'm here for you. Wake up, man!"

I sat up at his demand, scratching my head. My diary fell to the floor from the movement. Damien picked it up and handed it to me. A deep, hollow sensation buried itself in me.

"What's dat?"

"Nothing." His brow wrinkled as though he knew I was lying. "It's just a scrapbook for my work at uni. Anyway, who told you I was here?" I tried to change the subject. I slid my diary beneath the pillow.

"Lakiesha."

"Lakiesha?!"

"Really and truly, that doesn't matter. The point is you're carrying my baby in there, and I couldn't let you go through this alone. I love you, Steph. No matter what you think about me, please just know dis, I will never stop loving you. NEVER!"

I didn't know how to respond. I wanted to cry. I felt helpless. Wailing like a baby seemed like all I could do right then. I had no other means of expressing my discontentment. Water filmed my eyes, streamed down my face and my shoulders slumped. I panted squeakily and uncontrollably. I blanketed my face with one hand and my tummy with the other.

"Miss Johnson, are you OK?" I didn't even hear the curtain draw back, I just saw a blurry vision of a woman clad in dreary navy-blue scrubs.

I tried to get a sentence together, again and again. The words lost in my gasps. Damien interposed. "She's fine, just a bit upset. I'm her boyfriend. It's a sad time for both of us."

The freckled-faced nurse nodded understandingly. Her eyes flickered as she tucked curly tresses of brown hair behind her ears and left. Damien hugged me, and I didn't have the energy to make him stop.

"Steph, you don't have to do this. We can try again. Continue like we were before, this time be a family. I'll get a job and make you my proper wifey." He unthinkingly attempted to kiss me. I turned my head so robustly it frightened him off of me. "What?" he questioned. "Don't you want what I want?"

I shook my head.

"Well, you can't want dis! Look at you, about to murder our fucking child, and you're crying like a fucking baby knowing what you're doing is wrong. And den, you wanna come chat to me like you're all morally correct when you're about to murder my child! You ain't no different from my brovver or any ovver murderer out dere. I'm offering you a way out of dis, and you're refusing it, and for what?"

"I don't love you the way you love me anymore, and I don't want you in my life."

"So if you don't give a shit about me den why're you FUCKING crying like you do—you BITCH!" He lunged for me, gripped onto my neck, tried to strangle me. Security burst in and restrained him. His anger fought to drown his hurt, but it surfaced for survival, and beads cascaded from the corners of his eyes. Security escorted Damien out. It was a noisy exit.

The freckled-face nurse towered over my bed, checking me over. "I'm OK," I clarified, trying to pace my breathing. "Could I just have some space for a bit?"

She nodded and left.

Damien's last words haunted me. I tried to answer the question. Why was I crying if it weren't because of him? My being in love with him died out a long time ago. Instead, what held me together with Damien was understanding, loyalty, and losing love for myself. And that was why I cried. I cried because of me. My baggage, my own traumas that enabled me to create excuses that accepted this shady version of love. The anger I felt towards myself for making a decision that I knew didn't serve me. Didn't fit into who I'd evolved and wanted to be. I knew I was about to do something I'd probably regret later in life. But I had to do this. I *had* to. I had to take a life to save a life. I felt wholeheartedly then that I'd rather be dead than live the rest of my life with a reason for Damien to be in it. I prayed repeatedly for forgiveness...

"You all right?" Stella asked, holding a March edition of Pride magazine as my eyes broke open.

"Rah! How long have I been out for?" I looked around, trying to come to terms with where I was and what had happened.

"It's after two. Your sisters will be here soon, half two, they said.

Oh yeah, and Shariece is picking us up at five—she couldn't get out of work any earlier. Steph, what's wrong wiv you?"

"Nuffing. I just had a nuts dream, that's all. You haven't told Lakiesha or anyone about this, have you?"

"Are you nuts? Don't be stupid. Why would I do that?"

"I know, I know, sorry, that was a stupid question."

Still reeling from the intensity of my dream with Damien, I held onto my head as two nurses collected me and wheeled me into a small room adjacent to the operating theatre. One was the same freckled-face nurse who was in my dream. The other, a solid motherly spirit with bosoms fit for pillows, a shady weave-on that I knew I could fix, and a Nigerian accent. A touch of guilt entered the atriums of my heart with the thought that Damien knew nothing of this pregnancy and termination. I hadn't seen him since he threatened my life a few weeks ago and didn't want to give him any reason to come back into my life. Freckles inserted a tube into the back of my hand whilst Bosoms made up the solution before leaving, which Freckles then pushed into me through the injected tube.

"You might feel a little unusual soon; you should be out in around twenty seconds."

"No, I won't," I let burst and didn't know why I allowed it burst but let it burst anyway.

She wheeled my bed through, and I saw white apparatus and white lights and…and…I think that was Dr. Newton. Something was trying to take me under, but I was strong. Strong enough to withstand love, strong enough to withstand the anaesthesia. I wouldn't let it get me.

"Hello again, Steph; see you in a little while…and she's…out." He said matter-of-factly.

"No, I'm not," I slurred. "No…I'm…nn–"

I was out…

"*Steph! Steph! Steph...wake up now.*" A voice penetrated my unconsciousness.

I opened my eyes. Everything moved quickly past me. The foot of my bed crashed through a set of doors. Soon I was back on a familiar ward greeted by friendly faces.

"Happy Birthday, Steph. How you feeling?" Charlene asked, stroking my shoulder and handing me a gift in a Selfridge's bag.

"Yeah, are you all right?" Safire added.

I wanted to respond, show appreciation, but I couldn't. I nodded, pointing for Charlene to put the bag on the floor.

Stella smiled meekly, not uttering a word.

I felt my deflated belly and knew that it had gone. That constant full feeling of abundance and life had gone leaving me empty. My thoughts ploughed into the removal of my baby. I imagined the forceps pulling it out by its tiny legs, it...he...she, covering its face with its tiny hands immersed into a new frightening experience. I blurted out a sound that swiftly became the initiation of an avid and heartfelt cry erupting from the deep wells of my stomach. The arms of my sisters quickly snaked about me. I could feel their concern. Stella's eyes reddened, and she hung her head trying to disguise her pain.

This lasted a short while until Safire saw to Stella, confused by the graveness of her upset. Charlene turned their way whilst still rubbing my back as I calmed myself down. I went over to Stella and embraced her, whispering in her ear, "I'm sure this pain will go away one day," and she held me tightly, crying and shaking her head.

CHAPTER TWENTY-NINE

MY DESTINY

15th November 2001 – Home, Forest Hill

Dear Di, it's taken a while for me to get here, but finally I feel like I've found myself. Being single provides the space to make retrospective conclusions, and the time to become at one with them. There's nothing like a good old clear out to remove the old junk that clutters, torments and suppresses the inner self. It's been a bumpy and scary journey, but thank God I'm finally here. I have a sense of agency and am deciding my own destiny...

An A2 piece of cardboard lay centred across my rug between, magazine and newspaper cut-outs, CDs and 2Pac's song lyrics for 'Dear Mama', fabric samples and fashion sketches, snapshots and copies of my previous diary entries. A pair of scissors was grouped with PVA glue, a hand-held mirror and random shells, twigs and barks I collected from my local park. I was producing a mood board. Cutting, sticking, and assorting material before applying them to the cardboard sheet. Sat, immersed in my creativity, under the dim yellow light of a lamp atop a white-painted cabinet box positioned in the corner of the living room. I hadn't quite worked out a clear direction I would take the course project I was working on, just instinctively followed through with my attraction to nature and materials of interest. Outside roman blinds covered bay windows, the November night stood motionless and silent like it were Christmas Day. My house phone rang.

"Hello?"

"It's me, Damien."

I hung up. It had been eight and a half months since we'd broken up for good, eight months since I terminated the pregnancy. I dropped the phone with wavering hands as though it were a creepy-crawly. The phone rang again. I stared at it for some time, then answered.

"*Hello*?"

"Steph, please don't hang up. Please! This will be the last time dat I phone you, I promise. I just need to get this off my chest once and for all." My silence permitted him to continue. "It's taken me over eight months to accept that we're never going to get back together. And I understand why. But you need to know that I've learnt so much from being with you and that I will always love you and never love again the way I loved you because I never want to experience this kind of pain again; trust me, this love hurts bad, man.

"I've started back on that business course, and I think I'm gonna do all right, but I need you to do me a favour: no matter how much your conscience may prick you to check in on me, even if it's years on—don't. I know you will always care for me even if you no longer love me. Well... dat's it really...I just thought it was important dat you knew dat. Y'get me?"

"Uh-huh." I didn't know what else to say.

And with that, he hung up. When I peered down at my reflection in the mirror, the competing aspects of my character unfolded. The times when I was happy, yet sad; immersed in love, yet shrouded by hate; privileged with a large, connected family, yet deprived without unity; I had been externally warm, yet internally cold, dead to the world. The villain and the victim. I hated that. Finally, I took the control to be neither the victim nor the villain.

At nineteen years of age, I had enough experience to equip me to try new methods of doing things. I had failed in enough areas in life to know what didn't work and was likely to stifle my progression. I was now prepared to learn and take responsibility for the choices that I made in life. If God felt me worthy or capable enough to have a child one day, I would know what to do differently. I would know what difference communication—open, honest, and rational communication—would have on a child. I would know what difference listening would have; hugs and kisses would have; forgiveness; violence; my partner and father to my child; my family and companions; education; independent thinking, and unconditional love. I would know the difference they would all have on a developing human being and would try my damned hardest to ensure my child or children broke the cycle of experiences I incurred.

A ring vibrated my space. This time it was my doorbell. The unexpected ring stirred me. Seldom, did I get unexpected visitors. I pulled the blind up and peered out of the window. I noticed Mum's car. My heart sank. I questioned if I were in the mood, the right, emotionally steady, calm and collective, headspace to engage with Mum. It was New Years day, almost a year ago, since I'd last seen her. Something must be up, I thought.

I opened the door, "What are you doing here?"

"Do I need a reason to see my daughter?"

"Yes," I smiled turning my back to ascend the stairs, "especially when I've not heard from you in…what, almost a year."

"Well, you can call me too, Stephanie."

"I didn't want to," I spat matter-of-factly, as I entered the living space and sat in the middle of my work.

Mum sighed with rolling eyes and a shaking head as she descended onto the sofa in a slump, "Maybe that's why I've not called. You don't make it easy, Stephanie, you know."

I rose my brow in an intended 'whatever' way, "OK, so again I'll ask, what are you doing here? Clearly, I've not wanted to see you, so why are you here to see me?"

"Must you be so cold, Stephanie? I'm your mum. I may not have been the best mum, but God only knows I tried my best. I tried to do what was right in the eyes of God with everything I had."

"Did your God tell you to favour your children based on the colour of their skin? To beat them senseless and shed blood from their skin? Some God you serve, Mum."

"I've never favoured any of my children. I treated them differently because you are all different. You are much stronger than Safire, Stephanie. More stubborn too. And any licks I gave you I did with love, trying to guide you in the right direction to avoid life giving you the kind of beating life gave me. I'm not saying I always got it right, cos I know I didn't. I had my own problems and challenges I was dealing with. But I did love you girls and raise you the best way I knew how to, and that was with licks."

I looked down, processing her words and my feelings simultaneously. "I'm sorry you had a tough life. But even when I accept the beatings you gave us, it didn't feel like you showed up for me at all, not like I needed."

"I tried to Stephanie, but you wouldn't always let me. You're still a lickle feisty pickney to me, and yet I'm still here. I've showed up today. I want to show up now."

Mum went to hug me. I flinched. Stiffened my body into a motionless tree. Too much, too soon. "I love you," Mum declared, which sounded a little alien to me, however I forced myself to accept her words and return her embrace.

"I love you too," I finally got out, "and you are appreciated."

The corners of Mum's mouth rose with excitement. She bore a full set of teeth like she were a child. I was interrupted by my phone for a second time.

I got up to my feet to see to it; left Mum smiling on her knees like a Cheshire Cat, "Hello?"

"Steph?"

"Yeah, who's this?"

"Tyrone."

My heart fluttered. The stress of recent events had started to take its toll on my hearing. "Sorry, who's speaking, please?"

"Steph, it's me. Tyrone!"

My eyes bulged, lips pursed wide open encouraging my right hand to cover my mouth.

"Stephanie, are you OK?" Mum asked.

"Yeah. Yeah...Oh-my-gosh. Mum, sorry, you've gotta go. I need to take this call."

"You OK?" she asked again, got to her feet, grabbed her bag from the sofa.

"Steph," Tyrone's voice echoed through the phone"

"Oh-my-gosh," I gushed again. "Mum, I fine. Sorry to rush things like this. It's Tyrone. I need to take this."

"Jason brudda," Mum slipped into her patois dialect, "Whe' 'im deh? Nah di States?"

"Mum, I can't do this now. Thanks for coming. Thanks for the chat. I'll call you tomorrow."

"OK, love you, Stephanie," Mum sung as she descended the stairs to leave.

I waved to her from on top of the stairs. As the door closed again I gushed, "Oh-my-gosh!"

"I know," Tyrone whispered.

"Oh my fucking gosh....what....when...oh my gosh..."

"I know, Steph. I know."

"Whe'...where are you?" I asked throwing myself across the sofa. My eyes glazed over with tears, and they streamed down my face.

"In London."

"Oh my gosh!!" I shrieked. "What the fuck happened to you? Why are you here and when did *you* get back?"

"Yesterday. Since then, I've been trying to get hold of you, but my brovver didn't think me seeing you would be a good idea—"

"Why?" I interjected, "Jason doesn't get to decide what's good for you or me!"

"I know," Tyrone empathised, "He's just trying to protect me. Doesn't want me getting caught back up in my feelings, in the life I lived before, and Macy said she didn't want me hurting you again. But I'm a changed man now. You know I never meant to hurt you, right?"

I didn't know anything. It had been over three and a half years since Tyrone walked out of my life and never contacted me again after I had served an eighteen-month prison sentence with him and then gave him my virginity. In that time, I had been in foster care, been to college, been in a relationship, had to face and rectify my past at university, and...Killer Man Joe. I was high off exhaustion. I've not yet even had the chance to process a weighty conversation with my mum. And there I was, tempting fate with another emotional battering.

"Steph, we need to talk properly. Can I come and see you?"

"I dunno. Who gave you my number?"

"Damien. I bumped into him earlier today. I said I needed to get hold of you, and he gave me your number."

"But he—"

"Don't worry about all that; I know. I know what you two had. I know what Damien did to my dad, but that's all done now. He knows I can't forgive and be bredrens with man for dealing with my family like that, even if he didn't know, but as I said, I didn't come back to partake in the life I used to lead. I came back to see my family and you, Steph. I need to talk to you, explain things. So, can I come and see you?"

I didn't want to get hurt again. I wasn't ready for another emotional terrain. Too soon. This was all too soon. I had loved and had loved again to no prevail. Maybe God was telling me something. I was nineteen years old with two serious relationships under my belt that had taken my heart through a battlefield. Perhaps I wasn't ready for love.

"Yes," I replied.

Twenty-seven minutes later, the vibration of the doorbell chimed in my ear for the second time this evening. I exhaled with eyes closed, and moist palms laid flat on my thighs. Would he look the same, be the same caring and considerate boy he was before?

Riingg!!

The bell chimed. I bolted down the stairs pumping with excitement before composing myself to open the door. A pure white tracksuit with the silhouette of a tick pictured across the chest greeted me. The heavy-duty leather of an Avirex jacket sat firmly on his shoulders. The black-rimmed glasses he wore made him look intelligent and more mature. A white woolly hat covered his hair.

Moments rolled by before either of us made a move, a beam sprawled across my face. My eyes began to fill again and tears spilled over my eyelids, racing down my cheeks to meet again at the corners of my mouth. Tyrone, who was over six feet and towering, wrapped long, protective arms about me. I was in a haven. Protected from the perils and parasites of the world. I nestled my chin into the depression of his neck, so his head rested over and against my face. My crying became audible. My chest panted. Wispy squeals emitted from my lips. Tyrone kept sniffing. He too cried. We stood in the doorway of the communal area for some time, holding one another closely. We had often enjoyed moments such as this. A chain rattled. My neighbour's door opened. My heart rate sped up. I turned and saw Maggie peeking between the small gap in the door.

"Stephanie, is everything OK?"

"Yeah, I'm fine thanks, Maggie. Am I making a lot of noise?"

"Well, not really, it's just that I heard you crying, my love. But if you're OK, I'll leave you to it." She went to close the door, then opened it back up. "Oh, but Stephanie, would you do me a favour please and close the door? All that cold draft's getting in and letting all the lovely heat out."

"OK, sorry about that." I shut the door and led Tyrone in behind me.

"Oh, thanks, love." Maggie closed her door and chained it back up.

We arrived upstairs without a word dispensed from either of our lips. We gazed at one another, holding each other's hands like schoolchildren.

"Nice place," he commented upon entering the living room.

"Thanks," I chirped.

"So your mum was here when I called. That's nice."

"What's nice?" I quizzed.

"Your mum. Here. With you," he uttered, staccato.

"Oh. Well, yeah. It was nice, I guess."

He beamed seemingly proud of me. I headed over to a stack of CDs, trying to think of a song that encapsulated the mood, my feelings. Out of two hundred or more CDs, my focus closed in on the white bar and red graphics of Xscape's *Traces of my Lipstick* album. I withdrew the CD with trembling hands, selected track six, 'The Arms of the One Who Loves You' and increased the treble and bass levels. I know, I know, it even felt cheesy at the time.

Even as I was seated on the floor facing south with my arms wrapped round folded legs, keeping my body shaped into a ball, I was hoping. And not for what I wanted him to do—I hadn't figured that part out as yet. My chin was rested on my knees. I rocked my head slow and steady to the baseline. I was engrossed by the lyrics. I hoped he might be too. As the bridge of the song tailored off, naked arms encircled me from behind. I felt like I was a child at school again. My emotions were running havoc, making my skin sensitive to touch.

"Steph," he whispered in my ear, "I promise you, I will never leave you again."

"Don't make promises you can't keep," I asserted, dropping my eyelids low.

"I'm not," He whispered, stroked my arms before he kissed the roof of my head. I smiled. My nerves calmed, replaced by a warm, fuzzy feeling. I snuggled into his arms.

He turned my body round to face him. "Look at me," he demanded, tenderly clasping my jaw. He stared into my eyes with assiduous poise. "Please believe me when I say I will *never*—do you hear me?—*never*, leave you again." I could not take my eyes off him.

We gazed at one another in a trance for some time before we slowly moved towards each other. He took me back to my adolescence when we first kissed properly outside of a council estate in Peckham in the presence of my sisters, cousin, Manic and the other Peckham Boys. I felt giddy. My eyelids fell to a close. Soft, smooth, full lips pressed against mine. A coral-reef tongue waved into my mouth, and his breathing came alive as though he were taking his last, dying breath. Small, gentle hands fingered through the thick kinks of my afro hair. I stroked the low-cut fade of his head with sprawled-open fingers, feeling around his evolved facial structure. The album rolled on as effortlessly as the clothes rolled off our backs. Our bodies and the different shades of our skin entwined. And I became him, and he became me, and we became one.

ABOUT THE AUTHOR

Photo credit: @kellielicorishmakeup

Monique Campbell grew up in 90s South London, part of London's second-generation Caribbean community where their identity was created through music, culture, and politics.

A young person who experienced foster care, Monique went on to carve out a professional business career in B2B sales that spans media, digital media, and cloud-based technology. Monique has contributed to *Brown Eyes, Sexual Attraction Revealed*, and *Hair Power Skin Revolution* anthologies.

She has an MBA from Warwick Business School, is a mentor to young women in or entering business and sales, and a proud mother.

To find out more about Monique and her writing, please visit:
moniquecampbell.com

You can also connect with her on social media:
instagram.com/oncebadintentions

Printed in Poland
by Amazon Fulfillment
Poland Sp. z o.o., Wrocław

32238445R00208

JUNKERS Ju 88

THE TWILIGHT YEARS:
BISCAY TO THE FALL OF GERMANY

JUNKERS Ju 88

THE TWILIGHT YEARS:
BISCAY TO THE FALL OF GERMANY

CHRIS GOSS

FRONTLINE
BOOKS

JUNKERS Ju 88
The Twilight Years: Biscay to the Fall of Germany

First published in Great Britain in 2018 by Frontline Books,
an imprint of Pen & Sword Books Ltd, Yorkshire - Philadelphia

ISBN: 978-1-47389-236-1

Typeset in 9.5/12pt Avenir
Printed and bound in India by Replika Press Pvt. Ltd.

Pen & Sword Books Ltd incorporates the imprints of Pen & Sword Archaeology, Air World Books, Atlas, Aviation, Battleground, Discovery, Family History, History, Maritime, Military, Naval, Politics, Social History, Transport, True Crime, Claymore Press, Frontline Books, Praetorian Press, Seaforth Publishing and White Owl

For a complete list of Pen & Sword titles please contact:

PEN & SWORD BOOKS LTD
47 Church Street, Barnsley, South Yorkshire, S70 2AS, UK.
E-mail: enquiries@pen-and-sword.co.uk
Website: www.pen-and-sword.co.uk

Or
PEN AND SWORD BOOKS,
1950 Lawrence Roadd, Havertown, PA 19083, USA
E-mail: Uspen-and-sword@casematepublishers.com
Website: www.penandswordbooks.com

CONTENTS

V

ACKNOWLEDGEMENTS

I would like to thank the following for their assistance in compiling this book: Robert Forsyth, the late Manfred Griehl, Alfred Price, Bernd Rauchbach, Ken Wakefield, Ray Lauderback and Ed North.

PREFACE

The preceeding volume to this book, *Junkers Ju 88: The Early Years*, looked at the service of this enigmatic aircraft through the Battle of France, the Battle of Britain and the Blitz as well as its use as a trainer. That volume also detailed its early history, as well as the relevant variants.

This second volume completes the Ju 88's history in the latter part of the Second World War, exploring its deployment in the Soviet Union, in the Mediterranean and North Africa, its use as a torpedo bomber and reconnaissance platform, the heavy fighter operations it flew over the Bay of Biscay and Mediterranean, and, finally, its use up to the end of the war which included being used as a 'piggy-back' bomber.

It should be explained that the decision was taken to not include a section on the Ju 88's operation as a night fighter, and instead concentrate on day operations and night bombing work.

Chris Goss,
April 2018.

GLOSSARY

Adj	Adjutant
Aufklärungsgruppe	Reconnaissance Wing
Bordfunker	Radio Operator
Beobachter	Observer
Bordmechaniker	Flight Engineer
Bordschütz	Air Gunner
Deutsches Kreuz in Gold	German Cross in Gold award Dornier
Ehrenpokal	Goblet of Honour-awarded for outstanding achievements in the air war
Eiserne Kreuz	Iron Cross (came in First and Second Class)
Ergänzungs	Training
Feindflug	Operational flight
Feldwebel	Flight Sergeant
Fern	Long range
Flak	anti-aircraft fire
Flieger	Aircraftman
Fliegerführer Atlantik	Air Commander for the Atlantic region
Fluzeugführer	Pilot
Flugzeugführerschule	Flying school
Freie Jagd	Free hunting fighter sweep
Frontflugspange	Mission Clasp awarded for operational flights
Führer	Leader
Gefreiter	Leading Aircraftman
Generalfeldmarschall	Air Chief Marshal
Geschwader	Group consisting three Gruppen commanded by a Geschwader Kommodore
Gruppe	Wing consisting three Staffeln; commanded by a Gruppen Kommodore. The Gruppe number is denoted by Roman numerals
Hauptmann	Flight Lieutenant/Captain
Ia	Operations Officer
Jabo	Fighter-bomber

Jagd	Fighter
Jagdgeschwader	Fighter Group
Jagdgruppe	Fighter Wing
Ju	Junkers
Kampfgeschwader	Bomber Group
Kampfgeschwader zur besonderen Verwendung	Normal designation for a transport unit
Kette	Three aircraft tactical formation similar to RAF vic
Kriegsmarine	German Navy
Lehrgeschwader	Technical Development Flying Group
Leutnant	Pilot Officer/Second Lieutenant
Luftflotte	Air Fleet
Major	Squadron Leader/Major
Me	Messerschmitt (used by RAF)
Nachtrichtenoffizier	Communications Officer
Oberfeldwebel	Warrant Officer
Obergefreiter	Senior Aircraftman/Corporal
Oberleutnant	Flying Officer/First Lieutenant
Oberst	Group Captain/Colonel
Oberstleutnant	Wing Commander/Lieutenant Colonel
RAF	Royal Air Force
Reichsluftfahrtministerium	German Air Ministry
Reichsmarschall	Marshal of the Air Force
Ritterkreuz	Knight's Cross
Ritterkreuz mit Eichenlaub	Knight's Cross with Oakleaves
Rotte	Two aircraft tactical formation; two Rotten made a Schwarm; commanded by a Rottenführer
Rottenflieger	Wingman
Schlacht	Ground attack
Schwarm	Four aircraft tactical formation commanded by a Schwarm Führer
Seenotflugkommando	Air Sea Rescue Detachment
Sonderführer	Rank usually given to War Reporters
Sonderfstaffel	Special Staffel
Stab	Staff or HQ formation in which Gruppen Kommodore and Geschwader Kommodore flew.
Stabsfeldwebel	Senior Warrant Officer
Staffel	Squadron (twelve aircraft); commanded by a Staffel Kapitän. The Staffel number is denoted by Arabic numerals
Technischer Offizier	Technical Officer
Unteroffizier	Sergeant
Werke nummer	Serial Number
Wettererkundungsstaffel	Weather reconnaissance unit (of squadron strength)
Zerstörer	Destroyer/Heavy fighter
Zerstörergeschwader	Heavy Fighter Group

PART 1
OPERATIONS OVER RUSSIA

Groundcrew working on Ju 88 A-4s of 9./KG 51 in Russia during 1941.

Mechanics working on a Ju 88 A of 4./KG 51, Russia, Summer 1941. Note the large radiator underneath the Jumo 211 J engine which necessitated a bulge to the cowling and identifies it as a Ju 88 A-4.

Opposite above: A second view of Ju 88 A-4s of 9./KG 51 in Russia. The nearest aircraft is coded 9K+KT and both aircraft have the yellow Russian front fuselage band. The spinner colours also appear to be yellow.

Opposite below: Said to have been photographed at Rhein-Main in 1940, this Ju 88 A of III./LG 1 (the unit's emblem of three birds flying over white and blue waves on a blue background is visible on the nose) has pale-painted Balkan front cowlings. This would therefore mean the photograph was taken from April 1941 onwards. The spinner colours are believed to be red, which would indicate 8 Staffel.

Opposite: A ladder is required by this mechanic to enable him to work on the top of the Ju 88's port engine.

The first of a series of four photographs showing Luftwaffe groundcrew working on a Junkers Ju 88 during operations in Russia in the summer of 1941.

Opposite above: A mechanic examining the Jumo engine of a Junkers Ju 88.

Opposite below: The final image in the set depicting groundcrew at work on a Ju 88 on the Eastern Front.

Mechanics discussing the intricacies of the Jumo 211 J engine.

Opposite above: A Ju 88 A-5 of 4./KG 51 fitted with two 900-litre auxiliary fuel tanks on the bomb racks. This aircraft is 9K+CM, which was flown by Feldwebel Robert Ciuraj, who can be seen on the left.

Opposite below: Another 4./KG 51 aircraft fitted with 900-litre auxiliary fuel tanks.

Armourers take a rest from loading 50kg bombs to a Ju 88 A-4, that coded 9K+JM, of 4/KG 51, Russia, 1941.

Seen from left to right are Leutnant Bernd Sartor (Beobachter), Oberfeldwebel Robert Ciuraj (Fluzeugführer), Feldwebel Albert Mittelmann (Bordschütz) of 4./KG 51. It has not been possible to identify the individual on the right. Sartor, Ciuraj and Mittelmann all went on to be highly decorated, all three receiving the Ehrenpokal. Sartor and Ciuraj, meanwhile, were also decorated with the Deutsches Kreuz in Gold, whilst Sartor also received the Ritterkreuz.

A Ju 88 A of 4./KG 51, in this case that flown by Feldwebel Robert Ciuraj, attacking a Soviet airfield with SD2 anti-personnel bombs, June 1941.

Another view of the cockpit
of Feldwebel Robert Ciuraj's
Ju 88 A.

An exterior view of the cockpit of
Feldwebel Robert Ciuraj's Ju 88 A
of 4./KG 51.

Oberfeldwebel Robert Ciuraj and Leutnant Bernd Sartor of 4./KG 51 pictured have a cigarette by a stack of 50kg bombs. They are both wearing 10-76B kapok life preservers.

This blurred photograph shows a Ju 88 A-4, coded 9K+FM, of 4./KG 51 in the Balkans in April-May 1941. The aircraft has the pale-painted cowlings used in Operation *Marita*, the code name for operations in this region.

Opposite above: A Ju 88 A-5 of KG 77. The individual aircraft letter of G is outlined in white, though it has not been possible to identify the Staffel. Note what appears to be a fuselage band under the fuselage cross which would indicate early stages of Operation *Barbarossa*.

Opposite below: A Ju 88 A-5, Wk Nr 2192 and coded V4+CT, of 9./KG 1. At 16.55 hours on 21 September 1941, this aircraft, which had been badly damaged by three Soviet I-153 fighters, ditched in Finnish territorial waters at Terijoki. The crew, Leutnant Otto Edler von Ballasko (Fluzeugführer), Unteroffizier Heinz Wasel (Beobachter), Feldwebel Josef Achatz (Bordfunker) and Unteroffizier Rudolf Kiesner (Bordmechaniker), were uninjured and soon rejoined their unit. On the tail are twenty-eight RAF roundel mission symbols and sixty red stars, with, below, a Frontflugspange indicating that this crew had been awarded this decoration. The aircraft carried the stylised Hindenberg signature on the nose and has the fuselage band under the fuselage cross. Another successful crew, all were awarded the Ehrenpokal and Deutsches Kreuz in Gold and Ballasko the Ritterkreuz.

15

The wreckage of a Ju 88 A-5 of KG 51 (the Edelweiss badge is visible) lying forlornly on a Russian airfield. There appear to be the remains of a second aircraft behind it.

In the cockpit of his Ju 88 A is Hauptmann Hajo Herrmann. Herrmann commanded 7./KG 4 (which became 7./KG 30 in October 1940), then III./KG 30 from August 1941 onwards, meaning that he flew in missions over the United Kingdom, Malta and then, in 1942, Russia. He was awarded the Ritterkreuz mit Eichenlaub and survived the war.

An unidentified Ju 88 A which has crash-landed in Russia during 1941 – note the stopped starboard engine. Unfortunately, the unit code cannot be seen.

Opposite: Hauptmann Hajo Herrmann pictured by the tail of his Ju 88 A.

A Ju 88 A-4 of 7./KG 30, that coded 4D+LR, photographed taking off in early 1942. Note the KG 30 diving eagle badge on the nose.

A Ju 88 A-4 of 8./KG 30 taking off or landing in wintery conditions in early 1942.

Groundcrew in front of a Ju 88 A of KG 30 on an airfield in Lapland, 1942. Once again, KG 30's diving eagle badge is visible on the nose.

These Ju 88 D-1s of 2 (F)./22 are believed to have been photographed at Borispol, Ukraine, in February or March 1943. The nearest aircraft would have been coded 4U+FK, the second 4U+AK, followed by KN+SI and then, in the distance, 4U+PK. KN+SI was a Ju 88 D-1, Wk Nr 430587 and became coded 4N+UK. It was reported missing following a mission to Kuban-Rossoch-Woronesch on 8 May 1943. At the time it was crewed by Oberleutnant August Heinrich (Fluzeugführer), Oberfeldwebel Heinz Helm (Beobachter), Feldwebel Hans Hauser (Bordfunker) and Unteroffizier Heinz Kotter (Bordschütz).

Opposite: A Ju 88 A-4 of KG 30 starting up at a very wintry airfield, 1942.

An unusual photograph of a Ju 88 A of KG 30 which had had both tyres shredded by enemy action. The aircraft sports a fuselage band over which one can see 4D for KG 30. It also appears to have heavily toned-down camouflage.

A Ju 88 A-4, Wk Nr 142338 and coded F1+GS, of 8./KG 76. The number beneath the '38' is the Ju 88 fuselage number. The arms of the city of Heidelberg were adopted in late 1942 as it was the birthplace of the Gruppen Kommandeur, Hauptmann Heinrich Schweickhardt. Formerly Staffel Kapitän of 8./KG 76, Schweickhardt took command of the Gruppe in the spring of 1942. He was flying this aircraft from Catania to Athens on 9 January 1943 when he reported engine trouble after combat, with Flying Officer Danny Blair and Flight Sergeant Ed Dawson of 253 Squadron, 100 kilometres west of Zante. He and his crew, Leutnant Hellmut Vollmer (Beobachter), Oberfeldwebel Josef Tölle (Bordfunker), Oberfeldwebel Erich Müller (Bordschütz) and Gefreiter Lothar Kunze, were all reported missing. Schweickhardt, Tölle and Müller had been awarded the Deutsches Kreuz in Gold whilst Schweickhardt also had been awarded the Ritterkreuz mit Eichenlaub. He was promoted to Major posthumously.

Opposite above: The immediate aftermath of a Soviet air attack on a Luftwaffe airfield in 1942. The Ju 88s are believed to be D variants flown by Aufklärungsgruppe (Fern) 100.

Opposite below: A Ju 88 A-4, believed to be from I./KG 77, which came to grief in Russia in the spring of 1942. This aircraft has been fitted with VS-11 wooden propellers, but has no markings to confirm unit or date.

A Ju 88 A-4 of KG 77. Note the 20mm cannon in the gondola. The significance of the pig artwork is not known. Note the double bands on the spinner which appear to be white.

Opposite above: A much colder crash-landing for this unidentified Ju 88 A-4. The spinner tips appear to be red and there is no sign of a fuselage band. Note the wooden propellers.

Opposite below: The Ju 88 A-8 was based on the A-4 and included the addition of fittings for anti-balloon equipment. However, it never went into production. The aircraft in this picture is, therefore, an A-4 intended as an A-8, with fitting points top and bottom of the nose for the anti-balloon equipment.

Another stricken Ju 88 A-5 in Russia in the spring of 1942. This aircraft still has metal propellers. Note the 'beetle' rear canopy. Just visible is a fuselage band and the aircraft's individual letter.

A Ju 88 A-5, coded 9K+FM, of 4./KG 51 that crashed somewhere in Russia in the summer of 1941.

A close-up of the damage to the rear fuselage section of 9K+FM – note how the F has been outlined in white.

After his Ju 88 A-5, Wk Nr 6143, had been damaged by ground fire during a low-level attack on Krosno on 26 June 1941, Feldwebel Wilhelm Pahner of 4./KG 51 managed to execute a belly-landing, despite having himself been wounded in the left arm, the bullet breaking his arm.

Opposite: Members of 9K+FM's crew in discussion with another officer or official after their crash landing.

On 29 April 1943, Ju 88 A-4 coded 9K+AM of 4./KG 51 suffered an undercarriage collapse at Bagerowo. Feldwebel Robert Ciuraj (Fluzeugführer), Leutnant Bernd Sartor (Beobachter), Unteroffizier Albert Mittelmann (Bordfunker) and Feldwebel Ossenschmidt (Bordschütz) were uninjured.

The first in a set of five images of a Ju 88 A-4 after it had crash-landed on the Russian Steppes in the winter of 1942-43. Unfortunately, heavy camouflage has prevented it being identified.

Another view of the cockpit section of the Ju 88 A-4 after it had crash-landed on the Russian Steppes.

A piece of flying clothing hangs over the side of the cockpit of the Ju 88 A-4. It would appear that the crew survived.

The barren countryside in which the Ju 88 A-4 crashed is vividly illustrated in this shot. Note also the apparent cannon or shell hole on the engine cowling.

That the aircraft was undoubtedly written-off following the crash is clear from this photograph that shows extent of the damage to the fuselage.

An unidentified Leutnant pilot standing next to, presumably, his Ju 88 A. He has been awarded the Iron Cross First Class and is the wearer of the Frontflugspange.

Opposite: An unidentified officer in front of a Ju 88 A-4 which appears to be carrying a single 900-litre auxiliary fuel tank. He is wearing a two-piece 'Channel' flying suit and a 10-30 inflatable schwimmveste. Attached to the inflation tube is an armband compass.

Officers inspecting a crash-landed Ju 88 A. The officer to the left is a Leutnant and holder of the Iron Cross Second Class, while the Major to his left has the Iron Cross First Class.

Heading east in the summer of 1941 are these Ju 88 As of III./KG 76. At least two are carrying four 250kg bombs externally.

A Ju 88 A of Stab III./KG 76, which can be identified by the yellow hornet emblem under the cockpit.

This Ju 88 A, coded F1+BR, was flown by Leutnant Dieter Lukesch of 7./KG 76, whilst it was based at Orscha-Süd in November and December 1941. Note the two kill markings on the rudder. Lukesch, who would later be awarded the Ritterkreuz mit Eichenlaub, shot down two Soviet fighters and two courier aircraft while operating in the East. Shortly after this photograph must have been taken, Lukesch was badly injured in a crash-landing of Ju 88 A-4 Wk Nr 8533, coded F1+HR, at Orscha on 15 December 1941. He did not return to operational flying until mid-way through 1942, and went on to survive the war.

Pilots and groundcrew pictured during the ceremony held to celebrate 7./LG 1's 1,500th operational flight, which occurred in the summer of 1942. At that time, 7 Staffel was commanded by Hauptmann Egon Freiherr von Dalwigk. Soon after, von Dalwigk was posted to Erprobungsstaffel 410 to help in the development of the Messerschmitt Me 410. He went on to command 16./KG 2, followed by V./KG 2. He survived the war.

At the time of the ceremony, III Gruppe was commanded by Ritterkreuz holder Hauptmann Hermann Hogeback (who can be seen front left). Note the last two digits of the Wk Nr, 72, on the nose of this Ju 88 A-4, which is believed to be Wk Nr 142172, which had the fuselage number R.0382.

Opposite: A photograph taking during the event held by III./LG 1 to celebrate the 5,000th mission of the Gruppe at Stalino on 29 September 1942. It is believed that by this date, III./LG 1 had become III./KG 6 but still retained the trappings of its former unit. In November 1942, III./KG 6 moved to Creil in France and began to convert to the Ju 88 A-14.

Hauptmann Hermann Hogeback congratulates officers on achieving the Gruppe's 5,000th mission. Hogeback would be awarded the Eichenlaub to the Ritterkreuz he is wearing. He survived the war.

A celebration for a 7./LG 1 crew. Note the III./LG 1 emblem on the nose of this Ju 88 A-4. The Hauptmann congratulating them is standing between two 250kg bombs.

A crash-landed Ju 88 D-2, in this case that with the Wk Nr 0868, as identified by the uncamouflaged panel on the nose. The date and location are not known but it is possible that this aircraft was transferred to the Hungarian Air Force between December 1942 and September 1943.

This crash-landed Ju 88 is believed to have carried the code 7A which would indicate Aufklärungsgruppe (Fern) 121.

A second view of the crash-landed Ju 88 that is believed to have carried the code 7A. Note that the aircraft has an Eastern front fuselage band and is either an A-5F or D-5 version.

The identity panel on this aircraft confirms it as a Ju 88 A-5F which had the Wk Nr 0422. As part of 5(F)./121, this aircraft crash-landed at Welikije-Luki on 5 July 1941. There were no crew casualties, but the aircraft suffered 60 per cent damage.

PART 2
THE MEDITERRANEAN THEATRE

A 1,000kg bomb seen on a Ju 88 A-5 of III./KG 30 at Gerbini in the spring of 1941. Around the nose of the bomb was a kopfring – this being a metal ring, triangular in cross section, designed to prevent ground penetration or to stop forward momentum hitting water.

Opposite: A Ju 88 A-5 of 8./KG 30 in a hangar at Gerbini in the spring of 1941. Note the yellow cowling rings and spinners. It cannot be confirmed whether the badge on the nose is III./KG 30's bat and moon emblem, which was still in evidence on this unit at that time.

A mix of 500kg and 1,000kg bombs can be seen in the foreground of his picture of another Ju 88 A-5 of III./KG 30 – which was, once again, photographed at Gerbini in the spring of 1941.

An unidentified Ju 88 A on a Mediterranean airfield in 1941. Unfortunately, the markings on the sidecar do not assist in the aircraft's unit identification.

Opposite above: A damaged building and Ju 88 at Catania, Sicily, pictured after the raid by the RAF Wellingtons on the night of 15/16 January 1941.

Opposite below: A calmer view of the airfield at Catania taken in the spring of 1941. In the background is a Ju 88 A, that coded 4D+DR, of 7./KG 30. The foreground contains a mix of bombs – nearest to the camera are Luft Minen while the remainder appear to be 250kg or 500kg bombs.

The scene at the Luftwaffe airfield at Catania, Sicily, early on the morning of 16 January 1941. The previous night, a force of nine Vickers Wellingtons of 148 Squadron attacked the airfield, the main target being the administrative buildings seen in the background. Ten aircraft and a hangar were claimed as destroyed, this Ju 88 A-4 of 6./LG 1, Wk Nr 3263, being one of them. The Germans reported that 3263 was 60 per cent damaged.

Opposite above: A Ju 88 A-5 of III./KG 30 on the airfield at Gerbini in the spring of 1941. Note the bullet or flak damage to the nose and the KG 30 diving eagle emblem.

Opposite below: A view of the same aircraft seen in the previous image. By this stage, however, the propellers have been removed and it looks as if preparations are being made to lift the aircraft.

Gefreiter Helmut Quehl (Bordmechaniker) and Gefreiter Johann Schneiders of 8./KG 30 in front of a Ju 88 A-5 of III./KG 30. The unit moved from Schiphol, Holland, to Gerbini, Sicily, in February 1941, returning to Melun-Villaroche in France in June the same year. In August 1941, III./KG 30 moved to Gilze Rijen in Holland. It was whilst operating from there these that these two men were shot down and captured on 23 November 1941. The combat, which involved a Beaufighter of 307 Squadron, took place above the outskirts of Plymouth.

An unidentified Ju 88 A. The starboard engine appears to have caused considerable damage to the fuselage, elevator and rudder as well as burning through the wing trailing edge behind the engine.

A Ju 88 A-4 of 2./Kampfgruppe 606. In December 1941, the Gruppe moved from Lannion in France to Catania in Sicily, by which stage it had converted to the Ju 88 A-4. The first combat loss for 2 Staffel was on 5 March 1942, this being a Ju 88 A-4, Wk Nr 1392 and coded 7T+JK, which was flown by Unteroffizier Friedrich Engelbert. Fifteen days later, the Staffel Kapitän, Oberleutnant Rolf Krieg, was shot down and killed by anti-aircraft fire over Malta. He was replaced by the very experienced Oberleutnant Walter Prüger. Prüger received the Deutsches Kreuz as an Oberfeldwebel on 30 January 1942 after which he was commissioned. He would receive the Ehrenpokal and Ritterkreuz posthumously having been shot down by fighters attacking Hal Far airfield on Malta on 6 July 1942.

An abandoned Ju 88 A-4/Trop, that coded +BT, pictured under what appears to be an RAF guard, probably in Tunisia in 1943.

Opposite above: In September 1942, Kampfgruppe 606 was redesignated I./KG 77 and came under the leadership of Hauptmann Rolf Siedschlag. It continued to operate from Catania and Gerbini until the spring of 1943. This is the Ju 88 A-4 coded 3Z+FK of Oberleutnant Walter Kipfmüller's 2 Staffel at Gerbini. Kipfmüller would be awarded the Ehrenpokal, Deutsches Kreuz in Gold and Ritterkreuz. He survived the war.

Opposite below: A Ju 88 A-4 of I./KG 77 pictured at Gerbini during October 1942. Note the name Fanny on the nose.

A second view of the captured +BT. Note that an MG 15 machine-gun has been strapped to the side of the fuselage by the rear bomb bay – an unusual and rarely seen modification. The meaning of RACT on the flame damper is unknown whilst. The first two letters of the code appear to be BS.

Groundcrew and armourers loading 250kg bombs on to a Ju 88 A-4 of 2./ Kampfgruppe 606 at Catania in the spring of 1942.

A Ju 88 D-1 of 3.(F)/33, coded 8H+KL, flying over a typical Mediterranean landscape. Note the gondola has been removed. This unit moved to the Mediterranean in November 1942 and remained there for much of the remainder of hostilities.

Oberstleutnant Hermann Schlüter hands over command of KG 77 to Major Wilhelm Stemmler on 16-17 February 1943. Behind is the Kommodore's Ju 88 A-4, which was coded 3Z+AA. Schlüter had previously commanded Kampfgruppe 606 and spent the remainder of the war in command of training units or staff jobs; it is thought that he did not survive the war. As for Stemmler, it is believed he was flying this Ju 88 A-4, Wk Nr 140454, when he was shot down and wounded by flak north-west of Sfax. He would be awarded the Deutsches Kreuz in Gold and Ritterkreuz and survived the war.

Damaged by flak during an anti-shipping mission in the spring of 1944, this Ju 88 A-17 – the A-4 Luft Torpedo (LT) and A-17 were identified by the torpedo control housing elongated bulge on the nose – of 3./KG 77 flown by Leutnant Ulrich Laubis has come to grief on landing. Note the distinctive camouflage and wooden propellers.

Opposite: A Ju 88 A-4 of I./KG 77. The aircraft appears to be carrying a mix of 250kg and 500kg bombs and has Mediterranean camouflage on the upper surfaces, with black on the lower surfaces. Note the 20mm cannon in the gondola, ideal for anti-shipping operations.

A second picture of Leutnant Laubis' aircraft after his crash-landing. Laubis was shot down by flak north of Cherbourg on 23 June 1944. Flying a Ju 88 A-17, Wk Nr 801814 and coded 3Z+LL, he was the only survivor from his crew.

This is a Ju 88 A-4 of 2./Kampfgruppe 606 which has suffered an undercarriage collapse at Catania in late 1941 or early 1942. This unit suffered a number of such incidents during this period, so it has not been possible to identify the incident with certainty.

As the Allies advanced in the Western Desert, many abandoned aircraft were discovered on desert airstrips. This Ju 88 of 1.(F)/121 appears to have been cannibalised by its previous owners to such an extent that it is not possible to identify it as an AS-5 F or D-1. It is believed that the airstrip is the one at Castel Benito.

In late 1942, 10./ZG 26 began operating Ju 88 C-6s from Trapani and then Practica di Mare in Italy. This was followed in mid-1943 by the formation of 11./ZG 26 at Eleuis. It is believed that these C-6s are from one of these two Staffeln and are operating over the Mediterranean in 1943.

Later in 1943, KG 77 began to convert to torpedo training. This photograph is believed to show the Ju 88 A-4 with the Wk Nr 142352. Coded 3Z+FR (factory code VM+DK), it was reported missing during a mission against Tripoli on 19 March 1943. The crew, Leutnant Fritz Schendel (Fluzeugführer), Feldwebel Johann Wolf (Beobachter), Obergefreiter Fritz Lüdecke and Unteroffizier Ehrenfried Voss (Bordschütz) were all killed.

This Ju 88 A-4 of I./KG 77 still carries the Kampfgruppe 606 cockerel badge. In the background is Mount Etna which would date the moment as mid-summer 1943. Note the typical underside Wellenmuster (wave pattern) camouflage scheme, for dusk/dawn operations.

PART 3
RECONNAISSANCE AIRCRAFT

Opposite: The absence of air brakes and under-engine bulge reveals these aircraft as Ju 88 A-5 Fs of an unidentified reconnaissance unit.

The code 4U+KL confirms that this aircraft was from 3.(F)/123. During the Battle of Britain, this unit was based at Buc near Paris but then moved to Granville in February 1941. A Ju 88 A-5 with this code, Wk Nr 0340, was lost during operations on 20 July 1941.

Opposite above: In the spring of 1942, 3.(F)/33 transferred from the Russian front back to Le Culot where it received newer Ju 88 A-5s. It flew a number of missions over and around the UK, whilst flying from Paris-Orly, but moved to Montpellier in November 1942, by which time it was also flying Ju 88 D-1 and D-5s.

Opposite below: Groundcrew working on the engines of a Ju 88 A-5 F of 3.(F)/33 under camouflage netting at Le Culot.

Photographed at Lanveoc Brest during the winter of 1940-41 is this Ju 88 A just about showing the codes letters FK, which could indicate 2.(F)/123. The unit moved to the Mediterranean in February 1941 where it would operate for the remainder of the war.

This Ju 88 A-5 F of 3.(F)/33 skidded off the runway on landing, running into a stack of 50kg bombs which did not explode – no doubt to the crew's great relief.

The code letters H8 on the fuselage of this Ju 88 reveals that the unit involved is Aufklärungsgruppe (Fern) 33. This picture was taken in the ceremony that marked the unit's formation in Germany in early 1941. At the time, it was equipped with Ju 88 A-5s.

Opposite: Seen at Paris-Orly in the spring of 1942 are Hauptmann Hans-Ulrich Michael (Staffel Kapitän), Oberleutnant Heinz Baumert and Oberleutnant Hans-Jürgen Fiebrantz, the latter two being Beobachters. Fiebrantz was the only one not to survive the war, being shot down off the Isle of Wight on 17 July 1942. At the time he was flying in Ju 88 A-5 8H+FL, Wk Nr 519. The victors were two Spitfires of 412 Squadron. Oberleutnant Helmut Kirchner (Fluzeugführer), Unteroffizier Hans Gelin (Bordfunker) and Unteroffizier Werner Koch (Bordmechaniker) were all killed with him.

A group of officers chatting during the event marking the formation of Aufklärungsgruppe (Fern) 33.

Opposite: Just over a year later, on 23 September 1943, 2.(F)/123 flew its 4,000th mission. This time the crew comprised Oberleutnant Franz Hessinger (Fluzeugführer), Oberfeldwebel Helmut Dörries (Beobachter), Oberfeldwebel Herbert Huster (Bordfunker) and Feldwebel August Fastenrodt (Bordschütz). This photograph was taken at Tatoi in Greece following their landing at 17.25 hours in Ju 88 D-1 coded 4U+LK.

It was on 23 August 1942, that 2.(F)/123 flew its 2,000th mission – the aircraft involved being flown by Oberfeldwebel Alfred Nitsch (Fluzeugführer), Oberleutnant Heinz Bournot (Beobachter), Unteroffizier Hans Merz (Bordfunker) and Gefreiter August Fastenrodt (Bordschütz). This is Nitsch's Ju 88 D-5 photographed at Kastelli, Crete, immediately after the flight. All four would be awarded the Ehrenpokal, though Nitsch would also be awarded the Ritterkreuz and Deutsches Kreuz in Gold. Nitsch was captured on 15 September 1943, whilst August Fastenrodt was killed on 29 February 1944. The 2.(F)/123 badge in the centre of this tribute is a black eagle carrying a telescope on a quartered red and yellow shield.

Another picture taken at Tatoi following Oberleutnant Franz Hessinger's landing at the controls of 4U+LK. Hessinger had begun flying with 2.(F)/123 on 23 May 1941 and by 6 August 1944 had flown 192 operational sorties for which he would be awarded the Ritterkreuz; Helmut Dörries received the same decoration shortly afterwards.

Oberleutnant Franz Hesslinger, Oberfeldwebel Helmut Dörries, Oberfeldwebel Herbert Huster and Feldwebel August Fastenrodt at Tatoi on 23 September 1943. Hessinger, Dörries and Huster would all be awarded the Ehrenpokal and Deustches Kreuz in Gold.

This is believed to be a Ju 88 T-1 of 2.(F)/123, that coded coded 4U+VK, which was photographed at Tatoi in 1944. This is now believed to be one of just three exceptionally rare Ju 88 D-5/Trops, and more specifically the one with the Wk Nr 430105, which was in Tatoi from October 1942 and possibly lost in an accident in July 1943. The main differences can be found in the fact that there are no bumps or bulges on the upper side of engine cowlings and this aircraft had BMW 801 D2 engines (smoother cowlings on topsides), not the BMW 801 G-1 engines as on the Ju 88 G-1, R-2, T-1, and S-1.

Opposite: The crew of Feldwebel Lothar Röhrich of 2.(F)/123 having landed at Athens-Tatoi at 10.34 hours on 16 October 1943. Röhrich had just completed a reconnaissance sortie to Leros in the Ju 88 D-1, coded 4U+CK, seen here. This flight was the 100th operational sortie for Feldwebel Valentin Morak (Bordfunker). Seen here, left to right, are Feldwebel Willi Wyrich (Beobachter), Feldwebel Röhrich (Fluzeugführer), Feldwebel Valentin Morak (Bordfunker) and Oberfeldwebel Rudi Kasprowski (Bordmechaniker). On 3 February 1944, Röhrich, Wyrich and Morak were shot down over Nicosia, Cyprus by Spitfires of 127 Squadron whilst flying a Ju 88 T-1, that with the Wk Nr 430921 and coded 4U+BK. Whilst Röhrich was killed, the remainder of his crew was captured.

The moment that 1.(F)/100's 1,000th operational flight came to a successful conclusion as the Ju 88 involved flies low over the unit's base, probably at Orscha-Süd some time in 1943.

Personnel from 1.(F)/100 greet the successful crew. This Staffel was formed from 1.(F)/Aufklärungsgruppe Ob.d.L at Orscha-Süd at the end of January 1943.

Pictured during the celebrations to mark 1.(F)/100's 1,000th operational flight, the officer in the peaked cap is the Staffel Kapitän, Hauptmann Hans Schech. Having been with the unit since the end of 1940, Schech was posted away on 26 February 1943, after which he was awarded the Deutsches Kreuz in Gold. Note the crudely applied winter camouflage on this Ju 88 D-1. Coded T5+AH, it is presumably Schech's aircraft.

From this picture, it is fair to assume that Hauptmann Hans Schech, on the left in the peaked cap, was the pilot of the aircraft involved in 1.(F)/100's 1,000th operational flight.

Opposite: A 1.(F)/Aufkl.ObdL crew pictured celebrating a milestone – which is believed to be the 250th flight of the Staffel. Feldwebel Georg Kölbl (Fluzeugführer) is seen here being carried from his Ju 88 D-5 (with VDM metal propellers). Note the weather-worn camouflage, radiator bulge under the engines and the letter V on the cowling. The date is spring to the early summer of 1942. Kölbl would be awarded the Ehrenpokal on 25 January 1943.

The whole Staffel poses for the camera to mark 1.(F)/100's 1,000th flight. Above the third zero is Hauptmann Hans Schech, who, in due course, was replaced by Hauptmann Erich Marquardt (he can be seen standing to Schech's right).

Unteroffizier Karl Herberth, Kölbl's gunner, looks embarrassed as he is carried away from his Ju 88.

An unidentified member of Kölbl's crew (Kölbl is holding the flowers) speaking to an equally unidentified officer. The Kölbl crew, which included Feldwebel Joachim Paul (Beobachter), Unteroffizier Rudolf Schmidt (Bordfunker) and Unteroffizier Karl Herberth (Bordschütz), having taken off from Orscha-Süd at 05.25 hours, failed to return from a reconnaissance mission in the Weliki-Luki-Semzy-Lomenossowo-Welish area on 6 July 1943. They were flying a Ju 88 D-1, Wk Nr 430684 and which was coded T5+CH.

Another image taken during the celebrations for 1.(F)/Aufkl.ObdL's 250th flight. The Ju 88 D-1 in the background clearly shows the letter V on the cowling – this denotes the overhaul level of the engines.

Opposite: Leutnant Paul Venn (right) ready to greet the Kölbl crew. Venn and his crew, Unteroffizier Hans Waldner (Fluzeugführer), Unteroffizier Karl Christner (Bordfunker) and Obergefreiter Peter Osietzki (Bordschütz), suffered an engine failure during a reconnaissance mission on 5 August 1942. Their Ju 88 D-1, Wk Nr 430134, subsequently crashed near Rudnjo. Paul and Osietzki were killed and the remainder of the crew seriously injured. The injured were taken to the Luftwaffe hospital at Smolensk where Waldner later died.

Leutnant Paul Venn shaking hands with Feldwebel Georg Kölbl. It would appear that one of his crew is to his right, the other two to his left.

It would appear that the whole of 1 Staffel is celebrating the 250th sortie, though the Staffel Kapitän, Hauptmann Hans Schech, is not evident in this picture.

This unidentified 1.(F)/100 crew has been awarded the Frontflugspange in Gold for 110 missions. Beneath the oversized award is the 1(F)/Ob.d.L emblem of a shield on which an eagle is looking at the earth, and which is also written 1.(F)/100.

Below and opposite: A more muted celebration is enjoyed by this 1.F)/Ob.d.L crew on the occiasion of their successful completion their 110th operational flight. The identity of the Hauptmann in the peaked hat is not known.

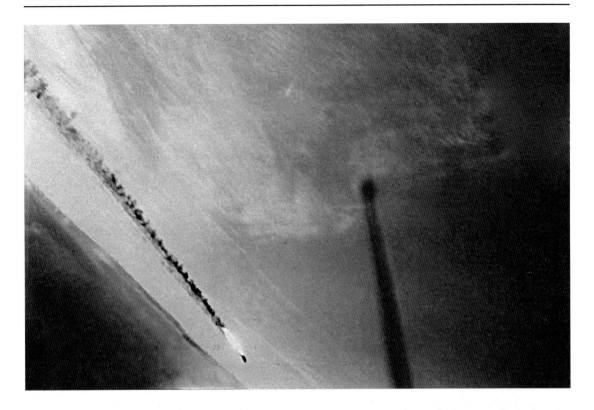

The moment that 4T+KH crashed into the sea. There were no survivors from the crew of Oberleutnant Ernst Stickel (Fluzeugführer), Inspekteur Johann Oeschsle (Beobachter), Oberfeldwebel Georg Nehr (Bordfunker) and Feldwebel Johann Kurth (Bordmechaniker). The pilot had been awarded the Ehrenpokal in December 1942. The Ju 88 managed to damage one of the Beaufighters, which burst into flames before crash-landing back in the UK.

Opposite above: The first of three photographs that reveal the fate of a Junkers Ju 88 D-1 of Wekusta 51 which was shot over the Bay of Biscay at 08.25 hours on 10 March 1943. Wettererkundungsstaffeln, which were also known as Wekusta or Westa, were Luftwaffe units of squadron strength used for weather reconnaissance. Their primary task was to collect weather data in areas that only aircraft could penetrate.

Opposite Below: The Ju 88 in question, Wk Nr 430406 and coded 4T+KH, was engaged by four Beaufighters of 248 Squadron, Coastal Command, one of which was flown by Lieutenant Maurice Guedj DSO, DFC, Croix de Guerre. A Free French Air Force pilot, Guedj had only been posted to the squadron, taking command of 'A' Flight, the previous day. He flew under the pseynedum 'Maurice' to avoid reprisals against his family.

Another Wekusta loss, but this time in the Mediterranean theatre. This Ju 88 A-4 of Wekusta 26, Wk Nr 140437 and coded 5M+Y, was shot down by crews of 252 Squadron eighty miles west of the island of Cyprus on 13 September 1943.

At 13.03 hours that day, Flight Sergeant Desmond De Villiers and Flight Sergeant W.P. Fryer took off from Limassol, Cyprus, in Beaufighter V8347 to provide fighter cover to four ships, one of which was the sloop Gander. Nine minutes later Flight Sergeant Alexander McKeown and Sergeant R. Dixon also took off in JL621, rendezvousing with the other Beaufighter shortly afterwards.

Despite the fact that the record of events in 252 Squadron's Operations Record Book makes no mention of what followed, the two RAF aircraft spotted a Junkers Ju 88 at position 35.09N 31.39E – the latter was flying at an altitude of 300 feet and on a course of 130 degrees. This was 5M+Y, which was flown by Feldwebel Fritz Wolters.

De Villiers attacked three times from the starboard stern quarter, closing from a range of 600 down to 400 yards, but his cannon jammed and only his machine-guns fired. However, he did notice a small piece break away from the Ju 88's port engine. McKeown then joined in the engagement, making eight attacks from the same range from both the port and starboard stern quarters.

A second camera gun picture taken during the attack on 5M+Y. In the face of the Beaufighters' onslaught, Wolters took violent evasive action, weaving and side-slipping as well as trying to corkscrew. McKeown anticipated a starboard turn and set the Ju 88's starboard engine on fire, after which the German aircraft made a perfect landing on the sea eighty miles west of Cyprus at 13.00 hours.

Two members of the Luftwaffe crew, and what was described as a rectangular box, were spotted in the water. In fact, all four men on board, Wolters, Unteroffizier Heinrich Schulze (Beobachter), Unteroffizier Hans Rader (Bordfunker) and meteorologist Dr Christian Theusner, were subsequently picked up by a high-speed launch and landed at Limassol.

The scene at 1.(F)/22's base at the time of the return of 4N+JH. Those aircraft with thinner blades are A-5 Fs, the ones with fatter blades are D-1s. Note also the Junkers Ju 90 landing or taking off in the background.

Opposite above: Two members of the crew of Ju 88 4N+JH of 1.(F)/22 pictured after their return to base and during the celebrations to mark the completion of their 100th flight.

Opposite below: The 'welcome party' waiting to greet 4N+JH and start the celebrations to mark the two crew members' achievement. Their unit's emblem of a puss in boots superimposed on the light blue and white shield of Kassel is visible on the nose of the aircraft taxying in.

Opposite: The Staffel Kapitän of 3.(F)/123, Hauptmann Helmut Höfer, pictured making a speech at Rennes on 23 August 1943.

The scene at Rennes on 23 August 1943, following the return of a Ju 88 D-1, that coded 4U+DL, of 3.(F)/123. The Staffel's 2,000th flight began at 16.43 hours that day when 4U+DL took-off and headed out over the Atlantic. The flight then continued towards to Ireland, on to England and then finally back to Rennes, where the crew landed after an uneventful flight at 19.40 hours.

The crew chosen for the 2,000th flight consisted of Oberleutnant Siegfried Müller (Fluzeugführer), Oberleutnant Günther Klien (Beobachter), Oberfeldwebel Siegfried Kirsch (Bordfunker) and Unteroffizier Roman Gastager (Bordmechaniker). All four had received the Ehrenpokal, whilst Gastager was also awarded the Deutsches Kreuz in Gold. It is believed that Müller was killed in an accident in October 1943, and Kirsch in February 1944.

A rare photograph, in this case a camera gun image, of a Ju 88 H-1 of 3.(F)/123. Having taken-off from Rennes at 16.00 hours on 31 July 1944, the last radio message from this particular aircraft, Wk Nr 430931, was received at 18.56 hours when the crew reported that they were about twelve miles west of Point du Raz, the latter being a promontory that extends into the Atlantic from western Brittany, France.

Just three minutes later, the Ju 88 was attacked and shot down by two Mosquitoes from 248 Squadron. There were no survivors, the crew of Feldwebel Paul Gruner (Fluzeugführer), Oberfeldwebel Günther Langenfeld (Beobachter), Unteroffizier Franz Banach (Bordfunker) and Unteroffizier Georg Quetscher (Bordschütz) all being killed.

The H-1 was a stretched D-1 with no ventral gondola, BMW 801 engines and with three cameras located further back in the fuselage. It had an increased range and was fitted with the FuG 200 'Hohentwiel' low-UHF band frequency maritime radar.

PART 4
TORPEDO OPERATIONS

A second photograph of the Stab./KG 77 Ju 88 at La Jasse. This aircraft particular is said to be that of the Geschwader Kommodore, who, at that time, was Major Wilhelm Stemmler. Stemmler normally flew the aircraft coded 3Z+AA.

Opposite: A Ju 88 A-17 of Stab./KG 77 pictured at La Jasse in southern France during the spring or early summer of 1944. Note the FuG 200 Hohentwiel aerials and the distinctive Wellenmuster wave pattern camouflage.

Leutnant Ulrich Laubis in a Ju 88 A-17 of 3./KG 77 at La Jasse in the spring of 1944. Laubis was shot down by flak north of Cherbourg on 23 June 1944, whilst flying Ju 88 A-17 Wk Nr 801814 and coded 3Z+LL.

This time Leutnant Ulrich Laubis is pictured looking out of the side window of another Ju 88 A-17 of 3./ KG 77. The white letter B on the gondola suggests that this aircraft was coded 3Z+BH. Note how the Wellenmuster camouflage pattern wraps around the upper and lower surfaces.

Leutnant Kurt Becker, Feldwebel Franke and Obergefreiter Skupsch of 2./KG 77, photographed at La Jasse early in the summer of 1944. This crew flew its first operational flight on the night of 11-12 April 1944 against a convoy, completing a further nine sorties by August that year. On 10 August 1944, 2./KG 77 became 2./KG 26 and moved to operate from Norway. Becker and his crew survived the war.

A Ju 88 A-4 LT of 8./KG 26, which, because of the losses it suffered in 1943, was referred to by its crews as a 'Suicide Squad'. This aircraft is painted yellow underneath the cowlings which shows it was operating in the Mediterranean at the end of 1943. The normal crew for this aircraft was Leutnant Fritz Massloh (Fluzeugführer), Unteroffizier Gottlob Hartmaier (Beobachter), Gefreiter Anno Körper (Bordfunker) and Gefreiter Anton Temmen (Bordschütz).

On 1 May 1943, this crew suffered engine failure during a mission and baled out of their Ju 88 A-4, Wk Nr 14464, without incident. On 21 October 1943, the same crew, minus Körper who was on leave and replaced by Leutnant Eberhard Eggert, was forced to bale out of Ju 88 A-4 LT Wk Nr 1722, coded 1H+FS, when it was hit by flak. They landed near Ibiza and were briefly interned.

Fritz Massloh would be awarded the Deutsches Kreuz in Gold. The whole crew survived the war.

A group of Ju 88 A-17s of 9./KG 26 pictured flying low over the Mediterranean in early 1944.

A Ju 88 A-17 of 3./KG 77 in the spring of 1944. Despite the camouflage, the individual code letter B is just about visible. Note that this aircraft has a Walter 109-500 Kraft-Ei jet pod under the wing, this being used for assisted take-off when it was carrying a heavy fuel load or using a short runway. Once airborne, the pod would be usually dropped. If both belly tanks were full, then it would be designated as a Ju 88 A-17 – more specifically, the A-17/A carried no belly tanks, the A-17/B was fitted with one tank (forward bay), whilst the A-17/C was equipped with two internal tanks.

A more traditionally camouflaged Ju 88 A-17 of 3./KG 77 that was photographed at La Jasse in May 1944. The torpedoes are F5b variants.

Opposite: The individual on the left is Obergefreiter Fritz Hermesmann (Bordfunker) of 9./KG 26. Experienced in torpedo operations, he was shot down in June 1943 in a He 111 H-6 LT, but was uninjured.

Hermesmann was captured on 18 June 1944, together with Leutnant Olaf Lüpke (Fluzeugführer), Unteroffizier Alfred Woiwode (Bordfunker) and Obergefreiter Edgar Mohr (Bordmechaniker), when their Ju 88 A-17, Wk Nr 801371 coded 1H+LT, was shot down, by ship's anti-aircraft between Cherbourg and the Isle of Wight, during an anti-shipping mission.

Oberleutnant 'Fred' Hauschnik's Ju 88 A-17 at Bardufoss in 1945. A Bordfunker, he was the Nachtrichten Offizier for both I./KG 77 and I./KG 26. His last mission of the war was on 18 March 1945, which he survived.

Opposite above: KG 77 was officially disbanded on 10 August 1944. The remaining crews formed KG 26, which then moved to Bardufoss in northern Norway – quite a change from the previous posting in southern France. This is one of the unit's Ju 88 A-17s photographed in February 1945.

Opposite below: These Ju 88 A-17s of I./KG 26 are pictured at Bardufoss starting up engines for a mission on 20 February 1945. The third aircraft is fitted with an auxiliary tank as opposed to a torpedo. The nearest aircraft is not equipped with a gondola.

Opposite above: A collection of Ju 88s at Bardufoss after the German surrender.

Opposite below: Another view of the scene at Bardufoss at the end of the war in Europe. All of these aircraft were scrapped shortly afterwards.

A Ju 88 of I./KG 26 taxying out at Bardufoss to attack an Allied convoy, RA 64, on 20 February 1945. In the crew is Oberst Ernst Kühl who had recently been given command of a Fliegerdivision based in Narvik. He was the holder of the Ritterkreuz mit Eichenlaub, Deutsches Kreuz in Gold and Ehrenpokal, and had flown 315 combat missions, most of them with KG 55.

Opposite: A pilot from 165 Squadron.poses for the camera in front of the same Ju 88 A-17 at Vaernes. This picture provides a good view of the FuG 200 'Hohentwiel' radar's aerial array. Note how the cover for the torpedo control has been removed

Among a mixture of aircraft captured at Vaernes in 1945 is this Ju 88 A-17, which is probably either Wk Nr 822897 or Wk Nr 822938 of II./KG 26. A total of four Ju 88s were surrendered at Vaernes.

PART 5
BATTLE OVER THE BAY:
V/KG 40

Ju 88 R-2s (note the BMW 801 engines) of I./ZG 1 in early 1944. V./KG 40 became I./ZG 1 on 13 October 1943. The first Ju 88 R-2 to suffer damage, that coded 2N+FH of 1./ZG 1, was involved in an accident at Lorient on 29 January 1944. The first combat loss of an R-2 was not until 11 April 1944. The aircraft in question, Wk Nr 751043 of 1./ZG 1, was being flown at the time by the Staffel Kapitän, Hauptmann Günther Moltrecht.

Opposite: A group of pilots from 14./KG 40 at Lorient in the summer of 1942. They have been photographed in front of a Ju 886 C-6. From left to right are: Leutnant Hermann Flothmann (killed 1 November 1942), Leutnant Herbert Hintze (wounded 16 January 1944), Leutnant Heinz Olbrecht, Hauptmann Hans-William Reicke (Staffel Kapitän, killed 30 January 1943), Leutnant Artur Thies (killed 22 March 1943), and Leutnant Helmut Messerschmidt (killed 11 April 1944).

A Ju 88 C-6 of 13./KG 40 showing the three MG 17 machine-guns and a 20mm cannon in the nose, as well as another two in the gondola. This aircraft is coded F8+RX and was the regular aircraft of Unteroffizier Hans Frank who would be killed in action fighting Beaufighters of 143 Squadron on 12 December 1943. He was flying a Ju 88 C-6 of 1./ZG 1, Wk Nr 750820 and coded 2N+DC, at the time.

A close-up of the nose of a Ju 88 showing the longer-barrelled MG 151 20mm cannon.

A Ju 88 C-6 of 13./KG 40, at Lorient in March 1943. This unit had few variations in camouflage and did not carry any unit badge. Some aircraft had kill markings on the tail or rudder.

Another Ju 88 C-6 of 13./KG 40, in this case the aircraft coded F8+MX. The M would have been in white; 14 Staffel used red Y and 15 Staffel Yellow X as their last letters.

Photographs of Ju 88 C-6s and R-2s of V./KG 40 complete with KG 40's 'world in a ring' emblem (black earth, pale blue sea, yellow ring) are rare. This could be a Gruppen Kommandeur or Geschwader Kommodore's aircraft, but this has never been confirmed.

Ju 88 C-6s of V./KG 40 on patrol over the Bay of Biscay in 1943. By mid-1943, the Gruppe sported a mix of camouflages, the new pale one being sported by the furthest aircraft.

Opposite: A Ju 88 C-6 of V./KG 40 taxies back to dispersal on its return from a sortie. The spinner colour would appear to be the yellow of 15 Staffel.

On 29 January 1943, two Ju 88 C-6s from V./KG 40, Wk Nr 360073 flown by Oberfeldwebel Johannes Kriedel and 360072 (coded F8+HZ) flown by Unteroffizier Paul Paschoff, were shot down by four Beaufighters of 248 Squadron; there were no survivors. This is the funeral pyre of one of the two aircraft.

Opposite above: A group of Ju 88 C-6s of 14./KG 40 taxying out to take-off on a mission. The pale camouflaged aircraft in the foreground is coded F8+NY.

Opposite below: The same group of 14./KG 40 pictured whilst taking off, possibly at Mérignac or Cognac.

The Ju 88 C-6 of 13./KG 40 seen in the background of this image, Wk Nr 360381 which was coded F8+BX, was one of three aircraft (the other two being Wk Nr 750419 and Wk Nr 750417) lost in an air attack on Lorient on 23 September 1943. A further four C-6s, a Bucker 131 and Fieseler 156 suffered varying degrees of damage.

Seen at Cognac is another 'pale' Ju 88 C-6, in this case the aircraft coded F8+HX. This was normally the personal aircraft of Unteroffizier Heinz Hommel.

Identifiable in this picture taken during 14./KG 40's formation practice are aircraft coded F8+RY, F8+NY and F8+AY. The last letter would appear to be red. The only recorded loss of an aircraft with these codes was Wk Nr 750412, coded F8+NY, on 25 September 1943. It was shot down by Mosquitoes of 307 Squadron resulting in the deaths of Leutnant Erhard Kromer and his crew.

Opposite above: This Ju 88 of 15./KG 40, F8+MZ, appears to have all of its letters a uniform colour.

Opposite below: A Ju 88 C-6 of V./KG 40 photographed by the crew of a Focke-Wulf Fw 200 C of 7./KG 40 over the Bay of Biscay during 1943.

Formation practice for the crews of 14./KG 40. It would appear that at least seven all-pale aircraft are in this group.

Ground crew refuel a Ju 88 C-6 of V./KG 40 during 1943. Whilst the aircraft's individual code is 'H', the Staffel letter cannot be discerned. Note the rear-facing defensive armament – the Ju 88 C-6 carried up to eight machine-guns/cannon.

An air-to-air shot of the Ju 88 C-6 coded F8+CY of 14./KG 40. It is believed that in addition to the letter 'Y' being in red, the band on the spinner was also red.

Oberleutnant Kurt Necesany, centre, of 14./KG 40 photographed after returning from the Staffel's 500th mission on 21 May 1943. For that sortie he flew the Ju 88 C-6 coded F8+RY – in this image clearly demonstrating that the 'Y' was a different colour to the letter 'R'. Note that the spinner has two red bands.

The 'welcome party' that greeted Oberleutnant Necesany and his 14./KG 40 crew on 21 May 1943. Necesany was killed in action following combat with a US Navy Consolidated PB4Y-1 Liberator of VB-103 on 14 February 1944. At the time he was flying Ju 88 C-6 Wk Nr 750967 and was the Gruppen Ia of I./ZG 1.

Opposite above: Unteroffizier Leo Wöber and Oberfeldwebel Kurt Gäbler of 15./KG 40. Gäbler was awarded the Deutsches Kreuz in Gold on 20 March 1944. When I./ZG 1 was disbanded in August 1944, Gäbler transferred to I./NJG 4. He was injured baling out of his Ju 88 G-6, Wk Nr 622132, near Osnabrück on 4 March 1945 when he ran out of fuel whilst returning from operations over the UK.

Opposite below: Unteroffizier Georg Ernst of 15./KG 40 pictured by F8+YZ. Just visible on the wing is one of the FuG 200 'Hohentwiel' aerials.

Two Ju 88 C-6s were forced to land in Spain following operations over the Bay of Biscay. The first was Wk Nr 360364 coded F8+HY of 14 Staffel. This was forced to land on 24 March 1943, with two of its crew mortally wounded, after a combat with a Halifax of 58 Squadron (which was also shot down).

The second was Wk Nr 360383 F8+PX of 13 Staffel, which suffered an oil leak in its port engine. The pilot was believed to be Oberleutnant Hermann Horstmann, the Staffel Kapitän, who soon returned to the unit. Horstmann, one of the most successful V./KG 40 pilots, was awarded the Deutsches Kreuz in Gold but was killed in action on 12 December 1943.

Opposite above: Leutnant Dieter Meister, on the right, Oberleutnant Hermann Horstmann, centre, and an unidentified army officer in front of a Ju 88 R-2 – the latter minus its spinners. Both Horstmann (Staffel Kapitän) and Meister were from 13 Staffel. Horstmann received the Deutsches Kreuz in Gold on 16 August 1943, Meister (who is wearing his) on 17 October of the same year. Horstmann would be killed in action on 12 December, while Meister lasted until 21 November 1944 when he was killed flying single-engine fighters with 10./JG 2.

Opposite below: A Ju 88 C-6 of 14./KG 40. The spinner ring is assumed to be red. It is believed that the pilot in the cockpit is Leutnant Knud Gmelin.

A rare photograph of a Ju 88 C-6 of V./KG 40 fitted with a 900-litre auxiliary fuel tank, these being useful for increasing an aircraft's range and endurance out over the Bay of Biscay.

Opposite: A crew from 13./KG 40 pictured after their return from a mission over the Atlantic on 4 September 1943. From left to right are Gefreiter Werner Göbler (Bordfunker), Unteroffizier Rolf Johenneken (Beobachter) and Unteroffizier Hans Frank (Fluzeugführer). Frank and Göbler would be shot down and killed, together with Unteroffizier Adolf Wirth, on 12 December 1943, by Beaufighters of 143 Squadron whilst flying Ju 88 C-6, Wk Nr 750820, 2N+DC. Two Beaufighters were claimed by Oberleutnant Hermann Horstmann and Leutnant Knud Gmelin, but three Ju 88 C-6s, including that of Horstmann, were shot down.

A Ju 88 C-6, believed to be F8+DY of 14./KG 40, pictured in the summer of 1943.

This Ju 88 C-6 of Stab III./ZG1, 2N+ME, would appear to have three kill marking, two RAF and one American, on the rudder. Note the fuselage band. III Gruppe was formed under the leadership of Hauptmann Hans Morr in March 1944 and it is possible this was his aircraft. Morr was awarded the Deutsches Kreuz in Gold in October 1943, but was killed in action whilst Gruppen Kommandeur of IV./JG 53 on 29 October 1944. In this image we can see Feldwebel Josef Mrechen, on the left, and an unidentified Gefreiter. Note the tail tip matches the fuselage band which is just visible on the left.

Opposite: There are eight kills, seven RAF and one American, on the rudder of this Ju 88 C-6 Wk Nr 750356 of I./ZG 1. It cannot be determined with certainty whose aircraft it was.

Another picture of Feldwebel Josef Mrechen (Beobachter) in front of 2N+ME of Stab III./ZG1. Mrechen was killed in action on 10 March 1941, whilst serving with 7./ZG 1, when his aircraft was shot down by Mosquitoes of 157 Squadron.

Another successful Ju 88 pilot was Leutnant Knud Gmelin, seen here on the left with his Bordfunker, Unteroffizier Gerhard Zimmermann of 13./KG 40. On 11 April 1944, Gmelin claimed three Mosquitoes and Zimmermann one off Lorient.

Gmelin (second from left) in front of his Ju 88 R-2, Wk Nr 750896, which was coded 2N+AH. To his left is Unteroffizier Gerhard Zimmermann, whilst to his right is believed to be Unteroffizier Wilhelm Dunkler (Beobachter). This crew was shot down in this aircraft on 9 June 1944, Gmelin dying of his wounds shortly after the crash-landing near Caen. The rest of the crew were wounded. All of Gmelin's 'kills', including the Mosquitoes on 11 April 1944, are marked on the tail.

One of the more unusual Ju 88 units that operated over the Bay of Biscay was Kommando Kunkel. Formed in November 1943 under the leadership of experienced He 111 and Fw 200 pilot Hauptmann Fritz Kunkel, its primary task was to intercept Allied aircraft at night. In June 1944, it became 9 (Nachtjagd) Staffel/ZG 1, before being redesignated 1./NJG 4 on 10 July 1944. Note the mottled camouflage and FuG 202 Lichtenstein aerials on the nose pof this aircraft, and the FuG 227 Flensburg aerials on the leading edges of the wings. The code letters 4C+AA indicate that this is Kunkel's aircraft. Kunkel did not receive any major decoration, but survived the war.

Preparations for the funeral of three unknown ZG 1 crewmen in the early spring of 1944. Note that the spinners and propellers are heavily camouflaged, something peculiar to Kommando Kunkel's Ju 88 C-6s.

Desperate times mean desperate measures. In an attempt to hide from Allied aircraft, this Ju 88 C-6 of ZG 1 has been heavily camouflaged.

During and after D-Day on 6 June 1944, the Ju 88s of ZG 1 flew daylight ground attack missions against the invasion forces. However, the unit suffered heavy losses. In fact, the attrition rate was so high that it led to the unit's disbandment at the start of August 1944. This Ju 88 R-2 of ZG 1, one of the many casualties, has managed to crash-land behind German lines. The date and crew names are not known.

The fate of this aircraft, a Ju 88 C-6 of 9(NJ)./
ZG 1, is known. It was shot down at 02.20
hours on 28 June 1944, crashing at Dancey,
near Chateaudun. The victors were Flight
Lieutenant Jeremy Howard-Williams and
Flying Officer 'Jock' Macrae of the Fighter
Interception Unit. The German crew of
Unteroffizier Werner Migge (Fluzeugführer),
Obergefreiter Hans-Joachim Köhler
(Bordschütz) and Obergefreiter Horst Michael
(Bordfunker) were all killed. The kill marks are
all RAF aircraft and are believed to reflect kills
for the whole Staffel, the only ones known
being those of 2 and 4 May 1944, claimed by
Leutnant Artur Ewert, and 27 May 1944, shot
down by Hauptmann Kunkel.

A close-up view of the nose section of the
ZG 1 loss.

PART 6
THE LATTER YEARS: 1943-1945

This is a Ju 88 A-14 of 6./KG 6 photographed at Cormeilles-en-Vexin in June 1943. The A-14 was a standardised cannon-attack bomber with a strengthened A-4 airframe. The officer standing under the aircraft to the left is Leutnant Walter Petrasch. Petrasch was killed at 01.30 hours on 23 February 1944, whilst returning from an attack on London. He, Unteroffizier Heinz Matz (Beobachter), Obergefreiter Norbert Cyron (Bordfunker) and Unteroffizier Ludwig Mackel (Bordschütz) all perished when their Ju 88 A-4 crashed at Beaucamp-Ligny near Lille in France.

Opposite: This Ju 88 A-4 appears to have suffered an engine failure in the starboard engine; the port engine seems to have been still turning, hence the blades are sheared and engine wrecked. The VS-11 broad chord wooden propellers of the stalled engine would shear in such a way, giving better survivability for the engine. The crew has jettisoned the rear canopy after landing. There is no visible fuselage band to indicate if the aircraft was in the Mediterranean or Russian theatres, but it seems to have a uniform dark camouflage for night operations.

The highly decorated and experienced Ju 88 pilot in the foreground of this photograph, which was taken at Beauvais in France in June 1943, is Oberleutnant Gerhard Lucke, Staffel Kapitän of 2./KG 6. Feldwebel Lucke flew with 5./KG 51 in France, the Battle of Britain and the Blitz. He then flew in the Balkans and was wounded in Russia at the end of June 1941. Oberfeldwebel Lucke was awarded the Deutsches Kreuz in Gold in July 1942, after which he moved to I./KG 77 in the Mediterranean. He became a Leutnant in August 1942 and was given command of 2./KG 6 which was formed from 2./KG 77 in September 1942.

By July 1943, Lucke had been promoted to Hauptmann and given command of 11./KG 6 at Brétigny. He remained with this Staffel until given command of IV./KG (J) 6, flying the Me 262, in December 1944. He survived the war having carried out 361 operational flights.

A Ju 88 A-14 of 6./KG 6 photographed by Leutnant Walter Petrasch in the vicinity of Cormeilles, June 1943. With Allied air superiority on the increase, such flights became a dangerous occupation.

Opposite above: Whilst this image is not the best quality, it is, nonetheless, historically important. It is thought to have been taken at Beauvais in August-September 1942. In the background is a Ju 86 R of the Hohenkampfkommando used for high-altitude reconnaissance of the UK. However, nearer the camera is believed to be a Ju 88 T-1, possibly coded T9+FH, which was operated by 1./ Versuchsverband OKL. The T-1 was essentially an S-1 used for reconnaissance.

Opposite below: Three highly decorated and experienced Ju 88 pilots, all of whom have been awarded the Ritterkreuz, photographed in early 1943. From left to right are: Oberleutnant Rudolf Puchinger, Staffel Kapitän 8./KG 6 (killed in action as Gruppen Kommandeur III./KG 6, 13 June 1944); Oberst Walter Storp, Kommodore KG 6; and Hauptmann Hermann Hogeback, Kommandeur III./KG 6. Storp had already been awarded the Eichenlaub, whilst Hogeback would receive his in February 1943, the same month that Puchinger received the Ritterkreuz. Behind them is a Ju 88 A-14.

In late 1942, Junkers modified the 'A' variant, resulting in the high-speed Ju 88 S serries. The ventral Bola gondola was removed, thus reducing the crew to three. There was a smoothly-glazed nose with radial-ribbed supports instead of the 'beetle's eye' of the A-version. The bombsight was a small periscope under the starboard nose. Armour plating and defensive armament were reduced as much as possible and it was powered by the improved BMW 801 G-2 engines – which, along with the GM-1 nitrous-oxide boost equipment, meant that this was the fastest of all the Ju 88 variants. One of the first units to receive this aircraft was I./KG 66.

Opposite: On 22 July 1943, Oberleutnant Karl von Manowarda of 1./KG 6 (second from right) flew the Ju 88 A-14 seen here, coded NJ+FA, from Foggia in Italy to Istres and then on to Villaroche. This photograph was taken just before they took off from Foggia at 07.27 hours.

Von Manowarda first flew operationally with 5./KG 2 on 15 October 1940, and until May 1943 had flown the Do 17 and Do 217. He would fly the Ju 88 for just two months before converting to the Ju 188 E-1. He and Feldwebel Heinrich Kaiser (Beobachter; second from left), Oberfeldwebel Ernst Fröhlich (Bordfunker; far right) and Oberfeldwebel Paul Schmaler (Bordschütz; seen here in the centre), together with Feldwebel Horst Wolf, would be shot down over Hampshire, on 15 May 1944, in a Ju 188 A-1, Wk Nr 3E+MH of 1./KG 2. Badly wounded, von Manowarda and Fröhlich were the only survivors.

Seen at Foggia, Italy, in the summer of 1943 is this Ju 88 A-14 flown by Leutnant Henning Gulde of 7./KG 6. Note the very dark camouflage with the Wellenmuster pattern. Gulde would be given command of 7./KG 6, but was killed flying an Me 262 with 7./KG (J) 6 at the end of April 1945.

In 1944, II./KG 76 was flying Ju 88 A-4s as pathfinders and target illuminators over the Mediterranean from Istres and Salon.

It is believed that the nearest aircraft is Wk Nr 822630 F1+JP, which was shot down by a Beaufighter of 108 Squadron whilst returning to Salon after an attack on a convoy. Staffel Kapitän Oberleutnant Hans Ebersbach (Fluzeugführer), Obergefreiter Edgar Fay (Beobachter), Oberfeldwebel Fritz Schwartz (Bordfunker) and Unteroffizier Othmar Grober (Bordschütz) were all killed when the aircraft crashed at St Martin de Crau. Ebersbach had already been awarded the Ehrenpokal and Deutsches Kreuz in Gold and would be promoted to Hauptmann, receiving the Ritterkreuz posthumously.

A Ju 88 A-4 coded B3+KH of 1./KG 54 photographed by Leutnant Hans Sickfeld of the same Staffel. Leutnant Sickfeld was reported missing on the night of 29-30 July 1944 whilst attacking Le Mesnil in northern France. No sign of his Ju 88 A-4, Wk Nr 3665 and coded B3+CH, or its crew were found.

During the time Sickfeld was with 1 Staffel, it lost two B3+KHs: Wk Nr 800939, whilst attacking Bristol on 20 April 1944, and Wk Nr 883900, shot down during a shipping strike in the Seine Bay on 20 June 1944. After Sickfeld's death, the Staffel lost one more aircraft coded B3+KH – that with the Wk Nr 1100, which suffered an engine fire near Paris on 16 August 1944.

Opposite above: Wing Commander Keith Hampshire and Flying Officer Tom Condon of 456 Squadronare pictured inspecting the remains of a Ju 88 which they shot down at Walberton, West Sussex, on 24 March 1944.

Just ahead of the cross is a small 3E and after it a letter A – which indicates that this is 3E+AP of 6./KG 6 (some records say it was an A-4, others an A-14). It was flown by 30-year-old Hauptmann Anton Oeben, the Staffel Kapitän, who was the only survivor. Feldwebel Otto Bahn (Beobachter), Unteroffizier Gerhard Drews (Bordfunker) and Unteroffizier Heinrich Ehrhardt were all killed. By this stage of the war, the unit's camouflage was either like this or dark with pale waves.

Opposite below: Parked in a hangar at Avord is a Ju 88 S-1 of I./KG 66. Formed in the spring of 1943, under the leadership of experienced pathfinder pilot Hauptmann Hermann Schmidt, this unit did not receive its Ju 88 S-1 until the end of the year or early 1944. Schmidt would receive the Ritterkreuz in April 1944 and survived the war.

By May 1944, Luftwaffe crews were being rushed through training. This is a Ju 88 A-4 or A-14 of IV./KG 6 seen at Lüneburg. Fähnrich Herbert Knospe (with hat) would fly operationally with 2./KG 6, having by then converted to the Ju 188 A-2. However, due to losses suffered over Normandy, he and his Gruppe flew back to Germany at the start of September 1944. From left left to right are Unteroffizier Alfred Hartung (Bordfunker), Obergefreiter Gustav Stör (Bordschütz), Knospe, and Obergefreiter Hannes Bruns (Beobachter). At the age of 23, the oldest in the group was Hartung, whilst the youngest was Knospe, who was just 19.

A Ju 88 S-1 of I./KG 66 showing the unit's distinctive mottled camouflage on the upper surfaces and black underneath. The unit code was Z6+.

Running up its engines at Dedelsdorf is this Ju 88 S-3 of I./KG 66, clearly illustrating the unit's distinctive mottled camouflage pattern. The S-3 had Jumo 213A liquid-cooled in-line engines as opposed to the BMW radial air-cooled engines of the S-1. Note that the only marking visible is the fuselage cross.

This is believed to be a Ju 88 S-3 which has come to grief at Celle in Germany. The engines would indicate an S-1 although the camouflage is a different mix to that used by KG 66. The aircraft individual letter is prominent on the fuselage.

Opposite above: The date on the photograph of this Ju 88 S-1 of I./KG 66 is 19 March 1944. By now, I./KG 66 was opeerating a mix of aircraft, with 1 and 3 Staffeln flying the Ju 88 S-1 and 2 Staffel the Ju 188 E-1. By July 1944, the S-1 had been replaced by the S-3.

Opposite below: Another engine run for a Ju 88 S-1 of I./KG 66. Note what appears to be an auxiliary fuel tank inboard of the port engine. KG 66 would carry aircraft individual letters on the leading edges inboard of the engines.

The aircraft of II and III./KG 54 were based at Bergamo in Italy at the time of this photograph, which was taken around December 1943. From the end of January 1944, they returned to Germany and were used for Operation Steinbock, a series of attacks on major towns and cities in the UK.

This Ju 88 A-4/Trop, Wk Nr 1214 and coded B3+PL, of 3./KG 54 has landed not in the Mediterranean, but in Essex. It took off from Wittmundhafen to attack London on the night of 18 April 1944, but its port engine was hit by flak and caught fire. The crew, Unteroffizier Heinz Brandt (Fluzeugführer), Unteroffizier Max Oppel (Beobachter), Obergefreiter Walter Kobusch (Bordfunker) and Gefreiter Heinz Oberwinter (Bordschütz), became disorientated and landed at RAF Bradwell Bay. The letter 'P' just visible in this picture is outlined in yellow and the KG 54 Totenkopf shield cam be seen on the nose. Once again, the upper surfaces are a mixture of green and grey whilst under surfaces were black.

Another late-war KG 54 loss – in this case a Ju 88 A-4 of 9./KG 54 that was shot down by flak at Colleville-sur-Mer, Normandy, at 04.00 hours on 13 June 1944. At the time it had been involved in attacks on Allied shipping supplying the invasion beachhead. Just visible on the fuselage is B3+, which indicates KG 54, and after the cross is the letter 'H'.

American personnel, including what appears to be a US Navy photographer, inspecting the wreckage of B3+HT at Colleville-sur-Mer. Obergefreiter Franz Schrapel (Fluzeugführer), Obergefreiter Bruno Schlag (Beobachter), Unteroffizier Kurt Gerber (Bordfunker) and Obergefreiter Heinz Lemke (Bordmechaniker) were all killed. Trophy hunters have already removed the tail swastikas.

The first of three remarkable stills taken from the camera gun footage captured by the Hawker Typhoon flown by a Belgian pilot, Flying Officer Charles Detal DFC of 609 (West Riding) Squadron, on 30 January 1944. At the controls of JP582, Detal was one of seven pilots from his squadron detailed to take part in Ramrod 498 – a two squadron mission (the other being 198) which 609 Squadron's ORB described as 'the biggest Typhoon victory of the war'.

A second still from Flying Officer Detal's camera gun footage, showing just how low his attack was made.

The 609 Squadron Typhoons had taken-off from RAF Manston at around midday. The squadron's ORB takes up the story: 'The 7 Typhoons of 609 [were] billed to sweep Montdidier–Malun–Bretigny, 198 doing likewise further west. First event is when, some miles S. of Amiens, F/O Detal takes time to squirt at a Ju 88 on the ground. This burst nicely into flames, and for the first time an attack is recorded with a 35mm camera, which produces fine stills which even show "types" running away. Others, Detal reports, remain rotted to the spot. A Ju 52 this time escapes his attentions. Detal thereafter follows the vectors given to the squadron by the C.O. [Squadron Leader J.C. Wells DFC], but does not catch up again.'

The last of the still from Detal's Typhoon. His target appears to be a Ju 88 S-1 of I./KG 66. He landed safely back at Manston at 13.40 hours. Detal was killed in an accident near Acklington, Northumberland, on 23 March 1944.

Flying Officer Detal was not the only 609 Squadron pilot to attack a Ju 88 during Ramrod 498 – as this image, the first of three camera gun stills from Squadron Leader Johnny Wells DFC's Typhoon, JR386, reveal.

At the end of the war, remains of Ju 88s could be found abandoned across Western Europe. Photographed in Germany in July 1945 is this Ju 88 A-4 with standard late war Wellenmuster camouflage and the letters 'DT' on the front of the gondola showing it was a 9 Staffel aircraft, but which unit is not known.

Opposite above: A second still taken as Squadron Leader Wells closes in on his target. Once again, the narrative can be drawn from the 609 Squadron ORB: 'Next "step" is Roye airfield, where the C.O. finds another Ju 88 being refuelled. Aided by Flying Officer Shelton [in JR312], who comes in close behind, he destroys this, and this time even the 16mm camera records the dispersal of the crews.' Once again, the target appears to be another Ju 88 S-1.

Opposite below: One can only contemplate the thoughts going through the mind of the member of Luftwaffe groundcrew pictured here behind Squadron Leader Well's target on 30 January 1944. The ORB continues: 'He [Wells] goes on to damage another a little further on (F/O Shelton declares the first was an Me.110 but is definitely refuted by the film). Meanwhile W/O Buchanan [JR300] damages a third Ju 88 and F/O Moulin [JR379] knocks pieces off the roof of a dispersal hut.'

Captured German aircraft pictured by an RAF officer at Lübeck-Blankensee in the immediate aftermath of the German surrender in May 1945. In the foreground is 1H+KM, a Ju 88 A-17 of 4./KG 26. It has a cut out in the flap so that the FuG 10 trailing aerial keep clear of the torpedoes.

The aircraft behind 1H+KM is a Ju 188 A-3 LT, Wk Nr 190327 and coded 1H+GT, of 9./KG 26. This aircraft first flew at Halle-Leipzig on 12 July 1944, and on 9 October 1944 was reported as being at Gotenhafen-Hexengruind with III./KG 26 – but not yet converetd for torpedo operations. On 8 May 1945, Oberleutnant Heinz Ebbinghaus and his crew flew from Gardermoen in Norway to surrender at Lübeck. The Ju 188 was assigned the serial number AIRMIN 113 and flown to Schleswig on 8 August 1945. It then headed to RAE Farnborough on 27 August 1945. It was scrapped in November 1947.

PART 7
THE JU 88 'MISTEL'

Previous page: The Mistel, this being the German for 'Mistletoe', was the larger, unmanned component of the composite aircraft configurations developed by the Luftwaffe in latter stages of the Second World War. The composite comprised a small piloted control aircraft, usually a fighter, mounted above a large explosives-carrying drone, the Mistel. As a complete unit, these composites were referred to as the Huckepack ('Piggyback') – but were also known as the Beethoven-Gerät ('Beethoven Device') or Vati und Sohn ('Father and Son').

This is a Mistel 2, probably of II./KG(J) 30, which is believed to have been photographed at Oranienburg in March 1945, during operations against the Oder and Neisse bridges. The Ju 88 G has the shorter, later warhead, with SHL 3500 fuse. Both aircraft have drop tanks (900-litre and 600-litre). It is possible that with the extra fuel this may have been an aircraft intended for a long-range flight to hit Soviet power stations as the Germans were still planning such moves in February-March 1945.

A view of aircraft on the Junkers airfield at Bernburg. This was the scene which welcomed troops of the US 9th Army's 113th Cavalry Group when they arrived there on 16 April 1945. On view are a Mistel S3C and a Ju 88 G-10 with fuselage-mounted support frame fitted ready for conversion into a Mistel. Note the latter's 'stretched' fuselage.

A Mistel S2, which comprised Fw 190 A-8 '97' and Ju 88 G-1 W.Nr.590153, pictured at Merseburg in May 1945. The Ju 88 bore the code 'C9', denoting an aircraft previously of NJG 5.

What appears to be a Mistel 2 or S2 pictured at the end of the war in Europe. Interestingly, a Focke-Wulf Fw 190 in the Imperial War Museum's collection, that with the Wk Nr 733682, is a Mistel survivor. It was captured by British forces in 1945. The aircraft retains the Kugelverschraubung mit Sprengbolzen (ball joints with explosive bolts) fittings underneath that attached it to its Junkers Ju 88 partner.

Opposite: A closer view of the Mistel S2 captured at Merseburg in May 1945. The S2 was a trainer version of the Mistel 2.

Opposite: A close-up view of the nose sections of the same captured Mistel 2 or S2 seen in the previous image. The main Mistel warhead was a shaped charge of nearly two tons in weight. The use of a shaped charge was intended to result in a penetration of up to seven metres through reinforced concrete.

Another example of a captured Mistel 2 or S2. Some 250 Mistels of various combinations were built during the war, but they met with limited success. They were first flown in combat against the Allied invasion fleet during the D-Day landings, targeting the British-held harbour at Courseulles-sur-Mer.

Above: There is some confusion surrounding this photograph. The Bf 109 F is clearly Wk Nr 10130 CD+LX. The number 5 on the tail of the Ju 88 A-4 identfies it as KI+CI/5T+CK, but underneath the codes would indicate GD+LN which is White 7. In any event, both were shot down on the night of 14 June 1944.

Oberleutnant Albert Rheker of 2./KG 101 was posted as missing whilst operating the combination of Bf 109 Wk Nr 10096 VE+TP and Ju 88 KI+CI/5T+CK. Oberfeldwebel Heinz Lochmüller, meanwhile, was reported killed whilst flying Bf 109 Wk Nr 10130 CD+LX and Ju 88 GD+JN.

One of the pair though it is not certain which one, fell to the guns of Flight Lieutenant Walter Dinsdale and Flying Officer John Dunn of 410 Squadron RCAF. They shot their victim down at 23.40 hours twenty-five miles south-east of Caen, Normandy.

Below: The first 'Beethoven' combination. This consisted of the Bf 109 F-4 coded CI+MX and a Ju 88 A-4. The combination was used extensively to conduct successful separation trials at the DFS 'Ernst Udet' at Ainring in early 1944.

MISSIONARY MAN

BAD MOON RISING

MISSIONARY MAN CREATED BY GORDON RENNIE & FRANK QUITELY

MISSIONARY MAN

BAD MOON RISING

GORDON RENNIE
Writer

FRANK QUITELY ★ SIMON DAVIS ★ GARRY MARSHALL ★ SEAN LONGCROFT
Artists

FRANK QUITELY
Cover Artist

Creative Director and CEO: Jason Kingsley
Chief Technical Officer: Chris Kingsley
2000 AD Editor in Chief: Matt Smith
Graphic Novels Editor: Keith Richardson
Graphic Design: Simon Parr & Luke Preece
Reprographics: Kathryn Symes
PR: Michael Molcher
Original Commissioning Editor: David Bishop

Published by Rebellion, Riverside House, Osney Mead, Oxford OX2 0ES, UK
www.rebellion.co.uk

ISBN: 978-1-907992-23-0
Printed in Malta by Gutenberg Press
Manufactured in the EU by LPPS Ltd., Wellingborough NN8 3PJ, UK.
First Printing: August 2011
10 9 8 7 6 5 4 3 2 1

Printed on FSC Accredited Paper

A CIP catalogue record for this book is available from the British Library.

For information on other *2000 AD* graphic novels, or if you have any comments on this book, please email books@2000ADonline.com

To find out more about *2000 AD*, visit www.2000ADonline.com

INTRODUCTION

By rights, *Missionary Man* shouldn't have worked.

The strip was an old fashioned Western, yet it was appearing in the *Judge Dredd Megazine* - a science fiction anthology where all the stories were set 122 years in the future. The writer was Gordon Rennie, who'd had only a few strips published when *Missionary Man* was commissioned in 1992. The artist was Glasgow illustrator Frank Quitely [a.k.a. Vincent Deighan], who'd been writing and drawing comedy strips for *Electric Soup*.

But there was something about this combination that clicked. Like lightning in a bottle, *Missionary Man* was unique, exciting and dangerous.

Why unique? This strip was unlike anything else in the Meg, owing more to the hard-bitten ethos of John Ford films than it did to the world of Dredd. Sure, there were mutants and monsters, even a spaceship, but they were concessions to where *Missionary Man* found itself. Unlikely redemption, unforgiving vengeance and unholy deliverance were the hardcore of Gordon Rennie's Bible-quote spewing mixture of piss and anger.

Why exciting? Just look inside these pages and see the stunning visual stylings of Frank Quitely. In an era when aspiring British comics artists all felt obliged to paint their pages in various shades of mud, he choose to tell stories with outstanding drawing skills. His eye for page layouts was a breath of fresh air after too many stale Bisley clones.

Why dangerous? *Missionary Man* was a gamble. Two emerging talents, a strip that defied reader expectations, and a choice of genre that spat in the face of the usual world of Dredd spin-offs. All these things could have backfired spectacularly – but they didn't, thank Grud. *Missionary Man* was a rootin', tootin' and six-shootin' hit. It changed the mighty Megazine for good.

Here endeth the lesson.

David Bishop
15th June 2011

SALVATION AT THE LAST CHANCE SALOON

THE TEX CITY OUTER TERRITORIES.

THE BIG COUNTRY.

AND ALSO THE *BAD COUNTRY.*

A HARD LAND BREEDS HARD MEN, AND A MAN GOT TO *WALK TALL* IF HE WANTS TO SURVIVE OUT HERE.

TAKES A *MIGHTY TALL* MAN TO TAME A HARD LAND.

ONLY A *FOOL* WOULD TRY TO TAKE THE LAW OUT TO THE BADLANDS.

HOWDY, STRANGER!

WELCOME TO DUKESVILLE—THE BEST LIL' *FREETOWN* IN THE WHOLE TERRITORIES! YOU NAME IT, WE'VE GOT IT!

SO WHAT BRINGS *YOU* HERE, STRANGER?

A FOOL--

-- OR A *MADMAN.*

SALVATION.

L-LORD HAVE MERCY!

SO MUCH *SIN*, SO MANY *WEAK SOULS* SUCCUMBING TO THE *WICKED WAYS* OF THE WORLD!

THEY ARE ALL *LOST SHEEP* WHO MUST BE RETURNED TO THE FOLD.

ONE WAY OR ANOTHER...

LOOKS LIKE IT MUST BE MY *LUCKY DAY*, UNLESS THERE'S ANY MORE BETS...

NO? WELL, I GUESS I WIN *AGAIN*--

PERHAPS YOU CAN ADD *THIS* TO YOUR WINNINGS?

WHAT'S THE MATTER, BOYS? *STAKES* A LITTLE TOO HIGH FOR YOU?

OUTLANDS MARSHAL

YOUR CREDIT'S *NO GOOD* HERE, MARSHAL, AND YOU'RE *WAY OUT* OF YOUR JURISDICTION. THIS IS A *FREETOWN* AND YOU TEX-CITY JUDGE-BOYS AIN'T GOT NO *BUSINESS* OUT HERE!

THE NAME'S *PREACHER CAIN* AND MY BUSINESS IS *THE LORD'S* BUSINESS. I GO WHEREVER HE CALLS ME, AND RIGHT NOW I'M HERE TO SAVE THE SOULS OF ALL YOU *MISERABLE SINNERS*...

WELL, 'PREACHER', HOW'S ABOUT YOU AN' THE LORD GET BACK ON YOUR HORSE AND RIDE ON OUTTA HERE 'FORE WE'RE LIABLE TO DO SOMETHING *NASTY*...

IT *PAINS* ME TO HEAR YOU *MOCK* THE LORD AND THE CHRISTIAN WORKS OF HIS HUMBLE SERVANTS—

--SO I GUESS I'M GOING TO HAVE TO GIVE YOU BOYS ONE OF MY 'SPECIAL' SERMONS!

HERE ENDETH THE LESSON.

WELL, LOOKS LIKE I GOT MYSELF A *CONGREGATION* HERE...

I GUESS YOU FOLKS ARE WONDERING WHAT I'M DOING OUT HERE IN *THE TERRITORIES* — A LAWMAN IN A PLACE WHERE THERE AIN'T NO LAW?

WELL, YOU'LL BE GLAD TO KNOW THAT I AIN'T *INTERESTED* IN THE LAW...

I'M HERE TO BRING *THE WORD* TO YOU GODLESS SINNERS!

THE LORD HAS GIVEN THIS LAND FOR US TO MAKE INTO A *NEW EDEN*, BUT YOU PEOPLE ARE TURNING IT INTO THE *SAME OLD HELL* THAT YOU LEFT BEHIND IN THE MEGA-CITIES...

I'M SERVING NOTICE ON YOU FOLKS THAT YOU BETTER START LOOKING TO MENDING YOUR WAYS *REAL SOON* 'FORE THE *RIGHTEOUS WRATH* OF THE LORD IS VISITED UPON Y'ALL...

LOOK TO *THE GOOD BOOK* IF YOU *TRULY* WISH TO REPENT--

GIRLS · CROG GUNS AND GAMBLING ALL WELCOME EVEN MUTIES! THE LAST CHANCE SALOON

— OPEN IT UP AND SEEK THE SALVATION *WITHIN*...

HOWEVER, I ADVISE YOU TO DO SO *SOONER* RATHER THAN *LATER*, FOR THE LORD SOMETIMES MOVES IN *SUDDEN* AND MYSTERIOUS WAYS...

THE ANSWER IS IN THE GOOD BOOK.

GOOD DAY TO Y'ALL NOW...

HE'S ONLY *ONE* GUY—WE JES' GONNA LET HIM *RIDE* ON OUTTA HERE LIKE THAT'?

YOU GONNA STOP HIM, LIKE'?

HEY--

--THIS BIBLE'S MAKING SOME KINDA *TICKIN'* NOISE...

'RIGHTEOUS WRATH OF THE LORD'!

'SUDDEN AND MYSTERIOUS WAYS'!

'THE ANSWER'S IN THE GOOD BOOK...'

SHOOT--

"—THAT PREACHER FELLER WEREN'T KIDDING NONE, NEITHER!"

'... AND HE LOOKED DOWN TOWARD SODOM AND GOMORRAH AND TOWARD ALL THE LAND OF THE VALLEY AND BEHELD, AND LO, THE SMOKE OF THE LAND WENT UP LIKE THE SMOKE OF A FURNACE.'

AMEN.

'And the Lord put a mark on Cain, lest any who came upon him should kill him. Then Cain went away from the presence of the Lord, and dwelt in the land of Nod, east of Eden.'

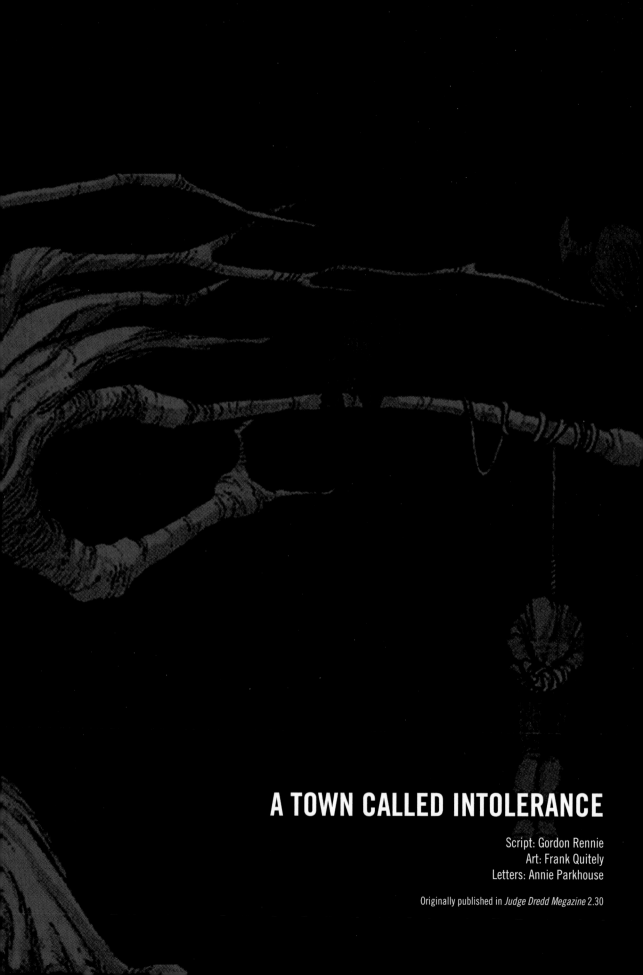

A TOWN CALLED INTOLERANCE

Script: Gordon Rennie
Art: Frank Quitely
Letters: Annie Parkhouse

Originally published in *Judge Dredd Megazine* 2.30

'PREACHER CAIN. REVEREND RIGHTEOUS. THE MISSIONARY MAN.'

'SOME FOLKS SAY THAT HE'S THE ANGEL OF DEATH HIMSELF, OUT TO PUNISH ALL US WICKED SINNERS!'

'MIND YOU, I ALSO HEARD TELL THAT HE WAS JES' SOME MAD OL' TEX-CITY JUDGE WHO GOT RELIGION AN' TOOK THE LONG WALK OUT INTO THE TERRITORIES TO CONVERT ALL US GODLESS HEATHENS!'

'KINDA HARD TO SAY WHICH STORY IS MORE LIKELY, REALLY...'

'EVEN I AIN'T TOO SURE, AN' I RECKON I KNOWS HIM BETTER'N ANYBODY, ON ACCOUNT O' BEIN' HIS DEPUTY, AN' ALL...'

'YEP, I REMEMBER THE FIRST TIME I MET HIM. I WAS JES' KINDA HANGIN' AROUND ONE DAY WHEN HE HAPPENED ALONG...'

WELL, WHAT HAVE WE HERE?

DON'T WORRY, FRIEND--

--ME AND THE LORD GOT BETTER THINGS IN MIND FOR YOU!

GET ON UP THERE, BOY! YOU AND I GOT **WORK** TO DO!

W-WHAT... HEY, AIN'T I SUPPOSED TO BE *DEAD*?

NOT *ANY MORE* YOU AIN'T. THE GOOD LORD HAS SEEN FIT TO GIVE YOU A CALLING TO *GREATER THINGS*...

WHAT'S YOUR NAME FRIEND?

JOE, SIR. LATE OF THE TEX-CITY 'BUFFALO SOLDIER' MUTIE IRREGULARS, AN' THE BEST SCOUT, TRACKER AN' GILA MUNJA HUNTER IN THE WHOLE DAMN TERRITORIES!

WELL, 'RESURRECTION JOE', WHAT'D THEY STRING YOU UP FOR?

BEIN' *UGLY* ON A SUNDAY, SIR!

SINCE WHEN WAS THAT A HANGING MATTER?

FOLKS IN THESE HERE PARTS GOT A *REAL* DOWN ON MUTIES...

SEEMS TO ME THAT THOSE *GOOD FOLKS* MAYBE NEED A LITTLE REMINDER 'BOUT THE *UNIVERSAL BROTHERHOOD OF MAN!*

C'MON. A MAN DESERVES A DRINK WHEN HE'S JUST COME BACK FROM THE DEAD...

YOU CAN'T TAKE ME IN *THERE* — THAT TOWN'S *SEGREGATED!*

NOT *ANYMORE* IT AIN'T...

I'VE TRIED BEING *REASONABLE* WITH YOU PEOPLE, BUT I AIN'T GONNA *TURN THE OTHER CHEEK* ANY LONGER...

HA HA HA HA HA -- EH?

REVEREND, *LOOK OUT!*

MUCH OBLIGED...

GODDAMN *MUTIE-LOVER!*

BEG PARDON, MA'AM...

AY, YOU AIN'T LIKE NO KIND F *LILY-LIVERED* PASTOR I VER CAME ACROSS 'FORE. OU AIN'T GOT NONE OF THAT IVE-TALK 'BOUT *LOVE 'N' PEACE,* AN' STUFF LIKE THAT...

JES' WHAT KINDA PREACHER-MAN ARE YOU, ANYHOWS?

I'M PREACHER *CAIN.*

THIS HERE LAND IS THE *PROMISED LAND.* IT'S A CHANCE FOR US ALL TO *START AGAIN.*

BUT FIRST SOMEBODY GOTTA *CLEANSE* IT. SOMEBODY GOTTA CLEAR ALL THE *SNAKES* AND *VIPERS* OF TEMPTATION OUT OF THIS NEW EDEN...

THAT'S WHAT *YOU* AND *I* ARE HERE TO DO.

DEPUTY

MOUNT UP, TROOPER! THERE AIN'T NO REST FOR THE *WICKED,* AND PRECIOUS LITTLE FOR *THE RIGHTEOUS* EITHER!

FRANK QUITELY

YESSIR!

YOU KNOW, JOE, I THINK THIS *COULD* BE THE START OF A *BEAUTIFUL FRIENDSHIP...*

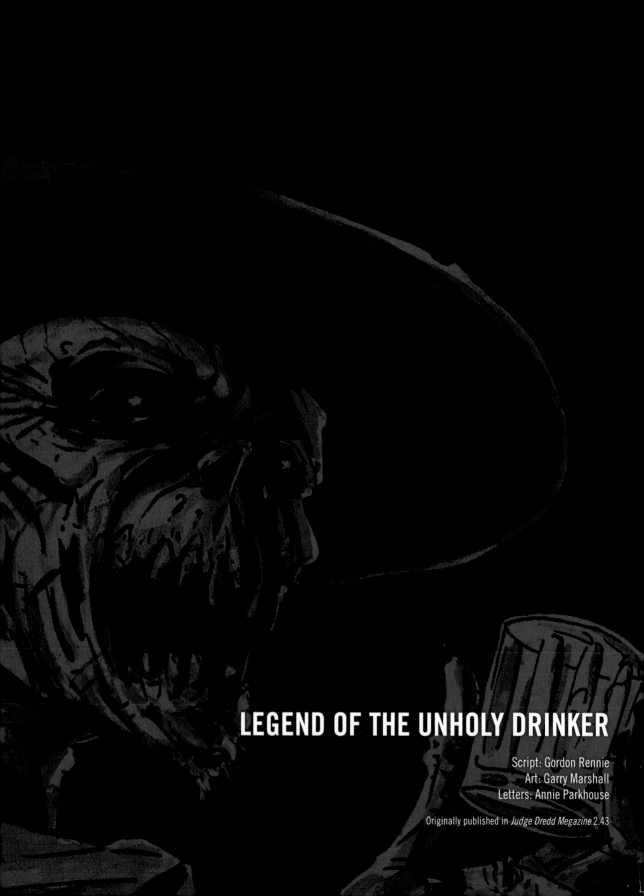

LEGEND OF THE UNHOLY DRINKER

Script: Gordon Rennie
Art: Garry Marshall
Letters: Annie Parkhouse

Originally published in *Judge Dredd Megazine* 2.43

BACK IN THE SALOON...IT'S *HORRIBLE!*

WONDER WHAT *THAT* WAS ALL 'BOUT?

ONLY ONE WAY TO FIND OUT...

♪ OH GIVE ME A HOME WHERE THE BUFFALO ROAM AN' THE *RIPPERJACKS* CAN'T PICK MY BONES! ♪

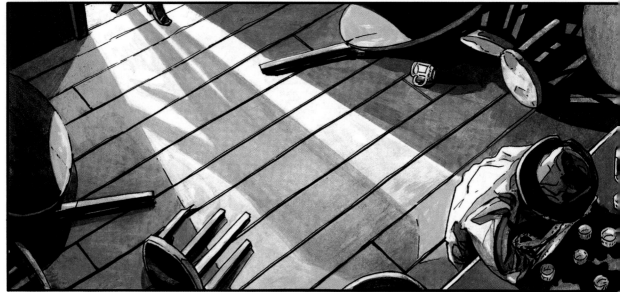

WHAT'S THE MATTER, BOYS— DON'T YA FEEL LIKE *JOININ'* IN?

SET 'EM UP, PAL! MY CREDIT'S STILL GOOD HERE, AIN'T IT?

Y-YESSIR!

WHAT SEEMS TO BE THE TROUBLE HERE?

AIN'T NO TROUBLE HERE, MARSHAL! CAN'T A FELLER ENJOY A *QUIET* DRINK ON HIS OWN WITHOUT THE LAW INTERFERIN'?

LORD HAVE MERCY--

ZOMBIE!

GUESS NOT...

SHOOT— OW'S A FELLER POSED TO DIGEST HIS LIQUOR ROPER WHEN YOU T A BELLYFUL' LEAD IN HIM?

AN' LOOK AT THAT— YOU DONE GONE MADE ME SPILL ALL MY BREW! RECKON THE LEAST YOU COULD DO IS BUY ME A COUPLE MORE IN COMPENSATION...

OK...THIS NEXT ONE'S ON ME--

HOLD ON, THERE, REVEREND— THIS FELLER DON'T SEEM TO BE DOIN' ANY REAL HARM, AN' AH RECKON HE'S GOT A POINT--

JUDGEMENT DAY?

GOTTA BE.

HELL, BUT THAT WAS ONE *BAD TIME!* I TOOK OFF FOR THE HILLS FROM THE DAY IT STARTED AND DIDN'T COME BACK DOWN TILL IT WAS ALL OVER. JUST ABOUT SLEPT THROUGH THE WHOLE DAMN THING!

WHAT WAS *YOU* DOIN' THAT DAY?

WORKING.

SO WHAT'S IT LIKE--BEIN' DEAD, I MEAN?

IT'S BAD. REAL BAD. EVEN WORSE THAN BEIN' SOBER, MAYBE.

THAT'S WHY I GOTTA KEEP DRINKIN'--TO *FORGET* WHAT IT WAS LIKE BEIN' BURIED DOWN THERE IN THE DARK...

WHAT 'BOUT YOU, MARSHAL--

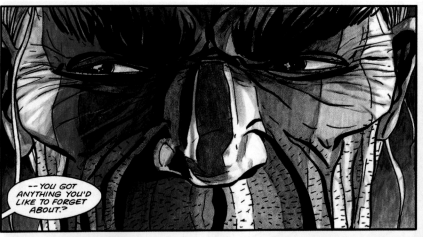

THE END.

BAD MOON RISING

Script: Gordon Rennie
Art: Frank Quitely
Letters: Annie Parkhouse

Originally published in *Judge Dredd Megazine* 2.50-2.55

SOMETHING WAS COMING.

THE PREACHER COULD FEEL IT ALL OVER.

HE HAD SENSED THE STIRRING AMONGST THE DARK THINGS OF THE DESERT AS THEY STARTED TO CREEP FORTH FROM THEIR SECRET PLACES.

SOMETHING WAS COMING.

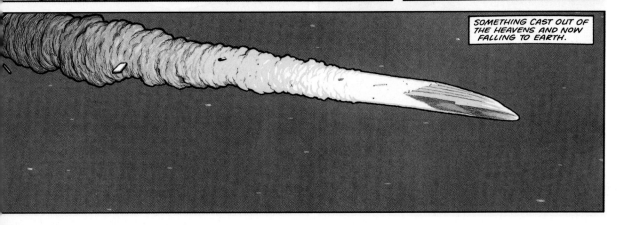

SOMETHING CAST OUT OF THE HEAVENS AND NOW FALLING TO EARTH.

JESUS!

HELL, BUT THAT WAS *CLOSE!*

PERHAPS, BUT *MIND YOUR LANGUAGE* IN FUTURE, DEPUTY. PANIC IS NO EXCUSE FOR *PROFANITY...*

THE LORD HAS GIVEN US A SIGN, DEPUTY. THERE'S *THE INJURED* TO BE TENDED TO AND *THE DEAD* TO BE GIVEN A DECENT CHRISTIAN *BURIAL!*

DON'T KNOW WHAT THE *BIG HURRY* IS ANYHOW--

"--THAT'S *GILA MUNJA* TERRITORY OUT THERE. THEM L'IL DEVILS WILL PICK THAT WRECK CLEAN 'FORE WE EVER GET THERE.

"AIN'T A PRETTY SIGHT TO SEE WHAT A PACK OF THOSE THINGS CAN DO TO A MAN.

"I MEAN, AIN'T *NOBODY* GONNA BE LEFT IN ONE PIECE 'MONGST ALL *THAT* MESS!"

WELL, YOU KNOW WHAT THEY SAY...

A *GOOD* LANDING IS ONE YOU CAN STILL *WALK AWAY* FROM!

"WORST THING 'BOUT GILA MUNJA IS THAT USUALLY YOU DON'T EVEN KNOW THEY'RE THERE UNTIL THEIR TEETH IS BURIED IN YOUR THROAT.

"ONLY THING THAT CAN SEE, HEAR OR SMELL A STALKIN' GILA MUNJA IS *ANOTHER* GILA MUNJA..."

WELL, *HELLO BOYS!* READY TO *GET IT ON?*

"AND WHEN THEY COME AT YOU, YOU BEST ALREADY HAVE MADE YOUR PEACE WITH YOUR *MAKER*, 'COS THERE AIN'T GONNA BE NO TIME AFTERWARDS."

"BELIEVE ME, THERE AIN'T *NUTHIN'* FASTER THAN A STRIKING GILA MUNJA.

"AN' IF THE CUT DON'T KILL YOU STRAIGHT OFF, THEN THEIR *POISON* SURELY WILL."

"THEY GOT STUFF SPREAD ON THOSE CLAWS THAT'LL BOIL A MAN'S BLOOD, ROT THE FLESH FROM HIS BONES AN' FREEZE HIS HEART 'FORE HE EVEN KNOWS HE'S BEEN CUT.

"NEVER HEARD TELL OF A LIVING THING THAT SURVIVED A CUT FROM ONE OF THOSE THINGS.

"LEASTWAYS, *NUTHIN' HUMAN...*"

COME, MY LITTLE ONES, DON'T BE AFRAID...

COME TO *DADDY!*

DRINK OF IT, ALL OF YOU. THIS IS THE *BLOOD OF OUR COVENANT,* AND IT IS BUT A *BRIEF TASTE* OF ALL THE BLOOD THAT IS YET TO COME!

NO SURVIVORS, JUST LIKE I SAID. BUT PLENTY OF TRACKS. *GILA MUNJA*, MOSTLY. AND *SOMETHING ELSE*...

WHAT?

KINDA HARD TO SAY. IT AIN'T GILA MUNJA, BUT IT AIN'T A MAN NEITHER...

ANYWAY, THE WHOLE LOT OF THEM HEADED OUT INTO THE *GERASENES BADLANDS*. THAT'S SOME PRETTY MEAN PLACE TO BE GOIN' *WALKABOUT*.

SAY, WHAT THE HELL HAPPENED HERE, ANYHOWS?

"HIM THE ALMIGHTY POWER HURLED HEADLONG FLAMING FROM THE ETHEREAL SKY WITH HIDEOUS RUIN AND COMBUSTION DOWN TO BOTTOMLESS PERDITION. THERE TO DWELL IN ADAMANTINE CHAINS AND PENAL FIRE..."

WHAT'S THAT? MORE FANCY *BIBLE-TALK*?

NO, JUST PART OF SOME OLD POEM.

EVIL SIGNS AND PORTENTS, JOE. SOMETHING *CAME DOWN* HERE LAST NIGHT, AND NOW THERE'S GONNA BE *BAD TIMES* A-COMIN' FOR US ALL...

"AND WHAT ROUGH BEAST, ITS HOUR COME ROUND AT LAST, SLOUCHES TOWARDS BETHLEHEM TO BE BORN?"

THAT ANOTHER ONE OF THEM OLD POEMS?

"YES, THIS ONE'S ABOUT THE COMING OF THE *ANTICHRIST!*"

SOME STORM! NEVER SEEN THE LIKE OF IT 'FORE...

"THINGS FALL APART; THE CENTRE CANNOT HOLD; MERE ANARCHY IS LOOSED UPON THE WORLD..."

WHATEVER CAME DOWN HERE THE OTHER NIGHT AIN'T OF THE NATURAL ORDER OF THINGS. IT CARRIES NOTHING BUT *DISASTER AND CHAOS* IN ITS WAKE.

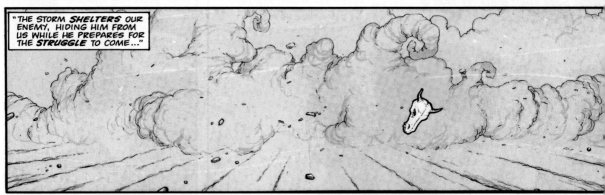

"THE STORM *SHELTERS* OUR ENEMY, HIDING HIM FROM US WHILE HE PREPARES FOR THE *STRUGGLE* TO COME..."

WE MAY NOT SEE HIS FACE, BUT WE MAY STILL KNOW HIS *DEEDS*...

HOW YOU GONNA DO THAT? *DIVINE INSPIRATION*?

NOPE. THE *FLIGHT RECORDER* AND SHIP'S LOG THAT I SALVAGED FROM THAT WRECK THE OTHER NIGHT.

DELIVER US, OH LORD, FROM THE ANGER OF THE ELEMENTS!

LOOK DOWN UPON THIS GATHERING OF YOUR FAITHFUL FLOCK AND WATCH OVER THEM ALL, I BESEECH YOU! WE HUMBLY COMMEND OURSELVES TO YOUR DIVINE PROTECTION.

"SEND US A SIGN OF SALVATION.

"SEND US AN ANGEL OF MERCY TO WATCH OVER US!"

THIS IS A HARD LAND, BUT THESE ARE GOOD PEOPLE, AND THEY HAVE COME OUT HERE TO DO YOUR BIDDING BY BRINGING LIFE TO THE LAND ONCE MORE. IN RETURN, ALL THAT WE ASK IS --

HEH HEH HEH...

ROOM FOR *ONE MORE*?

WELL, THIS IS *NICE!* HERE YOU ALL ARE, ALL *SAFE AND SNUG* IN HERE WHILE YOU LOCK THE DOOR ON ALL THE OTHER *POOR AND HUNGRY* TRAVELLERS CAUGHT OUT IN THAT *DREADFUL* WEATHER!

IS THAT WHAT YOU CALL *CHRISTIAN AND NEIGHBOURLY* BEHAVIOUR?

W-WHO ARE YOU? WHAT DO YOU WANT?

I'M THE *BEAST OF THE BADLANDS*, I'M THE *MUTANT MESSIAH*, I'M THE *DEMON OF DELIVERANCE*, I'M THE *ANGEL OF ANNIHILATION*, I'M *MR BAD MOON RISING!*

MY NAME IS *LEGION*, FOR WE ARE MANY, AND I'M HERE TO BRING *SALVATION* TO YOU ALL!

HAHAHA HAHAHA

'MY NAME IS LEGION, FOR WE ARE MANY.'

THAT'S ALL IT EVER SAID ABOUT ITSELF, AND THAT'S ALL THEY EVER FOUND OUT ABOUT IT FROM THE DAY THEY CAUGHT IT DURING A ROUTINE SWEEP OUT IN THE TEX-CITY BADLANDS.

THE JUSTICE DEPARTMENT GENETICISTS SAID IT WAS SOME SORT OF FREAK *SUPER-MUTANT.* THE ROGUE RESULT OF ONE-IN-A-BILLION DNA.

THE PSYCHOLOGISTS WENT CRAZY OVER IT — AN UNPARALLELED CASE OF *DEEPCORE HOMICIDAL PSYCHOSIS* AND SPLIT-PERSONALITY, EACH ONE MORE *MALEVOLENT* THAN THE LAST.

PSI-DIVISION SAID IT WAS JUST PLAIN *EVIL.* THEY LOST THREE GOOD JUDGES, TRYING TO SCAN ITS MIND. THE LAST ONE BABBLED SOMETHING ABOUT 'DEMONIC POSSESSION' JUST BEFORE HE DIED OF MASSIVE HEART FAILURE.

WHATEVER IT WAS, NONE OF THEM KNEW WHAT TO DO WITH IT. SO THEY LOCKED IT AWAY, WHERE IT SPENT ITS TIME JUST GIGGLING TO ITSELF.

SOME NIGHTS IT HOWLED AT THE MOON AND ATE BITS OF ITSELF. WHATEVER IT CHEWED OFF HAD ALWAYS GROWN BACK BY THE MORNING.

FINALLY, THEY DECIDED TO EXECUTE IT.

THEY EXECUTED IT *FIVE TIMES,* AND THE MORE THEY TURNED UP THE JUICE, THE MORE IT GIGGLED WHEN IT WAS ALL OVER.

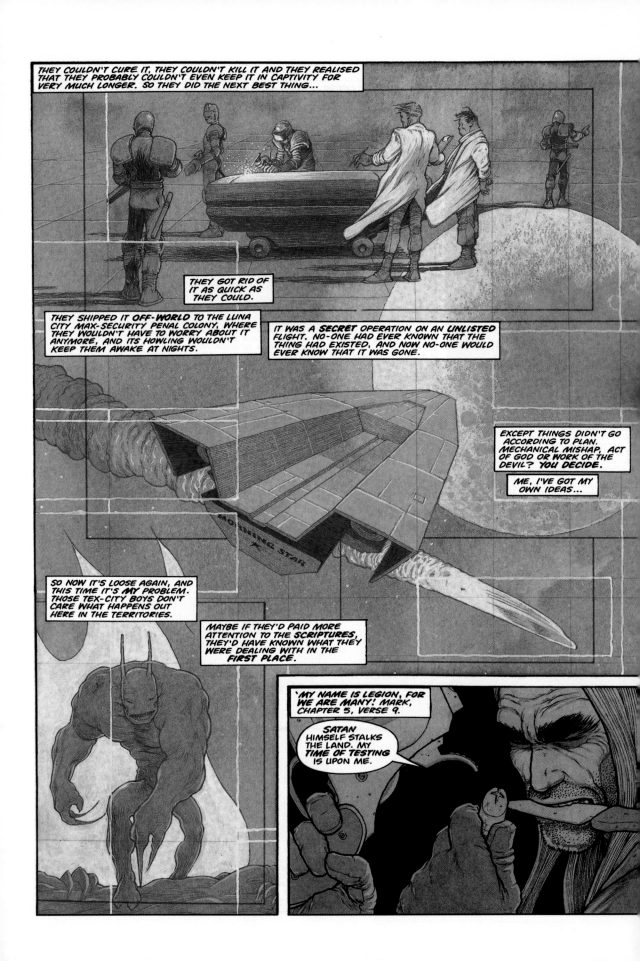

'THE LORD SHALL FIND ME READY. I SHALL NOT FAIL IN MY FAITH.'

WELL, BOYS, DIDN'T I PROMISE YOU PLENTY OF *FUN AND FROLICS*?

MEAN, *THIS SURE* BEATS THE HELL OUT OF THAT *LOAVES AND FISHES* ROUTINE!

AND WHAT DOES OUR *NEW RECRUIT* THINK OF OUR *LITTLE SOIREE*?

SUCH A *HEARTY APPETITE,* REVEREND! SEE? IT'S REALLY NOT SO BAD ONCE YOU TRY IT...

YOU'LL LEARN THAT ABOUT A LOT OF NEW THINGS, BEFORE I'M DONE WITH YOU...

BROTHER SIMON!

UUNGH?

BROTHER SIMON, HOW'S ABOUT GETTING UP TO TH' BELL TOWER AND *RINGING OUT THE JOYOUS NEWS*?

IT'S TIME TO CALL THE FAITHFUL TO PRAYER!'

ALL ACROSS THE TERRITORIES AND THE CURSED EARTH BEYOND, THE TOLL OF THE BELL IS HEARD, BEARING PROMISES OF THE PLEASURES AND HORRORS TO COME.

AND LEGION'S *DARK DISCIPLES* CAME IN ANSWER TO THE MYSTIC CALL, TURNING THEIR FACES TOWARDS THE LIGHT OF THEIR MASTER'S MOON.

STORM'S LIFTED, BUT SOMEHOW IT DON'T MAKE ME FEEL ANY BETTER...

AND WHAT'S HAPPENED TO THE *MOON*!?

IT'S TIME...

"...THE JACKALS ARE CRAWLING OUT OF THEIR HOLES.

"IT'S TIME FOR YOU AND ME TO GO *BATTLE* WITH THE BEAST, DEPUTY!"

WE SET OUT AFTER THEM AT *FIRST LIGHT* THE NEXT MORNING. IF THAT'S WHAT YOU WANT TO CALL IT.

DIDN'T TAKE US TOO LONG TO FIND WHAT THEY'D BEEN UP TO.

WHAT'S IT SAY?

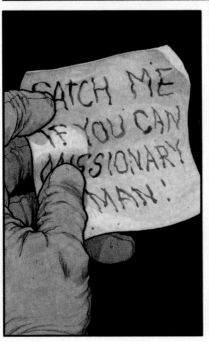

CATCH ME IF YOU CAN MISSIONARY MAN!

SO WE RODE ALL THROUGH THE NIGHT, WITH THAT BIG OL' *BAD MOON* LEADING US ON FROM ONE *DEAD PLACE* TO ANOTHER.

DIDN'T NEED TO BE NO *HOTSHOT TRACKER* TO FIGURE OUT WHICH WAY THEY TOOK. JUST ONE *LONG TRAIL* OF BURNED-OUT FARMSTEADS, AMBUSHED WAGON-TRAINS AN' WHOLE TOWNS RAZED TO THE GROUND.

AN' NUTHIN' BETWEEN ALL THIS BUT POISONED WATER-HOLES, BLIGHTED CROPS AN' DISEASED CATTLE WITH THE MEAT ROTTIN' OFF THEIR BODIES. IT WAS LIKE THE WHOLE LAND HAD TURNED *SOUR* IN THE WAKE O' HIS PASSING.

STRANGE THING WAS THAT IN ALL THAT TIME, WE NEVER FOUND EVEN ONE BODY. LEAST, NOT UNTIL WE GOT OUT INTO THE *CACTUS BADLANDS.*

AND THEN WE FOUND THEM.

THEN WE FOUND THEM ALL.

"THE LORD IS MY SHEPHERD. I SHALL NOT WANT. HE MAKES ME LIE DOWN IN GREEN PASTURES. HE LEADS ME BESIDE STILL WATERS. HE RESTORES MY SOUL."

BUT EVEN THAT WASN'T THE WORST THING--

NO, WORST THING WAS THAT SOME O' THEM DEAD 'UNS WAS STILL TALKIN'!

"HE LEADS ME IN PATHS OF RIGHTEOUSNESS FOR HIS NAME'S SAKE."

WELL, LOOKEE HERE--

--THE HOLY FOOL AND HIS PET MONKEY--

--ON THEIR WAY TO FIND THE BIG BAD WOLF--

--LIKE TWO LITTLE LAMBS TO THE SLAUGHTER!

"EVEN THOUGH I WALK THROUGH THE VALLEY OF THE SHADOW OF DEATH, I SHALL FEAR NO EVIL. FOR THOU ART WITH ME. THY ROD AND THY STAFF, THEY COMFORT ME."

RECKON THEY DON'T STAND A CHANCE--

--RECKON THEY'RE DEAD MEAT.

COURSE, IT WAS ALRIGHT FOR HIM. HE HAD HIS BIBLE TO SEE HIM THROUGH A THING LIKE THAT.

BIG MOMMA'S BOYS!

NO-HOPERS!

PAIR OF LOSERS!

BUT SOME OF US HEATHENS NEEDED SOMETHING A LITTLE STRONGER...

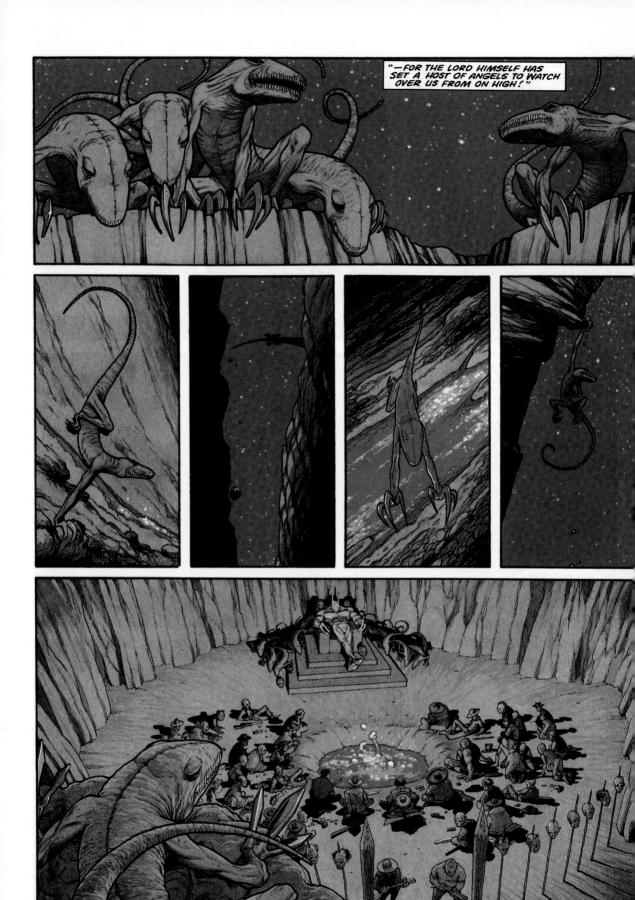

"—FOR THE LORD HIMSELF HAS SET A HOST OF ANGELS TO WATCH OVER US FROM ON HIGH!"

RrrrrrR...

NOW, BROTHER MATTHEW, DON'T BE SO TESTY!

LET'S HEAR WHAT BROTHER ISAIAH HAS TO SAY FOR HIMSELF...

AH! I WAS WONDERING IF HE WAS EVER GOING TO GET HERE...

AND JUST WHEN I WAS WORRIED THAT I WAS BEGINNING TO GET A LITTLE BORED...

TIME TO GATHER THE GANG TOGETHER, BOYS--

--NOW WE'RE REALLY GOING TO HAVE SOME FUN!

FRANK QUITELY

AMBUSH!

NO KIDDIN'!

CAN'T GO BACK NOW. GOTTA GO FORWARD... SOMEHOW I THINK THAT WAS PART OF THE PLAN—

LOOK!

WHAT DO THE SCRIPTURES SAY ABOUT THIS SORT OF SITUATION, REVEREND?

'YOU WILL NOT FEAR THE TERROR OF THE NIGHT, NOR THE ARROW THAT FLIES BY DAY, NOR THE PESTILENCE THAT STALKS IN DARKNESS, NOR THE DESTRUCTION THAT WASTES AT NOONDAY!'

'A THOUSAND MAY FALL AT YOUR RIGHT HAND, AND TEN THOUSAND AT YOUR LEFT HAND, BUT DEATH SHALL NOT COME NEAR YOU!'

'YOU ONLY HAVE TO LOOK WITH YOUR EYES TO SEE THE DUE RECOMPENSE OF THE WICKED!'

YOU JUST GOTTA HAVE TRUE FAITH!

SHOOT, I GUESS IT'S TRUE WHAT THEY SAY, AFTER ALL —

'ONLY FOOLS GO WHERE ANGELS FEAR TO TRED.'

MIND YOU, LOOKIN' AT THE MESS HE WAS GETTIN' HIMSELF INTO ALL OF A SUDDEN, I WAS KINDA REMINDED OF *ANOTHER* ONE OF THEM SAYINGS —

'THE BIGGER THEY ARE, THE HARDER THEY FALL.'

NOT THAT I HAD MUCH CALL TO *BOAST*, NEITHER...

REVEREND!

STILL, I'LL GIVE THE REVEREND HIS DUES.

YOU CAN ALWAYS DEPEND ON HIM TO GIVE IT HIS BEST SHOT.

AND HE SURE AS HELL DON'T KNOW WHEN TO QUIT!

'LET THEM BE TURNED BACK AND CONFOUNDED, WHO DEVISE EVIL AGAINST ME! LET THEM BE LIKE CHAFF BEFORE THE WIND, WITH THE ANGEL OF THE LORD DRIVING THEM ON!'

'LET THEIR WAY BE DARK AND SLIPPERY, WITH THE ANGEL OF THE LORD PURSUING THEM!'

MY, QUITE THE LITTLE BIBLE SCHOLAR, AREN'T WE?

GOT SOMETHING APPROPRIATE IN MIND FOR ME?

'DELIVER ME, O LORD, FOR THOU DOST SMITE ALL MY ENEMIES ON THE CHEEK—

THOU DOST BREAK THE TEETH OF THE WICKED!'

PSALMS THREE, VERSE SEVEN.

VERY FUNNY—

BUT I'M THE ONE WHO CRACKS THE JOKES AROUND HERE!

WHAT'S THE MATTER, OLD MAN? I CAN'T HEAR YOU LAUGHING. MAYBE I HAVEN'T TICKLED YOUR FUNNY BONE ENOUGH YET...

COME CLOSER. I WANT TO SEE THE LOOK IN YOUR EYES WHEN I REACH UP FOR YOUR *HEART* AND PULL IT OUT THROUGH THE HOLE IN YOUR *BELLY!*

WHAT DO YOU SAY TO *THAT*, MISSIONARY MAN?

IS THAT--IS THAT THE BEST YOU CAN DO?

NOPE--

--THIS IS *!*

NICE TRY, OLD MAN—

—BUT IT LOOKS LIKE YOU JUST DUG YOUR OWN GRAVE INSTEAD!

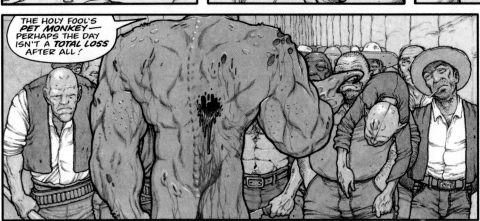

THE HOLY FOOL'S *PET MONKEY*— PERHAPS THE DAY ISN'T A *TOTAL LOSS* AFTER ALL!

LOOKING FOR A *NEW OWNER*, LITTLE MONKEY? WELL, I THINK I CAN HELP YOU OUT THERE...

COME WITH ME, THEN. HAVE I GOT A *TREAT* FOR YOU!

FRANK QUITELY

LAST THING I REMEMBER WAS SEEIN' THE REVEREND GOIN' DOWN 'MONGST A WHOLE PACK O' MUTIES, AN' ME RIDIN' OFF TO THE RESCUE.

WAKEY WAKEY, LITTLE MONKEY...

GUESS I MUSTA MISSED SOMETHING IN THE MEANTIME.

WELCOME TO THE PARTY!

POOR LITTLE PIGGY, I IMAGINE THIS ALL MIGHT COME AS SOMETHING OF A SHOCK TO YOU — WAKING UP AND FINDING YOURSELF ALL ALONE WITH THE BIG BAD WOLF!

STILL, YOU CAN'T SAY I DIDN'T WARN YOU THIS WOULD HAPPEN...

THE PREACHER..?

HIM? OH, HE'S YESTERDAY'S NEWS NOW, I'M AFRAID. A TRAGEDY, AND NO MISTAKE!

BUT LET'S TRY AND LOOK ON THE BRIGHT SIDE...

'...BUT WE'LL CERTAINLY GIVE YOU A HEAD-START!'

WELL, I THINK THAT'S LONG ENOUGH, DON'T YOU?

'CRY HAVOC, AND LET SLIP THE GODS OF WAR!'

AND ALL THAT JAZZ...

I KNEW I DIDN'T HAVE A HOPE.

NOT A HOPE IN HELL.

BEST I COULD WISH FOR WAS THAT THEY WOULD FINISH ME OFF QUICK, 'STEAD OF TAKIN' THEIR TIME 'BOUT IT, AN' PLAYIN' 'BOUT WITH ME A LITTLE FIRST...

GUESS ALL I COULD DO WAS PRAY.

PRAY FOR SOME KIND OF MIRACLE.

'I call upon thee, O Lord, for deliverance.'

'You are my rock and my fortress, the stronghold in whom I take shelter from my enemies.'

'I call upon thee, O Lord, to give me strength.'

'Strength to cast off the weight of my torments.'

'Strength to raise myself up from the desolate pit and once again set my feet upon the earth.'

HAD TO KEEP MOVIN'!

HAD TO KEEP HIDIN'!

COULDN'T LET THEM SNEAKY L'IL DEVILS GET A FIX ON ME...

LEASTWAYS, THAT WAS THE GENERAL IDEA...

CRITTER HAD ME COLD, BUT IT MISSED OUT ON THE DEATH-STRIKE. LOOKED LIKE IT WAS GONNA BE THE SLOW WAY AFTER ALL.

AND THEN, JUST WHEN I RECKONED THINGS COULDN'T GET ANY WORSE--

OH
LORDY--

-- PLEASE
JUST LET IT
BE QUICK!

THEN SOMETHING STOOD
UP AN' COVERED UP THE
MOON.

I WAS MIGHTY GLAD
THAT I COULDN'T
RIGHTLY SEE WHAT
HAPPENED NEXT.

ALL I COULD HEAR WAS
THEM NOISES, AN'
THAT WAS BAD ENOUGH.

STRANGLED YELPS, WET
RIPPIN' NOISES AN' THE
NASTY SNAP OF BONES
BREAKIN'.

AN' WHEN IT WAS
ALL OVER, THERE
WAS JUST HIM
LEFT STANDIN'
THERE.

DEPUTY,
YOU AND I
GOT SOME WORK
TO DO...

WHAT
YOU GOT IN
MIND?

'DIVINE RETRIBUTION.'

BACK SO SOON, BOYS? DIDN'T THE LITTLE RUNT GIVE YOU SOME GOOD SPORT?

STILL, I HOPE YOU SAVED A FEW CHOICE MORSELS FOR ME...

HERE--

--WHY DON'T YOU SEE FOR YOURSELF!

MY BOYS! LOOK WHAT YOU'VE DONE TO MY LOVELY BOYS!

JUST YOU AND ME LEFT NOW. JUST LIKE IT SHOULD HAVE BEEN FROM THE START.

IT'S TIME FOR THE FINAL RECKONING 'TWEEN US...

IT'S TIME FOR ABSOLUTION.

WHAT MAKES YOU SURE THAT A GUN'S GOING TO MAKE ANY DIFFERENCE THIS TIME?

BECAUSE THIS TIME IT'S LOADED WITH *SILVER BULLETS* MELTED DOWN FROM A HOLY CROSS.

WH--

GOING TO SHOOT ME AGAIN, JUST LIKE LAST TIME? YOU *BIG MEN* WITH YOUR *BIG GUNS* ARE ALWAYS SO *PREDICTABLE!*

YEP. RECKONED THAT MIGHT GET A RESULT...

NO!

YOU'RE NOT THE ONLY ONE WITH THE *CHEAP TRICKS!*

I SEEN THE REVEREND SHOOT, BURN, BLAST AN' BLESS THAT THING, AN' IT STILL AIN'T DEAD.

NOT QUITE SO COCKY WITHOUT YOUR LITTLE *TRINKET,* ARE YOU?

IF THE REVEREND CAME BACK FROM THE GRAVE AN' HE STILL COULDN'T KILL IT--

WHERE'S ALL YOUR *GIMMICKS* NOW?

--THEN WHAT KINDA CHANCE DID I HAVE?

BUT IT DOESN'T HAVE TO END THIS WAY, YOU KNOW. YOU CAN STILL WALK AWAY FROM HERE IN ONE PIECE.

ALL YOU HAVE TO DO IS FALL DOWN AND WORSHIP ME...

SOUND *TEMPTING?*

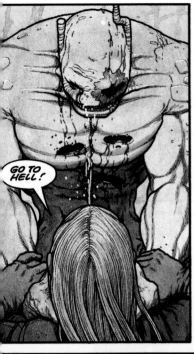

GO TO HELL!

OH, I SHALL, BUT NOT BEFORE I FINISH ALL THE WORK I'VE BEEN *SENT* TO DO!

MAYBE I WAS INSPIRED BY SOME OF THAT *BIBLE-TALK* THAT THE REVEREND WAS ALWAYS JIVIN' ON ABOUT--

MAYBE YOU JUST HAVEN'T *SEEN THE LIGHT* YET...

LET ME OPEN UP YOUR EYES AND *ILLUMINATE* YOU!

'BLESSED BE THE MEEK, FOR THEY SHALL INHERIT THE EARTH.'

BUT MAKE SURE THAT YOU NEVER LET ONE O' THEM GET BEHIND YOU!

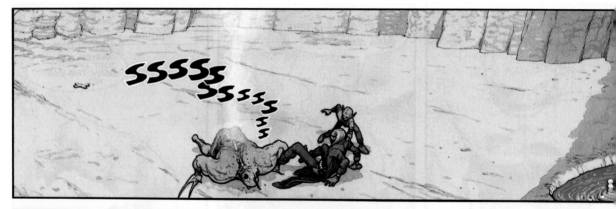

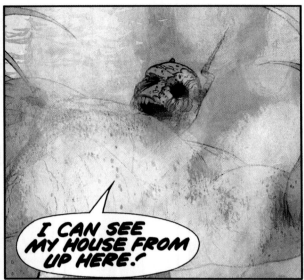

'AND THE DEVIL WAS THROWN INTO THE LAKE OF FIRE AND BRIMSTONE ALONG WHERE THE BEAST AND THE FALSE PROPHET ALSO LAY, THERE TO BE TORMENTED DAY AND NIGHT FOR EVER AND EVER...'

'REVELATIONS', RIGHT?

MAYBE I'LL MAKE A *TRUE* BELIEVER OF YOU YET, DEPUTY!

BUT WHAT WE GONNA DO 'BOUT *THEM?*

NOTHING.

LET THEM *CRAWL BACK* INTO WHATEVER HOLES THEY CAME OUT OF IN THE FIRST PLACE. LET THEM *BEAR WITNESS* TO WHAT THEY SAW HERE...

SO IT'S ALL OVER?

YES--

--IT'S OVER.

FRANK QUITELY

SEASON OF THE WITCH

Script: Gordon Rennie
Art: Garry Marshall
Letters: Steve Potter

Originally published in *Judge Dredd Megazines* 2.56-257

JACOB

JACOB CARTWRIGHT

NO – PLEASE... IT WASN'T MY FAULT!

I HAVE COME FOR YOU

GRUDDAMN IT, I SAW YOU KILLED ONCE ALREADY –

– SO WHY WON'T YOU STAY DEAD!

YOU KNOW WHY

NNN-AAAAHHGH!

NICE PLACE
YOU BROUGHT US TO...
THOUGHT YOU SAID FOLKS
IN THESE PARTS WAS
CIVILISED?

THEY ARE.
*RAINBOW'S
END* IS JUST
ABOUT THE MOST
PROSPEROUS TOWN
IN THE TERRITORIES.
LAND'S SO RICH, YOU
CAN GROW JUST
ABOUT ANYTHING
ON IT.

YEAH?

WE'LL
TAKE THIS ONE
INTO TOWN. MAYBE
THINGS WILL BE
BETTER
THERE...

AND
THEN AGAIN
— MAYBE
NOT!

GONE
TO
TEXAS
CITY

YOU SURE
THERE AIN'T
TWO TOWNS
CALLED RAINBOW'S
END IN THESE
PARTS?

TEX
CIT
or
BUS

THIS IS A *LOCAL BUSINESS,* MARSHAL, AND YOU AIN'T GOT NO PLACE HERE!

FOLKS IN RAINBOW'S END ALWAYS LOOKED AFTER THEIR OWN AFFAIRS, AND THAT'S THE WAY THEY'LL CONTINUE!

FINE. C'MON, DEPUTY...

SO WHAT WE GONNA DO NOW?

YOU HEARD WHAT THE MAN SAID, JOE — THEY DON'T NEED OUR HELP FOR ANY LAW-WORK...

BUT HE DIDN'T SAY ABOUT OUR *OTHER* BUSINESS OF ATTENDIN' TO FOLKS' SPIRITUAL NEEDS...

'MAYBE IT'S ABOUT TIME WE STARTED HEARING SOME FOLKS' CONFESSIONS.'

EVENING, YOUR HONOUR...

I BROUGHT YOU A LITTLE SOMETHING TO HELP RELIEVE YOU OF ALL *BURDENS OF OFFICE* THAT SEEM TO BE TROUBLIN' YOU SO MUCH THESE DAYS...

I — I DON'T KNOW WHAT YOU'RE TALKING ABOUT —

SEE, SHE STARTED COMING BACK FOR *US* — ALL THE ONES THAT HAD BEEN THERE THAT NIGHT — AND TAKING US ALL. ONE BY ONE. IN WAYS YOU WOULDN'T BELIEVE...

BUT NOW *YOU'RE* HERE, MARSHAL, AND I KNOW YOU AIN'T GONNA LET HER TAKE ME LIKE SHE DID ALL THEM OTHERS, ARE YOU?

ARE YOU?

A MAN REAPS WHAT HE SOWS, MR MAYOR, AND THEN HE'S GOT TO STAND ALONE IN JUDGEMENT FOR IT WHEN HIS TIME COMES.

MAYBE ONE LAST ACT OF *REPENTENCE* MIGHT STAND HIM IN GOOD STEAD WHEN HE'S CALLED TO ACCOUNT...

ME AND THE DEPUTY HERE STILL GOT A LOT OF BUSINESS TO DO THIS NIGHT, SO WE'LL TAKE OUR LEAVE AND BID YOU GOODBYE —

—'SPECIALLY AS I DON'T EXPECT WE'LL BE SEEING EACH OTHER AGAIN...

JOE, GO GET A LANTERN AND SOME SHOVELS—

WHERE'D YOU THINK YOU'RE GOING WITH *THAT*, MARSHAL?

GOT A LOST SOUL HERE IN NEED OF *SALVATION*. RECKON IT'S TIME TO LAY HER *AND* THIS WHOLE TROUBLE TO REST TONIGHT...

THERE AIN'T *NO WAY* YOU'RE GOING TO BURY THAT *MURDERING BITCH* HERE 'MONGST OUR KIN. BEST THING TO DO WITH HER IS BURN EVERYTHING THAT DIDN'T BURN THE FIRST TIME AND SCATTER THE ASHES TO THE WIND!

SHE CAST A CURSE OVER ALL OUR LAND AND KILLED HALF THE BEST MEN IN TOWN. WOULD HAVE GOT THE MAYOR TOO IF HE HADN'T *BLOWN HIS BRAINS OUT* FIRST—

THEN MAYBE THERE'S HOPE FOR HIM YET. CAN'T SAY THE SAME ABOUT THE REST OF YOU, THOUGH...

JOE..?

THANK-YOU, JOE. ANYONE ELSE WANT TO REGISTER A *COMPLAINT*, SEE THE DEPUTY HERE. IN THE MEANTIME, ALL OF YOU BETTER LISTEN UP GOOD...

THE ONLY CURSE HERE IS THE ONE YOU BROUGHT UPON YOUR-SELVES FOR THE KILLING OF AN INNOCENT WOMAN. ALL THEM THAT DONE THAT KILLING ARE DEAD NOW, BUT AS FAR AS I'M CONCERNED, THE REST OF YOU ARE ALMOST EQUALLY AS GUILTY...

'COS YOU ALL *KNEW* ABOUT WHAT REALLY HAPPENED TO HER. YOU JUST DIDN'T CARE, NOT AS LONG AS IT MEANT THAT THE 'CURSE' WAS GONE AS WELL. WHAT DOES ONE WEIRD MUTIE-WOMAN MORE OR LESS MATTER ANYHOW, YOU FIGURED...

HER VENGEANCE ENDS TONIGHT, BUT *MINE* IS JUST BEGINNING. YOU ALL GOT TILL *SUN-UP* TO GET OUT OF TOWN...

THEY ALL *LIT OUT* SOON AS YOU WAS GONE, THE WHOLE *TOWN-LOAD* OF 'EM! SHOULD HAVE SEEN IT — A GENUINE L'IL *EXODUS*...

SO WE ALL FINISHED HERE, NOW?

WELL, THE FUNERAL'S OVER—

—BUT NOW IT'S TIME TO HOLD THE *WAKE!*

OUTLANDS MARSHAL

THERE...

...THAT OUGHT TO JUST ABOUT DO IT!

RECKON SO!

BUT I STILL DON'T GET IT... THE MUTIE-WOMAN, WHAT WAS SHE ANYHOW?

PROBABLY JUST A *LATENT PSYKER* – I SEEN PLENTY OF HER STRAIN BEFORE. ALL MUTANTS LIKE HER AND ALL SHUNNED AND HATED FOR BEING SOMETHING THEY DON'T UNDERSTAND THEMSELVES...

FAR AS I'M CONCERNED, SHE WAS JUST ANOTHER *VICTIM*—

—ANOTHER VICTIM OF THE EVIL THAT MEN DO...

FORGIVEN

THE END

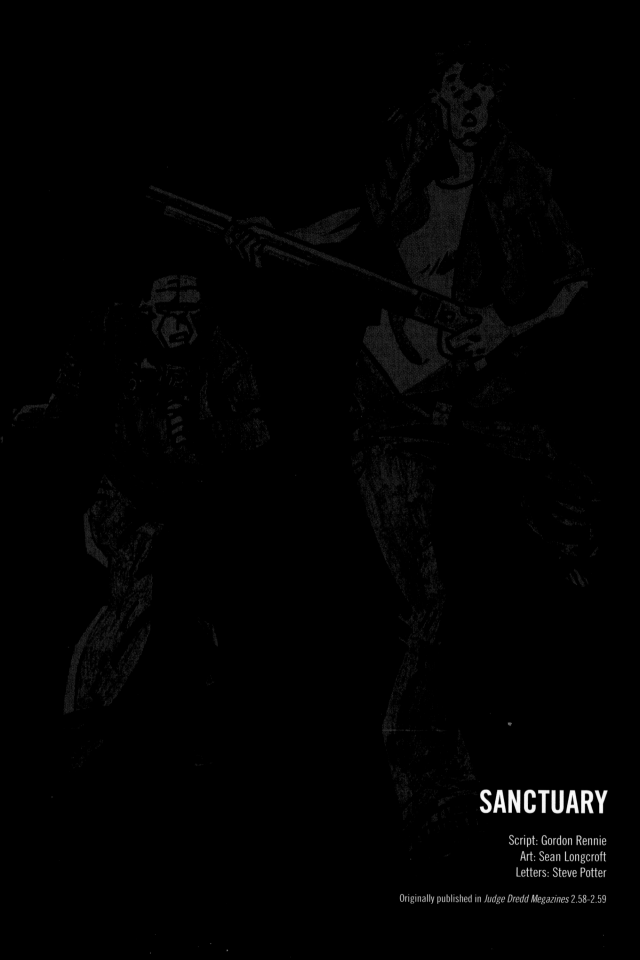

SANCTUARY

Script: Gordon Rennie
Art: Sean Longcroft
Letters: Steve Potter

Originally published in *Judge Dredd Megazines* 2.58-2.59

BARK! BARK!

WHAT IS IT, MA?

RIDERS! YOU CHILDREN WAIT IN HERE WHILE I SEE TO THIS...

STEP ON INTO THE LIGHT AND STATE YOUR BUSINESS, OTHERWISE I'D ADVISE YOU TO BE GETTING BACK ON YOUR WAY *REAL* QUICK...

SORRY FOR THE INTRUSION, MA'AM, 'SPECIALLY AT THIS LATE HOUR, BUT ME AN' MY FRIEND HERE WOULD BE MUCH OBLIGED OF SOME ASSISTANCE...

WELL, I GUESS YOU BOYS BETTER COME INSIDE...

WE WAS *BUSHWACKED*, MA'AM. ME 'AN THE REVEREND HERE WAS ON THE TRAIL OF SOME *BADLANDS BANDITS*. WE FOUND 'EM ALL RIGHT, BUT NOT THE WAY WE INTENDED —

'FRAID THE REVEREND TOOK A FEW HITS WHILE WE WAS MAKIN' OUR GETAWAY...

BEG PARDON, MA'AM, BUT YOU GOT ANY *MENFOLK* HERE WITH YOU?

ONLY MY HUSBAND —

— BUT HE'S OUT THERE IN THE YARD.

BROUGHT US OUT HERE FROM TEX-CITY TO FIND A BETTER LIFE, BUT THEN HE DROPPED DEAD OF *RAD-PLAGUE* SIX MONTHS LATER, LEAVING ME AND THE CHILDREN TO FEND FOR OURSELVES...

THAT'S *RIGHT UNFORTUNATE*, MA'AM, 'COS I WAS KINDA HOPIN' FOR HIS HELP —

"—'COS I'M FAIRLY SURE THAT THEM BUSHWACKERS IS STILL ON OUR TRAIL!"

CISSY, YOU TAKE YOUR BROTHER AND YOU MAKE SURE THE TWO OF YOU STAY IN YOUR ROOM...

OK, MISTER, YOU BROUGHT *TROUBLE* TO MY HOME, AND NOW YOU'RE GONNA HELP ME MAKE IT GO AWAY AGAIN...

YOU KNOW HOW TO HANDLE THAT THING, MA'AM?

YOU THINK A *LONE WOMAN* CAN LIVE OUT HERE WITHOUT KNOWING HOW TO SHOOT A GUN?

NOW —

— WHAT *KIND* OF TROUBLE WE TALKING ABOUT?

REAL MEAN MUTIE KILLERS, MA'AM — *HALLOWEEN JACK AN THE TRICK-OR-TREAT GANG!*

TOMMY, GET AWAY FROM THE WINDOW 'FORE MA COMES THROUGH!

DON'T WORRY, CISSY —

— THERE AIN'T *NOTHING* OUT THERE 'CEPT THAT BIG OLD STORM...

'—HE'S OUT THERE HUNTING THEM.'

MAN, TWO-HEADS WAS RIGHT — THAT OLD MAN IS PROBABLY DEAD ALREADY...

'DON'T LET ALL THAT BIBLE-TALK FOOL YOU —'

'THE REVEREND IS A NATURAL-BORN KILLER.'

'FACT IS, HE TAKES TO KILLIN' LIKE HE WERE THE ONE THAT INVENTED IT...'

YAAAA-AAAAGH!

HEAR WHAT I MEAN?

THAT'S ONE. HOW LONG YOU THINK THE OTHER TWO WILL LAST?

SHUTTUP, LITTLE MAN —

WANNA BET?

NO —

—THIS IS MY HOME, AND THERE'LL BE NO MORE KILLING HERE.

LITTLE LADY LIKE YOU SHOULDN'T BE MESSING WITH GUNS, MA'AM.

PUT IT DOWN NOW AND MAYBE I'LL GO EASY ON THE KIDS WHEN THIS IS ALL OVER...

THERE —

— LET THAT BE AN END TO IT.

MISSIONARY MAN
RETURNS
'THE UNDERTAKER
COMETH !'

THE UNDERTAKER COMETH

Script: Gordon Rennie
Art: Simon Davis
Letters: Ellie De Ville

Originally published in *Judge Dredd Mega-Special* 1994

"-- AND TELL HIM I LEFT HIM MY CALLING CARD."

DIED JUST AFTER SUNDOWN, JUST LIKE THAT BOUNTY HUNTER SAID...

PUTREFACTION HAD SET IN BEFORE HE WAS EVEN DEAD. NEVER KNOWN ANYTHING TO DO THAT, NOT EVEN GILA MUNJA VENOM ...

SO WHAT KILLED HIM?

THIS.

I'VE DUG MORE BULLETS OUT OF MORE BODIES THAN I CARE TO REMEMBER, BUT I AIN'T *NEVER* SEEN ONE LIKE THIS BEFORE. FAR AS I CAN TELL, THIS THING'S MADE FROM ONE-HUNDRED PERCENT PURE *POISON!*

WHAT'D YOU RECKON IT IS, REVEREND?

JUST WHAT THE MAN SAID, DEPUTY--

--IT'S A CALLING CARD. SOME KIND OF *CHALLENGE.* LOOKS LIKE SOMEONE'S THROWING DOWN THE GAUNTLET TO ME ...

COVER GALLERY

JUDGE DREDD

THE M INE

NEW STORY!

Introducing the
MISSIONARY MAN!

FREE GIFT!

Double-sided MEGA
POSTER inside!

No.29 May 29–Jun 11
FORTNIGHTLY
£1.25

UNFORGIVING!

GORDON RENNIE

Gordon Rennie is one of 2000 AD and the Megazine's most prolific creators, with co-creative credits *for Caballistics, Inc., Glimmer Rats, Missionary Man, Necronauts, Storming Heaven, Rain Dogs* and *Witchworld*. He has also written *Daily Star Dredd* strips, *Judge Dredd, Harke and Burr, Mean Machine, Past Imperfect, Pulp Sci-Fi, Rogue Trooper, Satanus, Terror Tales, Tharg the Mighty* and *Vector 13* and most recently *Absalom*.
Outside the Galaxy's Greatest Comic, Rennie has written for anthologies *Heavy Metal* and *Warhammer Monthly*, as well as *Species, Starship Troopers* and *White Trash*.

FRANK QUITELY

Superstar artist **Frank Quitely** first wowed *2000 AD* fans with his work on Shimura and *Missionary Man. He* broke into the US comics' scene, working with *2000 AD* writer Grant Morrison on *Flex Mentallo* and *JLA: Earth 2.* The pair would continue to collaborate on such titles as *New X-Men, We3* and *All-Star Superman,* the latter two titles winning various Eisner Awards between 2005-2007.

SIMON DAVIS

Simon Davis' unique, angular painted style has been a fixture of *Sinister Dexter* for some years now, since his *2000 AD* debut on the series. He has also found the time to create *B.L.A.I.R. 1, Black Siddha* and more recently *Ampney Crucis Investigates,* as well as contributing to *Downlode Tales, Judge Dredd, Missionary Man, Outlaw, Plagues of Necropolis, Tales of Telguuth, Tharg the Mighty* and *Vector 13*. His non-*2000 AD* comic strip work includes DC's JLA: *Riddle of the Beast.*
Simon is also a successful portrait artist and was short-listed for the 'National Portrait Gallery BP Portrait Award' in 2008.

GARRY MARSHALL

Garry Marshall has worked on two strips – *Missionary Man* and *Vector 13* – for *2000 AD,* collaborating both times with writer Gordon Rennie.

SEAN LONGCROFT

Sean Longcroft's work for the 'Galaxy's Greatest Comic' includes *Judge Dredd* strips for *Judge Dredd Lawman of the Future* and the *Judge Dredd Mega Special 1995,* as well as a *Missionary Man* strip in the *Judge Dredd Megazine.*